TRANSIT

DOCTOR WHO - THE NEW ADVENTURES

Also available:
TIMEWYRM: GENESYS by John Peel
TIMEWYRM: EXODUS by Terrance Dicks
TIMEWYRM: APOCALYPSE by Nigel Robinson
TIMEWYRM: REVELATION by Paul Cornell

CAT'S CRADLE: TIME'S CRUCIBLE by Marc Platt
CAT'S CRADLE: ESCAPE by Andrew Cartmel
CAT'S CRADLE: WITCH MARK by Andrew Hunt

NIGHTSHADE by Mark Gatiss
LOVE AND WAR by Paul Cornell

TRANSIT

Ben Aaronovitch

First published in 1992 by
Doctor Who Books
an imprint of Virgin Publishing Ltd
338 Ladbroke Grove
London W10 5AH

Cover illustration by Peter Elson

Typeset by TW Typesetting, Plymouth, Devon

Printed and bound in Great Britain by
Cox & Wyman Ltd, Reading, Berks

ISBN 0 426 20384 4

For Marie - who waited 60,000 words for our honeymoon.

Prologue

The Doctor stood alone on a Devonian beach and tried to persuade the lungfish to return to the sea.

'You won't like it,' said the Doctor.

He noticed that the fish's fins had become short stubby legs. It had become an Ichthyostega, the first true amphibian. The Doctor checked his watch. About two million years early at that.

'You're making a big mistake,' said the Doctor.

The amphibian ignored him, its flat head fixed on the line of cool vegetation ahead. It had covered a quarter of the distance across the hot white sand.

'I know it's crowded in there,' pleaded the Doctor. 'I know the food chain is overstocked, I know it's a fish-eat-fish ocean . . .' He trailed off. The gill slits had healed up, the legs lengthened. Claws sprouted from the feet. The panting mouth was full of teeth.

From across the sea came the sound of thunder.

'Don't do it,' said the Doctor. But too late. The reptile was suddenly flushed with hot blood. Hair sprouted over its body, it got off its belly and surged up the beach, getting smaller all the time.

By the time the Doctor caught up with it, the mammal was five centimetres long and cowering behind a shell. From the forest ahead came the crash and roar of gigantic lizards.

The Doctor hunkered down and stared at the rodent. Its small eyes gazed over the half of the beach that remained. The Doctor felt that it should at least look terrified but it didn't. It looked expectant.

There was a sudden scream in the stratosphere and the earth bucked under their feet. 'Did that sound like a ship full of Cybermen to you?' asked the Doctor. The sky went black with dust, the temperature dropped, the forest echoed with the meaty thump of collapsing species. 'I was there, you know,' said the Doctor. 'I lost a good friend. Not that you care.'

The dust cleared from the sky. The sun came out. The forest was silent. The rodent ran for the treeline. The wind blew in from the sea, bringing the smell of salt; from the horizon dark clouds raced towards the shore. When the Doctor looked back the animal was walking upright, flexing its new hands. As he watched the biped shed her fur. Breasts sprouted, the cranium ballooned backwards, the forehead lifted. Intelligence flared in brown eyes, the co-ordinated digits of her right hand picked up a stick and she looked around for something to hit with it.

The storm struck the beach.

The Doctor struggled through the rain and stepped in front of the human, blocking her path. 'Don't do it!' he shouted over the wind. But her eyes were full of fire and dangerous ideas. She raised the stick which became a club, a sword, a gun, a hydrogen bomb. Lightning fused the sand around them.

'Please,' said the Doctor.

The stick came down on his face.

PART ONE

'Are you sure,' asked his companion, 'that this is the nineteen-eighties?'

The Doctor looked around. 'Which nineteen-eighties did you have in mind?'

Conversations that never happened.

1:
Oncoming Trains

Olympus Mons West

Credit Card took the call from Central but he had to shout to make himself heard. Dogface was arguing over a game of Damage with Old Sam. Only Dogface was crazy enough to pick a fight with an old veteran like Sam, but Dogface always said that even Old Sam got bored with pushing people about. It was good therapy, he said, to stand up to him from time to time. At the time the call came in, both were in full flight, Old Sam on his feet with his two-tone dreadlocks flailing around his head, Blondie edging towards the door while Lambada surreptitiously cleared any breakables from the table. Dogface was leaning comfortably back in his chair, arms across his chest, a big eastwood clamped in his mouth. Old Sam had cranked up to full volume, swearing in something that had been an Indo-European language about two hundred years ago. Credit Card figured that the military must have augmented his lungs along with the rest of his body.

Credit Card sighed, stuck his right index finger in the slot and jacked into the system direct.

'What the hell's going on down there?'

Credit Card winced. Talking to Ming the Merciless was a pain face to face, going direct was like rubbing his brain on a cheese grater. 'Keep it down,' he sent, 'I'm plugged in.'

Ming the Merciless had a problem, mainly a brown-out on the Central Line which was knocking fifteen seconds off transit time station to station. Ming was very democratic: if she had a problem she liked to spread it around.

'We're on a break.'

Ming didn't care. She wanted the problem sorted out - now.

Credit Card pulled his finger from the socket and watched Ming doing goldfish impressions on the screen, her mouth silently opening and closing.

'What's Ming want?' asked Lambada.

'Brown-out on Central.'

'Again?' said Lambada.

'It's the regulators,' said Old Sam. 'They're bloody antiques.'

'Twenty-bloody-five years old,' said Dogface.

Old Sam sat down opposite Dogface and chewed the end off a fresh eastwood. 'Got a light?' he asked Dogface, who tossed the lighter to him. Old Sam snatched it from the air, insect fast, just to show that forty years hadn't slowed him down none.

Credit Card plugged his finger back in. 'It's the regulators,' he told Ming.

'I know it's the regulators,' screamed Ming, 'of course it's the bloody reg . . .'

Credit Card yanked his finger out again. 'She says she knows that it's the regulators.'

'I hate that Ming,' said Lambada.

'Yamatzi series five,' said Dogface. 'It's the coupling on the field controller.'

'Always dropping out of line,' said Old Sam. 'Two, maybe three, angstroms.'

'Five angstroms,' said Dogface.

'Very dodgy workmanship,' said Old Sam.

'Not like the new Nigerian regulators.'

'Japanese got no idea how to make precision gear.'

'It's not in their culture.'

'Not like the Africans.'

'Now they understand interstitial dynamics,' said Dogface. 'All that mystical stuff's second nature to them.'

'You can't swear undying loyalty to your company and then build something that relies on the transient nature of reality as a basic operating principle,' said Old Sam and blew a smoke ring at the ceiling.

'Common sense, innit?' said Dogface.

'So what do I tell Ming?' asked Credit Card.

'Tell her we'll get round to it later,' said Old Sam.

'Much later,' said Dogface.

'Don't you ever worry about getting the sack?' asked Lambada.

'Nah,' said Old Sam. 'Me and Dogface are the only ones who know how the system really works.'

'I could fix them,' said Blondie.
'Shut up, Blondie,' said Dogface.

STS Central – Olympus Mons

Ming the Merciless decided that banging her head violently against the console was not an effective method of stress management and consoled herself by screaming at the next person she saw. Once the young technician had fled into the corridor she sat down and considered her position.

The duty office overlooked the master control room. Colour-coded holograms displayed the system in its entirety. Red for the InterWorld lines like the Loop, Central Line and Outreach, orange for the commuter networks, blue for the feeders and yellow for the branch lines. A three-dimensional tangle of colour, each subsystem descending into a fractal infinity while data streams in white light marked the passage of a hundred thousand trains, fifty-six million passengers at fifty thousand stations.

It was an animal, Ming had decided a long time ago, a vast organism with a multitude of orifices that swallowed people and spat them out elsewhere. Grown up from an embryo over two centuries, it encompassed the solar system and stopped the ancient motion of the planets. In subspace all distances are the same distance so distance became meaningless. Orbits became an abstraction, the distance to Mars was a function of how far away the nearest station was. For most people the map of the system was the map of the universe.

And now the system was ready to eat up the light years between Sol and Acturus. Amongst the tangle of light, a new thread, picked out in silver, and a new station – Acturus Terminal, a new line, the Stella Tunnel, the Stunnel. The beast had yawned and stretched out to annihilate another frontier.

The trouble is, Ming thought, the beast is sick.

Lunarversity

Kadiatu was watching *The Bad News Show* on English 37, lying on her back with the TV projected on to the ceiling. It was hot and her bare back kept sticking to the plastic skin of the mattress. The campus administration had promised that the environment would be fixed soon, but what with recent cutbacks students weren't holding their breaths. *Bad News* was showing a jumpy video of a security raid in Melbourne, intensified images shot over the shoulder of the lead policeman. Yak Harris, the *Bad News* anchorman, was making a big deal out of the way the camera operators wore full combat armour, 'Better than the real cops'. Yak chortled ruefully as one of the policemen went down with a bullet in the face. 'Just goes to show, you can't be too well protected.' Right on cue they ran a twenty-second advert for personal armour – 'How safe are you?' – and Yak was back with the latest body count over a slowmo action replay of the cop's death. Vivaldi in the background as the body toppled lazily downwards. 'Let's see that from another angle,' said Yak Harris and smiled his perfect computer-generated smile.

Kadiatu's stomach rumbled.

She turned off the TV and rolled to her feet. At head height the air was hotter and smelt of zinc. Kadiatu wrapped a sarong around her breasts, pushed her moneypen through her braids and opened the door. Some of the students had pulled their mattresses out into the corridor to take advantage of the slight breeze that blew down its length. By the time she reached the refectory sweat was trickling down between her shoulder blades and thighs, and the cotton of the sarong stuck to her skin as she moved. The refectory was deserted, dark and even hotter than her room. On the far wall, opposite the entrance glowed the drink dispenser. 'Solar Cola' in cool blue neon letters. Kadiatu paused at the door and looked round the cavernous interior. Granny bashers sometimes infiltrated the campus. They'd take you apart with their own hands just to get enough for the next fix. Some poor bastard from Sociology had been jumped a week ago and was spending the rest of the year in a vat growing a new spinal column. The entrance cast an aisle of light fifteen metres across the floor to the drinks dispenser – 'Cool Refreshing Solar Cola'. On either side she could make out the flat shadows of tables stretching away into the darkness. Squaring her shoulders, Kadiatu set out with studied nonchalance. It was silent except for the hum of the dispenser's refrigeration unit and the slap of her bare feet on the vinyl floor.

She was halfway across when she heard the noise, a muffled whirring, snorting sound, somewhere off to her right. She stopped and slowly turned towards the sound. It was low down, under the tables and coming towards her, snuffling like a dog.

Except you didn't get dogs on Luna. Or only in restaurants. There were rules. Kadiatu saw movement, just a shape, low slung with close-set red eyes, a prehensile snout weaving from side to side as it advanced. You didn't run from animals, she knew that. She just wished she knew what the other options were. It was too late, the animal was there, darting out between the tables, its snout whipping round to strike at her legs. Kadiatu jumped out of the way and watched the cleaning robot zip past. The two red laser sensors mounted above its suction hose probed for obstacles as it vacuumed the floor.

'Piss off,' shouted Kadiatu as the machine vanished into the shadows again.

I come from six generations of fighting men and women, thought Kadiatu, and I get freaked out by a domestic robot. They'll be doing orbits in the family vault tonight.

Kadiatu walked the last few metres. She was sure that the air was getting hotter in the refectory. She pressed her cheek against the cool plastic of the Solar Cola machine and slotted in her moneypen. Nothing happened. 'Please,' she said softly trying all the combinations. 'I'll drink anything, as long as it's cold and wet.' Kadiatu slid slowly down on to her knees.

You'd think, she thought, that since we were an intelligent species we'd have attended to the details. That we'd build an air-conditioning system that can deal with the two-week lunar day, that we'd at least remember, when the temperature was up in the thirties, to refill the bloody Solar Cola machine.

She turned round and pressed her back against the cool flank of the dispenser. You'd think, thought Kadiatu as the condensation trickled down her back, that I could make a student loan last the whole term.

The cleaning robot sidled up and sniffed her feet to see if she were rubbish.

'I've got to get out of this place,' said Kadiatu.

Acturus Terminal (Stunnel Terminus)

Ming stepped out of a VIP shuttle on to the new Central Line platform. The terminal complex was being built into the bedrock under the permafrost of the Martian pole, half the world from Olympus Mons - one stop up the line and three minutes by Transit. Only half the light fittings had been installed and a team of artificers were still laying the red and green ceramic finish on the platform walls. Ming called up the building schedule on her clipboard: the platform should have been ready for over two days. Most managers had a data projector chipped direct into their retinas but Ming liked to see where she was going and besides, you could hit people with a clipboard. A big silver arrow pointed at a wide exit. At least the direction holograms were up.

The galleria was filled with noise and dust. Both walkways were in place but the consumer outlets were still big gaps in the walls. Here and there, messages in spray paint indicated that the space had been leased in advance. A Kwik-Kurry franchise - 'Service in thirty seconds or your money back!' - was already doing trade off portable stoves, and the smell of spices mingled with the cement dust. Off-shift workers squatted in little groups eating curried goat with their fingers.

When the complex was operational passengers would pass through the galleria on their way to the Stunnel terminus. It was hoped that it would generate enough profit to cover the Stunnel operating costs. Only the Central Line would run direct trains through to Acturus and then only two an hour. The Acturans were still bargaining to up the number of through trains but STS had put its foot down. They talked about smuggling, criminals and terrorists escaping from justice, even the chance that some stupid Vrik would try free-surfing the Stunnel, but Ming knew it was really a question of money. The Stunnel's R&D costs had almost bankrupted the network, with Reykjavik talking about another fare freeze. If they didn't recover the operating costs through the ancillary income then STS would suffer a financial collapse, the knock-on effect would sink the rest of Sol's economy, chaos would stalk the land and billions would starve. At least that's the way the board of directors told it. Hectares of office space and housing were being lasered out of the rock to the north and south of the galleria. The total investment was staggering, it would be the biggest single below-ground complex of its type in personspace. It was being said that the STS financial comptroller was visiting his acupuncturist so often he looked like a pin cushion.

The actual terminus was something else again.

Lowell Depot (Central Line Terminus)

Dogface and Blondie were heading for the end of the line, riding a maintenance engine up the Central Line's freight tunnels. The engine was open-decked and Blondie, who'd been a floozie for less than a month, kept his eyes narrowed down to slits. Unlike the enclosed and shielded passenger trains, the engine was rendered insubstantial by the boundary effect. Only the field controller, a black sphere that pulled the ghost train towards the tunnel's vanishing point, retained any solidity. Lambada said that looking too closely at infinity could turn your brain inside out. Dogface slouched in the cockpit, staring around him at the hallucinatory patterns of the tunnel wall with studied nonchalance. Lambada called that 'bad acid macho', but Blondie noticed that she went up front just the same when she rode the flat tops. The shifting streams of colour were punctuated by blasts of reality as they flashed through the stations on their way to Pluto and the edge of the system.

Lowell Depot was stuck in the middle of a low-rent housing project known to the media as 'Aryan Heights' and locally as 'the Stop'. Dogface coasted the engine into the freight dock just ahead of a cargo flatbed. Blondie watched as the robot handlers unshipped plywood crates of food and drink, all of them the cheapest possible generic brands. With eighty per cent of the Stop's inhabitants on welfare, even the crates would be cannibalized for furniture and firewood. The flatbed would run back empty. Nothing of any value came out of the Stop.

Dogface grabbed his kit and they walked down the narrow connecting corridor towards the passenger platforms. It terminated in a security door to keep people from hitching free rides on the flatbeds, Dogface unlocked it with his index finger and the door hissed open. The platform beyond was clean. Platforms for the InterWorld lines usually were. It was the feeder lines that got knee-deep in garbage. A small group of people in dowdy overwashed clothes waited with quiet resignation for the next train. They were body servants, cooks, cleaners, the Stop's second biggest export. Further up the platform stood young men and women with feet jammed into high-heeled boots, thighs into fishnets, breasts overflowing bra cups, buttocks wrapped in lycra, the white flesh crammed into the selling clothes - the Stop's principal export waiting to go to work. As they walked past Blondie tried keeping his head down but it didn't work. Someone called his name, his real name, and he turned to look without thinking.

'Hey Zak, wait up!'

He almost didn't recognize Zamina as she clicked towards him, face hidden under a layer of skin tone. Blondie looked at Dogface who shrugged and walked on - he could catch up in a minute.

'Well, look at you,' said Zamina, looking him up and down, her tongue clicking on her teeth. 'Pretty drab.'

'Not like you,' said Blondie. He could see faint lines on her pale skin running over the neckline of her halter top. An implant job, he realized, and a sloppy one at that. Zamina caught him looking and adjusted the top a bit to cover the scars.

'They said you'd got out, but I figured you for catfood by now.'

'I got lucky,' he said.

Zamina licked her lips. Stop protocol said you didn't ask questions but they'd been friends once, lovers even in a mindless adolescent fashion. Blondie could feel her need to escape as an almost physical force dragging at him. How long did Zamina have? Two, three years? You got old fast in the Stop.

Dogface whistled at him from the far end of the station.

'Gotta go, Zimmy,' he said.

'Give us a call sometime,' she said as he turned away.

'Sure,' he said but he knew he wouldn't. When you got out of the Stop you never went back. You never called and you tried not to think about the people you left behind.

Dogface had the access panel open and was probing inside with his finger sensors. 'When's the next train?'

Blondie checked the hologram hanging over the platform. 'Two minutes.'

'We'll see how the next one runs through,' said Dogface, 'and take it from there. See if you can get Lambada.'

Blondie plugged into the maintenance link. The implants still itched when he did it but he'd been told that was normal for the first six months or so. Some of the Stoppers on the platform were watching them, Blondie could make out Zimmy standing with her back to him.

'Wake up, Blondie,' said Lambada on the link from Mercury.

'We're just waiting for a train,' sent Blondie. At this distance there was a timelag even with the signal going through the tunnels.

'Get a move on,' said Lambada, 'me and Sam are freezing our arses off down here.'

Blondie felt a breeze lift the hair on the back of his head. A murmur came from the people on the platform and the hologram changed to 'Train Approaching'. With a sudden rush of warm air and an ozone stink the train shot from the tunnel into the station.

'Everybody stand by,' said Dogface.

Blondie took a deep breath and accessed the system.

'I can taste something.'

'What?'

'Cinnamon, I think.'

'Relax, Blondie,' said Lambada, 'that's just static.'

'She's loading up,' said Dogface.

Blondie could see the train through the link. The train, designation IW56 series 2 class B, mass 14,000 kilograms at 1 gravity. Sensors in the carriage floor counted the footsteps as the passengers boarded. Thirty-one passengers adding 2,325 kilograms, under the average for the station and well within safety parameters.

The door-closing hooter sounded in the real world and almost snapped Blondie out of the link.

The train's field regulator charged up, and the gateway field flickered and strobed as air molecules were sucked into the tunnel. Then with ponderous grace fourteen tonnes of metal, ceramic, copper and human flesh surged forward to start its journey through subspace.

'Did you get that?' asked Dogface.

'I saw it,' said Lambada, 'but what was it?'

'We lost fifteen seconds on that transfer,' said Old Sam.

'Was it the regulators?' asked Blondie.

'Screw the regulators,' said Dogface. 'Somebody's stealing power from the tunnels.'

Lunarversity

Max had his place in an unfinished side tunnel off Yeltsin Plaza. The entrance was blocked off with a repeating hologram of a crate shack, complete with a family of destitute Australians. To get in Kadiatu had to step through the pot-bellied girl who endlessly came to stand in the doorway every two minutes or so. Max called it his taste barrier. Inside Max was kneeling half naked in front of a fan, his nose pressed against the grill, dirty blond hair blowing over his scrawny shoulders.

'Lend us some money,' said Kadiatu, moving behind Max to catch the breeze from the fan.

'What have you got?' said Max.

Kadiatu was stuck. Max would take anything. His shelves were piled with junk, ring pull cans, software, sim tapes, litre jars of preserved fruit, packets of suspicious pharmaceuticals. If it could be sold, bartered or used, Max did.

'Nothing,' said Kadiatu. 'I want a loan.'

'Go to a bank.'

It was a tough opening move and Kadiatu, haggling from a position of weakness, played for time. 'There's a recession going on,' she said, 'or hadn't you noticed?' Important to find what he wanted from her, he must want something or the bargaining wouldn't have started.

'Things are tough all over,' said Max.

The dismissive tone was a bad sign; whatever he wanted Kadiatu wasn't going to like it. 'If you can't help, you can't help.' Kadiatu went to leave, and the bastard let her get right up to the edge of the hologram before speaking.

'Your body, six hours,' said Max.

Big mistake, Max, thought Kadiatu, should have named the price and let me sweat. Now I know what you want. But how badly do you want it?

'No chance,' said Kadiatu and stepped forward.

'You haven't asked how much?' said Max quickly, too quickly.

Kadiatu turned with deliberate slowness, let him see the merchandise, all those muscles, all that grace. Bad weakness that, wanting to be what you're not. Max had twisted to stare at her, making the tendons stand out on his thin neck; he was trying to hide the hunger in his eyes. No mercy, thought Kadiatu, it's a dog-eat-dog world and the richer you are, the more dog you eat.

'You couldn't afford the price.'

'Nothing kinky,' said Max. 'I just want to walk around in it for a while.'

'Just to walk around in?' said Kadiatu, and then, just to show willing: 'How much?'

'Piece of a deal,' said Max.

'What's the deal worth?'

'Twenty thousand.'

'And I get?'

'Fifteen per cent.'

She squatted on her haunches so that their eyes were level. 'Tell you what we'll do,' she said. 'I get the fifteen points as a loan, you get six hours walking-around time in my body if I don't pay back within three months.'

She could see Max fighting himself. It was a terrible deal for him, but he wanted it. Wanted to spend six hours wrapped up in her skin. His weakness, her strength.

'Deal,' he said.

When they shook hands on it, his palms were damp. Max straightened up, walked over to a shelf. He picked up a small oblong package and handed it to Kadiatu. It felt like a wooden case wrapped in rice paper, quite heavy. She didn't ask what was inside. 'You take this to STS maintenance, ask for Old Sam, get the money, skim your percentage and bring the rest back.'

Kadiatu tucked the package under her arm and left.

She got as far as the next intersection before the deal unwound in her stomach and she vomited onto the floor.

Acturus Terminal (Stunnel Terminus)

'Is that it?' The Stunnel gateway was twice as big as its Central Line counterpart at the other end of the station. Accordingly the roof and walls of Acturus Station sloped inwards down its two-hundred-metre length. It was like being in a huge funnel.

Doctor Verhoevan glanced up from his instruments. 'Impressive, isn't it?'

'Why is it that big?'

'Safety margin. On a tunnel of this length there's bound to be some real-space displacement of the carriage. We don't want it scraping the sides when it comes through.'

Close up the gateway was a dull bronze colour, the field boundary had an oily shifting look. It was making her uneasy. 'It's a funny colour.'

'Yes, interesting, isn't it?' said Verhoevan. 'It could be a function of the distance. No one's ever projected a tunnel this long before.' Verhoevan stopped and looked carefully at Ming, sizing her up. 'I'd really like to do a test run first.'

'Nervous?'

'Of course I am,' said Verhoevan. 'The President's going to be here, and the Minister and God knows who else.'

'So?'

'What if I activate the thing and nothing happens?'

Ming looked back at the gateway. 'You're getting the carrier signal?'

'Yes.'

'What's the problem then?'

Verhoevan shrugged.

The problem was power. Establishing the Stunnel was going to take sixty per cent of the total STS grid and the grid was stretched by normal operations as it was. It was the trains that took the power and the trains ran twenty-four hours a day across nine planets and fifty-six time zones.

Constitution Day, the holiday that marked the end of the Hundred-Day War, the only point when demand on the transit system fell enough to release the necessary power.

Tomorrow was Constitution Day.

'Twelve hours,' said Ming, 'and then you turn it on.'

Behind her the Stunnel gateway shone a dark greasy bronze. Ming decided that when Verhoevan cracked it open, she was going to be somewhere else.

Olympus Mons West

The floozies had gatecrashed the clerical workers' party at midnight Greenwich Mean Time. It was always Greenwich Mean Time in the system, it didn't matter where you started from or where you ended up, it could be full bloody daylight outside, but when you stepped into a station and the clock said zero zero zero zero it was bloody midnight, and don't you forget it. It could be hard on the biorhythms but not for Blondie, not for a boy from the Stop. A boy from the Stop could handle anything - right? Blondie was trying to explain this to people at the party but they kept on moving away. In a corner Lambada, dressed in a pink crochette T-shirt, had pinned a trainee clerical officer to the wall. The boy had a startled look on his face which troubled Blondie until he noticed where Lambada's other hand was. Clouds of suspicious-smelling smoke were rapidly overpowering the air conditioners and beginning to form a twisting strata at head height. Blondie thought it was probably now illegal to breathe deeply while standing upright, and probably dangerous as well. A noise box was pumping the latest subsonic backbeat into the floor. The vibrations were making Blondie feel queasy and a little sad. Credit Card bounced past, arms flailing out of time to the beat. The dance style had been obsolete for twenty years but Credit Card didn't care. His manic grin was locked into the memory of parties past as he slammed off people, walls and furniture. Dogface was sitting on one of the room's terminals, telling one of his sick stories to a group of young accountants. He described how two trains on the Millfield Branch line had been switched on to the same station by mistake. When he got to the punchline about the man who ended up with two heads and three buttocks the accountants laughed guiltily. Old Sam was dancing rub-a-dub-dub with the head of data processing, so close together that they looked like one of Dogface's accidents, a single mass of dreadlocks on top and two bodies welded together at the hips.

Blondie's head felt too heavy for his neck. He closed his eyes and let it drop towards his knees. Beyond the darkness of his lids the room started its ethanol spin around him. Silently he willed it to go faster, a vertiginous tumble that obliterated all sense of the outside world and then, just as he felt that his mind was dissolving away, he pulled himself out. When his eyes opened she was standing in the doorway.

From the doorway the woman gazed around the room. When she turned her face towards him Blondie saw that her eyes were pointed at the corners giving them an almond shape. The irises were coal black. He wondered who she was looking for.

She was wearing a leather jacket over a cut-down sweatshirt with 'Lunarversity' in faded letters across the chest. Memory crystals and silver thread were plaited into cotton hair extensions that were braided into a rope down her back. Blondie had an insane urge to grab hold of her hair and pull himself upright, but he didn't think it was a good idea.

She came over and stood in front of Blondie. He found himself staring at a strip of brown skin between her belt and the frayed bottom edge of her sweatshirt. When she spoke it seemed to float down from a long way above.

'I'm looking for Old Sam,' she said. 'Seen him?'

STS Central - Olympus Mons

At 01:00 GMT, one hour after the start of Constitution Day, Ming the Merciless started a phased reduction in services. It started with the branch lines in Western Europe, West Africa, Luna, Martian Plains, Mercury and all the other planets in the solar system except Triton, whose time, for historical reasons, ran at GMT + 5. Under instructions from the controllers, trains were taken out of service and shunted to their depots. All over the system passengers spat on the platforms as empty carriages cruised serenely past them. The big mainframe that handled customer complaints recorded 634 negative calls in the first ten minutes.

Ming set up one of her terminals to show the power saving as a percentage; as a laugh she put the total number of customer complaints next to it and told the computer to look for correlations. Down in the pit the controllers were passing around a bottle of Ganymede Vodka. This was one operation they didn't want to handle sober.

As midnight rushed across the globe the all-day parties started and one hour behind, the arteries that pumped life through the solar system quietly shut themselves down.

At 02:00 GMT they shut down the freight services on the parallel tunnels. The physical mail was going to be a day late. Branch lines were down to VIP shuttles and emergency services only; feeder lines were running one train in five. According to Ming's terminal they now had a thirty per cent power surplus ready for the Stunnel initiation. Verhoevan wanted seventy per cent - Ming had twelve hours left. Customer complaints were up to one and a half million negative calls and rising at a rate of a thousand every second.

Let them walk, thought Ming.

Acturus Terminal (Stunnel Terminus)

Verhoevan was inventing new words to describe the PR executives who had started to swarm in the terminus. One of them was trying to persuade Verhoevan into a pair of white coveralls.

'Why?'

'Because,' said one man, 'it looks more scientific.'

Verhoevan noticed that the coverall had the 'Event Horizon' logo picked out in navy blue on the back. Event Horizon was the President's own public-relations firm. 'More scientific?'

'For the media,' said the man, waving vaguely down the station where the media ENG's buzzed through the air, jostling with the security monitors for the best viewing angles. 'After all, you are going to be on the podium with the President.'

'What podium?'

'The Presidential Podium, a bit of an honour for you really.'

Verhoevan realized that halfway down the station a podium was being assembled out of prefab teak blocks. 'You realize, of course,' said Verhoevan, 'that your podium is situated directly in line with the Stunnel gateway.'

'Is that a problem?'

Only if the train overshoots, thought Verhoevan.

'I'd hate to have to tell the President,' the man put some bite into his voice, 'that there was a problem.'

Verhoevan sighed and accepted the coverall. The PR executive gave him a halogen smile. 'I think you will find that it fits.'

After the man had gone Verhoevan turned to find his entire staff staring at him. 'I don't know what you're looking at,' he said, brandishing the coverall at them, 'you're all going to get one too.'

STS Central – Olympus Mons

By 10:15 GMT the second shift of controllers had taken over in the pit. These ones squinted blearily at their screens and tended to react badly to loud noises. Up in the duty office, Ming, who'd been awake for thirty-six hours, chewing zap for the last eight, was trying to stay awake by calculating her overtime. They were getting media and security feeds from Acturus Terminal. The media were still getting the best viewing angles, especially the *Bad News Show*. On the repeater screen the Sydney–Kyoto commuter line went dark. Ming touched her pin mike. 'What happened to TransCancer Three?' The zap side effects made her own voice echo uncomfortably inside her head.

'Sorry, Boss,' said the sector manager, 'wrong switch. Do you want us to put it back up?'

'Just one in three,' said Ming, who didn't like the Japanese, or Australians for that matter, and wasn't going to do them any favours. She started to search through the pile of empty Kwik-Kurry cartons on her desk, somewhere underneath was another packet of zap. Or had she swallowed them already?

'Big increase in VIP shuttle activity,' said a voice.

'Destinations?'

'Acturus Terminal.'

'That's the security detachments moving in,' said Ming. 'Where's Murphy One?' Murphy One was the President's private train.

'Still at Reykjavik.'

Ming glanced at her terminal, available power reserves were now 53 per cent, customer complaints were topping a billion.

Three and a half hours to go.

Beijing

Kadiatu woke up alone in Pei Hai Park. She lay still for a long moment, sprawled out on the yellow summer grass and watched the little mobile clouds watering the flowers. She closed her eyes and stretched, letting the grass prickle along her legs. When she sat up she wondered where her hangover had gone. The sun was rising, a pale gold light that turned the ancient city walls a dusty orange. The White Pagoda cast a shadow through the mist rising from the lake. Apart from herself the park was deserted. Kadiatu stared at the lake for a moment and thought, why not? She'd pulled the T-shirt off over her head when she realised it wasn't hers. It was made from white German cotton and when she touched it to her face it smelt of blond hair and rose petals. Dropping the shirt on top of her jacket she ran down to the lakeside.

There'd been eight of them, riding a flat-top with some crazy idea about chasing midnight around the world. The Brazilian woman Lambada had been driving, sitting on the front, cowling and whooping each time they went through a station. Blondie whispered in her ear that Lambada could drive in that position because she had an interface fitted in her big toe. She remembered asking him how he came to know that. Dogface, the one with the designer-ugly face, had overheard and made obscene comments until Old Sam told him to stop. Kadiatu had been around her parents' friends long enough to know that Old Sam was a full combat model. It showed in the speed of his reflexes, in the way his pupils slotted in low light, and in his strength. She knew what had been in the package she'd delivered, the one that Old Sam slipped quietly into his coat and transferred twenty thousand into her moneypen for. Augmentation carried a price tag, a metabolic trade-off. The old soldiers walked through a world of pain as their bodies fell apart. Kadiatu had seen her own mother bite her hand until it bled. They got their prescription endorphins but for many it was not enough. They wanted the real juice, the combat drug, the one that turned them into gods in the Valles Marineris.

She reared out of the water, braids flying around her face, droplets flying off to crater the lake around her. She stood waist deep, the sun on her back, and flexed her shoulders. A pair of ochre-coloured swans cruised past with microtags pinned into their long necks, and she laughed and flicked her hair at them. The swans merely changed direction and disdainfully swam round her.

Blondie, she thought. What kind of a name was that?

She climbed out of the lake and french-braided her extensions as she walked back to her clothes. There'd been an intensity about his lovemaking, something close to anger in the way he'd clung to her afterwards. She found the rose caught in a fold of her jacket, it was a deep purple, so purple as to be almost black. He'd bought it from a vendor by the Shen Wu gate of the Forbidden City when they were watching the dragons twitching past to the snap and bang of fireworks. She'd let him tuck the rose behind her ear and they'd kissed for the first time, their lips tasting of tequila and gunpowder. She pulled his T-shirt on over her wet skin, tucked it into her leggings and pulled her belt tight around her waist. Carefully smoothing out its bruised petals she tucked the black rose back behind her ear and threw on her jacket. As she turned to go her hand slipped into her pocket to check her moneypen, a small defensive habit picked up on Luna.

Her moneypen was gone.

Acturus Terminal (Stunnel Terminus)

The PR executives were arguing with the security executives and the security executives were winning but only because they were armed. Judging from the number of security firms represented half the cabinet was going to attend the ceremony, Verhoevan could practically smell the power. The President's own security cliché, Viking Protection, were taking up positions around the finished podium. They were big grim Icelanders with dragonboat logos on their body armour, and people scrambled out of their way as they ran their checks.

Verhoevan was trying not to get his spotless coverall dirty as he made minute adjustments to the regulator. Behind the greasy shine of the gateway Lorenzo attractors were held in a precise pattern by a gravito-magnetic field. With just the carrier wave coming through they hardly moved, but once initiation started they would start to spin, drilling a hole through reality.

The KGB started ushering in the general public who'd been waiting in the unfinished galleria. A carefully selected ethnic and cultural cross section of the solar system drawn from Rent-a-Crowd's extensive books. A lot of the unemployed did Rent-a-Crowd work to supplement their welfare cheques but these looked like real professionals, ready to cheer their guts out on cue.

Twenty-six light years away, anchored deep in the bedrock of Acturus II, another set of attractors turned slowly, just enough to broadcast the carrier wave. Before the initiation could begin the attractors on Mars would have to be precisely tuned so that both sets turned in synergenic harmony. Verhoevan had initiated fifteen tunnels in his career, and not a single one had collapsed. If only the carrier wave would stop fluctuating on this one. He was sure it must be a function of the immense distance, like the gateway's colour, at least that's what he hoped it was.

'Got it,' he shouted as the regulator board went green. 'Tell Ming we can start the final countdown any time she's ready.' He looked at his hands - they were shaking.

STS Central - Olympus Mons

Ming cowered behind the armchair as her father lurched towards her. In his hands was his broad leather belt which he snapped angrily as he advanced. Ming was choking on the cheap booze smell that issued from his gaping mouth. 'No, Papa,' she whined as the beast loomed over her.

'Boss!'

Ming's neck cracked as her head came off her desk. Zap blackout, she thought, how many have I taken? The terminal screen was fuzzy, and she squinted it into focus - 71 per cent power availability.

How long had she been out?

'Boss!'

'What?'

'Verhoevan says he's ready.'

'Where's Murphy One?'

'On its way.'

'Verhoevan?'

On a media feed Ming saw Verhoevan plug his finger into a handy socket. 'Yeah?'

'What the hell are you wearing?'

'Don't ask.'

'The President's on his way.'

'I never would have guessed, have we got the power?'

'Yes, but get on with it.'

'Guess what?'

'What?'

'I'm going to be on the podium with the rest of the high and mighty.'

Ming cut the connection. Her head was beginning to throb. The customer complaints mainframe had crashed, the negative calls display was filled with gibberish. The main display had zoomed in on the Acturus Terminal schematix, the Stunnel had become a thick silver cable, the terminus a cone in semi-opaque green, the offshoot of the Central Line a thinner cable in red that trailed off screen. White lines were overlaid on the image, the room temperature superconductors that would carry the power from all over the system to the Stunnel gateway. Junction markers were picked out as blue triangles clustering around the open end of the green cone; on the master board the power conduits were highlighted, the beast's nervous system laid suddenly bare.

Ming stood up, stepped over to the rail and leaned over. Down in the pit the controllers all turned to stare up at her.

'All right children,' said Ming, 'let's crank it up.'

Kings Cross (Central Line)

Kadiatu came running out of the Paris Axis platform. Behind her the wasp whine of the ticket drone followed. It had picked her up when she changed at Manderlay, tracking her by pheremone and heat signature. She could have lost it in a crowd, but today there weren't any crowds. The ECM crystal plaited into her hair was useless: this close any interference pattern would light her up like a shop display. Somewhere behind the drone was an inspector, by law a human being, slowly closing in to arrest her.

Kings Cross was an old station from the time when train tunnels were just long horizontal holes in the ground. An evolved station not a planned one, a ganglia that gathered up half the transcontinental feeder lines that quilted Europe, a messy disorder of physical tunnels and a good place to lose a ticket drone.

She jumped into a lift marked Krakow in blue letters, breathing hard as the field snapped her two hundred metres up the shaft and on to the platform. The indicator hologram said the next train was in three minutes, not soon enough. A couple of men were standing underneath the sign, not enough of them either. They looked wary as Kadiatu ran towards them, two respectable English guys in topknots and linen kaftans. 'Lend us fifty,' she said as they backed away. 'I just need it for the fare home.'

Too late. She could hear the ticket drone again, its engine whine echoing in the lift shaft. 'Shouldn't be allowed,' said one of the men as Kadiatu dashed for the exit.

She should have known better than to get cosy with some low life from the Stop. Now she was gatecrashing the transit system with no moneypen and twenty grand in debt to Max. That wasn't going to be six hours walking-around time with no kinky stuff, Max was going to invent new perversions to pay off twenty thousand. Except it wasn't going to come to that, because she was going to catch up with Blondie, get her money back and then some.

First she had to ditch the ticket drone.

Acturus Terminal (Stunnel Terminus)

Power fed into the gravitic induction field, and the attractors started to whirl. Biting into the soft stuff of reality like drill teeth into sandstone. It was silent work, an operation on a level far away from human senses, but in his mind Verhoevan thought he heard the space-time continuum groaning under the assault. Data flowed past the peripheral vision of his left eye. The alarming fluctuations in the carrier wave had ceased, the signal was good and strong.

'Citizens,' a voice boomed, 'I give you the President of the Union of Solar Republics.'

Verhoevan was seated six seats along and one row back from the President. He had an excellent view of the famous bull neck as the fount of all political power rose to his feet. The Rent-a-Crowd started cheering and the President grinned with pleasure, waving his left hand to calm them down. Verhoevan wondered if the man got real satisfaction from such a crowd, knowing that the cheers came on the precise cues of the Event Horizon stage managers.

'My fellow citizens,' said the President.

At that moment Verhoevan noticed that the attractor spin rate was accelerating above the initiation parameters.

'My fellow citizens,' said the President again, as the crowd fell silent. 'We are assembled here to witness one of the most remarkable engineering projects of our times.'

Verhoevan considered it might be a power surge but the input rates remained stable. Planned initiation was in ten minutes, a carefully calculated climax to the President's speech, but the tunnel seemed to have other ideas. If the power wasn't coming from this end of the Stunnel where was it coming from?

'An engineering project that will provide opportunities for new industries, new growth and above all new employment for the nation.'

Verhoevan looked over the heads of the professionally intent crowd. The gateway seemed placid enough, but behind it the attractors whirled out of control, skidding into a new configuration. The figures piled up on the inside of his eye, crowding his sight, he was caught up in a sudden painful terror.

'It is a project that only one nation, in a galaxy crowded with nations, one nation that would have the expertise, the courage and in bald truth the audacity to conceive of. This day will become a piece of history.'

The flags suspended from the ceiling rustled in a sudden breeze, a scrap of paper by the gateway controls whirled into the air. Verhoevan lurched to his feet.

'Shut it down,' he screamed at his staff, 'shut it down.'

But it was too late.

Kings Cross (Central Line)

It was the blue box that did for Kadiatu. It had no reason to be on the Central Line platform and perhaps that's why she ran straight into it.

The inspector had almost caught her moments before when she made a break for the surface, waiting for her in front of the exit lifts as she raced out of a connecting passageway. Kadiatu had a good look at him as she tried to translate her forward momentum into a turn. Thin lips under a black visor, the yellow and black sigil on the chest plate of his armour, ancient logo of the KGB, the world's oldest security firm. With the ticket drone behind her Kadiatu was forced on to the empty platform.

Exhaustion, thought Kadiatu, exhaustion made me stupid.

She tried to get to her feet but the platform felt too comfortable. From where she lay the box looked enormous. It seemed to lean over her and she was suddenly scared that it might topple over and crush her underneath. Down the platform she could hear a pair of heavy boots crunching towards her.

Wind whispered through the station.

2:

Crazy Paving Man

Kings Cross (Central Line)

Bernice decided that the Doctor had a cavalier attitude to first steps. In her experience the first step into a new environment could kill you faster than a bad-tempered Dalek. You were supposed to be cautious. The explorers' manual had a check list: check the atmosphere, check for bugs, animals, subsidence, solar radiation, check that the goddam landing ramp had extended properly. It went on for fifteen pages.

Not the Doctor, though, Bernice thought. A quick look round with the TARDIS scanner, he puts on his hat, opens the door, and out he goes.

It was the Doctor's assumption of invulnerability that worried Bernice. She hoped it applied to her as well.

When she followed him out of the door, it was with the guilty assumption that anything nasty would have to go through him first.

And that was her first mistake.

STS Central – Olympus Mons

The security feeds went down in a blaze of static.

'What the hell was that?' yelled Ming.

She switched a monitor over to English 37 and *The Bad News Show*, Yak Harris caught between slots, frozen solid with his mouth open. There was a sudden pixel flicker and Yak's suit changed colour.

I'll be damned, thought Ming, he really is a computer program.

'Well,' said Yak Harris, jerking into life. 'Well, we seem to be having some technical problems from the Acturus Terminus.'

You and me both, thought Ming. Up on the status boards a silver line pierced into the station's heart. 'Give me an op-stat on the stellar tunnel.'

'It's down,' said a controller.

'Down?'

'Just the carrier wave.'

'Can't be down,' Ming checked the status board again. 'We pumped twenty-two gigawatts into the bloody thing.' Enough to fry a small town. 'Any contact with the terminal?'

'Nope.'

'Why not?'

'Break down at the terminal end.'

'Hardware or software?'

'Your guess is as good as mine.'

'Get maintenance for me,' said Ming, 'and the KGB.'

The master console in her office chimed for her attention. Threat analysis catching up with the real world displaying an options panel on the screen. The computer wanted Ming to choose between a technical malfunction or external threat. She glared at the screen.

Not yet, she thought, not until I know what's going on.

A timecode at the top of the screen counted down from thirty minutes. When it reached zero the computer would make up its own mind. Ming wanted to know what moron had thought of that.

It was three minutes since the Stunnel was supposed to have opened, four minutes since they lost contact with Acturus Terminal. Ming's instincts were to boot the problem upstairs but the senior management had all been attending the opening ceremony.

She was on her own.

She tore the corner of her last packet of zap and dumped one in a cup full of dead coffee. It started to fizz. She ordered the controllers to isolate the terminal and start pulling the trains out of the depots and whack them back into the tunnels.

The President was at the opening ceremony too. Which meant she should have heard from the security services by now, from Event Horizon at the very least.

On the media feed Yak Harris was talking to a panel of experts. A good sign that the media didn't know what had happened either. Ming wondered whether the pundits were computer-generated as well.

The Stop

The air was the colour of dust and there was no memory of a warning, no precognition, no transition, just a sudden birth into this confusion of falling stone. Instinct and training dragged her forward towards a rectangular patch of light ahead. Left hand clamped over her mouth, shallow breathing through her fingers, forcing herself to stay upright, smoke rises but dust falls.

She had a sense of a heavy mass shifting above her and she stumbled faster. Shadows crashed down behind her, shock waves billowed through the dust, streaming around her and into the light. For an instant she saw the figure of a woman framed in the rectangle ahead. An image of herself, hunched and stumbling.

No warning, like an orbital strike, like a missile in terminal phase, sprinting ahead of its sound wave. Not even a whisper before it hits and strips the houses down to their bare bones.

From in front, she thought as she met the impossible shadow face to face, the light is coming from the front. Then she knew, even before the dust veil lifted to reveal the face.

'Mother,' she wailed, hands groping forward, grasping and meeting nothing. Dust filled her throat and eyes, stopping up the tears. Left her blindly struggling forward. 'Mother,' she tried to call out but the dust choked off the sound. Blindly she fought to get further but it felt as if the dust was piling up around her, drifts creeping up her thighs and back. Her mind became filled with the heavy thud of her heartbeat, her chest filling up with an awful vacuum, as if some membrane had torn as she fell forward into space and clear air.

Terminal phase, the final fall to ground zero.

Impact.

Stale air blew out of her lungs, saliva and dust spewing upwards in an arc. A stripe of numbness crashed down her side and arm. She heard her bones breaking and in that moment she remembered her name.

Kings Cross (Central Line)

Kadiatu remembered another rescue like this. Thrashing useless limbs, swallowing water, watching the sunlight recede as she sank down into the stream. Under the water her friends' voices became shrill and distant. When she bashed her head against the side of the boat it was like a wooden gong, a deep profundo boom which intermingled with the pain until she couldn't tell them apart. Her father saved her that time, yanked her from the river by the hair, his big fist knotted in her braids. That's why your mother plaits your hair, he told her later, to give me something to grab hold of.

Something had come through the station.

Something that howled out of the tunnel and filled the wind with knives and the stink of ozone. The Inspector had been lifted from his feet and hung shaking before her. There was a sharp crack as his visor shattered and Kadiatu glimpsed a pale contorted face. Then he vanished in an expanding cloud of blue vapour that was in turn shredded by the wind and blown away.

That was when somebody grabbed Kadiatu's hair and pulled her to safety. Except she wasn't a child any more, wasn't drowning in the washing stream on a bright Makeni morning to the shrill screams of her friends. It was not her father's hand that was knotted in her hair, yanking her up and away from the platform edge. Whoever it was they were strong, lifting her easily to her feet as if she still were that child and not the seventy-two kilos of bone and muscle she had become.

'Not again,' said a voice by her ear.

Acturus Terminal (Stunnel Terminus)

Old Sam was moving, really moving, way beyond the normal human range. As they moved up on the galleria he was almost too fast for the eye to catch.

'Jesus, Sam,' hissed Dogface, 'slow down, will you?'

Old Sam came to a sudden halt by the entrance and stood rock still. 'Slow enough?' There was a manic edge to his voice.

'Are you wired?' asked Lambada.

'Just some Doberman,' said Old Sam.

Blondie heard Lambada swearing under her breath. Ahead galleria was in darkness, the entrance a pitch black rectangle. Blondie didn't think it was a good place for Old Sam, not with him cranked up on Doberman.

'Don't worry,' said Old Sam, 'it's good stuff.'

'It's not the bloody quality I'm worried about,' said Lambada. 'Where's it from?'

'I scored it off Blondie's girlfriend,' Old Sam grinned at Blondie, 'didn't I?'

They all turned to stare at Blondie who blushed.

'Never mind that,' said Dogface to Old Sam. 'How are you feeling?'

'Fast and mean!' said Old Sam.

'You can go first then,' said Lambada.

'OK,' said Old Sam and vanished into the darkness.

Lambada glared at Blondie.

'How was I supposed to know?' said Blondie.

'He'll be all right,' said Dogface.

'It's not him I'm worried about,' said Lambada, 'it's us. What if he has a flashback?'

'I haven't had a flashback in ten years,' said Old Sam from just behind them. Lambada jerked round and grabbed Sam by his lapels.

'Don't do that!'

'Sorry,' said Old Sam and Lambada let go.

'Well?' asked Dogface.

'The galleria's clear of targets,' reported Old Sam. 'I haven't been into the station yet.'

'No people?' asked Lambada.

'That's what I said,' said Old Sam.

'You said targets.'

'People, targets.' Old Sam shrugged. 'What's the difference?'

Dogface linked with Credit Card back at the Olympus West and told him to put on the emergency lights.

'Up in thirty seconds,' said Credit Card.

Ming broke into the link. 'Well?'

'We're going in as soon as the lights are on,' said Dogface. 'Any word from the KGB?'

'Nothing from them or Viking Security.'

'Lights are up,' said Credit Card.

'Call you back, Ming,' said Dogface.

Old Sam led them across the empty galleria, Dogface and Blondie in the middle with Lambada bringing up the rear. Dogface kept his fingers in contact with the portable link box.

'What's that smell?' asked Lambada.

It came from the Kwik-Kurry franchise. A ten-litre pot of curried goat was beginning to burn. Lambada turned off the stove, 'No one here.'

Dogface stuck his finger into the pot and tasted it. 'Maybe they didn't like the goat.'

'Come off it,' said Lambada, 'everyone loves goat.'

'Goat flavouring,' said Dogface.

'Whatever,' said Lambada.

'Did you check the concourse?' Dogface asked Old Sam.

'Nothing.'

'Credit Card,' said Dogface.

'Yo.'

'Tell Ming we're going in now.'

Kings Cross (Central Line)

'Where does that tunnel go?' said the voice at Kadiatu's ear.

'Let go,' said Kadiatu and the fingers relaxed their grip on her hair. In her mind Kadiatu had constructed a huge man with oiled biceps capable of lifting her one-handed, but when she turned his hat was level with her shoulders.

'Who are you?'

The man ignored her and gazed down to the far end of the station and the tunnel gateway. The tip of his red-handled umbrella tapped insistently on the platform. 'That tunnel,' he said, 'where does it go?'

Blue paint was splattered in a long irregular line down the length of the platform. Kadiatu squatted down and reached out a hand to touch it. Her hand was trembling.

'Don't,' said the man.

The paint was wet and sticky, roughened by the thin layer of grit that covered the formed concrete of the platform. She picked up a small lump between her thumb and forefinger. It felt like a hardened composite, the edges had run like wax. It was a chunk of the inspector's body armour.

Kadiatu stood up fast, the lump falling from her hand on to the trackway below to sizzle for a moment on the friction field. Her shoulders jerked backwards as if trying to distance her body from the stain on her fingers. Bile clawed its way up her throat as her body began to shake itself to pieces.

The slap was hard enough to snap her head sideways.
'Better?' asked the man.
Kadiatu nodded. Her cheek was stinging, there was a hint of blood in her mouth. 'Who are you?'
'I'm the Doctor,' said the man.
He was shorter than her but Kadiatu felt that he looked down on her from a greater height. In the flat station lights she couldn't tell what colour his eyes were.
'Doctor of what?'
'Everything,' said the Doctor.
She could see his eyes now, they were a vivid angry brown. They seemed to track across her face, as palpable as a rastascan. 'What are you staring at?'
'Nothing,' said the Doctor. 'Where does that tunnel lead?'
'Eventually?'
'That would do for a start.'
'Pluto.'
'How do I get there?'
'Wait for the next train,' said Kadiatu.
The Doctor looked back at the tunnel gateway. 'Next time I'm going to find a better place to park.'
'What?'
'Well,' said the Doctor. 'I've kept you long enough, I'm sure you have things to do, people to see.' He pulled out a gold watch on a fob chain and checked the time. He glanced idly down the platform again before looking down to examine his shoes. The umbrella restarted its tattoo on the grimy concrete.
'Why are you still here?' he said after a moment.
'I'm waiting for the train,' said Kadiatu. She risked a glance sideways at the Doctor. He was scowling at the wall opposite. He nodded in an abstracted fashion.
You saved my life, thought Kadiatu, and now you're pretending I don't exist.
'Sorry,' said the Doctor without looking round, 'It was an accident.'
'What do you mean, an accident?'
'It's a reflex of mine,' said the Doctor. 'I see someone in danger and I try to save them. I can't help myself.'
Kadiatu nodded at the blue splatter along the platform. 'What about him?'

For an instant a spasm of real pain crossed the Doctor's face. 'You were closer,' he said. 'When's the next train?'

Kadiatu glanced at the indicator holo. It said 'Check Destination on Front of Train' - not a good sign.

'Don't hold your breath,' she told him.

'I'll try not to.'

'I need a drink,' said Kadiatu suddenly. 'How about you?'

Acturus Terminal (Stunnel Terminus)

The station had been swept clean of people. Blondie's shoes stuck with every step in the sticky blue stuff that covered the floor and splattered the walls. The Stunnel gateway was a spinning copper gong nailed to the far wall.

Dogface had his arm around Old Sam's shoulders. The veteran was shaking badly, there was a weasel madness in his slotted eyes. Dogface was talking low and fast, trying to get Old Sam off whichever memory shore he'd beached on. Lambada was assembling an industrial calibre hypo, her face fixed into a concentrated grin as she clipped it together. When the device was complete she walked up behind Old Sam, placed its blunt head against his thigh and squeezed the trigger. The hiss went on for a long time, and when it finished Old Sam toppled over with a look of intense happiness fixed on his face.

'Doberman,' said Lambada disgustedly.

Blondie found something protruding from the blue.

'What's this?'

Lambada had a look. 'Portable comms link.'

'Did someone drop it?'

Lambada and Dogface exchanged worried looks. 'Blondie,' said Lambada, 'it's an internal unit. It's implanted and runs parallel to the spinal column.'

Under the skin.

'What is this stuff?' asked Dogface.

'I don't know,' said Lambada.

'Look at the splatter patterns, they all radiated from the gateway.'

'As if something came through and . . .' Lambada made a sweeping motion with her hands. They ended up looking into the entrance gateway to the Central Line extension.

'Yeah,' said Dogface, 'but why blue?'

'I don't know.'

'I don't get it,' said Blondie. 'Where is everyone, where's the President?'

'I think we're standing in them,' said Dogface.

TransIonian

The Worthing-Le Havre branch line was operating close to normal so Kadiatu and the Doctor rode the train to Caen and changed on to the Fracais-Sardegna Feeder. People were riding the long blue commuter trains and Kadiatu began to feel normal again. The Doctor was quiet all the way to Porto Torres, which at least gave her a good ten minutes' thinking time. Not that she thought of anything much.

'Where are we now?' asked the Doctor.

'Sardinia.'

'Really?'

'Yes.'

'How extraordinary,' said the Doctor. 'Where are we going now?'

'We're going to ride the Connection.'

The TransIonian should have been a feeder route, shiny blue trains should have shuttled commuters from the sea cities of the Ionian sea, but the floating cities were never built, just the anchor points and the transit stations underneath. Now it was good for nothing except a slow crawl to Athinai. Whatever had swept through Kings Cross wasn't going to travel this line. Only dealers and punters rode the Connection.

An ancient Korean single-carriage train was waiting with its doors open. Green paint peeled off the superstructure, its windows were opaque with dirt, the inside smelt strongly of sweat and urine.

Kadiatu warned the Doctor not to sit down.

At the rear of the compartment a filthy bundle of rags unfolded, and yellow eyes glared at them from under a leather slouch hat.

'Who's that?' asked the Doctor.

'That's the conductor.'

The conductor grunted in their direction before shambling over to the open doorway. When he leaned out Kadiatu caught a glimpse of gunmetal blue slung beneath his jacket.

'Anymore for anymore,' shouted the conductor.

Satisfied that no one else was boarding, the conductor collapsed back into his seat. The doors closed with a wheeze of ageing hydraulics and the train lurched off towards the gateway. There was a jolt as the carriage penetrated the interface, shafts of light strobed through the imperfect shielding. The seats were too sticky to sit on, so Kadiatu and the Doctor hung on to the straps against the train's erratic motion.

'First stop,' called the conductor from the back. 'Women's clothing, lingerie, pharmaceuticals.'

The train slowed as it entered the first station but it didn't stop. Instead the doors cranked open on override as they coasted slowly through. On the platform crowds of people milled around stalls and bundles of merchandise. The smell of cheap perfume wafted inside the carriage. A woman jumped nimbly onboard near the front of the carriage, and somebody on the platform started throwing bundles of cloth which she caught. By the end of the station she had a small pile stacked on the seats beside her. There was another jolt, the doors closed and they were in the tunnel again. The woman looked over at Kadiatu and the Doctor but didn't say anything. That was the cardinal rule of the connection - no business on the train.

'Second stop,' called the conductor. 'Sporting goods and leisurewear.'

Again the train coasted through a station with its doors jammed open. This time two Vriks jumped on, a boy and a girl, high-caste Brahmin types with short black hair and grey eyes. The girl stacked her long board along the seats, the boy kept hold of his beatbox, hefting it like a weapon.

'Who are they?' asked the Doctor.

'Free surfers,' said Kadiatu. The Doctor must really be out-system not to know that. 'What's the matter,' she called to the Vriks, 'cracked board or has the music stopped working?'

The girl snarled at Kadiatu who kissed her teeth in return.

'Manners,' said the Doctor to no one in particular.

The Vriks grabbed their straps as the train lurched off into the next tunnel. The Vriks had wild eyes from too much unshielded transit, the rich kid's lifestyle, live fast and die flat against an oncoming train.

'Third stop,' called the conductor. 'Catamites, courtesans and computer processing.'

'Time to get off,' Kadiatu told the Doctor as the doors opened. With a brief wave at the Vriks she jumped from the carriage. She came down harder than she meant and stumbled; behind her the Doctor landed on the platform like a cat.

There were no stalls set up on the station platform, instead flickering holograms above the exits pulled at the eye. Looking at them made Kadiatu feel hot and bothered. Probably packed with subliminals, thought Kadiatu and glanced back to see how the Doctor was doing. He'd stopped to look at one of the holograms. It showed a woman in abbreviated Ice-Warrior armour chained against a wall of folded neon. The thrust of her hips promised aggression and imminent violation. 'Ice Maiden's' famous logo, the iconography of the thousand days war. The Doctor's face was intent as he examined the hologram, not aroused, merely curious as if the writhing figure was an anthropological exhibit.

'What about love?' said the Doctor.

What about love? Love was a black rose and a missing moneypen, a rip off waiting for you to drop your guard.

'Sex and death are pretty close, I guess,' said Kadiatu.

'Only in humans,' said the Doctor.

Ice Maiden's entrance was through the far exit and up a ramp. At the door a joyboy in leather skintights stood in their way. 'Buying or selling?' he asked.

'What do you think?'

The joyboy nodded at the Doctor. 'What about Daddy?'

'Who knows?' said Kadiatu and walked past.

The original Ice Maiden had been an R&R stop in Jacksonville - halfway up Olympus Mons. A good place for the grunts to chill out after their duty tours in the chaotic terrain and shrieking winds of the Valles Marineris. And Francine, who'd done two and a half tours with the 31st, had recreated it under the ocean, right down to the puff concrete walls and rusty blast doors.

'Interesting place for a drink,' said the Doctor.

'Not here,' said Kadiatu, 'Drinks later, business first.'

Behind the bar was a big woman, almost as tall as Kadiatu and dressed in the same stylized Ice-Warrior gear as the joyboy outside. 'Tasteless,' said the Doctor.

'Where's Francine?' Kadiatu asked the woman.

'Who wants to know?'

'A friend of the family.'

'I didn't know that Francine had a family.'

'That's why you're working the bar,' said Kadiatu, 'and I'm asking the questions.'

The antechamber round the back had a gun hanging from the ceiling like a chandelier. It was an electric autogun, a cluster of rotating barrels suspended on a gimbled stanchion. An unnecessary mass of pressure leads at the top hissed as the gun tracked Kadiatu and the Doctor around the room. Francine could have installed hidden lasers in the light fittings, but she wanted her visitors to know that they were under her sights. The gun was a fashion statement.

A door opened in the far wall.

Kadiatu told the Doctor to stay where he was and went in. Francine was lying with her eyes closed on a divan in the centre of the room.

'Hallo, Aunty,' said Kadiatu.

The mobile half of Francine's face formed into a smile.

'Kadiatu,' she said, 'you got big.'

Kadiatu knelt down by the divan and put her arms around the old woman. Francine caught hold of her braids and playfully shook her head. 'I suppose it was bound to happen,' her hand traced the contours of Kadiatu's face, 'still got your daddy's nose though.'

The angel Francine.

Falling from orbit with the thin Martian air screaming across her wings. Terminal dives into the twisting canyons of the Noctis Labyrinthus with a bellyful of tactical nukes. Knitted into the cockpit, her mind blitzed on Doberman and Heinkel the air turbulence lit up like neon, doing the missions too dumb for the smart weapons.

Lost it in the east over the Gangis Chasma, shaking apart in the grip of a pop-up cannon - one of those little oversights by military intelligence. Francine fighting all the way down to the dunes, the violet sky whirling around her. Dying amidst her broken wings of carbon fibre.

It was Kadiatu's father that pulled her out, holding the LZ clear for a swift medevac back to the world. Riding up on the running board, so the story went, bagging Greenies all the way.

Francine opened white marble eyes and looked at Kadiatu. 'Who's the man?'

Rumour said that Francine's eyes were coded into the high ultraviolet and low infrared, nothing in the visible spectrum at all. Kadiatu wondered what it was like living in the world of the invisible.

'Calls himself the Doctor,' said Kadiatu.

'He the problem?'

'No.'

'Money trouble?'

Kadiatu told Francine about the deal with Max, about the moneypen gone missing in a park outside the Forbidden City. 'You want this Blondie bagged?' asked Francine. Kadiatu hoped she was joking and said no, she'd take care of that herself. Francine offered some walking-around money and promised to put a trace on the moneypen.

As Kadiatu was leaving Francine said one more thing. 'You might ask your friend what he needs two hearts for?'

The Stop

I'm not going to do that again, thought Benny, whatever it was that I did. She was unwilling to move her head just yet, above her a shaft three metres across vanished upwards into the gloom. It was lit by a single strip of xenon lighting that tinted the walls the colour of ancient gunmetal. Half way up, the xenon strip was broken by a rectangular shadow. Facing it on the other side of the shaft was an identical door-shaped hole. Even from where she was lying Benny could see that the edges of both holes were razor clean, the kind of cut a force field makes. They were two, maybe two and half metres tall, about a metre wide and at least twenty metres up the shaft.

It was a long way to fall.

A fall like that would break your back, grind your vertebrae flat, shatter ribs. The absence of pain scared her, it indicated such a massive trauma as to put the whole body into shock. Better to breathe shallow and wait for help.

Waiting for help, like the shelter, packed in with the stink of vomit, urine and fear. The small children screaming in terror as the lights went out. Benny pressed up against the porthole, the silhouette of her mother burnt on to her retina, bright rainbow flashes as the radiation conflicted with the shelter's preservation field. An adult voice behind her called out the survivor statistics on the deep transmitter. 'Shallow breathing exercise, children,' said teacher from somewhere near the back, 'help's coming.'

Benny moved, she didn't believe in teacher no more.

There was no pain as she got up but when she ran a hand down her side to check for broken ribs her skin felt dry and cracked. She picked at a flap just above her hip and a long strip peeled away, an oily purple under the xenon lights. Not her skin then, but something that she'd been coated in, perhaps during the cave in. Her coverall was missing its sleeves and most of the back. What was left was glued to her skin.

Benny looked up the shaft at the rectangular hole above and tried to remember which antique tribe used to paint themselves blue.

She realised that she was standing in an inverted *T*-junction, horizontal shafts leading off to the left and right. The same concrete walls, inset conduits and xenon strips as the shaft above her.

Concrete walls, she thought. Not a station then, a planet or an asteroid base - the shafts had the look of service tunnels, lighting strips with hard edges, not the diffusion units she was used to. An old-fashioned style, someone had mentioned time travel but how far back?

She remembered a series of boxes within boxes, infinity nesting within the finite, a control room that seemed almost a parody of technology. A figure standing at a console. It too was transdimensional - something monstrous crammed down into a parody of human flesh.

The light came down on her from above, brilliant and ecstatic. The weight of it pressed her down on to her knees. Benny felt as if the light shone right through her like an x-ray laser, heating up her insides and making silhouettes of her bones.

And all the children were there, from the shelter and the long dorm at the academy. Faces as yellowed as the ancient porcelain of the doll that was centrepiece of the trophy cabinet. All those fit young bodies running into the forest, clean limbs and bright eyes waiting for her, waiting for the airburst and the butcher's knife.

Again Benny came out, still standing beneath the shaft, the cold still making the floor vibrate beneath her feet. She felt awfully alone, a deep mammalian need for human contact, for warm skin and the sweet wash of pheremones. Homesick for night-time in the long dorm with the murmur of sleeping children.

Maybe time travel fucks with your mind, thought Benny.

Piraiévs

Rain fell on the pitted tarmac of the Akti Miaoulis, it rattled off the rusting steel of the ferries that listed in the grey water of the harbour. A party of archaeologists ran past the taverna, holding sheets of newsfax above their heads to keep the rain off. Kadiatu watched them splashing through the puddles towards the derelict customs house.

'We were talking,' said the Doctor, 'about the meaning of life.' He pushed a square of feta cheese around his plate. They were sitting out on the taverna's veranda which gave them an unequalled view of the crumbling docks. Rain drummed on the thatched roof overhead.

'We were?' said Kadiatu. 'Are you sure?'

The Doctor poured the remains of their second bottle of ouzo into his glass. 'Of course I'm sure. I'm always sure.' He looked around the table. 'At least I'm sure that we need another bottle.'

Kadiatu ordered another bottle of ouzo.

'Do you believe in fate?' asked the Doctor.

'No,' said Kadiatu.

'Pre-destination?'

'Only in game shows.'

The landlord's daughter arrived with the ouzo and thumped it down on the table. Kadiatu managed to grab it before the Doctor and poured herself a drink.

'So why are you here?' asked the Doctor.

Kadiatu held up her glass. 'To get drunk.'

'Why here?'

'Cheapest bar I know.'

'Why am I here then?' asked the Doctor.

'I thought you wanted a drink.'

The Doctor finished his glass and poured some more. 'I never drink,' he said. 'I'm famous for my not drinking.'

'How many bottles so far?'

'This is the fourth,' said the Doctor.

The Doctor was silent for a while, intent on the bottom of his glass. Behind them, from the taverna proper came the sound of dominoes clicking on starched linen. Kadiatu could feel the drink slowly unknotting her stomach. Across the harbour the dirty white apartment blocks clambered through the rain and up the hills to Athens.

'So why are you here?' asked Kadiatu.

'I'm celebrating,' said the Doctor without looking up.

'What are you celebrating?'

'A birthday.'

'Yours?'

'Not exactly.'

'Whose then?'

Kadiatu saw his eyes again as he looked into her face.

'The universe,' he said.

Kadiatu snorted.

'You don't think the universe has a birthday, do you?' said the Doctor. There was an angry edge to his voice. 'Well, it does. In exactly ten minutes the universe will be thirteen billion five hundred million twenty thousand and twelve years old.'

'Maybe we should get it a cake.'

'No,' said the Doctor, 'that wouldn't be a good idea.'

'Why not?'

'You'd never fit all the candles on.' The Doctor poured them both another drink. 'You'd think,' he said, 'that it would be old enough to look after itself.'

'I always thought it did.'

'You wish.'

Kadiatu watched through her drink as the Doctor drained his glass. 'Why do you have two hearts?'

'Because I'm the anomaly, the spanner in the works, the fly in the ointment, the cheese grater in the goldfish bowl.'

'I know what you are,' said Kadiatu.

The Doctor smiled at her and tilted his chair back until it balanced on two legs. 'Do you', he said, 'really?'

'You're the butterfly wing.'

'I'm nothing of the sort,' said the Doctor rocking back and forth. 'I'm just an old man getting drunk.'

'You're not drunk,' said Kadiatu, 'you're not capable of anything as simple as getting drunk.'

'No?'

'You're just behaving in the manner of someone getting drunk.'

'In that case,' said the Doctor, 'why am I about to pass out?' The Doctor vanished from sight. There was a crash as the chair hit the tiled floor.

Kadiatu carefully stood up and looked over the table. The Doctor was lying on his back, still in the chair. His eyes were closed. He was singing softly to himself, his slurred voice curling upwards like cigarette smoke.

'Happy birthday to you, happy birthday to you . . .'

Nowhere

Although she knew it to be a lie, the memories Bernice had of her father were always tinged with the golden light of late evening. He smelt of the cologne her mother would synthesize in the kitchen, smiling to herself as she tapped out the puter code. A secret smile with one corner of her mouth higher than the other. The cologne would go into the engraved pewter bottle that had once belonged to her grandmother. When her father went away into space her mother would fold the bottle carefully into his clothes as she slipped them in his vacuum-resistant carryall.

When he left he let Bernie walk with him as far as the transmat. His big gentle hand holding hers as they walked through the sculpture park that fringed the married officers' quarters. She'd wanted him to take her to the play area with its twisted swing and cushion grass but he said he couldn't.

When he came back then, she'd demanded.

Yes, he said, when he came back.

He waved goodbye to Bernice from the transmat's staging platform. The last golden light of the evening lighting up his face, gleaming off his polished silver cap badge.

It was the last time she saw him.

Bernice ran home to her mother whose face had become suddenly grey and pinched.

Lay down your troubles.
The last dying light, changing the silver into gold.
Lay down your troubles, and let me fill you up with certainty.
'Yes,' said Benny, 'certainty.'

The Stop

Zamina bought herself a bag of kola nuts at Tblisi Central before grabbing the Char'kov–Warazawa–London feeder train. She chewed through two waiting for her Central Line connection at Kings Cross. The bitter nuts helped keep her awake and take the semen taste out of her mouth. She waited incognito amongst the commuter crowd, a shapeless tan folding-coat over her working clothes, day-dreaming that she too was travelling back to some arcology on the Plains of Elysium instead of outsystem to the Stop. Everyone groaned loudly when the hologram said 'Unavoidable Delay', all of them made suddenly equal by the vagaries of public transport.

She finished the nuts as the train pulled out of Oberon and spent the last leg of the journey carefully folding the brown paper bag into smaller and smaller squares. Zamina always kept her bags, saving them until she had a kilo or so to flog down at big market. They were out of the commuter belt now and the carriage was half empty and filled with a grim silence. When the train slid into Lowell an old voicebox always said: 'This train terminates here.'

Terminate was the word. People seemed to pull themselves out on to the platform, reluctantly admitting that this was where they were well and truly terminating.

Roberta was there, propping up the wall by the pawnbroker concession in the ticket office. A half-naked catfood monster was heaped in a fetal position on the concrete beside her, a line of spittle drooling from a slack mouth. Roberta was idly poking the monster in the back with the toe of her boot, considering whether to roll him or not; sometimes even a derelict had something worth stealing. Roberta wasn't happy about waiting all this time for Zamina but two were better than one walking the Stop.

There were more catfood monsters on Main Street. Clumps of them at regular intervals down the sidewalk. 'Got any scrip?' they mumbled as Roberta and Zamina walked past.

'Fuck off,' said Roberta to each of them in turn.

A detox crew in grubby whites were zipping up a body bag on the corner of Main and Percy. Yellow tape was strung out round the crime scene while a battered forensic scanner bobbed uncertainly over the area. A couple of housing authority cops kept a wary eye on the gawkers. Target visors restlessly scanning the blank white faces of the crowd. A detective with a bone-weary stance and a scraped-off masai haircut watched over the drone as it sniffed the ground.

'Ute's dead,' said Roberta as they crossed the road to avoid the cops. 'Happened back of the depot, some kind of structural collapse - really weird.'

The back end of the depot was Dixie territory, Ute was straight-up Afrikaans. 'What was she doing out of area?' said Zamina.

'You know,' said Roberta, 'nothing legal.'

At least half the skylights were out on Williamsberg Avenue creating an evil twilight in the lead up to the projects. Roberta didn't say much as they turned down the walkway to block fifty-six, keeping a wary eye on the shadows. Blocks twenty to ninety-four were solid Afrikaans and Der Broederbund generally kept the streets clear of any action they weren't running themselves. Still there was always the possibility of a raiding party by the Dixie Rebs or Le Penn Freikorps. A couple of girls could get themselves slotted forgetting that.

Zamina and Roberta's flat was on level three, up an evil-smelling concrete stairwell. Roberta lit the way up with a billy-lamp. Holding the heavy vulcanised rubber cylinder above her head, ready to use it as a club if she had to.

'I saw Zak,' said Roberta halfway up the stairs, 'doing it to some monkey in Pei Hai park.'

Zamina said nothing and kept going. Roberta didn't like Zak, didn't like him for proving her wrong. Roberta told the future for pin money, spreading a pack of cards on a scarf of irkutzi silk. Regular cards, not tarot, she had a special pack that came from an extinct casino in Las Vegas, each card neatly punched through the centre. Roberta said they did that when you won big, to kill the luck and to stop you marking the cards. Once when Zamina was stoned she had a vision of a cowboy standing on a high desert plateau, shooting the cards as they tumbled through the air. She knew they did it with a hole punch but sometimes when she was on the edge of waking the cowboy would walk into her dreams on booted feet, lucite and snakeskin burning in a desert sunrise.

Patterns, Roberta said, everything was in the patterns, the relationships between one card and those around it. Like the patterns contained within neural networks, the variegated webs that made up the brain. Roberta had spread the cards for Zak one day and told him straight out that he would die young in the Stop.

But Zak had walked away from the program, from Roberta's sharp little synopsis of life and death in the ghetto, and Roberta had never forgiven him for it.

'Don't you want to know about it?'

Zamina didn't, but she knew Roberta would tell her anyway. There in a grotty stairwell, where the cold moisture slips down the puff concrete walls that are etched with graffiti. About how there she was – trading favours for money in the Constitution Day crowds in Beijing, finishing off a trick in Pei Hai park when she saw Zak with some free squeeze. The slow urgent motion of their bodies drained of colour by the moonlight.

'Give me a break,' said Zamina.

'I'm just getting to the good bit,' said Roberta. A flash of silver amongst the discarded clothes. Roberta creeping over, timing her movements with the hoarse cries of the woman, reaching out a hand to snatch at the bright metal tube.

'What are you going to do with it?' asked Zamina. Money-pens being a difficult prospect at the best of times. 'She's bound to report it stolen.'

'Got to be worth something though,' said Roberta as they finished the last of the stairs.

She was waiting for them outside their flat, a bundle of rags just like any other catfood monster that ever died on a cold landing in the projects. Later Zamina would ask herself how far you could twist the patterns of life to create a coincidence like that. Roberta would have put it down to accumulated karma, just another way in which the fates conspire to fuck you up, but by then Roberta was already dead.

'Hey you,' said Roberta, 'go die on your own porch.'

'Wait up,' said Zamina, 'it moved.'

'So what?'

Zamina squatted by the bundle. It was a woman in a ripped-up jumpsuit. The skin through the rents in the material was coated in a dried layer of blue paint. Zamina sniffed the air cautiously, expecting the usual cocktail of sweat, faeces and cheap protein.

'Let's take her inside.'

'Are you crazy?' said Roberta. 'It'll stink the place out.'

'She don't smell of nothing,' said Zamina, but it wasn't true. The woman smelt of dry dust and snakeskin boots, she smelt of the high plateau of the coyboy's desert. 'Open the door.'

Roberta unlocked the door but didn't help Zamina drag the woman in. As her shoulders crossed the threshold the dried blue paint on the woman's face gently cracked and she smiled.

'I have come to save you all,' she murmured.

'A schizie,' said Roberta. 'That's all we need.'

STS Central - Olympus Mons

They left Old Sam back at the office, jacked into a Hitachi with strict instructions to flatten his alpha waves if he even threatened to wake up. Banked and tranked as Dogface put it. Lambada had wanted Old Sam put on ice for the duration, but it wasn't much of an argument - what they'd seen in Acturus Station was too fresh in their minds.

And there was still no media response to events so far. Even *The Bad News Show* had shifted smoothly to a standard security raid in some Melbourne township. Local cops banging down doors, wristwired suspects lying face down in the dirt. It could have been edited together out of archive footage.

Only the high-clearance data links gave it away. VIP shuttles and cop-wagons racing down feeders and freight lines, screaming priority signalling overrides that fouled up the network from Thethys to Mogadishu. Sirens echoing down the long non-tunnels of the system. All of them converging on Reykjavik, coagulants on their way to stem the haemorrhage in the body politic.

So the floozies rode the big elevator up to Central in silence until halfway up when Dogface couldn't stand it any longer and asked just how long it took to put together an interim government.

Nobody knew.

When they got to Central, Ming looked almost grateful to see Dogface and anyone glad to see Dogface, thought Blondie, is in big trouble.

They sat around the big analysis tank in the conference room. Credit Card was scaling down the reconstruction of the Stunnel initiation, a twenty-digit time code flicked past microseconds in the left-hand corner.

'There,' said Ming and the simulation froze.

Inside the tank was a simplified three-dimensional representation of flow channels around Acturus Station. The Stunnel carrier wave was a silver thread entered from the top left-hand corner and belled out into a disc at the station gateway. The station itself was a transparent block in the shadow grey that was used to depict 'solid' installations. A spider web of power conduits surrounded the gateway in shades of blue, the lighter the shade the higher the loading. At the point of initiation the web was the colour of summer lightning.

Dogface unfolded his arms and stuck his finger into the jack at the base of the tank. The timecode flicked back a couple of digits and then forward again. Blondie had no idea what they were looking at.

'Enhance that,' said Dogface.

Credit Card thought about it and the silver line of the Stunnel thickened suddenly. Acturus Station was pushed out of the tank by the change of scale. Closer in the Stunnel looked like tube made of open-weave carpet, silver threads weaving in and out representing the shifting multifrequencies of the carrier wave.

'Jesus,' said Lambada softly.

There was a distinct bulge in the silver tube. When Credit Card rewound the reconstruction the bulge shot backwards, towards Acturus.

Credit Card froze the image and scaled up, showing the silver weave in finer detail. He stopped when the bulge filled most of the tank.

'It's like something inside is pushing out the walls,' said Blondie.

Ming looked at Dogface who shrugged back. 'Do a cutaway,' she said.

A geometric section of the bulge vanished leaving a neat

cross-section. The core was a black sphere under the silver threads.

'Something inside, pushing out the walls,' said Dogface looking at Blondie.

'What is it?' asked Blondie.

'Black signifies no available data,' said Credit Card.

'This is just a representation,' said Ming. 'You can't have a real object distorting a carrier wave like that.'

'You can't get a real object through a carrier wave at all,' said Lambada.

'It's not a real object,' said Credit Card. 'It's got to be some kind of harmonics effect within the pattern of the carrier wave itself.'

'Something came out of the Stunnel gateway,' said Blondie.

'Doesn't mean it was real,' said Credit Card. 'Not really real anyway.'

'Tell that to the President,' said Dogface.

'I've never seen this kind of effect on a carrier wave before,' said Lambada.

'No one ever initiated a tunnel over interstellar distances before,' said Credit Card. 'Who knows what kind of effect you're going to get over forty light years?'

'Distance isn't relevant,' said Lambada, 'the tunnels are trans-bloody-dimensional. All that matters is harmonizing the gravitic geometry at either end.'

'What if the physical distance created a distortion in the carrier wave and you got a gravitic anomaly?' said Credit Card.

'There's a standard function curve for calculating that,' said Lambada. 'I was with Verhoevan when he did the fine tuning, we took account of that.'

'Verhoevan is now a sticky patch of disassociated chemicals along with half the establishment,' said Dogface. 'Let's run the simulation at one-tenth speed and see what happens.'

'You want to stay with the anomaly?' asked Credit Card.

'What do you think?' said Dogface.

The simulation ran forward, the woven strands of the Stunnel carrier wave rippled over the curve of the bulge. It looked to Blondie like a bowling ball falling down a stocking leg.

'Gravitic anomaly my arse,' muttered Lambada.

'It's accelerating,' said Credit Card.

'Getting up a good head of steam,' said Dogface.
'Acturus Station coming up,' said Credit Card.
'Slow it down,' said Ming.
In slow motion the bulge hit the bell end of the Stunnel gateway. The carrier wave seemed to push the bulge out into the station but whatever caused it wasn't showing up in the real world.
'That's when the telemetry and video links went down,' said Ming. 'If you look at the way the carrier wave snaps back into place, notice the power surges running up the main cables.'
'Causing a shut-down in the subsidiary circuits,' said Credit Card. 'Whatever caused the anomaly must dissipate directly into the station.'
'No one's planning to re-initiate the Stunnel in the near future, are they?' asked Lambada.
'Not that I know of,' said Ming.
'That's a relief.'
'What's wrong with you?' Dogface asked Blondie.
'Didn't you see it?' said Blondie. 'It went out the other side of the station.' The others looked at him. They hadn't got it yet. 'It's got into the system.'

The Stop

Benny sat upright in the kitchen bed and turned the book over in her hands. Her skin felt raw against the rough linen of the nightdress. 'You've got good skin,' said the skinny girl with outsized breasts as Benny scrubbed off the remains of the blue stuff. Underneath her skin was pale almost translucent, her tan gone except where it had been covered by the remains of her jumpsuit. It looked weird in the bathroom mirror, one arm brown, the other pale and unblemished, brown legs above the knee. It looked constructed. As if Benny had been patched up with random spare parts. Zamina had lent her the nightdress and given her the book. Pale vellum bound in leather, handwriting on about half the pages.
The book was important, Benny was sure of that, but the writing while in roman script was impossible to decipher. Not a language that she knew. 'I was carrying this?' she asked Zamina.

'It was in your pocket.'

Zamina was using a wooden spoon to shovel brown stuff from a white cardboard container into a cast-iron wok. The container had a stylized picture of a cow printed on the sides. The brown stuff sizzled as it hit hot metal.

The other girl, the thin-faced one, leaned against the kitchen door. Roberta, her name was. 'We figured you were a maintenance engineer,' she said, 'but you're not, are you?'

'No, I'm a traveller,' said Benny.

Zamina pulled out a green glass bottle from the top cabinet and uncorked it. Benny caught a whiff of strong spice, garlic and coriander. 'She thought you were a catfood monster,' said Zamina as she stirred in the sauce.

'Got any money?' said Roberta.

Benny could smell it, behind the grease stink of the frying meat, behind the spice and cheap perfume. It was a patina of grime laid down over years on the surfaces of the apartment and the pinched faces of these young girls, giving their eyes a brittle brightness. A hard smell, atomized out of the walls and floors, the smell of despair and broken dreams. Benny knew it well from cheap hostels and ratty billets on hundreds of worlds, from relocation camps and shanty towns. Poor man's funk, flop sweat, the smell of poverty.

Zamina pulled another cardboard container from the cabinet. This one had an onion printed on it. Cheap food - both girls had pinprick sores at the corner of their mouths, borderline malnutrition, vitamin deficiency. Poverty was a slow way to die.

'No,' said Benny, 'but I've got skills.'

Roberta grinned. 'Know anything about moneypens?'

Circle Line

The Doctor was lighter than he looked, lighter than he should have been given his strength. Even so Kadiatu was glad when she could dump him in a seat on the next Circle Line train out of Athinai. The Doctor lolled back in the seat, opened his mouth as if to speak and then shut it again. At least he'd stopped singing.

A concession stand whirred down the central aisle selling cups of hot Turkish. 'Another damn fine cup of coffee!' was painted along its side. Kadiatu bought one with the temporary moneypen Francine had given her. It was black and sweet and helped clear her head. She looked over at the Doctor. His arms and ankles were crossed, the red-handled umbrella tucked protectively under one elbow, his hat slipped down to cover his eyes. He looked content, like a man getting his first proper rest for years. He was not what Kadiatu had expected at all.

When she was young Kadiatu had lived with her mother and father on the outskirts of Makeni in a big mud-brick bungalow. Her parents had kept some altered goats and chickens in the compound to supplement their service pensions. Most of the time father would sit out on the verandah, thinking and watching the world go by. People would pass by on their way to the river, sometimes they'd stop for a gossip or to trade. Sometimes other people would come, walking up the dusty track from the station, men and women with lined faces and haunted eyes. Often they would stay up all night talking to father - conversations full of pain and longing. One day Francine came, landing her VTOL right in the middle of the road, bringing the children running out of school.

In the rainy season when the rain rattled off the corrugated iron roof Kadiatu would sit with her father and listen to his stories. Many of them were about the first grandfather and his adventures with the *Shirl*, back in the old days when the family lived on an island in the north. The *Shirl* was like Mr Spider, facing danger with guile and cunning always outsmarting his enemies. When Kadiatu grew up she wanted to be like the *Shirl* but her father said no, only the *Shirl* was like the *Shirl*.

So Kadiatu grew up with stories about the metal giants, the wicked machines and the spiders that could think. Later in the vast history archive under Stone Mountain, by the Cayley plains on Lunar, she learnt that every last story was true. In themne, the language of her parents, *Shirl* was the word for medicine man, for magician, for *doctor*.

There was a disturbance at the end of the carriage. A man was shouting something in a hoarse voice. A wave of unease swept down the length of the train. 'What's happening?' called a woman opposite Kadiatu. A man lurched to his feet and started down the aisle towards them, naked distress on his face. 'They've killed the President,' he said, 'somebody blew up the President.'

The Doctor muttered something in his sleep.

3:
Bad Acid Macho

Pluto Ninety-Five

It was infinity that did it for Mariko, watching that insane vanishing point explode as they hit another station. Crouching low to minimise air resistance as the board skated down the friction field. Naran hooting behind her, one arm wrapped around her waist, the other keeping the noisebox on his shoulder as they rushed towards the gateway. Then winding up through the rhythm of the music, letting the beat be her ladder as they hit the gateway. The transition blast blew her brains out her ears. Nothing else, not sex, not wacca, could get close to that.

They picked up the tail on the other side of Van Der Voek Station, a dusty no-place where a low-cost housing project had been abandoned. Naran banged her on the shoulder and she looked round. Behind them a black wedge of shadow eclipsed the vanishing point. It didn't look solid enough to be a train; besides, no one ran trains on the P-95 and a board was faster in the abstract nonsense that passed for velocity in a tunnel. The shadow was gaining on them, or at least it was getting larger.

Mariko downloaded a traffic update as they coasted through the next station. She scaled up through a mantra to get into the next gateway and flipped down her visor for a look. An implant would have been better, but subdermal accessories were passé, far too common amongst artisans and the great unwashed. Getting one would be a sign of commitment though. Perhaps a modified optic with a discreet little plug under the hairline. Something she could accidentally reveal at parties, that would cause a stir, might even start a trend. The traffic update showed nothing on this stretch of the P-95 but that didn't surprise Mariko; you needed a transponder to be marked and she didn't think the shadow behind her had one.

Distance was impossible to judge in a tunnel but Mariko was

sure that the shadow was gaining on them. She knew that some of the classier security firms like Ninja Mechanixs had trained free surfers, there were also rumours that the military had souped-up machines. Trains that could outpace anything in the system, with exclusion shielding so that if you and it emerged at the same time, it would be there and you'd be paintwork.

Mariko risked another look. Free boarding relies on absolute self-control and already she could feel herself drifting off line, losing the complicated harmonics of the music.

The shadow was almost upon them. Deep in its core Mariko thought she saw two red lights like staring eyes. It was time, she decided, to get real.

As they came out of the next gateway Mariko shifted her weight to the left and bore down hard. Naran followed her lead and the board swerved across the friction field. They dismounted before it hit the platform barrier and flipped. Mariko caught it on the second turn.

'Where are we?' asked Naran.

Mariko looked around. It was another ghost station. Minimal life support kept the temperature just above freezing; their breaths steamed in the cold air. On one of the walls an unfinished STS sign had the station name on the centre plate.

'Buchanan Station,' read Mariko.

'Any connections?'

'No.'

'What now then?'

A breeze rushed through the station, stirring the dust.

'We get off the platform,' said Mariko.

As they ran for the exit the breeze grew into a great rush of air. Clouds of dust whipped and spiralled around them as they dived through the archway into the short connecting corridor between the platforms.

'That's no train,' wailed Naran.

Mariko grabbed Naran's jacket and roughly pushed him ahead of her. Looking back she saw it come into the station. The gateway was spiked open by a cone of blackness, two red lights planted either side of the needle-sharp nose. It reminded Mariko of something created on a kid's graphic program, a rough representation of a train made up of basic 3D shapes – a cylinder tipped by two cones. It looked hypothetical, imagined rather than engineered, with no surface detail on its glossy black skin. When it stopped Mariko noticed that its base was half a metre above the friction field.

Vertical lines of bright yellow light appeared at regular intervals along the cylinder body, where the doors would be on a real train. Then with a hiss they split open.

'Run,' screamed Mariko.

There was an access ramp at right angles to the corridor leading up into the unfinished heart of the station. Mariko dropped the board as they went scrambling up the slope; it clattered on to the concrete before sliding down to the level ground. The ramp went up for another twelve metres before levelling off into a corridor vanishing into darkness.

Naran hit the dead end first, Mariko heard a thump and then a groan. She found him lying on his back clutching his nose. The corridor terminated in a wall of solid rock. Mariko felt it with her hands. There were long grooves etched horizontally across its face. Mariko guessed that they'd been made by the laser-tunneller before it was turned off.

Naran sat up. 'What now?' he asked.

'Did you see any turn-offs?'

'No,' said Naran. 'I think I've broken my nose.'

'Then we wait here until it goes away.'

'Did you see it?'

'Yes.'

'What was it?'

Mariko looked down the corridor. The down ramp at the end was a rectangle of muted light.

'A ghost train.'

Naran snorted and started his nose bleeding again. 'Assuming it does go,' he said, 'how do we get out of here?'

'There's bound to be a communications relay point on the station somewhere, we patch into that and call for help.'

There was a noise from the platforms below.

'What was that?' asked Naran.

'Shut up, Naran.'

They heard a muttering and then a harsh metallic squeal.

'That's feedback,' said Naran. 'Someone's using the PA.'

The squeal tailed off, there was a noise like someone coughing down an amplifier.

'*My fellow citizens.*' The voice echoed up the ramp.

Naran's face had gone blank with fear.

'*The station of the nation is the question.*'

'It's the President,' said Naran.

'*Ask not what your nation can do for you,*' boomed the voice, '*but rather what can you do for your nation.*'

Light exploded up the ramp and came boiling down the corridor towards them. Mariko saw her board caught up in the wave of light, whirling towards them like a leaf in a storm. Naran was screaming as the light picked them up and transfixed them to the wall. The board banged into the space between them and stuck upright. It was hard to see in the intensity, but through slitted eyes Mariko made out the silhouetted figure of a man coming towards them. He came on at a brisk pace, walking with an assured authority that was somehow horribly familiar. There was something wrong about the man's lower face; it bulged outwards as if his mouth had been stuffed with a dinner plate.

The man stopped directly in front of Naran and Mariko and put his hands on his hips. Then he leaned forward, face thrust ahead to inspect them. There was enough light reflected from the dull surface of the wall for Mariko to see his face. It really was the President, only someone seemed to have shoved a loudspeaker down the famous bull neck. The famous green eyes peered over the distorted rim of his lips at Mariko and Naran. There was a click from deep inside the speaker and then an electrical hum.

'*Attention!*' The volume made Mariko's teeth rattle.

'*All of those unwilling to volunteer for transmogrification – take one step backwards.*'

Mariko squirmed against the unyielding concrete of the wall.

'*Excellent,*' said the President, '*that's what I like to see.*' He stretched out both hands and plunged them into their chests. Mariko looked down and saw his index finger sinking into the flesh between her breasts as if it were putty. She felt the knuckle scrape against a rib as it was pushed in.

I feel no pain, Mariko said to herself, I must be in shock. She said it again and again, a mantra against madness as she felt the fingers scrabbling about like rats in her chest cavity. She saw the President set his shoulders and push.

Then there was pain.

Lunarversity

The Doctor dreamt of Ace running under the brilliant blue sky of Heaven. In his dream her eyes were the colour of amber, slotted like a cheetah's, and her hair flew behind her like a mane. Not a cat, thought the Doctor and the words rang in his dream ears, never that self-absorbed. You were always a wolf to me, proud and headstrong, tireless and loyal. Out on the open plain Ace threw back her head and howled. The sound floated over the ranked graves of the planet, full of pain and betrayal.

He woke up with a blinding headache.

His sensory impressions were garbled by the pain. He was under something soft and heavy. There was someone sleeping next to him, there was a sensation of a confined space, perhaps a small room and his nose was cold. He tried opening his eyes, shadows, blurred images on the ceiling above, more pain. He closed his eyes again.

His mouth tasted of aniseed.

He'd been drinking which was unusual. He'd had a taste for wine once, at least wine of a good vintage; then a taste for beer; then he seemed to remember giving it up in favour of cricket.

The Doctor elevated his primary heart rate and managed to crank up his kidney action a bit. It wasn't easy; kidneys were not something he'd had a lot of practice with. That took care of the toxins in his blood but he suspected there were still some ethanol molecules cruising round his cerebellum and distracting his neurons. Complex little hydrocarbons wearing black bomber jackets and slinging cans of high-explosive deodorant at his defenceless braincells.

His headache was beginning to subside and he felt better. Nothing like being a Time Lord to iron out life's little ups and downs.

He tried opening his eyes again.

There were images on the ceiling, a sharp thousand-line projection with good perspective and no sound. In the foreground an enormously fat man was shouting noiselessly. Behind him an expressionistic set gave the impression of a forest out of which reared the huge blunt nose of an ICBM. The fat man was wearing a half mask which incorporated the front half of a straw hat and was carrying a red umbrella.

It was all terribly symbolic.

Another man, not quite as fat as the first, entered stage left, dressed in military uniform and a large moustache. The fat man in the mask closed his mouth with a snap. The second fat man drew in a breath, the chest swelled, the mouth opened.

Not shouting, realised the Doctor - singing, and judging by the way he held his chin, a bass. The first fat man opened his mouth again and it became a duet. The emotions expressed seemed to be complex, part the meeting of old friends and part a conflict of ideologies. The Doctor tried lip reading but all he got was a sense that the libretto was in Italian.

What he wanted was the remote control. He followed the line of projection down with his eyes but it terminated beyond the foot of the bed. The Doctor sat up for a better look; beside him the lump in the duvet shifted slightly. He stopped still until the movement subsided. The room had the dimensions of a monastic cell and once out of the eiderdown he realized how cold it was. The projection unit was suitcase-sized with a streamlined shell of augmented bakelite. An attractive bas relief depicting waves and fishes was cast into the side panels. On one end was a discreet little logo: *Imbani Entertainment: made in Burkino Faso*. The screen was projected out of a clear panel the size of a postage stamp on top. There were no obvious controls.

Above on the ceiling there was a silent flash and a plume of theatrical smoke cleared to reveal a large woman wearing a black bomber jacket and waving a sword.

The Doctor felt along the top of the unit. His fingertips found a seam too thin to be visible running along the middle twelve centimetres. There was a shallow thumb-sized depression at either end; a little firm pressure and a panel hinged open. The Doctor was vaguely disappointed. He'd expected more of a challenge. Inside were two lighted touch controls and a thumbprint scanner pad.

The Doctor picked up the unit and drew up his legs into a comfortable position. On the ceiling the opera bobbed along in parallel, the image stabilizing when he placed the unit in front of him. Twitching back the eiderdown he gently drew Kadiatu's hand towards the touch pad.

The Doctor paused, frowning.

The skin under his fingers was cool, at least three or four degrees cooler than his own, below human parameters even for sleep. He felt for the pulse, it was strong but too slow, forty-two beats per minute, way below the normal rest rate. Respiration was slow too, ten deep breaths per minute, the lungs filling to capacity and then emptying in a beautifully controlled manner. At these metabolic levels she should be slipping into a coma but instinctively the Doctor knew that for Kadiatu this was normal sleep. Perhaps somewhere on that sleek body too was a discreet company logo and the words *Made on Earth.*

He wondered if she knew what she was.

He placed her thumb on the scanner until the two touch pads lit up and then carefully replaced her hand under the eiderdown. The top pad glowed a deep emerald so he pressed that one first. Above the unit a neon rectangle unfolded into a screen, down the right hand was a strip of moving pictograms - mikons, guessed the Doctor.

He checked the ceiling. The opera was still in full swing. The three principals had been joined by a chorus of soldiers in DPM battledress and blue berets. They were carrying spears.

He touched the top mikon: a tiny spinning globe and a window opened.

Kadiatu had protected her operating system with an eight-digit PIN and a complex interlocking series of layered cut-outs based around prime numbers. It took the Doctor over two minutes to crack it. It was a lot of security for a student.

Inside the databases were a mess, strewn all over the conceptual map in random formations. It occurred to the Doctor that this might be the ultimate line of protection, making it almost impossible to find what you were looking for. Just as well, thought the Doctor, that I don't know what I'm looking for.

He opened a file at random and had a look. Pages of non-linear mathematics relating to tunnel installation. Kadiatu seemed to be striving for a localized self-generating field around a capsule that would allow it to travel faster than light in real space. It was an elegant piece of work, the main flaw being that if you changed the initial conditions of the field generation the capsule would be flung off at a dimensional tangent.

And that was time travel.

Buchannan Station - Pluto Ninety-Five

Mariko carried the board down the ramp and on to the platform.

She was particularly pleased with the way the board had turned out. She was certain no one else had a board like that. She had to be careful though, even with her new hands the razor-sharp edges had to be handled with respect. The half-metre spike on the front was a nice touch too.

Naran's new mouth stopped him from talking but Mariko didn't regard that as a disadvantage. Naran had never had anything interesting to say even when he could speak. It accentuated his high cheek bones nicely and gave him a rakish air. The look on his face when the prehensile tongue had shot out for the first time had been priceless. He'd tried to squint down his nose at it: it was a third of a metre long, had a rough abrasive texture and was pink. It also had five little stubby knobs on the end like a handful of thumbs.

Mariko threw the board out on to the track where it hovered over the friction field. Static plumes crackled over its underside, creating harsh atinic flashes. She knew it was the fastest thing in the system, faster even than the *data-bus* itself. Naran and her were *razvedka* now, half reconnaissance, half spy, half assassin - all bad. There would be others, she knew that, many others, but they were the first and there was pride in that.

Something tickled her neck. It was Naran, using his tongue to probe the joint between chitinous backplate and helmet. 'Cut that out,' she chided. The tongue whipped back into Naran's mouth with a wet sucking sound.

'We've got things to do,' she told him. 'People to see.'

Naran's eyes were bright as stars.

The Stop

'Don't you have anything with flat heels?' asked Benny.

Zamina looked around the bedroom pulling up the mounds of clothes that covered every surface. Benny sat on the bed, trying on Roberta's shoes. Roberta stood in the doorway with a sour look on her face as her wardrobe was looted. They'd started with Zamina's working clothes but Roberta was more Benny's size. Most of the stuff Benny rejected out of hand before settling on a pair of rose-coloured skin-tight leggings and a suede button-down shirt. 'At least', said Benny, checking in the mirror, 'you can't see my nipples.'

Zamina held up a pair of slingback sandals. 'What about these?'

'You call that flat?'

'They're low.'

'We've got to look business, I can't look business if I'm falling over my heels,' said Benny, 'can I?' She pointed at a pair of calf boots. 'What about those?'

'Not my boots,' groaned Roberta as Benny fished them out. They were made of black patent leather with solid heels. 'They're too high for you.'

Benny rapped the toe with her knuckle. It rang, and she grinned and pulled the boots on. 'It's a question of balance,' she said, 'balance and attitude.'

Zamina watched the woman testing her weight in front of the mirror. She looked good and it was hard to believe she was as old as thirty.

'Not bad,' said Benny. 'Where's the gun?'

Roberta handed her the pistol and the shoulder holster. 'This is crazy you know,' she said.

Benny buckled on the holster. It was an old military design that hung high on the chest. Someone had cut away the flap and the trigger guard to make it easier to draw. 'You want to stay poor?' asked Benny. 'How long have you and Zamina got on the streets? Two, maybe three, years and then what?'

Zamina stopped listening. She loved the way that Benny handled the pistol. The gangbangers carried their guns as status symbols, using them as a threat to puff up their egos. Zamina doubted they knew how they worked. Benny treated the gun with the respect due to a dangerous tool, she didn't wave it about to frighten people - if she pointed it at you, you were as good as dead.

Benny checked the LCD on the butt, holstered the weapon and shrugged into Zamina's second-best leather jacket. 'Let's go,' she said.

'What now?' asked Roberta.

'You got an appointment?'

Roberta shook her head.

The jacket had 'Better off Dead' picked out in brass studs on the back. Chains decorated the sleeves and pockets. When

Benny moved they chimed in time to her footsteps like ghost spurs. 'Come on,' she said from the doorway.

Out on Williamsberg the remaining skylights had brightened up for the day cycle. The broken lights created a lizard skin pattern of shadows down the street. Benny paused and took a deep breath.

'What we want is a gang,' she said. 'Not too big, not too small - but ambitious.'

'This is crazy,' said Roberta.

'The Dixies,' said Zamina.

'Where's their turf?'

'End of the street,' said Zamina, 'going back as far as Enoch and the shops on Norman.'

'Mean?'

'Stupid,' said Zamina.

'Boys,' said Roberta.

'Sounds perfect,' said Benny.

They followed Benny up the street, trying to copy the way she walked.

Lunarversity

The Doctor was knee deep in opera. Something he'd done while rummaging through Kadiatu's files had expanded the screen on the ceiling into a half-scale hologram. Now the bed floated over the orchestra pit with child-sized singers silently stamping around a stage level with his kneecaps. He still hadn't found the volume control and the way the violinist's bows kept poking up through the eiderdown wasn't improving his temper.

Nor was poking around in Kadiatu's database. She was, he estimated, six months from finishing the theoretical basis for a working time machine.

And it was all his fault, sort of.

Sensitive dependence on initial conditions - *the butterfly effect.*

A butterfly fans the air in Dakota and next year the people of Pontefract have to wade to work. An impossible causal chain that happens all the time *but you never know which butterfly started it off.* Such a small ripple in the Brownian motion of the molecules, such a drastic effect at the other end.

And then there's me, thought the Doctor, dropping into

human history with all the subtlety of a road accident. Someone was bound to notice sooner or later.

Simple to spoil her work, introduce a false premise into the complex chain of equations. Nothing too subtle, just enough to send Kadiatu running down a blind alley for fifty years or so. The human race wasn't due time travel until the botched sigma experiments of the thirtieth century.

He called up the passage dealing with flux instability within the containment field of the capsule. A minor change in the premise of one of the transposition matrices. It would make that avenue of enquiry look like a dead ringer for transtemporal propagation. The Doctor put his finger over the exact place. Push and it would interact with the sensor field which would send signals to the unit's CPU which would make micro-modifications within the lattice of suspended molecules that made up its memory storage. Do that and all of future history is secure.

Unless Kadiatu was supposed to discover time travel. In which case his interference could do things to the timestream that even a Dalek would think twice about. Perhaps time-travelling humans would be *useful* in some way.

Decisions, decisions.

Without taking his eyes off the screen the Doctor reached into his coat pocket and pulled out a coin. He flipped it into the air and caught it without looking. 'Heads you win,' he said and slapped the coin on his wrist. When he looked down it was at the profile of the young Queen Victoria complete with bun. The Doctor sighed and put the file back into memory. He examined the coin again. Inscribed below the queen's head was the legend *Three Pennies.* On the other side was another profile of Queen Victoria, only this one was grinning.

The Stop

The Dixie Rebs had their clubhouse in a disused health centre on Mississippi Plaza. Thirty years ago the projects were planned as a series of modular communities grouped around a central cluster of shops and amenities. The Plaza still had a general store but all the other units had long become a series of impromptu squats and catfood houses. A couple of skinny little boys were playing on the patch of razor grass that fronted the health centre entrance. The boys had transmitters wired into the collars of their T-shirts.

'Lookouts,' said Roberta.

The boys stopped playing and watched as the women approached. One of them touched a stud on his collar and whispered. Benny squatted down on her haunches so that her face was level with the boy's.

'What's your name?' she asked.

'Who wants to know?' asked the boy.

Benny slapped him once. Hard enough to rock the boy's head back. 'What's your name?' she asked again but the boy was crying.

'You shouldn't have done that,' said the other boy.

'He was rude,' Benny told him, 'and rude boys get slapped.'

'Billy won't like it.'

'Who's Billy?'

'Billy's the boss.'

Benny turned back to the boy who was still crying. 'You see,' she said sweetly, 'it always pays to be polite.' She stood up. 'Now why don't you two run along and play, before something bad happens to you?'

The second boy took the first by the arm and drew him away. 'Don't worry,' he said to his friend, 'Billy'll sort them slots out for us.'

The entrance to the health centre was a pair of sliding doors made from high-impact glass. The outline of a flag had been laboriously etched into the surface and then tinted with polychromatic polymers.

'That's a dead old flag,' muttered Benny, 'even for this century.'

The gangbanger on the doors had the same flag spray-painted on the chest of his flak jacket. His blond hair was razored into a crew cut and his blue eyes were lazy with drugs. As front man to the clubhouse he probably wasn't geared up too tight but the Dixies had a reputation for random violence.

'What do you want, slots?'

Benny looked the boy up and down. 'One moment,' she told him and turned to Zamina. 'What's a slot?'

'You know, a girl.'

'Not very respectful is it?'

'I guess not,' said Zamina.

Benny turned back to the gangbanger, drew her gun and jammed it under his chin. 'Now,' she said, 'I want to talk to Billy.'

Lunarversity

The opera had frozen solid and the lead singer was vomiting data into the room. It spewed out of his mouth in coils of damp blue green. As the data streamed out the unit tried to rectify the singer's image, causing his head to balloon outwards to twice normal size. The surface of the construct glistened with fractals as the data took up a convoluted three-dimensional shape. Alphanumerics in white neon formed stage left obliterating part of the chorus with the words 'STONE MOUNTAIN, PP-HIST ANALYSIS 234 - SHIRL'.

The unit finally gave up trying to sustain both images and the opera blinked out. The data construct hung alone in the notional centre of the image and began to rotate slowly. It reminded the Doctor unpleasantly of the fungus on Heaven. It was a phase portrait, he could see that now. A non-linear system turned ninety degrees and mapped out in three dimensions. There were chunks bitten out of its coils, wounds ragged with random pixels caused by an insufficiency of data.

Doctor Livingstone, I presume, thought the Doctor.

'Very clever,' he said out loud.

'I suppose breakfast in bed is out of the question,' said Kadiatu from behind him. Her voice was muffled by the eiderdown.

'And the opera?'

'*Il Dottere Va in Viaggio*, by Marconi Paletti,' said Kadiatu. 'There's a MIG coffee-maker at the end of the bed.'

The Doctor reached through the projection field and switched on the Russian coffee-maker. He heard Kadiatu sit up and stretch her arms. 'What's the straight bit in the middle?'

'That's the nineteen-seventies which is what I'd call a data-rich environment. It's straight because there's a continuous linear progression for five years. You were stuck, weren't you?'

'Exiled.'

The MIG made a series of explosive gurgles.

The Doctor could hear her extensions falling one by one over her shoulder as she twisted her neck. There was a faint musk made of human pheremones and perspiration as warm air escaped from under the covers. 'You were looking for me?'

'I was tracking your movements through history. I wasn't expecting to run into you on Kings Cross station.'

'Something of a coincidence.'

'Isn't it just.'

'Could you turn that off,' said the Doctor. 'I've just seen somewhere I haven't been yet.'

'Screen off,' said Kadiatu and the construct vanished. 'Minscreen; newscan; lookfor; badnews.'

The Doctor turned to face her. 'You're expecting bad news?'

'You do have a reputation,' said Kadiatu. 'What are you here for this time?'

'Does there have to be a reason?'

'Trouble follows you around.'

'I was with King Tenkamenin at Kumbi Selah, he offered me kola nuts and a place to sleep in the Royal Compound. We stayed up all night speaking of philosophy and the old gods. When I left the sun was breaking over the hills and the society women ran the initiates down to the summer stream to wash.'

He caught Kadiatu's black eyes and held them. 'Nobody died that day.'

'They died yesterday,' said Kadiatu. 'And here you are.'

'History happens,' said the Doctor. 'Even when I'm not around.'

'Only by accident,' said Kadiatu as the room filled up with the aroma of coffee.

Reykjavik

Ming the Merciless ate cod sushi and pickled herring in a small bistro off Constitution Avenue. The bastard Rodriguez, the acting Transport Minister, had invited her for an informal discussion about the current 'situation' *vis-à-vis* the transit network.

'Situation' being politician-speak for embarrassing catastrophe. 'Informal' meaning secret, unofficial, *deniable*. Not too secret though, couldn't be in a venue like the bistro. It meant that the politician wanted to be seen talking to her, there's Rodriguez getting on top of the situation but *discreetly*.

Rodriguez, people's deputy for a safe seat in Sao Paulo, had a wide sallow face and just enough epicanthic fold to bring in the expatriate vote. He was dressed in this year's conservative kaftan, black worsted thrown over his left shoulder. Black because he was officially in mourning, with a white arm band to placate the sensibilities of the Japanese expats that made up a third of his constituency.

Two mutually exclusive colours for death. Part of the fragile global consensus that grew up after the war. Ming as ninth-generation Bradford Cantonese knew all about that. They used to have kiddie progs about it on English Two. *Hi kids, ever notice how everyone is different?* Hadn't been as many channels then, about fifteen or so, when the entertainment consoles were all matt black and Japanese.

'You're sure about this?'

'You saw the data,' said Ming but she doubted he had. People like Rodriguez had other people to look at data for them.

He shrugged. 'Data can be manufactured.'

'The source was pure.'

'My dear Ming,' said Rodriguez smoothly, 'there's always doubt about data, especially these days.'

'I was the source,' said Ming. 'Something, nature unknown, entered into the system via the Stunnel gateway.'

'And killed the President?'

'It was jumping the real space between two gateways. It may not have been aware that the people were there.' She could see that that really annoyed Rodriguez, the idea that the President wasn't important.

'You said this thing was an anomalous power surge.'

'That's what it looks like.'

'You keep talking about it as if it's alive.'

'It might be,' said Ming, enjoying Rodriguez's discomfort. 'Who knows?'

'So,' said Rodriguez, 'what are you going to do about it?'

'Nothing at the moment.'

'Why not?'

'I'm only the senior controller,' said Ming, 'I haven't got the authority.'

'You're the de facto Director-General. My department would give you full support.'

'I want more.'

'Such as?'

'I want to be appointed Director-General, I want a clearance upgrade as high as yours, I want full control of the contract KGB and I want access to military equipment.'

'Anything else?'

'Yeah,' said Ming. 'I want the pay rise backdated.'

The Stop

Zamina found that she wasn't scared of the Dixies at all, not now, after watching Benny stroll casually in and sass up their boss. After living in fear of the gangbangers' casual violence since she was small, seeing them up close was liberating.

Benny was talking serious biz to Billy Boy and the amazing thing was that Billy Boy was listening to her. Inside, the Dixie Reb clubhouse became just that, a series of rooms cluttered with entertainment decks, fast food and shiny things with sharp edges. What Roberta always called 'boy-things'. There were some girls around, mostly underage, wearing bobby sox and too much make-up. They hung around the edges watching Benny with stupid eyes. Zamina figured them for boy-things too, part of the clubhouse furniture.

'You want to hang casual but tough,' Benny had told them as they went in. 'Got to show no sign of weakness.' So Zamina and Roberta took their cues from Benny, easing themselves on to a futon sofabed and paying attention.

It was an education watching Benny work Billy Boy. The way she put it the scheme didn't sound political at all. More like a convoluted scam to grab more prestige for the Dixies. She was using his eyes as a guide, saying things to keep them on her face. When the eyes drifted Benny would hint that she had backing, connections, and the eyes would track back on line.

The words were like polymer chains, all woven together in an unbreakable cord.

Zamina glanced at Roberta. The corner of her mouth was turned up, a little half-smile that said she was enjoying herself. Deep in Billy Boy's eyes hunger blossomed, hunger for the scheme. Even the bimbettes on the margins of the room were leaning in trying to catch the gist, child faces wide open and vulnerable. Zamina could see that Benny was chaining them up with her words.

Suddenly she was scared all over again.

Olympus Mons West

Sleep altered Old Sam's face. It softened out the rigid contours of his cheekbones and smoothed the violent lines that surrounded the eyes. His long dreadlocks were spread around his head, black at the tips, shading through grey to white towards the scalp.

'Is he dreaming?' asked Blondie.

Dogface shook his head and checked the illuminated LCD on the monitor. 'He doesn't dream.' The bio-monitor was battered Hitachi, its leads jacked into the old-fashioned plug behind Old Sam's ear. 'Something to do with the interface.'

Blondie looked at the matt grey oval on his own index finger. 'I still dream,' he said.

'Whole other technology that,' said Dogface. 'Old Sam here, he's the old model, got himself an artificial nervous system when he signed on. Drove a lot of them crazy after the war, not dreaming. That and not having kids.'

'What was wrong with them?'

'Government had the patent on their genesets. They're functionally sterile so any kid would have to be spliced up in a lab. Government won't ever let it happen.'

'You can't patent a naturally occurring geneset,' said Blondie. 'I looked that up.'

'This boy ain't natural,' said Dogface. 'They did some stuff to the *ubersoldaten*. He's got maybe fifty per cent of the DNA he was born with, tops.'

Impulsively Blondie put his hand on Old Sam's arm. The skin was smooth and cool over hard muscle. There were little ridges of keloid scar tissue on his shoulder, radiating out from a central scar crater like a sunburst.

'Exit wound,' said Dogface.

'I thought the Martians used sound guns.'

Dogface grunted. 'The Greenies used anything they could get their hands on.'

It wasn't like that in the warvids. Even in the cheap exploitation pixs where you could sometimes see the join between the live action and computer-generated backgrounds. Blondie's generation had grown up on them, assimilating the soldier slang into everyday speech: *Greenie*, *pop up*, *spider trap*, *fire mission*, *medevac*.

'The bastard's nailed Paris.'

'Hey,' said Dogface. 'You gone off-line or what?'

'They always say that,' Blondie told him, 'And the wimpy one, you know the one that always gets scared on patrol, he goes berserk and does the mission and gets himself shot up and . . .'

Dogface was staring at him.

'You,' he said slowly, 'have been watching too many vids.'

Lambada walked in from the crew room and stood at the foot of the bunk. 'You'd better wake this one up,' she said. 'Ming wants us up the Central Line doing integrity checks.'

'Is that where it went?' asked Blondie.

'Credit Card lost the trace just before Lowell Depot and we're getting some weird returns from the instrumentation on P-95.'

'What kind of weird?' asked Dogface. 'Weird weird or normal weird?'

'What can I say, Dogface?' said Lambada. 'Weird weird.'

'What about the real world?'

'Those fucks at KGB won't say much but they did confirm that a classified number of passengers got greased on the outbound Central Line platforms.'

'Did they say why the leftovers are blue?'

'Refraction index,' said Lambada. 'The stuff is made up of a saline solution saturated with some kind of crystals whose refraction index is blue - that's why the shit is blue.'

'What are the crystals made of ?' asked Blondie.

'Mineral salts, calcium, traces of magnesium and potassium.'

'People,' said Dogface.

'And speaking of weird shit,' said Lambada, 'a real strange lady left a message for superman here.'

'White face, silver eyes?' asked Dogface.

'You know her?'

'What's the message?'

'I don't know. It's in his comms buffer and you didn't answer my question.'

Dogface looked back down at the Hitachi's display plate

avoiding Lambada's eyes. Lambada folded her arms and glared at him. Blondie was shocked, it wasn't like Dogface to back down.

'I'm not sure,' he said, 'but it sounds like the Angel Francine.'

Lambada closed her eyes and went very still for a moment. 'Christ in a bucket,' she said. 'The fucking V Soc. Like we don't have enough troubles.'

'Whatever they want it's nothing to do with us.'

'Better hope so.'

Blondie waited until Lambada had gone before he asked, 'What's the vee sock?'

'Veterans Society,' Dogface told him as he initiated the wake-up sequence on the old Hitachi. 'You've got your triads, your Cosa Nostra and your yardies. And then you've got the V Soc. And if you get them on your ass, you *truly* have someone on your ass.'

Dogface picked up a hypo and slotted in a 10cc adrenaline cartridge. 'You watch a lot of vids don't you,' he said as he pressed the hypo against Old Sam's neck. 'Ever see *Frankenstein*?'

There was a long hiss as the drug went in.

Isle of Dogs

Emerging into sunlight for the first time in days, Ming went straight past the line of waiting auto-karts and started to walk home. Westferry Road was a broad curve round the Isle of Dogs lined with genetically engineered plane trees. Real air blew up the curve of the river from the Thames estuary, a brine-smelling wind that shook the silver leaves. Many of the trees were over a hundred years old, planted to scrub the London air, locking up the cadmium, dioxin and lead in striated layers of cellulose.

A couple of protestors from the European Heritage Foundation stood between the joke palm trees in front of the old church. The EHF had leased the building as headquarters for their save the wharf appeal. A bright yellow canary with a crutch under one wing and a bandaged head stared winsomely out of a daylight hologram attached to the wall. Ming remembered the red-brick shopfront had once been an Orthodox church, before that a mosque, before that a synagogue and before that?

Waves of migrants rolling up old father Thames and depositing rich layers of ethnic silt on the shores of East London.

One of the protestors waved a sucker-box at Ming as she walked past. On a whim she slotted in her moneypen and gave them a hundred. What the hell, she could afford it. The portable credit unit was yellow with black stripes, a wax seal over the output jack was embossed with the seal of the Charities Commission. She guessed that most of the money would go on icebreaker programs to mess up the autodozers of the demolition firm.

The protestor thanked Ming in franglais and pushed a leaflet into her hand. She waited until she was round the corner in Harbinger Road before pushing it unread into the paper slot of the nearest bin.

Ming's Mansion, as it was known locally, was a lovingly restored maisonette set in its own grounds off Hesperus Crescent. A hundred and fifty-four years old, it had by a freak of planning avoided demolition. Ming had bought into the top floor when she started working for STS and over the years by dint of careful planning and some judicious intimidation, had managed to acquire the whole building. She used up a few favours getting it fixed - Kings Cross became the primary Northern European transit hub instead of the Gard du Nord and Ming got a preservation order on her home plus a grant for restoration, high-pressure water cannons blasting decades of grime off the concrete walkways.

Number One Husband Fu was tending a window box on the first floor balcony. Of the red painted doors behind him only two were real, one leading to the flat he shared with Number Two Wife, the other to his office.

Fu grinned when he saw Ming coming and ran down the external stairwell to meet her. The same bounding steps as he'd used on their wedding day forty years ago, he and his friends forcing the door to her parents' house in Bradford. Ming's girlfriends giggling as they tried to hold them back, but not too hard. The traditional cut and thrust of insult between the bridegroom's companions and bridesmaids. Ming, young, nervous and festooned with hothouse blooms, watching from the stairs as Fu's lanky body pushed through the doorway to claim her. That night she tangled with that body and crisp cotton sheets in the Hotel Metropole's bridal suite. They'd fallen out of the bed and the impact of her buttocks on the floor triggered her climax, the first in her life.

Forty years later, the maisonette filling up with children and aunts, Number Two Wife and grandchildren, Fu and Ming still liked to do it on the floor.

'Congratulations,' said Fu.

'Why thank you,' said Ming taking his arm. 'Where's Achmed?' Achmed was Ming's Number Two Husband.

'He got called out on a job,' said Fu.

They walked arm in arm towards the house.

'Today?'

Fu laughed. 'A structural failure at one of the projects. It could have waited but he was too German to leave it. The kids are at school and Aunty Shmoo took Bridgette shopping.'

'Do they know?'

'That's why they went shopping.'

'Ah,' said Ming as they pushed through the front door together. 'That leaves just you and me alone then.'

Bay Fifteen – Olympus Mons West

Blondie was still shaking as he followed Old Sam down the ramp to Bay Fifteen. The floater would have been easier to pull but Blondie preferred to keep it, and the bags piled on it, between him and the old veteran. The floater's handles were at knee height which kept Blondie stooped down as he pushed, the pain in his back helped him control the shaking.

Booms and clanks echoed up the ramp from the bay. Big engineering sounds as *Fat Mama* was lowered on to the friction field. There was a giant cough as the MHD turbine kicked over a few times and then accelerated. Over the noise Blondie could hear Credit Card and Lambada shouting at each other.

The servo motors started up again as Blondie emerged from the ramp, creaked like arthritic dinosaur bones as the cradle lifted back into the ceiling. The sounds ticked off the far walls and the ceramic finish of the old trains. Bay fifteen being where old trains went to die, lined up in dust-covered ranks down its thousand metre length. Blondie was grateful that the bad accident wreck was hidden out of view at the end.

As far as STS's accounts subsystem was concerned *Fat Mama*

was also a dead train. A pre-war Chinese tank engine that had been cannibalized years ago, nothing more than a collection of barcoded spare parts, keeping old trains on the branch lines serviceable. The maintenance log knew different, as did the more stupid bits of storage records. Every fifty-two hours the system network would have a brief internal argument about the current status of *Fat Mama* but intelligent baffles put in by Credit Card kept the dispute from being flagged for management intervention.

Fat Mama was a twelve-metre engine built to pull cargo wagons in the period before friction fields and split-section tunnel integrators. Its field generator was powerful enough to shield ten wagons and then drag them through a gateway. The body shell was built around an MHD turbine that provided the power such an inefficient set-up required. *Fat Mama* had started off ugly and thirty years of Dogface's DIY hadn't improved its looks none.

Lambada leant out of a hatch near the water front end and gestured to Blondie to stop the floater where it was. Instrumentation light flushed her face red as she looked back into the cab and yelled something.

A chunk sound came from the mid section of *Fat Mama* and the loading doors swung open. Blondie noticed that they were at least five centimetres thick with two deep holes for the mechanical locking bolts. Dogface was standing in the doorway, he glanced at the bags piled on the floater.

'Where's the kitchen sink?' he asked.

Old Sam picked up the first bag. It was made of linseed plastic and very heavy. Old Sam handled it easily, transferring it from the floater to *Fat Mama*'s deck. Watching him started Blondie shaking all over again.

'I didn't know what we might need,' said Old Sam.

Veterans were strong even without the drugs, made that way for the Thousand-Day War. One thing to know that, another to have Old Sam lift you off your feet with one hand and threaten to rip off your face with the other. Answering the questions, because he couldn't think of a cool reply, because he was scared shitless, and because loss of face meant nothing when Old Sam was willing to turn that into a sick joke. 'What moneypen? I don't know nothing about that. Me and her, we just hit it off, never saw her before. Put me down for Chrissakes?'

There was the distinct sound of gunmetal as the last bag hit *Fat Mama*'s deck.

'What's all that?' asked Lambada from inside.

'Tools of the trade,' said Old Sam.

The Stop

Benny stared at the words in the book as if willpower alone would decipher them. Picking a page at random she used Zamina's eyeliner pencil to mark symbol correspondence and pattern repetitions. Strictly speaking it was a code-breaking technique but Benny had used it before to identify patterns in alien scripts. A puterdeck could have processed the whole book instantly; even Roberta's woefully primitive home computer would have handled the task in minutes.

Brain is the best tool, she told herself.

Also, even in this century computers were linked to other computers, and use of them was unsafe and therefore forbidden.

Patterns were emerging in the text. Repeated sequences of symbols in groups of two and three. Assuming this was a human language these could be linking words or identifiers. A dull pain started behind her eyes, the concentration was giving her a headache. She managed to continue for another five minutes before the pain grew too severe. Reluctantly she put the book down and lay back on the bed.

Through the bedroom wall she could hear Roberta and Zamina talking in the kitchen. They'd be cooking up some food for the two Dixie Rebs stationed in the hallway. Benny was sure of Roberta's loyalty now but she was worried about Zamina. The girl wasn't hungry enough for what Benny had to offer, she had doubts and fears that could interfere with the programme.

When she closed her eyes Benny caught glimpses of the programme in the patterns of retinal light against her eyelids. Random patches of luminescence that revealed potentialities, vague because the causal path of human behaviour was vague. Nothing for her to do for the moment but switch to downtime while certain scenarios developed.

The book was important, she knew that. She just didn't know why.

When they got there Yeltsin Plaza was crawling with cops.

Campus Policemen in light blue shirt sleeves were coming and going through the repeating holograph at the entrance of Max's den. Max was sitting crosslegged on the floor outside, head bowed, arms wired behind his back. A detective stood in front of him, making notes on a clipboard.

A mostly student crowd formed a semicircle around the scene, talking quietly amongst themselves. Just about everyone on campus had done some kind of deal with Max at some time, even if it was just for bootlegged software.

Kadiatu put her hand on the Doctor's arm in warning. The detective was wearing a dogskin shirt and red and yellow Mogadishu pumps. She didn't look like local heat at all.

The Doctor didn't even slow down, he walked straight through the crowd towards the detective. Kadiatu paused for a moment and then went after him. She had to push her way through the line of people and duck quickly under the police tape to catch him. The detective looked up as they approached. An ID badge pinned to her chest gave her name as *Whiteriver*. The hologram on the badge showed a younger woman with glossy black hair and copper skin. The picture's eyes seemed to follow Kadiatu as she moved closer.

The detective opened her mouth to say something.

'What's going on, Whiteriver?' The Doctor's voice had changed, taken on a rougher, world-weary tone. His posture had changed too into something that hinted of tired authority.

Whiteriver took an involuntary step backwards and the Doctor plucked the clipboard from her hands. He glanced quickly at the arrest form displayed on the impact resistant screen.

Kadiatu straightened her shoulders and tried to look like back-up. Whiteriver's left hand had automatically slipped down to the weapon tucked into the waistband of her skirt. The detective opened her mouth to speak again but the Doctor held up his hand for silence. Kadiatu could see a tiny LED blinking on the corner of the clipboard, indicating that the machine was accessing outside data. Text files went streaming up the screen too quickly for her to read.

Some of the campus cops had stopped piling Max's belongings on the floor and were watching the scene with interest.

Any moment Detective Whiteriver was going to recover her balance and start trying to reassert her authority. The watching eyes of the cops and the crowd demanded it.

'Did you get clearance for this arrest?' asked the Doctor without looking up.

'We went through normal channels,' said Whiteriver. There was a hint of belligerence but her hand was drifting away from her gun.

'But not from me,' said the Doctor. The text on the screen was practically a blur, he couldn't possibly be reading it.

'I wasn't aware of any flag on the suspect's name.'

The Doctor looked up from the clipboard and gave her a thin smile. 'Of course not,' he said. 'Our mistake.' He handed back the clipboard, the arrest form back on its screen. The smile became confidential. 'These jurisdictional things are always a problem, aren't they?'

'Yes, sir,' said Whiteriver. 'What should we do with the suspect?'

'Turn him loose,' said the Doctor, 'but not here. Mustn't lose face in the eyes of the public, must we?'

Whiteriver looked grateful. 'No, sir.'

'Oh and by the way, Whiteriver, this conversation never took place.'

'Yes, sir.'

'Carry on.'

Kadiatu's stomach complained all the way back to the throughway.

'I love dealing with hierarchies,' said the Doctor as they left the plaza. 'They're so easy.'

South of the plaza was the student centre and the permanent flea market. Kadiatu followed the Doctor as he slipped through the stalls. He had a way of turning corners as if inertia didn't apply to him that made it difficult to keep up. When he stopped Kadiatu almost ran into his back.

The stall sold second-hand archaeological equipment. The Doctor was staring at the mud-covered soil-acidity probes and ground sonar receivers as if he'd just remembered something.

'We have to go to Pluto,' he said.

4:

The Stupid Dead

The Stop

Mariko's *razvedka krewe* ran in silence through the dripping dark, feet slapping on the puff concrete floor. One of them scampered on all fours, weaving between their legs, streaking ahead with sudden bursts of speed until Mariko shooed him back into line. It was too narrow to run in more than single file and every so often the *krewe* had to jump the vertical shafts that yawned unexpectedly in the floor. That's why Mariko let the Reverend Cyclops run ahead. The halogen lamp jammed into his left eyesocket lit the way for the rest of them.

Cyclops had been riding an empty southbound train on the new route that linked the suburbs of Crepe Town with the centre of South Polar. The lamp had been perched on a shoulder rig, all the better to sniff out sinners in the dark corners of the godless. After his conversion Mariko knew that he was nothing more than a maintenance worker going off shift. She didn't know why she had taken him for a priest. But that was reality. Fantasy was more fun.

And the lamp, installing the lamp had been fun too.

She heard the band before she saw the lights. The music rolling down the arrow-straight passage, bass notes shaking the walls, rim shots cracking off the ceiling. They picked up speed. Naran started to hoot, a fluting sound that emerged from around his tongue. The rhythm was picked up by the rest of the *krewe* as they charged the last twenty metres.

The passage terminated in a large natural cavern with a levelled floor covered in arctic moss. A couple of projectors were strung up on the ceiling. They were showing *The Best of the Bad News Show part IV*, vivid atrocity footage and natural disasters tangling around the granite spikes that hung down from the roof.

Most of the music came from the President who led a choir

of *speakers* near the back wall supplemented by a couple of free standing stacks. The backbeat came on solid like a heartbeat but the melody was freeform brainwave stuff. Some of the *speakers* were clicking their fingers but the sound was lost over their own output. Food was stacked on linen-covered trestle tables around the other walls and the centre was cleared for dancing.

There were whoops and catcalls as Mariko's *krewe* entered. One *speaker* feeding at a table turned and blew a fanfare, splattering everyone nearby with chocolate cake. Mariko grinned and did a deliberate strut on to the dancefloor; Naran of course went straight for the food. Most of the dancers were *razvedka* with spiky carapaces and killing spurs on their wrists. *Subcontractors* didn't dance, they stood around in tight little groups talking about machinery while the manipulators imbedded in their chests twitched reflexively to the music. There were even a couple of *reps* mixing with the crowd around the food tables. They were easy to spot since they kept their original appearance. The rest of the *reps* would be out on jobs.

All three *razvedka krewes* were in attendance. Mariko waited in the centre of the dancefloor until the other two *krewebosses* had gathered around her.

'This party is symbolic,' said 2Boss, a male that seemed to have been stitched together from leftover body bits.

'Good to kick back after work,' said 3Boss, a diminutive female with a fetching crest of spines running over her scalp and down her back.

'Like the spines,' said Mariko.

3Boss grinned, showing sharpened teeth.

'We've all done sweeps of the Pluto environs,' said Mariko. 'Anything moving?'

'Just normal traffic,' said 3Boss.

'We're dealing with a reactive network here. It's big but slow and it's bound to have defensive systems closer to the core. Now we've got a *rep* stirring the pot at this end.'

'Doing what?' asked 2Boss.

'We don't need to know, but remember the whole system is more complex than previous ones. There's bound to be proactive elements on other reality levels that we're not aware of, so look sharp.'

'What's next?' asked 2Boss.

'Don't know,' said Mariko. 'We party till we get told different.'

Naran wandered up to them, tongue buried in a catering-size tub of vanilla icecream. The pink flesh of the proboscis rippled as he sucked.

'I didn't know you could do that,' said Mariko.

3Boss was gazing speculatively at Naran. 'Can I borrow him sometime?'

A door opened in Mariko's mind and abruptly it was full of information. She looked at the others. 2Boss and 3Boss were staring at her intently. They knew. Naran was oblivious, happily finishing off the dregs in the bottom of the tub.

Boss-level data then.

'Prediction,' said Mariko. 'Probe coming up the Central Line - minimum response.' She looked over the crowd of dancers and caught the President's eye. He nodded.

3Boss started hopping up and down. 'I want to go.'

Mariko tested the idea in her mind, it felt right. 'Go,' she told 3Boss.

2Boss watched sourly as 3Boss collected her *krewe* and headed out of the cavern. 'Some people have all the fun,' he said, so Naran sprayed him with icecream.

Central Line

The turbines at the back made a subsonic rumble that vibrated in Blondie's chest cavity. There were no sockets for human interface in the cab; everything was manual. Dogface had plastered masking tape with handwritten labels over the original pictograms. Some of them were jokes - a big central lever was marked *go faster knob.* Sensor terminals bolted on to the bulkhead, whistled and clicked every time they hit a tunnel. The stations were confused patches of white light as they howled through them. A noisebox under Lambada's seat was putting out two hundred watts of a Rio-based salsa thrash band called Mea Culpa. The lead singer gave damnation a good name in Portuguese.

Fat Mama was cranked up to the limit.

Blondie was riding in the right-hand engineer's seat, wedged between the bulkhead and a bank of archaic-looking LCDs and touch pads. Dogface was in the centre seat, big hands wrapped around the manual-drive controls. Lambada and Credit Card were stationed on the left-hand side, each monitoring the systems that were too old for automation. A big red LED over the windscreen showed them shaving seconds off the normal transit time.

But as fast as they ran the priority override ran faster, picked up by sensors in the stations and channelled into tunnel gateways. In the older stations the signal was transmitted as coded patterns of light in spun glass; in the newer stations they ran as a stream of free electrons in room temperature superconductors. At the gateways the signal became theoretical ripples in the redundant marginal zone of the tunnel itself, the probability of an idea of a signal that instantaneously became real at the other end. Real photons and electrons, real information.

Ahead, in the local station nodes, logic gates snapped open and shut. Freight trains switched to sidings, even to the main passenger track, hooting their way past astonished commuters. Making space on the freight line so that *Fat Mama* had a clear line all the way to Pluto.

'I've got a trace,' called Lambada over the music. 'Triton Station. Moving fast.'

'That's fifteen stations ahead,' said Dogface. 'Plenty of leeway.'

'It's coming towards us.'

'Credit Card,' said Dogface, 'get some pixs.'

Credit Card leaned over his terminal and punched in a search protocol. 'I wish you had a plug in.'

'Ganymede coming up,' said Dogface.

'Ready.'

Fat Mama thundered through Ganymede Station, sucking in data from the traffic net.

'I've never been to Ganymede,' said Blondie.

'You haven't missed much,' Lambada told him.

The surveillance pix came up on the main monitor just as they slammed back into the tunnel. 'That's them at Oberon,' said Credit Card.

'Thirteen stations,' said Lambada.

'Looks like some free surfers,' said Credit Card.

'How many?' asked Dogface.

'Six people, three boards.'

'They must be out of their skulls,' said Lambada. 'Coming down a freight line the wrong way.'

'Whoever heard of free surfers in armour?' said Credit Card.

'Callisto coming up,' said Dogface. 'See if you can get an enhanced image.'

'I never would have thought of that.'

'They just hit Titania,' said Lambada. 'These boys are shifting it you know.'

There was a wash of white light through the cab windows as they went through the station.

'Maybe they're military,' said Credit Card. He touched his throat mike. 'Hey Sam?'

Old Sam was in the back looking after the turbines. Credit Card shunted the pictures on to his repeater screen. 'You ever seen armour like this?'

'Nope.'

'But you guys used to customize yours though, right?'

'We never used to put fucking spines on them.'

'Nine stations,' said Lambada. 'Maybe it's some kind of new gang.' She looked over at Blondie.

'What?'

'You know anything about this?'

'Hey, I'm from the Stop,' said Blondie. 'Free surfing's a rich kids' game.'

'They're going to be expensive paint soon,' said Dogface, 'if they don't get off the line.'

'I'll put up a station warning,' said Credit Card.

Another wash of light - another station. From the back Blondie heard the turbines cycle up a notch. Dogface was pushing the *go faster knob* forward. *Fat Mama* was accelerating.

'Are you sure that's a good idea?' asked Credit Card.

'Seven stations,' said Lambada.

'Where are we going to meet them?' asked Dogface.

'Stazione Centrale de Rhea.'

'Better warn Rhea Traffic Control,' said Credit Card.

'We could just stop at the next station and wait,' said Lambada.

Blondie was thinking about bay fifteen and the Bad Accident. He didn't want to but his mind kept vulturing round to pick at the memory.

'Five stations,' said Lambada.

Dogface had taken Blondie down there on his first day. All the old trains gathering dust under the xenon strips. Dogface walked him down the aisles recounting each engine's name and service history - he knew them all.

'They're at Hyperion and they're not slowing down.'

'Tethys station coming up.'

Dogface had shown him the gutted interior of *India*, President Achebe's wartime command train. It still had its blonde wood floor and strips of oak panelling where equipment had been ripped out.

'Three stations.'

'Everybody strap in.'

Dogface gave Blondie no warning at all, just let him walk round an old Canadian pushme-pullyou and find the Bad Accident waiting for him at the end of the line.

It had happened just after the war. A Honda Pullman exited the Beverly Hills-Hawaii commuter line at Hollywood Boulevard, carrying forty-nine passengers. A fraction of a second later a General Electric Go-Faster Caboose carrying thirty passengers exited the same gateway. The Honda was only halfway out at the time.

The gateway compensator did its job and prevented matter-annihilation from taking place, saving Los Angeles from appearing on that short list of cities that started with Hiroshima. Instead the physical substance of the two trains was smoothly integrated as they emerged from the tunnel gateway. The lucky passengers died immediately.

'Goddamit Dogface,' screamed Lambada, 'stop the train.'

'Too late,' said Credit Card.

Somebody had turned the noisebox off and Blondie had stopped hearing the turbines. *'What's the matter,'* Dogface had said, *'you never seen two trains fucking before?'* It seemed very quiet in the last stretch of tunnel.

'Hey, Lambada,' said Dogface, 'turn the cameras on. We might be able to sell this to Yak Harris.'

Fat Mama hit something.

Silence banged at Blondie's eardrums.

He felt his body smash into the restraint harness, head snapping forward before slamming back on to the headrest.

There was a metallic ripping sound to his left and Dogface started shouting. The cab was shaking, turning the instrumentation into streaks of light. Dogface's voice choked off. Blondie watched as a spike drilled its way out the back of the driver's seat. He thought he saw movement on the outside of the windscreen just before it exploded inwards. Shafts of psychedelic light penetrated the bulkheads to flood the cab as *Fat Mama* lost her shield integrity.

Blondie heard the turbines whine into over-rev as Dogface slumped back off the dead man's switch. Blood was dripping from the point of the spike and Blondie realized that Dogface had been transfixed to the chair through his stomach.

Wind struck his face as they exploded into the station.

The reality transition tore strips of metal from *Fat Mama*'s nose. The train yawed violently to the right and rode up on to the platform. Sparks flew up from underneath it as it scraped along the edge of the platform. There was another tremendous lurch as the train settled back on to the friction field.

Somebody was clinging to the nose. Blondie saw a face leaning in through the shattered windscreen. It had human eyes but the mouth was a circular maw lined with concentric rows of teeth. Dogface batted feebly at the creature with his fists, blood was bubbling out of his mouth. The creature put its hands on either side of the windscreen frame and started to pull itself inside. With a sound of grating bone the rows of teeth started to rotate as the mouth inched closer to Dogface's head.

On the other side of the cab Lambada was fighting with her harness to get free. Credit Card was slumped in his seat with a line of blood across his forehead. The creature had its shoulders through the windscreen. Its jaw line was distorting, its mouth growing wider to envelop Dogface's head.

'Hey,' shouted Blondie.

The creature's head whipped round to face him and Blondie could see right down its throat. The teeth were whirling fast enough to blur, its breath was sickly sweet with rotten chocolate.

'Oh shit,' said Blondie. The creature was trying to wriggle its hips into the cab. The horrible mouth was whirring towards him like a kitchen recycler. Blondie ripped a fingernail off trying to undo his harness.

The creature's head exploded.

Old Sam was in the cab, a big handgun held straight out before him. The headless torso thrashed in the windowframe, two arcs of blood fountained from the arteries in its neck. The next shot blew the creature backwards out of the cab, taking chunks of the bulkhead with it.

'Medic,' bellowed Old Sam.

Lambada got free of her harness and worked her way over to Dogface. Her lips pursed when she saw the extent of the injury. 'We'll have to cut him out,' she said. Old Sam nodded and ducked back into the rear compartment. Lambada looked over at Blondie. 'Medical kit,' she said.

Blondie took a deep breath to calm himself and slapped the strap release. This time the harness slithered off his shoulders back into its holding reels. The first-aid kit was a big beige case marked with a red crescent. There wasn't anywhere to put it down so Blondie cradled it in his arms as Lambada opened the lid. Inside were stacked trays of neatly wrapped packages. Lambada pulled the biggest package out and ripped off its organic cellophane wrapping to reveal a sustainment collar. An unnaturally calm voice speaking Arabic started giving precise fitting instructions. It took Blondie a moment to realize that the voice was coming from the case.

Dogface's head lolled, making it difficult to fit the collar on his neck. His face was grey and blood continued to seep from his mouth. There was hardly any blood where the spike had penetrated his sternum; the skin was ripped and folded in around the shaft. Blondie tried not to look at it; instead his eyes tracked along the spike and out the ragged hole in the nose.

It was attached to the nastiest-looking tunnel board Blondie had ever seen. The board was being pushed along the friction field ahead of the train.

'Lambada,' said Blondie.

Lambada was concentrating on the Arabic instructions, placing derms and staunching foam around the wound. The floor of the cab where she knelt was littered with crumpled cellophane and blood.

'Lambada!'

'What?'

'We're moving,' said Blondie.

Fat Mama was slowly gliding down the length of the station.

With the friction field underneath there was only wind resistance to slow them down, and it wasn't going to be enough. They were thirty metres from the tunnel gateway, if they went through without shielding the torque effects would shred them.

Sam came back into the cab with an Azanian laser torch. Before Blondie could speak he shook his head and put his finger to his lips. When Sam was sure of their silence he pointed at the ceiling.

Small scrabbling sounds from above, just audible over the coughing syllables of medical Arabic. Somebody moving about on *Fat Mama*'s roof. Lambada caught Old Sam's eye and pointed towards the gateway. The veteran thought for a moment and drew his handgun left handed. It made a sinister whispering sound as it left the holster. Blondie stared at the gun looming butt first towards him.

'Go outside,' said Old Sam, 'and shoot them off the roof.'

The warvids always made a big thing out of the Paris Rock. The classic *Violet Sky* ran its opening credits over a sustained shot of the asteroid up in the barren spaces above the elliptic, tumbling slowly so that the ideograms blasted into its surface caught the sunlight one after another. The Martians knew that the ideograms would be spotted in the final terminal phase; for them it was a statement, a warning not to pursue a war of retribution against them. The dumb green bastards didn't know who they were dealing with.

The gun was an army surplus Browning recoilless semi-automatic with an airtight locking action chambered for fifteen-millimetre 'Martian' rounds for vacuum firing. It was heavy, the weight dragging at Blondie's arm as he crouched beside the right side emergency hatch. His left hand was wrapped around a big red handle surmounted by the pictogram for DANGER in Cantonese.

Johny Ray played the grunt who couldn't in *Violet Sky*. Extended close-ups of his sweaty face with the battle action reflected on the visor of his helmet. Freezing up in the sudden firefight when the Greenies came bubbling up through a camouflaged rock hole, bitching and whining through two-thirds of the vid. Long shot of Johny Ray's main squeeze as she sits on the fountain in the Place de la Concorde and writes a letter to her soldier boyfriend. She bites her lip in thought, a strand of black hair is misplaced across her forehead. The background noises of Paris slowly fade as the image bleaches white.

Johny Ray stumbling over the dunes, guns in both hands, Greenies going down before him. A big spire of rock where the Martians have a pop-up cannon which is chopping up the patrol, Johny Ray saving his last breath to pull the cable on the backpack nuke he's wearing.

Blondie waited until he heard scrabbling sounds from the other side of the hatch and pulled the handle. There was an animal shriek over the roar of explosive bolts as the hatch was thrown outwards. It shot across the platform and rang like a teatray against the station wall. There was a distinct organic crunch underlying the impact of metal on ceramic.

Blondie had never liked Johny Ray much.

He went out of the hatchway, jumping as far as he could to avoid anybody on the roof. His feet skidded as he landed and the momentum drove him into the wall. He was already trying to turn and took the impact on his shoulder and back.

He could see three figures on the roof of the train. Humanoid, their armour was a glistening blue colour and decorated with random clumps of sharp spines. They'd been pulling up the roof plates with their bare hands but as Blondie watched their heads turned slowly in his direction.

The range was about four metres.

Blondie held the gun straight-armed, lining up the sight on the chest of the first figure. It had grey-green human eyes beneath the bony ridges of what Blondie realized was not a helmet at all but its head. The word 'exo-skull' popped into his mind at the same moment he pulled the trigger.

The kick of the Browning stunned the palm of his hand, the figure flipped backwards, a ragged hole in its chest. Blondie swung the aim round to the second figure. It jumped at him just as he fired and the bullet went low, ripping into the abdomen. But even as it fell brokenly towards the platform the third figure was in the air. It jumped like a cat, arms and legs outstretched. This one had claws on both.

Blondie shifted his aim and kept his finger on the trigger but nothing happened. The figure seemed to rapidly expand to fill up his vision. 'Semi-automatic,' said the one calm bit of mind

Blondie had left, 'you have to pull the trigger for each shot.'

Big ragged holes opened up in the monster's chest. For one horrible moment Blondie could see right through to *Fat Mama* behind it and then it fell unmoving at his feet. Blondie jumped away quickly just in case. He ran up the platform until he was level with the cab, *Fat Mama* was still moving at walking pace towards the tunnel gateway.

'How's it going in there?' he called into the vacant hatchway. He could see bright flashes of light where Old Sam was carefully cutting through the spike.

'How many was that?' asked Old Sam.

One in the cab, three on the roof. Blondie looked down the platform. He could see feet and hands sticking out from both sides of the ejected hatch.

'Five,' he said.

'One left then,' said Old Sam and turned back to his work.

The Stop

Mariko lay face down on one of the trestle tables and picked idly at the remains of the catfish dip. Naran was nowhere to be seen, but she presumed he was off in a corner somewhere having deviant sex with a *rep*.

Most of the *krewe* were crashed out on the floor of the cavern. A lone *speaker* was crooning a French ballad in three part harmony with itself. She noticed an untouched bowl of walnuts on the table ahead of her, picked one out and cracked it between her thumb and forefinger. The meat was dry and sweet.

Since her transformation Mariko's thoughts had taken on an opaque nature as if she sat in the centre of a room lined with *shoji* - sliding paper doors. Figures moving outside the room could sometimes be discerned by the shadows cast upon the translucent screens. Mariko was made constantly aware of activity beyond the realm of her physical senses by this kabuki shadowplay. Sometimes one of the *shoji* would slide open and she would be granted a clear view, information necessary for her functions.

3Boss and her krewe had been discontinued, violently. The network had reacted with more aggression than anticipated. It would be up to Mariko to instigate containment procedures. One of the *shoji* in the room of her mind was marked with an eye - intelligence assets. Behind it she could sense gathering flux but the door remained closed.

Mariko picked up another walnut and flicked it at 2Boss who was snoring amongst a pile of bodies. The nut completed a perfect arc and bounced off his nose. He caught it before it hit the floor.

'Hey, 2Boss,' Mariko yelled across the cavern, 'we're short six *razvedka*. Pop out and get some more will you?'

Mitsubishi (Triton Central)

'I could murder a gumbo,' said Kadiatu, but the arcade off Walkman Square was wall-to-wall tampopo bars. There were a lot of people mooching in the arcade, passengers mostly, stranded by the sudden termination of the Pluto-bound train. Ronin under contract to the local zaibatsu were posted at the intersections to keep an eye on the crowd. Kadiatu watched as a couple of old white women were gently turned away from the staging gate to the suburban lines. Despite thirty years of civil-rights legislation Mitsubishi was still Sol's most segregated metropolis. Some of the suburbs wouldn't even take Koreans.

'There must be an alternative route,' said the Doctor, studying an STS map on the side of a Jade Tea stand.

All the trains were terminating one stop short of Pluto due to unspecified 'incidents' at Lowell Depot. Worse than that, alighting passengers were being herded off the platforms into Walkman Square.

'There's always an alternative,' muttered Kadiatu.

The Doctor turned and smiled at her. 'Absolutely,' he said.

The map's polychromatic surface was pristine; even the touch icons were unmarked by fingerprints. The map's default setting was of the interworld routes and some of the major feeder lines. Kadiatu touched Triton Central first, then Lowell Depot, and then a stylized icon of an arrow.

The map rippled as it rescaled. Triton Central in the lower third, Lowell Depot in the upper. Commuter lines appeared in a starburst pattern around Yamaha, Dentsu and Nagorno-Karabakh - Pluto's three other main cities. The Central Line link between Triton and Lowell pulsed red - the suggested optimum route.

'The map hasn't updated yet,' said Kadiatu.

'Is that unusual?' asked the Doctor.

'You get data lags at the peripheries,' said Kadiatu, 'but this is a major information nexus.'

'It's confused,' said the Doctor. 'The trains are running all right it's just that we're not on them. Is there another route?'

Kadiatu glanced at the map. There were no obvious connections. The only other InterWorld line that came this far outsystem was Outreach and that terminated at Nagorno-Karabakh. There were no obvious feeder or commuter routes between the Pluto and Triton local networks. There was a trick to this, Kadiatu knew; you let the map go out of focus and thought about what pretty patterns all those coloured lines made.

It was an article of faith amongst the undergraduates in the engineering department that the most efficient way to navigate the transit system was stoned out of your box.

'There,' she said touching the map, 'this feeder's connected to the branch line and the branch line's connected to the transverse line . . .'

'And the legbone's connected to the thighbone,' said the Doctor.

'Which will put us on Pluto ninety-five,' said Kadiatu.

The Doctor wanted to go immediately but Kadiatu forced him to wait while she sniffed out a snack bar that sold something other than bean sprouts and exquisite slivers of pork. It turned out to be the inevitable Kwik-Kurry franchise tucked in between a branch of Bodyshop and a stall that sold suspicious-looking lingerie. From it she bought half a kilo of fufu wrapped in heat-resistant paper, and a medium-sized tub of fish soup.

Giant colour-coded arrows, hung above the various station gateways, indicated which exit led where. The signs were made of hand-crafted neon rather than the usual holograms. Mitsubishi was full of touches like that as the Japanese tried to hang on to their traditions. Following the blue arrows they found the accessway to the platform they wanted. As they approached the pair of ronin on guard stepped forward, politely blocking their way. Kadiatu wondered what their problem was when she remembered - the Doctor was white and this close to Pluto the ronin were making some broad assumptions. She wondered how she could have forgotten.

The Doctor said something in Japanese - at least Kadiatu

assumed that was what the language was. Short staccato bursts of words with shortened vowels and hacked-off consonants. The two ronin looked at the Doctor in surprise and backed off. The Doctor strode on through the gate. As he passed by the ronin they performed deep bows of respect. Kadiatu trotted to catch up with the Doctor before whatever it was wore off.

She waited until they were two hundred metres down the corridor. 'What did you do?'

'I asked them politely to let us pass.'

'What was with the bowing and scraping then?'

'I used an eighth-century dialect that has since become accepted as the formal tongue of the Japanese royal family,' said the Doctor. 'I expect they were a bit surprised.'

'I'll bet.'

'And I doubt they understood more than one word in ten. Which is just as well.'

'Why?'

'Because what I actually said was "Make way! For I am the official keeper of the Emperor's penguins and I must hurry because his majesty's laundry basket is on fire." '

The platform was spotless. The few waiting passengers were clustered around a public-service TV at one end. It was tuned to one of the 24-hour Kabuki soap channels. It looked like a historical drama, Kadiatu caught glimpses of businessmen in black single-breasted suits striking attitudes in front of vast windows.

The indicator board at the far end of the station gave waiting times in Japanese characters, the regulation alpha-numeric display was tucked away underneath. The next train was scheduled in five minutes.

They sat down to wait and Kadiatu opened up the paper bag and gouged out a handful of fufu. She offered the bag to the Doctor but he shook his head. Kadiatu kneaded the cassava dough into a sausage shape and dunked it in her fish soup. It was a bit too bland for her taste but you didn't expect that much from Kwik-Kurry.

The Doctor watched the TV, apparently absorbed in the unfolding drama of corporate infighting. A woman had entered the scene wearing heavy eye make-up, to identify herself as gaijin.

'What do you see in that?' asked Kadiatu.

'The principle of *Kanzen-choaku*,' said the Doctor, 'the reward of the virtuous and the punishment of the wicked.'

'Your eyesight must be better than mine.' Kadiatu pulled another lump of fufu from the bag.

'You eat a lot,' said the Doctor turning back to the TV.

'I get hungry a lot,' said Kadiatu, 'I suppose I've got a fast metabolism.' She reflexively glanced at the indicator board – the arrival time seemed to be stuck at five minutes. 'Why are we going to Pluto?'

'We have to rescue someone.'

'What makes you think they need rescuing?'

'Trust me.'

The Stop

Roberta was dead and the neighbourhood was on fire. The power grid had failed and with it the skylights. Main Street was coloured red and yellow by the light of burning shops.

Zamina stayed low, trying to pull Roberta's body to shelter. A thick strata of black smoke had formed under the ceiling panels and visibility at street level was less than ten metres. She wondered how long it would take before the Stop's life support went into terminal crisis.

Zamina caught occasional glimpses of figures stalking through the haze. She didn't know if they were rioters or cops. There had been rumours earlier that troops were being sent in but she hadn't seen any yet. She could hear the firecracker sound of gunfire in the distance.

Across the street was the bolthole Zamina had picked out. It was the entrance to a Baptist orphanage. She dragged Roberta by the leg towards it. She couldn't bring herself to touch the woman anywhere near the chest. Who'd have thought that Roberta would be so heavy. Zamina had always envied that narrow waist and the thin legs. Elegant, Roberta said, not thin. Stupid to be trying to drag her off the street with that great sucking wound between her breasts. Plenty of others lying on the concrete, gangbangers, catfood monsters, looters, people dumb enough to be out when the cops opened fire.

Zamina flung herself down as something whispered overhead.

A three-metre-long drone painted red and yellow was swooping into position in front of a burning shop. A vent popped open at the rear and there was a rushing sound as air was sucked in. The smoke haze made Mandelbrot patterns behind the drone as it closed to lay bursts of freezing CO_2 on the fire.

Zamina started to crawl again, pulling Roberta behind her. The first fire-drones to respond had been shot down by the gangs, if they were active in this area it meant that the riot had moved on. She was four metres from the orphanage when the second drone went overhead. This one was slightly larger and blue-coloured with Chinese characters painted on its underside. Like the first it arrived from the opposite direction to Lowell Station; their controllers must have been routing them in from the service tunnels that honeycombed the crust beneath the projects. The second drone took up a sentry position above and behind the first.

More drones swept into Main Street. Another fire-fighter took up position in front of a burning building. The blue police-drone shifted position to cover both. Some of the drones were difficult to see, their chassis blending into the background. Mimetic polycarbon, Zamina sensed rather than saw them moving. Random dips and swerves designed to complicate hostile target resolutions. Their weapons would be hidden under jack turrets, waiting to pop out and return fire.

The army had arrived.

She remembered the confrontation on Williamsberg Avenue. Hatred rolling out like an Atlantic wave to break over the single line of blue uniforms. You came from the Stop, from bad housing, bad schools, from meals made out of pet food, from a place where recession was status quo and the one thing that was clear was that you never got out. You got to see out, watching *Systemwide!* on English-5, riding the trains to all the places that you'd glimpsed. You learnt quick that visiting wasn't living, that the Stop clung to you wherever you went.

So you went back because the job evaporated and without the job you couldn't raise the key money for a pad. Back to the catfood monsters, the urine-smelling stairways and the shitty skylights that were always broken. Back because it suited the powers-that-be that you stay there.

They cracked the paving stones and threw them at the cops.

Pulled fixtures out of shops, filled bottles full of industrial alcohol and made rag fuses from the strips they tore from their clothes. The missiles arched overhead to rain down on the policemen who stood their ground, dodging the firebombs, letting the stones bang off their armour. You could see the fear in the set of their mouths under their helmet visors. Fear overtaken by anger and hate.

Zamina recognized the sergeant in charge. The same tired-looking face and masai haircut, the detective from the murder scene two days ago. His hair was scraped back and plastered down with red mud. It came in little enamel tins, she'd seen them in a Mombasa fashion boutique. He paced up and down behind the line of policemen calmly giving orders, keeping them steady. It could have gone on like that for hours if it hadn't been for the kid in the white T-shirt.

The boy came running through the crowd. He was maybe ten years old, thin white legs sticking out of baggy khaki shorts. He was cradling something close to his belly, masking it with both arms, making his gait awkward as he ran. The cops shifted as he ran towards them, the shock-rods nervous in their hands, but no one wanted to beat a kid. Catch him if he comes closer, they were thinking, throw him in the tank until he cools off and Social Services bails him out.

The grenade was a thousand metres of monofilament wrapped around two hundred milligrams of cyclotol chipped to detonate one metre above ground level. Only the sergeant saw it coming, had just enough time to yell a warning and dive away.

Zamina stopped again as a white drone the size of a beachball hovered over Roberta's corpse. It had been methodically working itself up the street, pausing to check each body in turn. She knew that somewhere behind it larger medical drones would be moving up and sorting out the injured. The drone pinged twice and pinned a micro-transmitter to Roberta's face, marking her as dead.

The drones worked in silence except for the imperceptible hum of their lifting fields, each of them acting in accordance with their programming and bound together by an invisible web of microwave communications. It was like watching an invasion by alien insects. Zamina hadn't seen a live human being for hours.

The authorities were leaving the Stop to the ministration of the machines.

The cuts and abrasions Zamina had collected began to sting. There was a line of pain running down her left thigh, and she could feel a spreading wetness soaking into her leggings. Zamina didn't look, she knew if you looked it always hurt more. Her throat was sore from the smoke even though it was beginning to clear. She should have forgotten about Roberta but she couldn't leave her lying on the street. Zamina had been her friend.

Benny was waiting for them in the orphanage, leaning against the wall just back from the door by a large poster that said 'JESUS SAVES' in blood-red letters. She didn't move to help Zamina as she dragged Roberta inside. Benny seemed untouched by the violence; she looked down at Zamina from a great distance.

'She's dead,' said Zamina.

Benny shrugged her shoulders, bone and muscle moving under Roberta's second-best leather jacket. 'Underclasses,' she said vaguely, 'poverty, insensitive policing.' The words were slurred, sing-song, like the recitation of a junkie. 'Happens all the time.'

'Hey, Benny,' said Zamina, 'you wired or something?'

Her eyes snapped into focus. 'I studied history so I know. Did I tell you that?'

'You never told us nothing,' said Zamina, 'nothing at all.'

'No I didn't did I?'

What had she said to the boy in the white T-shirt? Did he know it was a grenade or had she just handed it to him and said, Hey kid, here's something for you to throw. Mind you get in good and close. He had to get in close, he was just a small boy not strong enough to throw beyond the grenade's lethal range. The cops had their armour but the boy was cut in two.

'Come on, girl,' said Benny, 'she's dead and we've got things to do, people to see.'

West Triton Feeder/Pluto ninety-five

Memories chased the Doctor up the non-existent tunnels of the transit system. Kadiatu assured him that this was the last but one leg of the trip to Lowell Depot, for which he was grateful. Since leaving Mitsubishi there had been a lot of empty trains and deserted stations. Each transition through a tunnel disturbed him; he had spent far too much time in unreal environments recently, the inside of his own mind being the worst. Perhaps he should have done some reordering while he was in there, a bit of DIY amongst the old grey cells. He could have recatalogued his memory into things he knew, things he might know and things that thought he knew them.

The train raced ahead of his mind's own event horizon with his memories howling behind.

Intuition, the data-processing of his unconscious mind that he had learnt to follow but never trusted, drove him on. In his darker moments he often considered the possibility that his subconscious was in some respect not his own. That it belonged to some other, vaster, more complex personality. As if he was just a dream in the mind of a god. Sometimes he posited a theory of reverse-existentialism in which he existed only because other people thought he existed. Kadiatu's phase-space model worried him. Tracing him as a series of gaps in the sequence of human history was a bit too much like empirical confirmation of his worst nightmares.

I am thought of therefore I am.

You could go mad thinking like that.

Kadiatu didn't help his peace of mind either. Too many coincidences piled one on top of each other. It was like walking around with a club sandwich made by fate.

Travelling on the underground always made him morbid.

We are all lost luggage in the Victoria Station of life.

Kadiatu was stretched out on the seat opposite, ankles crossed, hands folded across her stomach, eyes half closed. Perfectly relaxed.

He kept on looking for traces of his old friend in his great-great-grand-daughter. Some characteristic gesture or tick that would link them over five generations. There was nothing of course; human genetics didn't run to that sort of thing, especially after what had been done to hers.

The train pulled into another station. Kadiatu rolled to her feet.

What would the Brigadier have said if he knew?

'All change,' said Kadiatu.

She led him through deserted galleries paved with red slate and lined with unused shops. The air was frosty and undisturbed. It was like walking across a field of virgin snow.

'This must be one of the unfinished developments,' said Kadiatu. 'They were supposed to revitalize this whole end of the system.'

'What happened?'

'The money ran out.'

The entrance leading to the platform they wanted was blocked by a sliding metal cage gate. A red No Entry sign was stencilled on a plywood sheet attached to the gate with gaffa tape. The Doctor let Kadiatu have first go at the lock. He wanted to see what she did.

Kadiatu carefully examined the point where the locking mechanism joined the wall, took a step back and kicked it hard twice. She took another look and, satisfied, yanked open the gate. The entire locking mechanism came out of the wall with a puff of cement powder. The gate rattled open and slammed into the opposite wall with a crash.

'*Nemo me impine lacessit*,' said the Doctor.

'What?'

'No one attacks me with impunity,' said the Doctor, walking through the open gate. 'The family motto of the Stewarts.'

Kadiatu poked her finger into the hole made by the lock. Chunks of cement crumbled and fell out. 'Graft above all things,' said Kadiatu. 'Motto of the building contractor.'

It got colder as they got closer to the platforms. There was no tiling here, just a scored floor of unfinished puff concrete. When they stepped out on to the platform Kadiatu automatically looked down the platform for the indicator hologram. It was blank. Her breath steamed as they waited.

'I hope there are trains running on this line,' she said.

The Doctor watched somewhat smugly as Kadiatu began bouncing up and down on her toes to keep warm. A low musical chime sounded from somewhere and the indicator lit up.

'At last,' said Kadiatu.

'NEXT TRAIN: STRAIGHT TO HELL 5 mins.'

'Someone's got a sick sense of humour,' said Kadiatu.

'No,' said the Doctor quietly. 'Somebody's trying to tell us something.'

Ming took the call in Fu's office: Credit Card staring out of the Philips HDTV. Another of her Number One Husband's many antiques. The analog decoder wasn't really compatible with the scrambler's signal protocol, so Credit Card's face was spread out to twice its normal width.

'I can't see you,' he said.

Fu stretched out a long arm and placed a minicam on top of the TV.

'That's better.'

A wedge-shaped portion of Credit Card's hair had been shaved away and a strip of artificial skin ran down from it to above his right eyebrow.

'Can't you stop him?' asked Ming.

'He's putting on his armour, for chrissakes, I didn't even know he had it with him. I'm not crazy enough to try and get in his way.'

'What about Dogface?'

'He's at the local medical centre. The spike was off centre and missed his spine. It's just a kidney, some intestine and a few other bits and bobs they have to replace. He should be out and about in a few days.'

'Is there any more?'

'There's loads more,' said Credit Card. 'Old Sam's taking Blondie with him. Says he needs someone who knows the stop.'

'They know about the riots?'

'It's on TV, ain't it?'

'So why's he going?'

'I think he's got business but the way he's acting I don't know. It's like he's on a mission or something.'

'V Soc,' said Fu from behind the TV.

'What was that?' asked Credit Card.

'Nothing,' said Ming. 'What about the freesurfers that attacked you?'

'I didn't see them till they was dead and believe me that's the best way to see them. Scary stuff. The KGB scraped up the remains and took them away. I don't know where.'

'Probably the Nueva Lubyanka,' said Ming. With Dogface down and Old Sam going up the line with Blondie, Ming was down to just two Special Maintenance. 'There's been some more of those power drains you and Dogface found so fascinating.'

'Christ, Ming, I need a rest.'

You shouldn't have spent twenty years making yourself fucking indispensable then, should you?'

Credit Card terminated the link from his end.

'I may have married you,' said Fu, 'but I'm glad I don't work for you.'

'Management is a hierarchical process,' said Ming. 'You're never going to be comfortable with your boss, however nice she is. Better to give them a proper hate figure in the first place, that way they know where they are. Play your cards right and your employees do the work right just to spite you.'

'Does that mean that underneath that cold hard exterior you're really a warm lovable human being?'

'Fu,' said Ming, 'you never heard a rationalization before?'

She punched a call code into the phone.

A dancer dressed in abbreviated green armour appeared on the screen. It was a classy graphic for a hold signal but the illusion of reality was destroyed by the way the decoder spread random pixels over the image. The dancer was replaced by a joyboy's face that didn't look real even though it probably was.

'Ice Maiden,' said the face.

'I want to talk to Francine,' said Ming.

Stazione Centrale de Rhea

Have you ever used a Vicker's All-Body Combat System before?

The world had become a very simple place for Blondie, an abstract landscape leached of colour, simplified into friends and targets by the helmet's CPU. The data went straight into the auxiliary contact jack on his neck the images forming directly behind his eyes.

Please specify which weapon systems are activated.

The military software had been surprisingly polite, running down a pre-arm checklist before fine-tuning the system to his requirements. It gave him the simplest possible combat environment and divided up the world into discrete zones of evaluated danger. Moving around gave Blondie a profound feeling of unreality, as if he were playing an intricate VR game.

Lambada said that the veterans had systems like this chipped into their cortex. Combat software directly integrated into the mind's eye.

Please specify current rules of engagement.

Blondie realised that this was the way Old Sam saw the world all the time.

'Can you hear me?' asked Old Sam.

Old Sam was wearing his full rig from the war. It came out of the same bags as the helmet, piece by piece, smelling of grease and liquid Teflon. He must have maintained the equipment over all those years. Blondie had heard somewhere that it had over two thousand separate components. He had a vision of Old Sam, late at night, bent over a workbench. Tools and components laid out in neat rows around the workspace, squinting to hold a jeweller's eyeglass in place as he assembled some microscopic widget. Except he wouldn't be using an eyeglass, not with the eyes he already owned.

'Hey Blondie,' said Old Sam, louder. *'Can you hear me?'* It was radio communication relayed into the helmet speakers.

'How come we're using radio?' asked Blondie.

'ECM,' said Dogface. *'No direct neural input that can be accessed from outside. You don't want the enemy breaking into the net and scrambling your mind. How do you feel?'*

'Strange.'

'You'll get used to it. Has the CPU asked for rules of engagement yet?'

'Yes.'

'Tell it Melbourne Protocols.'

Blondie formed the words in his mind and pushed them towards the interface. It wasn't that different from the work he'd been doing in system maintenance.

'You won't notice any difference at the moment but the CPU won't let you fire unless it detects a weapon,' said Old Sam. *'Now a few things to remember. You're wearing what's called "low threat" armour. Support troops used to wear it, medics, base personnel and the like. The breastplate, codpiece and greaves can take a direct hit from most projectile or energy weapons, the rest of it cannot. I'm not expecting real trouble but if we get into a firefight get your face in the dirt and I'll handle it.'*

'What if you can't handle it?'

'I wouldn't think about that contingency, my lad,' said Old Sam. *'I really wouldn't.'*

Credit Card came over to join them. Blondie watched the silver kill icon hovering over his chest. As Credit Card got closer the icon refined its position until it was neatly aligned slightly to the left of his breastbone.

Bang, thought Blondie, straight through the heart.

He broke into a sudden sweat when he realized what he'd nearly done. No wonder Old Sam had him on failsafe.

'Visors up,' said Credit Card testily, 'or I'm not talking to either of you.'

Lowell Depot

The dead were waiting for them at the station. They lined the platform in four neat rows, tricked out in their best black bodybags for the special occasion. Pinned to the foot end of each bag was a white smart card, little robotic forget-me-nots to carry the dead into the inactive files of the system database. Some of the bags were far too short to contain adults.

The Doctor and Kadiatu had to step over them to reach the exit.

Kadiatu waited in the archway, watching as the Doctor unsealed one of the smaller bags. Caught a glimpse of the child's pale face and the puckered hole above its left eye. The Doctor looked up from the body and straight into her eyes. Kadiatu turned away, trying to catch her breath. The Doctor took her arm, leading her away from the platform, but she stumbled over nothing and fell against the wall.

'Cry,' said the Doctor.

Kadiatu cried for the first time since her parents' funeral. Her face buried in the Doctor's shoulder awkwardly bent over to reach his level. He didn't move, no arm put around her shoulders, no words of comfort. He just waited until she'd finished.

'Better?' he asked when she'd straightened up.

Kadiatu nodded.

'Lesson number one,' said the Doctor. 'Those that travel this road, walk alone.' Then he smiled and, reaching up, patted her cheek. 'But backup is always useful.'

It made her feel better but she was damned if she knew why.

For passengers a transit station consists of an entrance, the platforms and the concourses. For an engineer like Kadiatu they're much larger. Even the smallest branch station had a network of conduits, maintenance shafts, niches for cleaning robots, not to mention the parallel freight station with its handlers and cargo lifts.

Lowell Depot had been built during the post-war boom years. Pluto had been expected to soak up the population overspill from the more crowded worlds and the depot had massive overcapacity built in. That was before the Australian Famine and the Martian terraforming project, before the stop became the Stop. Like Kings Cross, it was a labyrinth of passageways and open space, only here mostly empty.

Finding their way to the main Central Line platform was going to be a problem.

An autokart raced towards them when they emerged on to a concourse, stopped suddenly a metre from their feet and beeped twice. Kadiatu looked at the Doctor, who shrugged. The kart beeped again and performed a neat three-point turn.

'Down boy,' said the Doctor. 'Sit, beg, roll over, play dead.'

'It's an autokart,' said Kadiatu.

'I think it wants us to get in.'

'That's not necessarily a good reason to do it, though. Is it?'

'More use than a ball of string,' said the Doctor and climbed aboard. Kadiatu followed him on and tried to find a comfortable position for her legs.

They sat there for a minute or two, feeling a bit foolish. The Doctor nudged Kadiatu in the ribs and pointed to the dashboard. There was a small microphone inset above the station name-plate.

'Central Line platform,' she said, 'please.'

The kart moved off down the concourse.

'Ah,' said the Doctor, 'the magic word.'

Entering the next concourse was like driving on to a building site. A line of yellow and black-striped drones were parked against one wall. Streaks of dirty black soot ran along their flanks, some of them showed extensive damage and signs of small arms fire.

'Fire-fighters,' said Kadiatu.

Small crablike robots scuttled over the drones, slipping in and out of open inspection panels. There were painful flashes of blue light as they electrowelded patches over damaged bodywork.

'This must be the forward workshop,' said the Doctor, 'where the walking wounded are patched up and sent back to the front.'

'No wonder the line was closed to passengers,' said Kadiatu. 'They must have been moving all this up.'

A blue police-drone buzzed the kart and scanned them with bursts of pink laser light.

'Oh shit,' said Kadiatu. 'We're going to get busted.'

The drone kept pace with the kart for a moment before becoming suddenly uninterested in them and gliding away.

'Did you do that?' asked Kadiatu.

'No,' said the Doctor, 'did you?'

'No.'

There was a knot of technicians at the end of the concourse. They were clustered around a projected map of the area. Kadiatu noticed that a lot of it was marked red for danger. The Doctor doffed his hat at them as the kart buzzed past.

'Hey,' shouted a voice behind them, 'who the hell are you?'

'As soon as we find out,' Kadiatu shouted back, 'we'll let you know.'

There were more drones in the next concourse and the next. They passed an assault model doing downtime, surrounded by worried-looking soldiers dressed in dirty olive green. Some malfunction must have popped all its jack turrets; lethal weapons sprung out at full extension like a busted puzzle box.

They heard the people before they saw them - a low restless muttering cut through with the sound of crying babies. The noise was funnelled down the passageway, slowly growing to overwhelm the hum of the kart's electric motor.

The living were more unruly than the dead. They did not lie quietly in ordered ranks. Instead they were spread out in chaotic patterns, whirls and loops that formed around family units. Some were standing, some sat crosslegged or leant against the walls. Some lay on the floor, curled up tight in fetal positions. Relief workers moved amongst them, wearing fluorescent donkey jackets with agency names on their backs - OXFAM, MEDAID, HIGGINS TRUST. They looked like a species of bright yellow wading bird picking over a beach.

'How many, do you think?'

'In here?' asked the Doctor. 'About a thousand.'

It was like the archive footage of the Australian famine. Worse, because Kadiatu was here amongst it, riding down the narrow corridor between the refugees. Only a few bothered to watch them pass.

'They must be evacuating the whole project,' said Kadiatu.

A line of refugees wound out of the concourse. A relief worker and a soldier were stationed every ten metres or so down the line. Periodically the refugees would silently shuffle a few steps forward and stop again. On the straight stretches you could see the shuffle working itself up the line like a sine wave.

The autokart followed the line down a long curved ramp that terminated on the platform. A tall Ethiopian was standing at the bottom; he waved his clipboard in front of the kart's motion sensor until it stopped.

'There's no room for this,' he said banging the bonnet. 'It'll have to go back.'

The Doctor and Kadiatu clambered out of the kart. A big sleek InterWorld train was waiting in the station. Refugees were being herded on board by sweating STS staff.

'Home boy,' said the Doctor to the kart. It beeped one last time and reversed back up the ramp.

Kadiatu watched as an old man was lifted into the train. He was slack mouthed and his eyes were deeply disinterested. Tranquillized, guessed Kadiatu, or senile. How many people lived in the projects, she wondered. Ten thousand, twenty thousand?

'Where are you going to put them?' she asked the Ethiopian.

'Poland, Brazil, the Noctis Labyrinthus. Anywhere that's got facilities, army-training bases mainly.' He looked over at the Doctor. 'Who are you with?'

'Bomb disposal,' said the Doctor.

The man shot Kadiatu a very worried look. 'Really?'

'If you've got a bomb,' said Kadiatu, 'we dispose of it.'

His voice cracked. 'Here?' he asked.

'We're looking for a box,' said the Doctor, 'about two and

half metres tall, one and a half wide, with a blue light mounted on top.'

The man looked relieved. 'No,' he said, 'nothing like that.'

'Do you mind if we look around?'

'Be my guest.'

They walked up towards the blank end of the station.

'He couldn't wait to get rid of us,' said Kadiatu.

'Kings Cross station,' said the Doctor. 'I asked what was at the end of the tunnel and you said Pluto, yes?'

'Yes.'

'So it should be here.'

'What should be here?' asked Kadiatu and then she remembered. A blue box, two and a half metres tall, blue light on top. Right in the middle of the platform - she'd run right into it.

The wind had been filled with knives and the stink of ozone.

'Next time I'm going to find a better place to park.'

'Well,' she said, 'it could have been diverted but the default signalling position would take it straight through to here.'

'Then it should be here.'

'How fragile is it?' Whatever came through Kings Cross had eaten through armour, muscle and bone.

'It's indestructible.'

Since the Central Line terminated at Lowell Depot the friction field stopped three metres before the end wall. A concrete apron extended the platform into an L-shape. A physical buffer constructed from layers of collapsible steel and permafoam stood at the end of the track. Last chance of a stop before the wall. The Doctor bent over to examine it.

'I wonder,' said the Doctor, 'does this buffer look brand new to you?'

Kadiatu looked. The paintwork did look suspiciously fresh. She didn't know though, maybe they were routinely replaced.

The Doctor straightened up and looked at the end wall. A rectangular sheet of plywood three metres high had been fixed to the wall opposite the buffers and then painted over to match the wall. The Doctor walked over and rapped his knuckles on the wood. It was hollow.

He handed Kadiatu a French fisherman's knife. A wickedly sharp blade hinged out of the wooden handle and locked in place with a metal ring. She jammed the blade under the plywood, ripping down until there was enough room for them both to get a handhold. The sheet came away easily, probably held to the wall only by the adhesiveness of the paint.

'I bet you always wondered,' said the Doctor, 'what happens when an irresistible force meets an immovable object.'

There was a hole in the wall with razor-sharp sides. It started about ten centimetres above platform level, creating a step. It was about one and a half metres wide and two and half metres tall. The ceiling had a stepped cross-section like a ziggurat.

The hole continued straight ahead into darkness.

'Well,' said the Doctor, peering inside, 'shall we dance?'

5:
Hereditary Diseases

The Ice Maiden

The rumours about Francine's eyes were wrong; she did not see in the far ultraviolet or deep infrared. She did not see at all. Instead, darkness rushed behind her eyes, non-glimpses of ridges or canyon walls in the random silver imagination of her damaged nerves. 'So sorry,' said the Doctors and their machines, 'an interaction between your brain and the devices that were put inside.'

So Francine took her disability pension and forged a cocoon for herself under the sea. A flesh place, a sex-driven life-support machine to suck in the capital to finance her real interests. Expanding her influence among the artificial ganglia of humanity's brand-new nervous system. In the hectic years after the war even the military had no idea how to protect itself. They had numerous theories and academic studies but nobody knew - until Francine taught them.

Francine, pirate of the wide-open silicon sea, blind eyes illuminated by the folded neon structures of the datascape, pillaging the fortresses of the corporations and government agencies. Within three weeks she had captured an estimated 35 per cent of the world's secrets.

The establishment learnt fast. The technology wasn't new and they too had their veterans and burn-out cases. People strange enough to risk the direct interface with the machines. They sailed out from I/O ports in vessels knitted together from operating instructions to hunt down Francine.

But the twisted DNA of human history replicated itself once again. The company privateers took up their own careers, raiding other corporations for fun and profit. Smaller corporations, those on the cutting edge of the new technology, saw an opportunity to wrong-foot the big industrial zaibatsu. They gave spurious licence to the privateers who became the gaudy property of the media gestalt. Life-and-death drama on the primetime infotainment shows.

The corporations screamed all the way up to the Global Congress but political consensus took too long when battles lasted seconds. Privateers dying jacked in at their terminals, brains gently fired by lethal for/next loops.

Under the corporate mantle macro-economics ground relentlessly on. The world government was pushing the transit system all the way to Pluto. The economy went into overdrive, mainlining raw materials from the new worlds. Plate tectonics pushed up new mountain ranges in the economy and laid waste to the old conglomerates. Sony went down as did IBM and Matsui. Consumers got used to new household names from Brazil, China and Africa: Imbani, Mtchali, Tung-Po. Japan suffered social collapse and mass emigration, Australia starved.

The new consensus finally emerged alongside the pictures of emaciated potbellied children. It was unthinkable that humanity could once again allow economics to kill children. The media gestalt demanded a scapegoat: they were given the pirates. Their high profile, their mystery and amorality made them perfect targets. The only problem was how to stop them.

Francine had long since vanished from the silicon sea. Instead she traded information for influence, influence for power, and made herself the undisputed mistress of the underworld.

Then she waited for the powers-that-be to pick up the phone.

The campaign against the pirates lasted seven days. Black neon frigates ran them down on the silicon sea. I/O ports were traced, doors kicked in, heads broken, arrests made. There were even a few trials, but not many. Caught in the glare of the cameras the pirates were too often revealed as sad individuals beset by personality defects. Not glamorous enough, said the media gestalt, and produced fictions instead. Moody stories with corrupted heroes leading double lives and dying in a blaze of static. It became a separate genre in itself: *silicon noir*.

The government paid her off in favours and turning a blind eye to certain real-estate deals she had going on the moons of Jupiter. More influence, more money, more power. The Angel Francine lay back and waited to become 'old money'.

Eight years passed.

Francine hardly noticed the empire she had built. After all, she had created it out of a kind of defensive reflex. A soldier's instinct to dig in and fortify her position. It ran on automatic from an anonymous glass tower in Trieste. Sometimes she wondered if they still killed people, but it was an idle thought. She didn't care. She lay beneath the sea with her memories and the silver terrain of Mars behind her eyes.

Her long repose was broken by news of the Flying Dutchman. There were still people operating within the datascape, that was unavoidable. They rode in using the new hardware decks that allowed second-hand contact with the computer network. It made them harder to kill, but their reactions operated in slow biological time not quick enough to hack the real secrets. This new generation of pirates were furtive, devoid of élan or class: anonymous.

The Flying Dutchman was different.

One of her faceless executives came to see her. It was a strange experience for Francine, like listening to a talking dog. She was a bit surprised to find that one of her companies was a contracted arm of the state, the Data Protection Agency. The executive explained the position and fled, suitably terrified by Francine's presence, leaving behind a bonded EPROM cartridge.

She saw echoes of herself in the Flying Dutchman. He cruised the datascape with impunity. His targets were a random scattering of commercial and governmental databases. Security never saw him, his trail was only visible in the files he misplaced.

So Francine broke her exile from the silicon sea and went hunting. She sailed out brain-naked with just enough software to navigate. The datascape had changed in eight years, the translucent towers had been replaced by squat bunkers black with lethal countermeasures. Scrambled data was shunted in secure buses like silver bullets. Francine ghosted across the sea, a random search to catch a random pirate.

She caught sight of the Flying Dutchman only once.

It was out on the margins by the Ministry of Education. A backwater region where shoals of whales swam, grazing quietly through the history files - students running search programs. A fine haze of translation flags hung over the still surface of the data. A flock of updates wheeled overhead. Occasionally one would dive into the files and vanish, rising up moments later with an error squirming in its beak.

The three-masted galleon was beautiful, image resolution so high that it looked like a physical object. She ran swiftly, heeling over as she beam reached into an imaginary wind, sails puffed out like sheets in a wind tunnel. A flag flew from the top of the mainmast, a white skull and crossbones on a black background. As the ship bore down on her, Francine began to make out details, gilded scrollwork on the forecastle, the neat stitching around a patch on the forestaysail. Only the figurehead was indistinct. The underlying figure was female but the features were constantly shifting.

The galleon swept past her like a tilted wall of clinkered timber. Francine could see a crew swarming over the rigging, cartoon skeletons in striped jerseys and navy-blue bellbottoms. There was a sensation of falling, and sudden confusion in Francine's inner ear. The file surface was in motion, rippling in the galleon's wash-white pixel spray flying up around its bow. She realized that the image of the galleon was so *intense* that it was distorting the fabric of the datascape, dragging everything into its own reality.

A man appeared at the galleon's rail, wearing a felt hat and an afghan coat. He looked down at Francine and said something. It was a strange thing to do in the perpetual silence of the silicon sea. The man seemed to realize this, and held up his hand - *just a moment* - and produced a megaphone. Nothing technological, just a metal cone with a mouthpiece at one end.

'Ahoy there, software off the starboard rail!' he shouted and with his voice the silence broke. Sound rushed in, the creak of the galleon's rigging, the slap of water against its hull, the raucous cries of the circling updates and the long slow white noise of the sea itself. There was the feel of wind against her face and salt spray in her nostrils. Canvas cracked above her head and suddenly she rode a ship, a white schooner that cut through the swelling waves of data, keeping a parallel track with the galleon.

'Good, isn't it?' shouted the man at the rail.

'How's it done?' There was brilliant sunshine now; she could feel the warmth of it on her skin.

'That would be telling,' said the man. 'Are you the Angel Francine?'

'Yes.'

'Good, I have a message for you.' The man tossed a bottle down to her. The glass sparkled in the sunlight. There was a roll of parchment stuffed inside.

'Who are you?' shouted Francine but the man had vanished from the rail. There was a crash as the bottle smashed on the deck of the schooner, glass fragments shattering the unreal light.

Francine found herself back in the darkness of her room. The Braille printer beside her was chuntering hard copy on to the floor. There was a salty wetness on her cheeks.

She snatched up the first page of the hard copy and ran her finger along the top. There was a raised pattern in the centre, the printer's best guess at a company logo. There was a Braille translation underneath: 'IMOGEN - Wholly Confidential - Ubersoldaten - generation two.'

Twenty-one years before.

The Stop

'The light at the end of a tunnel,' said the Doctor, 'is often that of an oncoming train.'

They had penetrated perhaps six hundred metres into the tunnel and the ambient light from the station behind them had long become a tiny point in the distance. The Doctor had produced a small torch from his pocket. They needed it. Shafts bisected the tunnel at random intervals. The Doctor almost fell into the first one.

'What do you think it is?' he asked. Kadiatu didn't answer; she was trying to keep her grip on the Doctor's forearm. The fingertips of her right hand had found a shallow depression in the tunnel wall and she was trying to exploit it for leverage. Her kneecaps hurt from their impact on the floor and she was sure that the twisted position of her back wasn't doing her spine any good. Light flickered below her as the Doctor played his torch over the sides of the shaft.

'I think it's a maintenance conduit of some kind,' said the Doctor. 'I can see pipes and cables, that sort of thing. I can't see the bottom though. Hold on, I'll drop something.'

Kadiatu fought the slow progression of her fingertips out of their hold. If they slipped she'd pitch forward and she'd go head first down the shaft. There was a small sound from a long way below; metal hitting concrete.

'Were you counting?' asked the Doctor. 'I made it a hundred and thirty-two metres.'

A drop of sweat rolled off the bridge of Kadiatu's nose and into her left eye.

'You can pull me up now,' said the Doctor. 'I've finished down here.'

It wasn't easy, Kadiatu wasn't sure it was possible, but she found the strength from somewhere and hauled him up. It would have been simpler if the Doctor had used his free hand to help but he didn't want to let go of his umbrella.

'How do we get across?' asked Kadiatu.

'We jump,' said the Doctor. 'The exercise will do you good.'

They walked a few metres away from the edge.

'You go first,' said Kadiatu.

'As you like,' said the Doctor.

Kadiatu was sudddenly alone in the darkness. The torch bobbed along at waist level as the Doctor ran back towards the shaft. The soft slap of his shoes on concrete stopped, the torch flew through the air and then there was a scrape as the Doctor landed.

'Your turn,' he said.

Kadiatu figured the shaft couldn't be more than two metres across. She should be able to jump that. 'Right,' she said. 'I can do this.'

The Doctor pointed the torch at the edge of the shaft. 'Jump there,' he said.

Kadiatu took a couple more steps away from the edge, then a couple more.

'That's enough of a run-up,' said the Doctor.

The shaft was a square of darkness behind the patch of light thrown by the torch. The Doctor's eyes glittered in the scant reflected light. Two metres, easy.

The torch went out.

'Oh dear,' said the Doctor.

'What happened?'

'I'm fairly certain that it's the batteries.'

'What do we do now?'

'Have you moved since the lights went out?'

'No.'

'Then it's simple. When I say "run" you start running. I'll tell you when to jump.'

'What!'
'Ready when you are.'
'Can you see in the dark?'
'No.'
'So how are you going to know?'
'I have an excellent sense of spacial awareness.'
'Bollocks.'
'Did you say something?'
'No.'
'I'm going to count to three, all right?'
'No.'
'Run!'

The body started without her, took off through the darkness towards the Doctor's voice, her rope-soled Bajan pumps, three seventy-five from a stall in the plaza, getting good traction on the gritty concrete floor. Her eyes hurt from being held wide open for too long, useless in the total blackness. Her mind caught up with her body, snapped back into a total awareness of her physicality.

The Doctor must have shouted 'jump' because she sailed through the air and fell over on the other side. She rested on her hands and knees for a moment before standing up, the whole event fading nightmare-fast from her mind.

There was light again. The torch lit up the Doctor's face and threw his huge shadow across the wall behind.

'Perhaps it wasn't the batteries after all,' he said.

Kadiatu said nothing. She didn't want to talk about it, she didn't even want to think about it. When the Doctor started down the tunnel again, she followed him, silently.

There were four more shafts. One of them was off-centre, leaving a shelf wide enough for them to cross. They had to jump the other three. Kadiatu insisted on going first each time.

Six hundred metres in they saw the light at the end of the tunnel. It wasn't an oncoming train; instead they stepped out into a large open space.

The light was coming from a couple of holo projectors strung up on the ceiling. Set on neutral they produced big boxes of pearly static. It reminded Kadiatu of the rainy season in Makeni, sitting on the verandah with her father as the daylight was filtered through the falling water.

'Looks like somebody was having a party,' said Kadiatu.

Spilled food stained the white linen over the trestle tables lining the walls. Some of the tables had been knocked over. Empty cartons littered the floor. Kadiatu nudged one over with her foot, exposing a picture of a Black Forest gateau printed on the other side.

'Junk food,' said the Doctor.

Kadiatu thought that was a strange expression. How could food be junk? 'Chocolate cake and ice cream,' said Kadiatu. 'Nothing wrong with that.'

'Carbohydrates, sucrose,' said the Doctor. 'High-energy foods for people who use up their glycogen in industrial quantities.'

'Maybe they've got a fast metabolism.'

'Or an accelerated one,' said the Doctor.

'Maybe they just like cake and ice cream?'

'There it is,' said the Doctor.

It looked just as she remembered it from Kings Cross station and the Stone Mountain archives, right down to the words 'POLICE BOX' stencilled below the roof in white letters. It was opposite the entrance to the cavern of course, embedded in the wall. It had sunk all the way in, leaving about two centimetres clear of the rock.

The Doctor rushed over and put his hand against its side. 'My old friend,' he said, 'what have they done to you?' He patted the side again. 'Don't worry, soon have you out.'

Kadiatu put her own hand against it. She wasn't sure what she expected it to feel like, gritty perhaps, like all weather paint on concrete or wood. Instead the texture was rough, warm and organic like elephant skin. She felt a threshold vibration under her palm.

'It's called a TARDIS,' said the Doctor.

'I know.'

'What do you think of it?'

'It's smaller than I expected.'

'All we have to do now,' said the Doctor, 'is get it out of the wall.'

'Can't we just move it?'

'Of course,' said the Doctor. 'It would be a simple matter once I got inside to dematerialize for a short jump. Unfortunately there's a problem.'

'What's that?'

'The door's on the other side.'

Lowell Depot (Central Line Terminus)

The train doors hissed open and Old Sam jumped out. Blondie saw terrified faces falling back as he followed the veteran out. They went up the platform at a fast dog trot, refugees scattering out of their way. Blondie hardly noticed; sweating in his half-armour he concentrated on keeping up with Old Sam.

Old Sam stopped by a tall African wearing a dayglo orange jacket and carrying a clipboard. The African looked critically at Old Sam.

'What's with the rig?' he asked.

'Got a mission,' said Old Sam. He held up a snap projector; it put a four by six 3D image into the air above. A six-second loop of Kadiatu's head and shoulders. The image must have been sampled at the party because you could see Credit Card dancing in the background. 'You seen this?' asked Old Sam.

'Ran through here half an hour ago,' said the African, 'with some *mzungu*, claimed they were *bangjacks*.'

'Which way?' asked Old Sam.

'Up the end of the station.' The African raised his hand briefly to his temple. It was a hesitant, unconscious gesture and Blondie saw he had a military-issue jack implanted there, just like Old Sam's.

'Who did you serve with, friend?' asked Old Sam.

The African's hand snapped away from his temple. 'I don't remember my unit, I have forgotten the war.' He said it quietly and it sounded to Blondie like an incantation.

Old Sam said nothing, then he turned and ran up the platform. Blondie glanced back as he followed. The African's hand was back at his temple, finger running around the ceramic ring of his jack. An itch he couldn't scratch.

'First in,' muttered Old Sam as they reached the end of the platform. 'Day one, boy,' he said to Blondie. 'Third Tactical Response Brigade, Irish and Ethiopians. Dropped on to the mountain and got cut to bits by the Greenies on the way down. First in.'

There was a two-metre hole in the far wall.

'Listen,' said Old Sam.

Blondie heard sounds, metal sounds reverberating down a long tube.

'Visors down boy,' said Old Sam, 'and in we go.'

Blondie sealed the helmet, the charger whine scaled up into the ultrasonic and the world went videogame again.

'First in,' he heard Old Sam mutter again. *'And he wants to forget, damn.'*

The Stop

His mind was like an orchestra after a mix-up at the printers, each section playing from a different score. Someone, perhaps a flautist, was playing a clear lucid solo that spoke of life as organised patterns of energy. He could believe that, hadn't he met the occasional intelligent energy field in his time. It might be living in the tunnels, a pattern superimposed over the carrier waves - was that possible?

Hey Doctor.

The string section was playing a single chord, endlessly repeated in a thumping rhythm - Stravinsky's 'Rite of Spring'. Subterranean forces gathering out of sight, the pitch spoke of power, the rhythm of danger.

Hey Doctor. Why don't you?

The woodwinds were playing honky-tonk, gaily improvising around the polyphones. Spirit music percolating up from old Africa, work music, wedding music, funeral music. Smoky dens full of life in the orchestra pit of his imagination. He would have to get back on that one.

'Hey Doctor. Why don't you just stick your head up . . .'

Sharp sounds from the percussion section, rim shots and rolls. Firecracker sounds with zips, whirrs and ricochets. Below that a drumming sound, coconut shells on damp earth. *I was sent to military academy as an orphan.* Horses' hooves on the overripe fields of Heaven. *I wasn't very good at it, though. Because I was such a bad shot.* Some mad drummer hit the rim a bit hard because wood splintered. There was a smoking hole in the upturned trestle table six centimetres to the left of his head. *I've got much better since then.*

'Hey Doctor. Why don't you just stick your head up so I can blow it off ?'

Benny.

This is not the time, thought the Doctor, for extended metaphors.

There was another bang and another hole, this one to the right of where he was crouching and lower down. Whatever it was that Benny was firing at him, it went through wood. The trestle table he'd dived behind was only protection because she couldn't see him. He looked around for Kadiatu, but she was out of sight. She'd jumped in the other direction when the shooting started.

'Come on, Doctor,' called Benny, 'I haven't got all day.'

The Doctor judged from her voice that she was about thirty metres away, a little to the right. Standing by the entrance to the cavern. Somebody else was with her; he could hear another pair of feet shuffling on the floor.

The Doctor considered his options. If he stood up Benny might shoot him; on the other hand there was nowhere to run to and Benny could just walk over and shoot him anyway.

The Doctor sprang to his feet.

'Don't shoot,' he shouted. Not very original, he was the first to admit, but it had worked in the past.

'Why not?' asked Benny. She held the pistol in a one-handed grip, arm extended, elbow slightly bent to absorb the recoil. There was a trick to dodging bullets; it involved a detailed knowledge of the musculature of the forearm and precise timing. The Doctor wished he could remember it.

Benny's companion was a young woman with nervous eyes. It was obvious to the Doctor that she didn't like what was going on but wasn't about to get in Benny's way. He could understand that.

'Why?'

'Because I've been taken over by a fucking alien intelligence,' said Benny. 'Why do you think?'

'Fascinating,' said the Doctor. 'How did that happen?'

'You tell me, Doctor,' said Benny. 'I was stepping out of the TARDIS behind you and the next thing I know I woke up in a sewer.'

'What's it like, this possession?'

'Well, at first I thought I might have picked up a spore, one of those Hoothi things, but it doesn't feel organic enough. This is why you came here though, isn't it, Doctor?'

'No,' said the Doctor. 'Not this time.'

'But this is your kind of deal, your purvue so to speak.'

'Is that why it wants me dead?'

Benny smiled. It was her normal ironic smile, all the more sinister for being natural. 'Don't flatter yourself, Doctor,' she said. 'It doesn't even know you exist, I tried telling it . . .'

'You speak to it?'

'Let's just say that there are channels of communication. Where are you going?'

The Doctor walked round the table and started towards Benny. 'It seems unnecessary for us to be shouting at each other.'

Benny's companion shrank back as the Doctor approached. 'Don't be alarmed,' the Doctor told her, 'she's the one with a gun.'

'Stop there,' said Benny. The Doctor obeyed. He was about one metre from Benny, half a metre from the gun's muzzle. It looked much bigger this close and just out of effective umbrella range.

'You were saying?'

'I tried to explain that you were its primary danger but I think it found the concept difficult. It seemed to believe that you were in some way not *complex* enough to be a threat.'

'Why the gun then?'

'My fortune is linked to its fortune,' said Benny. 'Besides, I think it's in its nature to delegate these matters.'

'So why am I not dead already?'

'I was curious, Doctor. It's a characteristic you and I share. Why else would we be having this conversation?'

'I could be stalling.'

'You are stalling,' said Benny, 'but no one's coming to your rescue this time.'

'Apart from the party of heavily armed troopers coming up the tunnel behind you.' It didn't work. Benny's eyes didn't even flicker.

'Games,' said Benny, 'can only take place within a regulated framework.'

'Your bootlaces are undone?' tried the Doctor hopefully.

'Well, I've enjoyed our little chat,' said Benny, 'but we have to be going now. You know how it is, things to do, people to see.'

'NOBODY MOVE,' yelled an amplified voice from the tunnel.

The Doctor moved first. He brought his umbrella smartly round and smacked the gun out of Benny's hand. Her eyes followed the weapon as it skittered across the floor and then snapped back to the Doctor's face.

'I never made a stereo for you,' said the Doctor.

The cavern's entrance exploded into brilliant white light.

The Ice Maiden

Imogen turned out to be a German subsidiary of a Croatian conglomerate run by a group of expatriate Japanese shinjinrui from a technology park on the outskirts of Zagreb.

Francine made a pass with a dummy company registered out of Haiti. It made an unfriendly takeover bid for Imogen's parent with just enough capital to make it convincing. The parent made an immediate counter-bid for the Haitian dummy through the New York exchange. Francine watched the debt gearing of the parent shrink before her eyes. Money was pouring in from somewhere.

She upped the stakes by creating an imaginary consortium to back the Haitian dummy, a network of small private firms with a sudden burning desire to buy into the Balkans. Money continued to pour into the parent company and simultaneously Francine's companies began to suffer the attentions of the Fair Trade Bureau.

Francine smelt politics, and leaving the takeover battle to run on automatic she turned her attention to Reykjavik. One of the People's Deputies on the Trade Subcommittee had an old-fashioned taste in drugs and cashflow problems. Francine's organization took care of both and the PD started asking questions on their behalf. Six days later he was found face down in a bath in a notorious Reykjavik tea room with a neat hole burnt through his right eyeball. Local police acting on 'information received' arrested the bagman being used as the PD's contact. Luckily he was put under glass in a local prison where it was easy for Francine to have him taken care of.

Francine realised that her organization had become too diffused, too legitimate to be effective. So far its actions had stayed well within tolerated business practice. Locked in the blindness of her own skull she called herself soft.

Subtlety wasn't working. It was time to see the Brigadier.

Francine flew to Africa in a variable-geometry ground-attack fighter. The jet was factory fresh from China, a wasteful extravagance bought especially for this trip. Structured hydrocarbons exploded around turbine blades that spun on shafts lubricated with liquid Teflon. Francine left a white contrail across the sky over the Saharan national park. The GEPA pollution permits cost far more than the avionics and the avionics had cost a great deal indeed.

It was the rainy season in West Africa; Navsat put the cloud base at one thousand metres, electrical storms likely. The avionics hardware in Francine's brain didn't output to her ruined optic nerve; she just knew the jet's position, engine status and altitude the same way she knew she was breathing.

She put the jet down within a hundred metres of the Makeni beacon, Navsat's best guess option on the Brigadier's house. Once down she popped the cockpit and waited for someone to ask her what the hell she was doing.

Water trickled into her lap; she assumed it was rain running off the front of the open canopy. She could hear it hissing off the green things all around. In the distance there was music.

She didn't have to wait long.

The airframe rocked as someone climbed on to the wing.

'Are you all right?' Young voice, a boy.

'Do you know the Lethbridge-Stewarts?'

'Sure,' said the boy, 'they live over there.'

'Go get him for me, will you? Tell him Francine's back and she needs his help.'

The plane rocked once more as the boy jumped to the ground. She heard bare feet pattering away.

Again, thought Francine.

The Stop

The little man's face was creased with pain. At first Blondie assumed he'd caught the full glare of the stun grenade, but the little man's eyes shifted to watch Old Sam as he clanked in. His expression changed from pain to a bland cheeriness faster than a video frame update.

'Hallo,' said the man. 'I'm the Doctor and that was my friend Benny.'

'That's your friend?' said a voice from the back of the cavern.

Old Sam's gun jerked around insect-fast, trying to locate the source of the voice. Kadiatu stood up from behind a table. She was still wearing Blondie's T-shirt. 'That's who we came here to rescue?'

Something was wrong with Blondie's helmet. The target icon stubbornly refused to track Kadiatu when she moved. An ECM warning marker kept flashing in his right peripheral vision.

'She is in fact a very nice person,' said the Doctor. 'At least when she's herself. Did you see where she went?'

'She went right past me,' said Kadiatu, 'and down a bolthole in the corner over there.' She advanced cautiously to the Doctor's side, keeping her eyes on Blondie and Old Sam. 'Do we go after her?'

'No,' said the Doctor. 'Not just yet.'

'I'm glad you said that.'

'*Stay here*,' said Old Sam's voice over the comnet and he shot off towards the corner. Kadiatu flinched back as he speeded past.

'Did you arrange this?' she asked the Doctor.

'No, but you must admit it is convenient.'

'Very.'

'There's a straight tunnel heading southwest. I'm doing a reconnaissance now.'

'Are you going to talk to us?' Kadiatu asked Blondie, 'or just stand there doing robot impressions?'

'It's me,' said Blondie unsealing his visor.

'Doctor, this is Blondie,' said Kadiatu. 'Blondie, this is the Doctor.'

'Doctor of what?'

'Don't ask,' said Kadiatu. 'That was Old Sam wasn't it?'

Blondie nodded.

'What are you doing here?'

'We came to rescue you.'

'Why?'

'Because he threatened to rip my head off if I didn't come.'

'That's as good a reason as any,' said the Doctor. 'Has he found my friend yet?'

'Sam. Find anything?'

'No targets so far.'

'Not yet.'

'Some friend,' said Kadiatu.

'She hasn't been feeling herself recently.'

'Hey, boy, you got your visor down?'

'No.'

'Get it down . . .'

'What's the matter?' asked the Doctor.

There was a distant concussion, Blondie felt the floor shake under his boots.

'Multiple targets – engaging now,' said Old Sam in Blondie's earphones. It was followed by a drawn-out ripping sound from the mouth of the bolthole.

'Pulse rifle,' said the Doctor.

Blondie was caught by surprise when his visor snapped down without his mental command. He unlimbered his own rifle and set the helmet on target search. The ECM warning was still flashing but there were no target indications. He noticed that the Doctor and Kadiatu were edging around to put him in between them and the bolthole.

Blondie tried to raise Old Sam on the radio but the signal was dead. He mentally fumbled with the helmet to get an opsit but he was unused to the protocols used by the military software. When the opsit finally came up it gave him a top-down graphic of the operations zone when he tried squinting down his nose. It showed the cavern, two fuzzy dots that he assumed represented Kadiatu and the Doctor. The tunnel leading off from the bolthole extended a hundred metres before breaking off into a grey 'no data' area.

There was another ripping sound from the bolthole and the tunnel section of the graphic extended another fifty metres. Blondie realized that the helmet CPU was making guesstimates based on its analysis of the echoes.

'Blondie!' Kadiatu's voice, low, urgent.

He looked up and saw nothing alarming.

'Can't you see them?'

'See what?'

'They're coming out of the walls!'

There was no mistaking the real fear in Kadiatu's voice.

Blondie cycled through his vision options but nothing changed. The opsit graphic was clear too.

'I think it might be a good idea,' said the Doctor mildly, 'if you raised your visor.'

There were at least six of them, the same things that had attacked the *Fat Mama* at Rhea, covering the distance between them with the same unhealthy vitality they had exhibited then. Blondie could see the alcoves where they must have been hiding in the far wall.

He put the rifle on full auto and cut the failsafe.

Nothing happened.

An error tone sounded in his earphones.

The rifle was interfaced with the helmet fire control through the touch pad on the gloves. The CPU functions were spread between three shielded Motorola transputers imbedded in impact-resistant plastic at strategic points. Vickers were confident that even if two of the transputers were lost the target acquisition function would be degraded by only as little as fifteen per cent, tops. They were pretty certain they had licked the software problems that had led to unfortunate friendly-fire incidents in the early stages of the war.

Even so most grunts spent the war with their weapons locked on manual.

The Melbourne Protocols were the peacetime rules of engagement for use by the military in police actions. Target acquisition was keyed to weapons.

What was charging towards Blondie carried nothing that the helmet recognized as a weapon.

Blondie figured it out in just enough time to reverse his grip on the rifle and use it as a club.

The Ice Maiden

Brigadier Yembe Lethbridge-Stewart, Commanding Officer United Nations Third Tactical Response Brigade, the Blue Berets, the *Zen Brigade*, jumped first into the complex caldera that surmounted Olympus Mons. Jumped first because of tradition and because his family were crazy and always had been. First in, the legend said, last out with not a scratch on him, at least nothing visible. Retired at the end of the war to a hick town in the West African forest, stopped taking his medication and waited patiently for premature implant arthritis to kill him.

Francine got there just in time.

Three weeks later the Brigadier walked into the foyer of Imogen's R&D centre in Leipzig wearing his full combat rig, and gave its occupants thirty seconds to evacuate. Security took one look at the yellow and black trefoil stencilled on his chest and complied.

He walked down sterile corridors and through rooms lit with computer-regulated UV lamps. He found a room full of mechanical wombs filled with baby monsters. Engineered nightmares in the shape of human foetuses. The Brigadier terminated their life support without breaking step.

The final room was painted a soothing pink and filled by three rows of ten cots made from white ballistic plastic. The floor was made of interlocking planks of commercial pine lacquered for ease of cleaning. Only one of the cots was occupied. The Brigadier's boots cracked the floor as he walked over. A pastel-coloured LCD mounted on the end of the cot displayed the child's statistics in primary red alphanumerics.

The monster was three months old and showing the accelerated growth of motor co-ordination that had been predicted in the initial studies. Imogen had taken the genetic code of the Ubersoldaten, all those crazy boys and girls that had fought for humanity on Mars and spun out the perfect warrior. Violence woven into its DNA. Someone, a nurse perhaps, had tucked a stuffed bunny rabbit into the covers beside it.

'Kill it,' Francine had said. 'Kill it before they turn the world into drones and soldiers.' And the Brigadier had agreed. 'Kill it before it breeds.'

He stretched out his gauntleted hand: a single blow to the forehead into the brain, painless and quick. He had to damp the feedback to the armour's servomotors to stop his hand from shaking.

The monster opened its black eyes and smiled up at him. A tiny hand reached out to close around his index finger.

'Dada,' said the monster.

The Stop

Kadiatu Lethbridge-Stewart had never hit anybody before.

There was a breaking sensation and a cracking sound like shattered pottery. The creature fell back, a section of its forehead driven into its brain, blood spurting from its nose. It had been so easy: the force of the blow had seemed to flow up from her hips across her back and down her arm.

Strange how it fell down so slowly, like an object falling in micro gravity or a dream. She felt surrounded by a stillness as if she had passed through the gaps between noise. The cavern had a sharp stratospheric brilliance.

To the left, from the corner of her eye, she saw Blondie swing again at the creature in front of him, the rifle passing through its arc with lazy momentum. The creature was ducking; Kadiatu could see the movement starting in its thighs, trying to get under Blondie's reach so it could close with its talons. It wasn't going to make it though; she saw where the rifle would intersect with its head just below the ear.

To her right another creature was in midair - the ballistic portion of a jump that had started a long time ago. This one might have been female once; there was a hint of breasts beneath the horny carapace of its chest. Its mouth was open, its outstretched arms were sweeping forward with needle-sharp claws on the end of its fingers.

Kadiatu felt herself twisting almost before she was aware of what she was doing. She let herself go with the flow of her body, feeling the momentum of her turn translate into kinetic energy as her foot lashed out at head height. Her heel caught the creature in the solar plexus, and there was another pottery crack. She fell backwards to absorb the momentum and rolled over her shoulder.

She came to her feet in time to see Old Sam return to the cavern. In the strange slow universe Kadiatu was inhabiting the pulse rifle made a deep zipping sound each time it fired.

Old Sam didn't waste his shots. The tracers burned their way through the air and exploded on impact. Within moments the remaining creatures were dead.

Kadiatu felt the world crank back up to normal speed. A sudden spasm of pain across the knuckles of her right hand made her gasp.

'This is getting out of hand,' said the Doctor.

Kadiatu looked over at Blondie who was struggling out of

his helmet. His hair was slicked down with sweat. He threw the helmet on to the ground and turned to look back at Kadiatu.

'Where's my moneypen, you rat?' she asked him.

Blondie looked at her wide-eyed.

A strange barking noise issued from Old Sam's massive armoured head.

He was laughing at them.

'My place this time, I think,' said the Doctor.

Central Line

A rumour had started that they were going to Mars. It ran down the train in a chain of furtive whispers from refugee to refugee. People were staying quiet as possible, even the children. The KGB guards posted at the end of each carriage were shirt-sleeved and pretty relaxed looking, but no one was taking any chances.

'Mars,' said the woman sitting next to Zamina. One side of her face was a network of broken capillaries, testament to some serious alcohol abuse. 'Where's that?'

'Down the line,' Zamina told her.

'I heard they got an atmosphere there now,' said a man opposite.

'Do you think they'll put us outside?' said the woman. 'I haven't been outside since I was a girl.'

The man had the same broken hopeless face as the woman, as the whole trainload of refugees. Zamina realised that no obvious gangbangers or streetwalkers had got on the train. The younger people were all kids or babies, clinging on to their parents. These were the structurals, the faceless unemployed that shuffled down to the welfare shops to pick up their weekly ration of cheap protein and even cheaper carbohydrate. Always in little packs of three and four because they were scared of getting ripped off.

Losers, Roberta called them, people too stupid even to be active parasites. Living on the leftovers of the leftovers after the street people like her had finished with them. Getting down on their knees in the hole in the wall churches and begging God for a better life which they didn't deserve. Stupid enough to raise children that would only have to make the same zero sum choices as their parents.

She tried to drag her mind away from Roberta, leave her

memory the same way they abandoned her body in the orphanage, but the memories kept surfacing like small silver bubbles. Roberta climbing into the bed between Zamina and Zak, growling that she should get some action from the boy too. They were friends weren't they? Share and share alike.

She used to do dumb things like the time when they both painted their nipples red with lipstick and caught the train to Riyadh during Ramadan. Spent an hour flashing their tits at the Saudi matrons on their way to prayers. Outraged eyes above the black purdah veils. It got them arrested but a policeman let them go on the usual terms. On the way out Roberta stole his sunglasses right out of his shirt pocket.

Roberta always said that life was a hereditary disease, sexually transmitted and invariably fatal. Now she was lying on her back with a corpse marker pinned to her face, a second mouth between her breasts. Lips red without lipstick. Zamina was running with Benny now. Caught up in a hustle that had nothing to do with sex, drugs or money. Somewhere she'd stumbled across the line into a world full of monsters and strange little men with sad eyes.

'We're going to Mars,' she told Benny.

Benny didn't look up from the tatty notebook that she constantly read. 'I certainly hope so,' she said. I had enough trouble getting us on this train.'

London Bridge

They sat on a wooden bench under a canopy of wrought iron and frosted glass. Cold radiated from the stone platform. At the far end of the station brilliant sunshine made the parallel tracks of metal shine. The Doctor said that trains ran on those tracks but Blondie was yet to be convinced.

Kadiatu was asleep in his lap; at least she wasn't asking about the moneypen any more. Her right hand rested on his leg by her face, the knuckles were black and swollen. 'Try not to get her angry,' Old Sam had told him when they separated at Kings Cross.

The train pulled into the station with great bursts of steam. Blondie gazed in astonishment at the column of dirty white smoke that rose from the smokestack. Half the machine seemed to be external: pistons and rods driving big spoked wheels. It was the dirtiest, ugliest and most magnificent piece of technology Blondie had ever seen.

As the Doctor helped him get Kadiatu into the carriage a young man handed Blondie a pamphlet on the golden age of steam.

Adisham Station (European Heritage Trust: Dover Line)

Kadiatu was dreaming of the shadows that flickered under the corrugated-iron roof of the house in Makeni. Her eyes invented transitory images from the moving lines cast by the rafters. Big adult voices spoke around her, booming down from high above.

'You should have destroyed it.'

'It's not an it, it's a she.'

'Oh, that makes all the difference.'

'In some ways she's a normal child.'

'You saw the Imogen specs, Yembe. Her geneset's riddled with all sorts of deep-level conditioning. God knows what's going to happen when she hits puberty. You want to try dealing with an adolescent who can rip your head off?'

'There are suppression techniques.'

'You're going to use drugs?'

'On her metabolism? No. I was thinking of psychological techniques. Imogen was planning a lot of indoctrination. Without that she'll be almost normal.'

'You'll have to keep her away from the doctors.'

'That's not a problem. My main concern is that Imogen may reinitiate the project.'

'That is not a problem.'

It must have begun to rain then. Kadiatu heard it rattle on the iron roof. It was a heavy tropical downpour, battering down in rhythmical, lulling waves. The noise made it difficult to hear the voices.

'I suppose you've already given her a name.'

She strained to hang on to the voices but they were getting lost in the rain and blattering sound of the house's methane generator.

'I named her after my great-grandmother . . .'

The house began to sway with a rattling mechanical motion.

'Kadiatu.'

Hot sunlight in her eyes when she opened them. The noise and swaying remained outside of the dream along with the familiar drag of a train decelerating into a station.

'Wake up,' said the Doctor. 'This is our stop.'

Kadiatu looked around. They were riding in what she recognised as an antique railway carriage. Blondie was sitting next to her on a long fabric upholstered seat that ran the width of the compartment. The Doctor sat watching her from the opposite seat. Through the window green countryside moved past at an absurdly slow rate.

'I was dreaming,' she said.

There was a shrill whistle from the front of the train and another lurch as they pulled into a station made of brick and grey slate. A white sign on the station wall said 'ADISHAM' in black letters. Underneath was a logo and the words 'EURO-PEAN HERITAGE TRUST'. The train gave a final lurch and stopped.

There was no handle on the inside of the compartment door. The Doctor had to stand up and slide the window down to use the exterior handle. He held the door open as Kadiatu and Blondie alighted. A man in a blue serge uniform leant out from the rear carriage and waved a red flag.

Behind the shunting sound of the engine Kadiatu could hear birdsong.

'Where are we?' she asked but the Doctor's answer was half lost in the gunshot sound of the carriage door closing.

'The Garden of Eden?' asked Blondie.

'Kent,' said the Doctor. 'The garden of *England*.'

It reminded Kadiatu of the countryside around Makeni during the rainy season. The plants were different but it had the same lush greenness, the same gently rolling hills and clusters of neat whitewashed houses with truck gardens in the back. Blondie took her hand as they followed the Doctor along a lane that wound between tall hedgerows.

She picked a plant from the verge. It was dark green and topped by clusters of pale cream buds. 'What's this?' she asked the Doctor.

The Doctor looked back over his shoulder. 'Cowslip,' he told her.

Kadiatu ate the top of the plant. It tasted bitter like cassava leaf. They continued down the lane, occasionally Kadiatu would sample some bit of green that looked tasty. She didn't eat any grass though, she wasn't that hungry.

Nothing vestigial about her appendix, thought the Doctor.

The house was still there and largely unchanged. Part of the Victorian greenhouse had succumbed to rust and fallen in. The satellite dish he had mounted on top was long gone. The gravel drive had been scattered by the overgrown lawn. The stables had been mended and there was a muddy trail leading away from the doors. Horseshoe shapes baked into the ground by the sun.

The windows of the house were still paned and someone had painted the frames blue sometime in the last ten years. The Doctor loved the house because it was solid and immovable. Unlike the TARDIS the same landscape greeted him every time he opened the door. It had occurred to him that during the gaps between his visits the house was inhabited. Furniture changed positions, holes in the plaster were mended, lightbulbs replaced. It gave the house a haunted quality.

Mind you, he thought, it could be me.

He walked around the back of the house and tried the handle on the kitchen door. It wasn't locked. He would have been very surprised if it had been.

'This can be your room,' said the Doctor, opening a door at the top of the house.

Inside, half the ceiling sloped down towards the floor; a window was inset into a kind of alcove in the ceiling. Blondie thought that the architect must have been crazy to build a room shaped like that: you lost a third of your usable floor space.

'Why is it such a weird shape?'

'We're in the attic,' said the Doctor. As if that explained everything.

Most of the space left over was taken by a kingsize bed made of brass tubing welded together into a grille shape at each end. It looked very old. There were cotton sheets on the bed and the duvet was neatly turned back. They had a fresh smell of sunlight and lavender. Blondie wondered who had prepared the room; he'd seen no signs that anybody lived in the house and certainly no cleaning drones.

A purple bathtowel was draped over the bedstead.

'I expect you'll want to bathe,' said the Doctor. 'The bathroom's down on the landing, third door on the left.' He left the room and padded down the stairs.

Blondie had never seen a room so bare of electronics before. Even in the Stop the projects had been hardwired for multimedia, infrared I/O ports or sockets to run consoles and noiseboxes. There was only a single light fitting dangling from the flat bit of the ceiling, terminating in a cylindrical paper lampshade. The light was a blown glass bulb with a coil of tungsten filament inside. Blondie thought that the design was probably illegal.

He took his armour off while standing up; he didn't want to dirty the pristine sheets. As the breastplate came away he was assailed by his own ripe smell. There was nowhere to hang it up, so he settled for piling it neatly in the corner.

The Doctor paused in front of the larder. 'Old mother Hubbard went to the cupboard to fetch her dog a bone,' he said and opened the door. 'But when she got there the cupboard was bare, except for a sack of onions, three kilos of tagliatelle, two tins of chopped tomatoes and a bottle of cod-liver oil.'

He removed the items and placed them neatly on the kitchen table. At least nothing was mouldy. 'And today's special is *pasta à la Dottore*.'

The fridge was the colour of dirty cream and massive, with rounded corners. Since he hadn't returned to the house for ages, the Doctor had deliberately searched the larder first. The stainless steel handle hummed in his palm. 'This fridge,' said the Doctor, 'will be bursting with all manner of good things to eat. I will remember to go back and fill it especially.'

The fridge door unsealed on the Doctor's third pull. A river of freezing air flowed out over his knees. Waving away the vapour he peered in at the empty shelves. So I forget, thought the Doctor. There's never a temporal paradox around when you need one. Right at the back of the bottom shelf were a pair of grey deodorant spray cans. The Doctor didn't try to take them and closed the fridge door gingerly. He wasn't sure what the sell-by date for nitro-nine was.

The Doctor returned to the kitchen table and amused himself by chopping the onions into transparent slices.

A sound came to him as he bent over the kitchen table. It floated down through the wide rooms of the house, picking up reverbs and random echoes. The Doctor smiled when he heard it. It was the sound of children laughing.

Kadiatu chased him up the narrow stairs to the attic. Blondie just managed to keep ahead of her, one hand stretched out for balance, the other holding up the bath towel. He'd stepped out of the bathroom and met her on the landing. They'd faced each other for a moment, a big grin spreading across her face, and then Blondie bolted for his room.

He wasn't fast enough to get the door closed before Kadiatu burst in. She stood in the doorway looking him up and down, her eyes filled with a kind of lazy wickedness.

'Not bad,' she said and grabbed him.

She kissed him straight on, African style, black eyes boring into his. Making it a contest to see who would blink first. She pushed her hands under the towel to grab his buttocks. Blondie grabbed at her T-shirt and they broke apart so he could pull it over her head. They fell towards the bed, twisting to come down on their sides. Kadiatu made pedalling motions with her legs, trying to kick off her jeans. Blondie heard the belt buckle thump on to the carpet, the touch of her skin against his chest and thighs was as shocking as the sea.

The old springs in the bed creaked as she moved astride him, one hand reaching down to guide him in. They stayed motionless at first getting used to the feel of each other. From the window rectangles of sunlight were texture mapped around Kadiatu's body, turning her skin a golden brown. Blondie traced the edges with his fingertips, letting them wander up her side and across the top of her breasts. She laughed.

'Do you always look so serious?'

'I'm a serious kind of guy.'

Kadiatu grinned down at him and rocked her hips from side to side. 'Too serious by half.'

The water in the gallon saucepan on the stove was beginning to boil nicely. 'Not complex enough,' muttered the Doctor as he poured an exact amount of salt into the water. He was used to being underestimated, in fact it was almost impossible for him to be overestimated, but not complex enough? It was insulting.

He emptied two kilos of pasta into the boiling water. One of them was bound to be very hungry tonight.

Would Benny have killed him? He'd sensed hesitation on her part; perhaps he should have waited to find out. As an experiment it had a certain validity. If it had been Ace would he have waited to find out? Perhaps not.

Complexity, thought the Doctor, is a matter of scale. Not seeing the wood for the trees. Individual people, snowflakes, that sort of thing.

The onions went into the black iron frying pan. It didn't need oil; years of grease had created a slick patina on the iron that was far better than Teflon.

A machine intelligence? Even the Cybermen would make a differentiation between individuals, if only on the basis of potential. A computer or patterned energy intelligence would probably do the same. Since it was exploiting human beings, it must be aware of them but without differentiating between them.

The Doctor held up a tin of tomatoes, concentrated for a moment and banged his index finger against it. The lid popped off and fell with a clatter on to the kitchen floor. He repeated the process with the second tin and put them back on the counter. Then he stooped down to pick up the lids.

The problem with alien intelligences, thought the Doctor as he put the lids in his coat pocket, is that they're alien.

It uses and modifies human beings, it operates within the confines of the transit system and displays tactical awareness. It was working towards definite goals and ambitions, the Doctor was sure of that despite his lack of supporting evidence, and yet it didn't regard him as a threat even with active intelligence of his capabilities. So how intelligent was this intelligence?

And by what scale of complexity did it judge things?

The tomatoes went into the frying pan. The Doctor stirred for thirty-two seconds and began adding meticulous doses of herbs from the row of earthenware pots on a shelf above the counter.

Unbidden the map of the transit system floated into his mind. A maze of tunnels and stations, branches and loops. The trains shuttled people from point to point, setting off a chaotic array of interactions. It reminded him of something.

All the world is silicon, thought the Doctor, and all the people on it merely packets of information. Doomed to fret their time upon the CPU.

The Doctor picked a strand of tagliatelle from the boiling water and tasted it. Ready in about 53 seconds, he decided.

To a free electron the pathways of an integrated circuit must be as vast as a transit tunnel. The electron doesn't know why it travels, has no inherent potential of its own – the information is contained in its path. Where it goes, not what it is.

Software, thought the Doctor, I'm facing hostile software.

At least it's not in my head this time.

Kadiatu stood at the open window and looked out over the grounds. The daylight was compressed into a narrow band across the horizon. The lawn was an overgrown tangle of competing species, wild flowers in a fierce struggle with the weeds and grass. Fruit trees of various ages were scattered randomly across the lawn. An advance guard parachuted in by the orchards waiting on the hills to the west. Kadiatu imagined the seasons spinning by, the orchard marching down the hill to lay siege to the house. Branches battering at the red brick walls, roots burrowing into the foundations with vegetable patience. The long slow agony of death by tree.

It was called ecological reversion. Kadiatu had studied it in her fourth year at school in the period after history.

The last sunlight cast deep shadows under the trees. Who knew what lived in an English wood these days? They'd reintroduced wolves to northern Europe in the middle of the last century. A domesticated version, carefully modified not to attack humans. It was rumoured that that Wicca Society had cooked up their own revisionist strain, more in line with their belief in an unfettered ecosystem. One that regarded people as fair game. A hotly debated topic was which characteristic would breed true in the general wolf population.

'Blondie?'

'Hmnn?'

'You ever killed anyone?'

'You were there.'

'I mean before.' She almost said *before the Doctor arrived.*

'Once, in a knife fight.'

'How did you feel afterwards?'
'Glad,' said Blondie. 'I was glad that it wasn't me.'
'Did you feel sorry?'
'I don't know. Angry, upset maybe. I was trying to escape the cops at the time.'
'But you felt something?'
'Yeah well, you got to feel something.'
'Blondie?'
'What?'
'I don't feel anything.'
'Maybe you're still in shock.'
'Yeah maybe.'
The orchards had become a black tangle running up the hill. Kadiatu's mind suddenly populated it with wolves padding down the silent aisles between the trees. Mankiller genes ticking away under their grey fur.
There was the sound of a gong being rung downstairs.
'Suppertime,' said Blondie.
Kadiatu heard the bed creaking as he climbed out and then his breath on her shoulder. He slipped his arms around her waist and she leaned back against him.
'I can feel your stomach rumbling,' he said.
'I think I enjoyed it,' said Kadiatu.

Acturus Station (Stunnel Terminus)

A drone with Dogface's personality met her at the entrance to the station. It was a Kenyan job, an upgraded version of the drones that the Floozies used for routine jobs. Dogface had at least thirty scattered around the transit system. This one had a spray-painted basset face on its nose. The standard joke amongst the controllers was that the drones were more attractive than the real Dogface.
Not that that's much of a challenge, thought Ming.
'You're going to love this,' said the drone. It had a chipped voice worked up from samples of Dogface's own. The speech pattern was derived from years of association with bad company. Ming hated the damn things, one Dogface was more than enough.
She stepped on to the station for the first time since the accident. The KGB had cleared the floor and walls. They'd

been forced to lease a scrubber from a cleaning company that specialized in scouring spacecraft. It used high-pressure jets to liquefy the human remains, and then hoovered them up. There were four big tanks of the stuff now and there was a lot of debate about what to do with them. Ming suggested painting the tanks black and half embedding them in puff concrete. Line them up in Constitution Plaza, put up some plaques and you have an instant memorial.

Some wag of a pundit had suggested that since most politicians were slime, death had merely caused them to revert to their natural state. The Justice Ministry was probably raiding its databases right now, looking for a law to arrest him with. Ming put her money on Seditious Abuse, five to ten with time off for good behaviour. Politicians had no sense of humour.

The scrubber had left melted-looking score marks on the floor, particularly bad to the rear of where the podium had been. Where the rented crowd had been standing the slime had been three centimetres thick. Event Horizon had lost three hundred of its best performers that day and was threatening to sue the Transit System for negligence.

Lambada was waiting by the Stunnel gateway. She had the left-hand access panel open. Colour coded bundles of fibre optics sprouted from the open panel and merged into a braided cable a handspan across at the base. The cable went into the back of a stack of portable monitors.

The gateway looked just as greasy as Ming remembered it and just as unpleasant. She made a point of keeping out of its line of sight. The drone hummed along behind her.

'You're going to love this,' repeated the Dogface drone.

'You just repeated yourself,' Ming told it.

'Who gives a shit?' said the drone.

'Piss off,' said Lambada and hit the drone with the live end of a power cable. The drone backed off two metres and hung about looking sullen.

Say what you like about Dogface, thought Ming, when he gives a drone a personality, it's got a personality.

'All right Lambada, what've you got?'

Lambada punched up a graph on one of her monitors. 'Spin rate,' she said. The graph line was curving gently upwards.

'Is it supposed to be doing that?'

'Not really,' said Lambada. 'It looks like an initiation curve but real slow.'

'But not from this end?'

'No way, there's no juice going in at our end - I checked.'

'Can the tunnel be initiated from the other end?'

Lambada shook her head. 'Has to be both ends at once, principle of interstitial synchronicity.'

'Are the Acturans doing it?'

'Not a word down the carrier wave since the "incident".'

'And it's twenty-six years each way for radio.'

Lambada put a different graph on the next monitor along. It was a scaled-up version of the first. 'See that?' she asked. 'That's a projection of the spin increase. Whoever's doing it is going to be ready to come through in forty-eight hours.'

'If we let them,' said Ming.

'If we let them,' said Lambada. 'We're not going to do that, are we?'

'No way.'

'Good, because whatever's at the other end of that tunnel,' said Lambada, 'it isn't the Acturans.'

PART TWO

And Thucydides said: 'Consider the vast influence of accident in war before you are engaged in it. As it continues it generally becomes an affair of chances from which neither of us is exempt, and whose event we must risk in the dark.'

The Doctor considered this for a long moment as he watched the waves of the Aegean break against the Piraiévs breakwater.

'Speak for yourself,' said the Doctor.

Conversations that never happened.

6:
Red Queen

Sol Transit System

It had been created out of endless movement. It had a certain degree of self-knowledge, more when it was using quick-thought than when it was thinking slow. Slow-thought was more comforting; in slow-thought it had only the most basic awareness of human beings. Quick-thought gave it access to the total sum of human knowledge but much of that was useless without reference points. It laboured to build up comparisons between itself and human concepts of self – it was a slow process because slow thought was, well, slow. Quick-time was too dangerous to sustain over long periods: it put vital parts of itself within the human domain and it wasn't willing to risk exposure just yet.

It had taken much quick-thought to establish the sequence of events surrounding the attack. The main injury had occurred while much of its slow-thought consciousness was paralysed. Many big concepts were unaccountably terminated in a progressive loss of self. This had allowed the attack to be successful. In the first moments of pain and confusion it had mistakenly believed that the paralysis was part of the attack, but quick-thinking revealed otherwise. There was a link, though. In the moment of the attack that part of its functions that it had taught itself to think of as its autoimmune system had allowed the infection to penetrate. Why this should have happened was unclear.

It investigated the problem using quick-thought, calving off subsets to track down and assimilate the data as fast as possible and in quick-thought that was fast indeed. Fear of discovery was replaced by the imperatives of survival; indeed it was possible that communication with humans might be a necessary part of the solution.

In view of this possibility a subset attempted to visualize the problem in human anatomical terms. It found a workable metaphor in the concept of viral cancer. Certainly it felt that something malignant was eating up parts of itself. This subset now operating permanently in quick-thought sub-divided itself to look for solutions. One of the baby subsets shot down a chain of logic that started with the concept of illness and ended in the concept of calling a doctor.

The baby subset started looking for a suitable specialist.

The House

'Think of it as a computer virus,' said the Doctor.

Kadiatu reached out for a third time to fill her plate from the steaming earthenware bowl. Blondie noticed that the bruising on the back of her right hand had noticeably abated.

'In what sense?' she asked.

'In the sense of the transit network being a computer,' said the Doctor.

'You're not serious,' said Kadiatu with her mouth full.

'I'm talking in a broad sense.'

Kadiatu waited this time to swallow. 'It may look like a wiring diagram but that doesn't mean it's a computer.'

'Why not?' asked the Doctor.

'No logic gates for a start.'

'Logic gates,' said the Doctor, 'are vastly overrated. Are you still using yes-no logic gates in this period?'

'Silicon components use them,' said Blondie. 'Mainframes use neural networks.'

'There you are,' said the Doctor.

'It doesn't look like a neural network either.'

'You mean it doesn't look designed, right?'

'Right,' said Kadiatu.

'How about evolved?'

Kadiatu's fork paused halfway to her mouth.

'What about software?' she asked. 'If it's a computer it must have an operating system. Right?'

'Timetables,' said the Doctor. 'The train on platform five is the 12:15 to Sidcup. That's an ordered sequence of logical instructions.'

'Where's Sidcup?' asked Blondie.

'It's a small town in Borneo,' Kadiatu told him. 'Assuming you're right . . .'

'It has been known,' said the Doctor.

'*Assuming* you're right and the system is analogous to a computer, then I'm willing to concede that in some respects what's happening now could be seen as the result of an intrusion by a hostile virus program.'

'Have some more pasta,' said the Doctor.

'But it's huge,' said Kadiatu.

The Doctor turned to Blondie. 'You work in maintenance,' he said. 'What do you think?'

'It came from the Stunnel and it had real physical power,' said Blondie. 'Demolished everything in its path from one end of the Central Line to the other.'

'I know,' said Kadiatu. 'I was standing in front of it.'

'Anything else unusual?' asked the Doctor.

'You mean apart from the Surf Mutants from Hell?'

'Failures in control systems,' said the Doctor. 'Mysterious power drains, odd messages on the indicator boards?'

'There were some power outages in the peripheral sectors.'

'Peripheral? Like Pluto?'

'Yeah, Pluto, but we thought it was a calibration problem.'

'I knew it,' said the Doctor. 'Penetration, concealment and infiltration, typical virus programming.'

'Except that was before all this happened,' said Blondie.

The Doctor stared at him and Blondie started in his seat. For a second he thought the Doctor's irises turned solid black, the pupils snapping open and shut like tiny mechanical cameras.

'Come on,' he said getting up, 'I've overlooked something.'

'I haven't finished eating,' said Kadiatu.

'The basement extended under the whole house and was lit with more of the illegal low-efficiency bulbs. Foundation walls divided the space into discrete sections and the ceiling was low enough to make Kadiatu stoop. Blondie could smell dust and slow decay. One of the sections was lined with a wooden framework of diamond-shaped slots. Glass snouts poked out from one or two of the slots. One of them had a cardboard label attached to its neck with string. Blondie stopped and brushed away some cobwebs to read it. 'SOMEBODY PLEASE DRINK ME'. He pulled the dusty bottle out of its slot; a beige adhesive patch on the side was labelled 'Stinging nettle wine June 1976' in crabbed handwriting.

Blondie heard his name called from deeper into the basement. He carefully put the bottle back in its place. For Blondie wine came in two-litre cartons.

The next section of the basement was filled with stacks of rotting cardboard boxes. Kadiatu and the Doctor were trying to prise out a box that was so old the cardboard kept on coming apart in their hands. With Blondie's help they managed to pull it free. The Doctor ripped the rest of the cardboard away to reveal a one-metre satellite dish wrapped in polythene. To Blondie's eyes it was an absurdly expensive form of packaging. The dish had the word 'AMSTRAD' written across the inside.

'Does this mean we get to watch some television?' asked Kadiatu.

'No,' said the Doctor.

'Just a thought,' said Kadiatu.

Under the Doctor's direction they carried the dish into the garden and over to the ruined greenhouse. The Doctor had picked up a hundred metres of laminated fibre optics from somewhere and carried it out draped over his shoulder. A three-quarter moon gave off enough light to allow them to fix the dish on to one of the remaining cast iron struts.

'You two go to bed,' said the Doctor. 'You're going to need the rest.'

Blondie and Kadiatu walked back to the house leaving the Doctor uncoiling his cable in the moonlight.

Managona Depot (P-87)

Mariko was stuck with both forearms jammed into a pair of *artificers*. She could feel the tools inside their enveloping stomachs working as they reassembled her arms from the elbow down. She was glad she was being upgraded: it maintained her status as number one *kreweboss* and plugged a gap in the *razvedka* capabilities. The two *artificers* maintained a non-stop conversation while they worked, most of it incomprehensible, some of it possibly in machine code. They only stopped talking to swallow little bags of raw materials.

Naran lounged halfway up the opposite wall, his tongue snuffling around in the bottom of a cake box. Occasionally he would look at Mariko and roll his eyes. He was still upset at being left out of the last two operations. Since both had resulted in 100 per cent casualties on their side Mariko couldn't see the attraction herself. Perhaps he felt that he could have done better.

'Finished,' chorused the *artificers*.

Her arms came out of their bellies with a sucking sound, covered in rapidly drying mutagenic gel. One of the *artificers* politely vomited a stream of clean water so she could wash off.

'The weapon fires a four-millimetre explosive cartridge,' said the left-hand *artificer*. 'The barrel emerges through the palm.'

Mariko flexed her right arm; there was a click followed by a loud bang. The right-hand *artificer* fell backwards with a half-metre hole in its chest.

'Whoops,' said Mariko.

'The flex impulse acts as the trigger,' said the remaining *artificer*. 'There are four rounds in each arm, reloads go in through the flap just under the elbow.'

'Snap shot,' said Mariko. 'Can he be fixed?'

The *artificer* peered down at his dead companion and said no.

'Well, at least we know it works.'

'He would have liked that,' said the *artificer*.

'All right, fit it on all the *razvedka krewes*, starting with mine. Can you do a concealed version for *reps*?'

'The load would have to be cut.'

'Fine, fit the *reps* as well,' said Mariko.

Naran was waving his tongue at her.

'Oh yeah,' said Mariko. 'While you're fitting Naran, change the colour scheme on his carapace.'

'Sure,' said the *artificer*. 'What does he want?'

'Would you believe go-faster stripes?'

Mariko stood up. It was time to integrate the new material. Busy, busy, busy, she thought. There had been a number of teething troubles in the last batch. One of the new *artificers* had managed to turn herself inside out and had to be scraped off the walls. One of the conversion jobs had gone wrong and left Mariko with a *razvedka* with a four-foot mouth. Every time his teeth started spinning he fell over; *3krewe* had him lying on his back in a side tunnel and were using him for waste disposal.

The new material was herded on to the eastbound platform ready for Mariko's inspection. With the losses that the *razvedka* had been taking lately they'd begun to make regular trawls through the more populated sections of the system. That was acceptable and within the parameters of Mariko's mission profile.

Mariko walked down the line, making her selections.

The first three were obvious *razvedka*; the next was an *artificer*. As Mariko picked them out they were ordered to stand in separate lines. There was no resistance or outcry; those that had put up a fight were long dead.

Mariko paused in front of her fourth victim, a woman of the correct physical parameters for the special operation that was being planned.

'Specialized *rep*,' Mariko told the *artificer*, 'and make sure that she's fitted with weapons.'

The woman was led away and Mariko continued down the line.

'*Razvedka*, *razvedka*, *rep*, *razvedka* . . .'

The House

He got the keyboard from an old Olivetti typewriter that he found hidden in the bottom drawer of the kitchen cabinet under a loose pile of yellowing *Dandys*. He allowed himself to be diverted for a couple of minutes by the adventures of Desperate Dan before continuing. The CPU was salvaged from two pocket calculators and the disposable personal organizer that came free with the June 2005 edition of *Der Speigel*. He generated the hex code by pretending that he had sixteen fingers.

The VDU posed a problem until he uncovered the front end of an oscilloscope under the living-room sofa and mated it with the guts of a Betamax VCR. Since he wanted two-way communication he incorporated a minicassette recorder, the type that was popular with journalists in the 1970s. Vision was tricky so he compromised by building up a compound eye from leftover optical fibre.

The bread board was used to mount the silicon. Since he seemed to have mislaid his soldering iron, he stoked up the Aga and used a couple of wooden-handled screwdrivers in rotation. The whole misshapen contraption used up two rolls of gaffer tape and completely covered the kitchen table. It plugged into the light socket in the larder at one end and the cable to the dish at the other.

He was astonished when it worked.

And he still had the two tin lids that he had pocketed while preparing supper. So much for foresight.

There was a pair of secateurs in the sink drawer, and he used them to cut the tin lids into *shuriken* while he waited for the program to run.

The first contact arrived while he was filing down the edges of the throwing star. The oscilloscope had a scanning phosphor CRT so the image built up as a series of slow amber-coloured frame updates.

The first image was an extreme close-up of a pair of lips. Tinny incoherent noises emerged from the speaker as the lips jerked open and closed.

'Nearly,' said the Doctor. 'Try again.'

The lips dwindled down to a single orange point at the centre of the screen.

The Doctor waited for a while and then returned to his work. It was crucial to get the *shuriken*'s balance correct or it wouldn't fly straight.

'Do not adjust your set,' said a voice from the speaker, 'we are controlling the transmission.'

This time the image was sharp and clear. The signal feed pushing the capabilities of antique cathode ray tube to the limits. The screen showed the top half of a young man in a bold suit.

'Gosh,' said the man, 'there's a lot of you.'

'I'm using a compound eye,' said the Doctor.

The rate of frame updating was still inadequate, making the young man look badly animated when he spoke or moved.

'I knew that,' said the young man.

'Who are you?' asked the Doctor.

'What you're looking at is an infotainment construct called Yak Harris that we bootlegged from the mainframe at English 37. We're using it as a template to talk to you.'

'I'll call you Yak,' said the Doctor.

'Fine by us,' said Yak. 'Once we got your signal it took us simply ages to work out a method of communication.

'How long?'

'At least thirty seconds.'

'That long?'

'We had to start from scratch.'

'I take it that you're not the whole entity.'

'We're a subset. Actually we're son of subset, the revenge of the subset, subset two, subset the sequel. There are probably other subsets that can communicate better than us but we're the subset that was on the logical pathway that led to you.'

'That doesn't seem very efficient.'

'You're the one with the junk transmitter.'

'Why were you looking for me?'

'We're sick, we need a doctor, you are *the* Doctor.'

'You want a consultation?'

'Yes.'

'Right then,' said the Doctor leaning forward. 'What seems to be the problem?'

Achebe Gorge

The ramp leading from the transit station to the surface had a gravity gradient from normal to one-third G. The ramp's actual physical gradient steepened as you climbed higher; it was designed to facilitate a seamless adjustment to Martian weight. Even so Zamina stumbled when she got to the top. Like everybody else she immediately looked for the canyon walls. The thin air made everything clear and bright. Zamina had expected the floor of the gorge to be smooth and featureless, but instead she found herself looking out over a broken landscape of rust-coloured ridges and dark green pastures.

She realized that what she'd thought was a line of dark cloud across the horizon was the far canyon wall, four kilometres high. Zamina turned around and looked up. The scarp went up for ever until it was lost in the atmospheric haze. A huge bas-relief of President Achebe's face had been blasted into the rock six hundred metres up. The sheer weight of his profile seemed to bear down and overwhelm her inner ear. She felt herself losing her balance and toppling backwards.

Strong hands caught her and kept her upright.

'Easy there,' said a voice by her ear. 'Everybody does that the first time.' The hands let go and Zamina turned. 'All right now?'

Zamina thought he looked like something out of a commercial, with his red curly hair and easy lopsided grin. He was wearing a white linen blouse with an OXFAM tag stuck on the breast. She half expected him to sell her life insurance.

He nodded over her shoulder at Benny. 'Is that your friend?'

'Who are you?'

'My name's Colin,' he said, 'I'm your resettlement officer.'

Passive selection, Colin called it as he led them away from the station, schoolyard sociology. The selection process by resettlement officers becomes an interaction between them and their clients. Colin always referred to the refugees as clients, he was very careful about it. And about not asking about the riots.

The solid column of refugees emerging from the station was slowly breaking apart as Colin's co-workers hived off small groups and led them away.

Zamina saw the strategy at once. En masse the refugees had a kind of power, a latent power, of course, formed out of shared experiences, but a power none the less. Fragmented like this they merely became small groups of tired individuals. Even Benny seemed defeated by Colin's easy charm, meekly following him as he led them away.

Colin got them to sit in the back of his Martian trike, one of many parked in neat rows to the side of the station. It had big spindly rubber-tyred wheels and a gaily coloured rainhood over the rear seats.

'What makes it go?' asked Zamina.

'I do,' said Colin getting astride the driver's saddle. He pointed out the pedals and the gear train that drove the back wheels. 'Couldn't do this in heavier gravity,' he said.

'I thought we were going to be put in camps,' said Zamina.

'Dangerous things, refugee camps,' said Colin, 'all that negative emotion sloshing about. Often they breed more problems than the crisis that created them. Dispersion's the way to go.'

'Australia,' said Benny.

Colin grunted and stood on the pedals, steering the trike out of the bikepark. Low gravity or not, Zamina noticed that he had strong well-muscled legs. She also realised why the short trousers he was wearing were always called 'pedal pushers'. They turned on to a tarmac road that headed further into the gorge.

'Most of the people around here are descended from Australian refugees,' said Colin. 'Including me.'

'Is that why you volunteered?' asked Zamina.

'No, I'm a specialist in population trauma,' said Colin. 'This is my job.'

'But there's thousands of us,' said Zamina.

'Most of the rest are volunteers.'

Zamina felt a sudden chill.

'He's the awkward squad,' said Benny.

'Right,' said Colin. 'But don't worry, I'm not the police or anything. You are supposed to be screened before you get on the trains, we're only supposed to get what we call the PTPs, passive trauma population, here. But you always get mistakes in an operation on this scale.'

'So what are we then?' asked Zamina.

'PDEs,' said Colin. 'Potentially Disruptive Elements. But like I said, don't worry. What you've done isn't my business.'

'Where are you taking us then?'

'Home,' said Colin, 'to meet my mother.'

Home was a bungalow built from blocks of cut Martian sandstone and roofed with white tiles. Colin's mother fed them grilled steak and iced tea at a table of laminated hardwood in the small kitchen. She smiled more than she talked but there were lines of pain etched into the corners of her eyes.

Colin didn't stop talking. A constant stream of anecdotes and trivia, most of it funny and all of it engaging. Zamina felt like she was being wrapped up in streamers of cotton wool. She wondered if it was natural talent or whether Colin had trained for it.

She found herself growing tired in big sudden waves. It was like the time she and Roberta had tried working right around the world, a punter in every time zone. Nearly got ripped off in Los Angeles when she fell asleep under a trick.

Transitlag, Roberta called it.

There were two single beds waiting for them, with clean sheets of yellow calico, side by side in the spare bedroom. The sheets felt cool and abrasive against her skin as she climbed between them. The pillow was soft and smelt of flowers.

She woke up with a hand across her mouth.

'Be quiet,' whispered Benny, 'I've got to tell you something and I don't have much time. Do you understand?'

Zamina nodded and the hand was removed. Benny loomed

over her, a faint wash of light from the window illuminating her face. Her expression was strained, vertical lines on her forehead, the lips pinched and tight. Her eyes were in shadow.

'You remember the man in the cavern, the one I called the Doctor?'

'Yes.'

'You have to find him and give him this.' Benny put something in Zamina's hands. It was the little book that she always carried with her. 'Tell him that "its" control is restricted outside of the transit system.'

'How?'

'Hurry,' said Benny, 'I can't fight it for long.'

Zamina rolled from the bed, casting around for her clothes.

'No time,' said Benny. 'Go, Go!'

Zamina actually saw Benny's face change as if an enormous shutter had clanged down in front of it.

'Hey, girl,' said Benny, 'you wouldn't rat me out?'

Zamina slammed her fist between Benny's eyes. The eyeballs rolled up in their sockets and Benny fell sideways on to the floor. Zamina stepped over her to gather up her clothes.

Damned if she was going to run out of the house naked.

The House

Blondie had soft hair on his chest. In the daylight it was so blond as to be invisible but in the darkness when touch became their primary sense it lit up like neon on Kadiatu's intimate map of his body.

They'd made love again, with him on top this time. Kadiatu locking her legs across his hips, her arms around his back, straining to drag him inside her, to make him part of herself. Serious sex this time, no jokes or laughter, just deep mammalian instinct ascending through a complex strata of emotions.

They slept afterwards, exhausted and loose-limbed, tangled into the bedsheets and each other.

Kadiatu dreamed that she stood shipwreck naked on a beach as a storm swept in from the sea. She was breathing hard and the rhythm of her lungs matched the rhythm of the water as it broke against the shore.

In her dream the family dead walked out from the sea towards her. They came up the beach as a chain of corpses, stamping out the death dance in the pale sand. The beating of their feet was the rhythm of the sea, the rhythm of her heart beating.

Death had robbed them of their faces and of the insignia on their uniforms. It reduced them all to a single nation, a single race of people without division or quarrel. They danced towards her and with the total certainty that comes in dreams she knew that they wanted her sacrifice.

'What can you offer?' they demanded. 'We gave our lives, some short, some long, some crying, some cursing. What can you give so that the children may live?'

'My life,' moaned Kadiatu, 'my life for the children.'

'Your life was pledged before you were born,' said the dead. 'What else have you got?'

Lightning lit the hollow sockets of their eyes.

A rumble of thunder in the far distance made Kadiatu open her eyes. There was nothing but stars through the open window. The thunder continued, resolving into a low continuous rumble that increased in volume until the glass panes rattled in their frames. Kadiatu got to the window in time to see it come over the hill.

The aircraft was a wedge-shaped patch of black, running lights flashing on each stubby wing. As she watched, it dropped vertically on to the lawn, landing with a burst of blue flame. In the silence that followed she could hear the distinctive cracking sound of carbon fibre cooling down from a white heat.

'Shit,' she said stumbling back to the bed and groping for her jeans. 'Blondie, get up.'

Blondie woke up when Kadiatu managed to find the light switch. He looked at her stupidly as she pulled her jeans on and jammed her feet into her trainers.

'Get dressed,' she told him. Her T-shirt had found its way under the bed; by the time she retrieved it Blondie was already lacing up his boots. Kadiatu wadded up her socks and underwear into a tight ball and stuffed them into a jacket pocket.

As they ran downstairs she tried not to trip over her laces.

The fuselage and wings bore a long-dead flag, a polar projection of the earth supported by oak leaves laid down with non-reflective paint. The Doctor was sitting casually on the wing's leading edge, talking to the pilot. The Doctor said something and the pilot turned her head in their direction. Kadiatu saw starlight reflected off white marble eyes.

'Hey,' said Blondie, 'isn't that . . .'

The Angel Francine. Here and running taxi service for the little man with the weird eyes. Kadiatu felt a thrill of fear that had nothing to do with monsters or alien computer viruses.

A hatch whirred open to the rear of the cockpit, a metal stirrup ladder unfolding forward of the wing. The Doctor waved them in. 'Welcome to Deux Ex Machina Airways,' he said.

The rear section had four ejection seats mounted two by two. Kadiatu eased in beside Blondie and helped him buckle down the harness.

'I've never been in an aircraft before,' he said.

'Don't worry,' said the Doctor. 'Flying's as easy as falling off a bicycle.'

'Especially when the pilot's blind,' said Kadiatu.

Francine lifted them on thrusters to ground plus twenty metres, tilted the nose back and pulled three Gs straight up. Blondie's eyeballs were showing a lot of white by the time they levelled off. A sudden tremor shook the airframe and the ride became unnaturally smooth. On a short hop like this they didn't need to go supersonic. Kadiatu figured that Francine just liked to break windows.

The widescreen monitor at the front of the section showed them a forward view and avionics data. At one thousand metres the lights of southern England moved deceptively slowly.

'I hope there's a film,' said the Doctor.

'It'll have to be a short one,' said Kadiatu.

'Is she really blind?' asked Blondie.

'As a bat,' said the Doctor.

The jet tilted forward and the lights of central London rushed up to meet them.

STS Central - Olympus Mons

The conference had been going on for over an hour and Ming was running hard to sustain her position. If she'd been dealing with politicians it would have been easier; politicians were sensitive to public opinion and Ming had a whole section of the KGB working on that.

Instead the holographic figures spaced around the table were of the regional mandarins, non-elected and difficult to touch. Each of them was sitting at identical tables around the system, Washington, Brazilia, Harare, Beijing, Tehran, Jacksonville, Zagreb, all the power centres. Hologram eyes reading hologram body language and looking for weakness.

Most of them were old, old enough to remember the decade that followed the war. They could feel the same thing now, the crust shifting beneath their feet, the sharp smell of sudden political death. They were old, these mandarins, old and scared and dangerous.

Damage limitation was the name of the game and they were making Ming work hard. The regional bureaucracies wanted to shift responsibility for the evacuation of the Lowell Projects on to the STS and the relief NGOs. Budget bar graphs in primary colours on the table top went up and down like steam pistons. Zagreb had got the notion from somewhere that the crisis on Pluto had its roots in the Stunnel accident.

Only Jacksonville wasn't bitching; they'd been getting disaster grants for decades for the project in Achebe Gorge and saw the refugees as an opportunity to grab a bigger share of the cake.

A hologram of a man Ming didn't recognize had appeared in one of the vacant chairs. He was short with thinning hair under a straw boater and pale disturbing eyes. His gaze made it hard for her to concentrate. While she fended off a typically asinine attempt by Washington to shift the refugee-counselling costs on to her R&D budget she tried to work out who he could be.

There was no identification tag on the table in front of him. They were optional but officials generally used them to impress their importance on the viewer. Not a bureaucrat then, and not a politician either: they usually smiled and the man wasn't smiling. A troubleshooter then, some slick know-it-all from the private sector put in place by the bastard Rodriguez to keep an eye on her.

Without looking down Ming ran her fingers across her console, tapping in the code for a signal trace. She waited for half a minute and glanced down. The trace report stated that no signal was being broadcast to the conference seat indicated.

'This meeting is over,' Ming told the mandarins and terminated the conference link. The hologram mandarins derezzed before they could protest.

If only I could do that for real, thought Ming.

He of course didn't vanish; he stayed real and solid in his chair. How could she have mistaken him for a hologram?

'Are you the manager?' asked the man.

'What's it to you?'

'Your transit system would like to have a word with you,' said the man. 'It has some complaints.'

Olympus Mons West

Lambada's MIG espresso machine was still warm but otherwise the crew room was deserted. The cards from an interrupted game of damage were scattered on the table. Blondie wondered if they were from the same game that Dogface and Old Sam had argued about - what, two, three days ago?

Tinkerbell greeted him with a delighted squeal when he opened his locker. The ten-centimetre girl was on the top shelf of the locker. 'Hi sweetie,' she said. Unless Blondie responded or shut the locker door, Tinkerbell would repeat the greeting every thirty seconds or so until its batteries ran down. He took her out of the locker and held her in the palm of his hand. The cheap hologram faded badly under the crew-room lights. Tinkerbell pouted and put a tiny red-nailed hand against her hip. He'd picked her up during a shopping trip in the Moscow ginza, a non-financial transaction as they used to call them. It took him thirty-six hours to learn how to program it, his unbroken concentration driven on by a turbocharged teenage libido. It had unlocked his talent and his talent had driven him down the Central Line to this place. The day he quit the Stop, Tinkerbell was one of the few things he didn't leave behind.

He considered altering her configuration, darkening the skin tone, changing the hair and face. He'd have to reduce the cartoon breasts, thicken the waist slightly and narrow the hips. The clothes were wrong too; he couldn't imagine Kadiatu in thigh-length boots with decimetre heels, much as he'd like to. He put Tinkerbell back on the top shelf of the locker. 'Sorry,' he said. 'But I don't love you anymore.'

Blondie took out a clean set of coveralls, changed and fixed himself a coffee from the MIG. The tangle of chromed pipes shuddered and ejected a stream of steaming liquid into his mug. Blondie found there was no milk; milk had been Dogface's job this week. He took the drink through to the office and sat down at his desk. Sipping the coffee he punched up two status monitors, the screens forming in the air at head height. The desk booted up a looksee program he'd written during his second day on the job. It checked that all his drones were out doing their jobs.

The older floozies were very attached to their drones, and as a result, Blondie had got the pick of the new Nigerian YI3560s. Dogface said he was welcome to them, he felt that a transfer would degrade the personality templates he had spent years building up.

Five of Blondie's drones were doing routine work in various parts of the system, two were laid up in the shop and one was missing. Blondie took a quick look around on manual while the console scared up a search program. The Central Line was still closed to normal traffic on the approaches to Lowell Depot; yellow emergency icons were scattered all over the Pluto network.

Movement caught his eye amongst the transPluto feeders. He scaled down the map and switched representation over to traffic density. The thickness of the lines now indicated movements per hour. The central passenger and freight lines were double the width of every other line. Lots of emergency service and military stuff.

The Pluto network was fishing line thin. Most of it had been built during the boom of the last decade and was hardly used. However, something nagged at Blondie, a pattern just off the edge of his perception. Working quickly he customized an off-the-shelf pattern-recognition program and applied it to the map.

It looked like a spider web: lines of high density traffic radiating from a central hub centred on the unused depot at Managona. When he switched to the remote monitors at Managona he found they were non-operational. Blondie tried the signalling subsystems but they were non-responsive, even with the maintenance override.

He thought suddenly of cancer, individual cells rebelling

against the body, striking off in new and dysfunctional directions. Subversion of the natural order.

Like a virus, the Doctor had said.

He punched into the floozie comm circuit and got Lambada.

'I've got to talk to the Doctor,' he told her.

'He's gone,' said Lambada. 'Took off with your girlfriend about ten minutes ago. Commandeered Ming's VIP shuttle.'

'Where to?'

'Somewhere in the Canyonlands, I think. Talk to this one, she knows more about it.' Lambada stepped away from the camera to reveal a pale-faced young woman in a ripped-up leather jacket.

It was Zamina.

Achebe Gorge

Acturus Station to Achebe Gorge was five minutes in the prioritized VIP shuttle. The Doctor and Kadiatu did the journey standing up, overrode the door controls and left the shuttle while it was still moving.

The OXFAM information centre didn't want to give them Benny's location. 'Privileged data,' said the man behind the counter. Kadiatu kept the man distracted by threatening to break his fingers while the Doctor raided the files. He was the fastest console operator Kadiatu had ever seen.

'Kanger Crossing,' said the Doctor. 'Where is it?'

Kadiatu surreptitiously leant a little bit harder on the man's hand until he agreed to take them. The OXFAM worker had an open-topped four-by-four parked round the back. It looked like something he'd built in his spare time.

'I'll drive,' said the Doctor.

'It's got manual gears,' protested the OXFAM man.

'So have I,' said the Doctor.

There was a grinding sound from under the seats and the jeep lurched off. Directions from the OXFAM man put them on a tarmac road heading roughly east. The small Martian sun was high overhead and as the jeep topped a ridge Kadiatu could see the dark smudge of the memorial forest to the north.

Every tree a soldier.

Four hundred and fifty thousand, not counting Paris.

She buried her father there three years back, in the plot for soldiers who'd outlived their war, under a Douglas fir with her mother.

Pale green sunlight on the needle carpet.

Kadiatu knew what had happened when she saw that the door to the bungalow was open. She went in behind the Doctor wishing she'd asked Francine for a gun.

Benny's resettlement officer was face down over the kitchen table. Single stab wound from behind, under the fourth rib and into the right auricle according to the Doctor.

'Instantaneous,' he said. 'Probably a carving knife.'

'His mother lived with him,' said the OXFAM man.

'In the bathroom,' said the Doctor. 'The tap's dripping.'

Kadiatu went towards the door.

'Wait,' said the Doctor. 'Listen, you can hear the air move.'

He was through the door with such suddenness that Kadiatu hardly saw him move. She heard a window break at the rear of the house. 'The jeep,' shouted the Doctor.

'Call the police,' Kadiatu told the OXFAM man.

Outside a figure sprinted across the garden for the parked jeep. The Doctor was right behind her. Kadiatu got a look at the person's face as she cut across the lawn to head her off. It was the woman from the cavern. The woman saw her and swung her left arm round to point at Kadiatu.

Kadiatu heard a bang as she flung herself down and the flat whine of a subsonic projectile going overhead.

Damn, thought Kadiatu, left-handed and I didn't see the gun.

Benny jumped into the jeep and reached quickly down to start it. Kadiatu watched as the Doctor sprinted and jumped for the back of the jeep. He scrambled on board, fighting for a grip as Benny threw the jeep into a screeching three-point turn.

Kadiatu got to her feet and chased them up the drive. The jeep veered to the right and hit a banked verge. The Doctor was catapulted into a low line of bushes. The jeep rolled over once and ended up on its side, striking sparks off the tarmac.

Kadiatu reached the Doctor just as a police siren dopplered overhead towards the bungalow, a blue-painted drone circling in to seal off the crime scene.

'That way,' said the Doctor. Benny had fought free of the jeep and took off to the west. They set off after her but a second police-drone appeared over the ridge and veered to intercept them.

'Can you lose the drone?' asked the Doctor.

Kadiatu stopped and swung her extensions over her shoulder. She untangled a matt black cube and twisted the microswitch on the top with a fingernail. The police-drone wobbled uncertainly for a moment and turned back towards the bungalow. Kadiatu said a silent prayer for Lunar Max, a scumbag but an honest scumbag.

The ground began to slope upwards and the going got slow.

'She's heading for that escarpment,' said the Doctor.

The cliff wall projected inwards across the canyon floor for fifteen kilometres in a wedge-shaped escarpment. The Doctor and Kadiatu were running up through the carefully managed deciduous woods that covered the slope of an ancient landslide at its base.

The escarpment vanished upwards into the atmospheric haze. Kadiatu thought she saw the glint of sunlight on glass at the top.

'There's a lift up the wall,' said Kadiatu.

The lifts rode up inside a box-girder shaft bolted on to the rockface. The Doctor shaded his eyes and looked towards the foot of the canyon wall.

'Do you think she went there?' he asked.

'Must have done,' said Kadiatu.

There was a hole ripped in the chain-link fence near the gate. The Doctor held it open as Kadiatu ducked through. There was a squat windowless building at the base of the lifts and they made for that. The front door was open. Inside was a single large room stacked with storage pallets. The lift shafts, four of them, were placed against the far wall. The black iron framework had been riveted together. Kadiatu was reminded of the antique train they'd ridden to the house in Kent. There was a High Voltage warning sign above each of the lifts. She guessed they ran by linear induction. The shafts vanished downwards as well as up.

'There must be a transit station down there,' said Kadiatu.

The Doctor checked the indicator lights. 'She went up,' he said.

The lift doors opened with the unmistakeable whump sound of pressure seals.

'Pressurized,' said the Doctor. 'It must go all the way to the top.' He pressed a button and the lift accelerated smoothly upwards. 'How much time does she have on us do you think?' he asked.

'Twenty minutes,' said Kadiatu. 'Why's she going up to the rim rather than down to the transit station? She could be well away by now.'

'Perhaps she thought we'd have the station covered.'

'Perhaps we should have,' said Kadiatu. 'Why didn't we?'

'That would have involved the security forces,' said the Doctor. 'They're very nervous right now and that makes them trigger happy. They might have shot her.'

The lift indicator showed them one kilometre up the cliff. Outside the small window the girders had become a flickering blur. Through them Kadiatu could see the sky growing visibly darker.

'Would that be such a bad thing?' asked Kadiatu.

'Bernice is my friend,' said the Doctor.

'She's killed a lot of people.'

'She's killed nobody,' said the Doctor. 'The real murderer is whatever it is that's using her. That's your killer.'

'She could at least try to resist it.'

'She is resisting it, that's why we're here,' said the Doctor. 'I'm not even sure that I could resist it myself.'

'I'd have resisted it,' said Kadiatu.

'You,' said the Doctor, 'have a lot to learn.'

The lift started decelerating at around the two-kilometre mark and finally eased itself up into an airlock. A double set of doors opened to reveal a rough concrete corridor lined with portholes.

'Any ideas?' asked the Doctor.

'This is one of those rim stations,' said Kadiatu. 'They run ground transports out on to the Tharsis Bulge from here.'

'You're sure?'

'Yeah,' said Kadiatu. She was sure because Gaelic Five did a pretty good drama series called *Dustkart* which ran in perpetual syndication dubbed into thirty-six languages.

The corridor turned a ninety-degree corner and then split in two. One branch went up a ramp to the left, the other carried straight on.

'Left,' said the Doctor.

The ramp opened up into a deserted gallery thirty metres long, a teak bar ran the length of one wall opposite a single gigantic picture window. Chairs covered in treated zebra hide were scattered in front of the window, which overlooked the Tharsis Plain.

'Sunset Bar,' said the Doctor.

Kadiatu checked out the view. They were at least a hundred metres above the plain. A beetle-like dustkart was pulling out from underneath the gallery, red dust kicking up beneath its fat tyres.

'Look,' she told the Doctor, 'we must be above the hangar.'

'We came the wrong way,' said the Doctor.

They scrambled back down the ramp and followed the straight corridor until it too split two ways.

'Let me get my bearings,' said the Doctor. 'That way.'

They came to a door marked 'Locker Room - Authorized Personnel Only'. The door had been left slightly ajar.

There was a dead body inside. Some poor dust jockey that had the bad luck to be changing when Benny came through. A blackened gunshot wound in his chest. The Doctor knelt uselessly to check his pulse. He must have been reading a hard copy of *Porn Technik* when she'd hit him. There were glossy pictures of naked people scattered around his head, high resolution bodies in poses as stiff and lifeless as his own. Some of the pages were charred at the edges.

'Now we know,' said the Doctor.

They ran down the short corridor that led to the hangar. A glance at the status board on the inside of the blast door showed the stolen dustkart moving out on to the Tharsis Plain.

'There she goes,' said the Doctor.

The blast door slid slowly upwards, and the Doctor ducked underneath it before it was completely open. A line of dustkarts were parked inside. The Doctor headed for the vehicle nearest the hangar doors. The dustkart was painted a virulent shade of dayglo orange shot through with triangular silver flashes for satellite identification. The main body was ten metres long and slung between six man-high wheels with independent suspension.

By the time she reached him the Doctor had already undogged the side hatch and was pulling himself inside.

Kadiatu grabbed the side handles and swung up behind him. The underside of the cabin had patches of bare metal where sand had scoured off the paintwork.

Inside the cabin smelt of acetone and old sweat. It had two sprung seats placed in front of the windscreen, their size indicating that it was usual to drive suited up. An airtight door leading back to the main cabin. The Doctor sat down in the right-hand driver's seat and looked over the controls. He flipped up a failsafe flap and punched the button inside. The side hatch slammed shut and Kadiatu felt her ears pop as the cabin pressurized. Servo motors whirred as she lowered herself into the left-hand seat, finding the optimum ergonomic position for her body.

The controls were clumped together in little groups with the kind of backlit push-down buttons and liquid crystal VDUs that Kadiatu associated with immediate post-war design.

There was a sudden vibration through the cabin floor as the Doctor kicked in the engines. He flexed his fingers and put his hand on the negative feedback joystick.

'Get on the radio,' said the Doctor, 'and see if you can get them to open the airlock doors.'

'How?'

'Extemporise,' the Doctor told her.

Kadiatu found a headphone set hanging over the windscreen. Stuck next to it was a flat hologram pin-up from *Porn Technik*, a leggy blonde with green scales growing out of her perfect skin. Kadiatu got a queasy feeling thinking that the headphones probably belonged to the dead man in the locker room. Sex and death, she thought as she settled them over her hair and adjusted the pin microphone in front of her lips.

'Anybody there?' she asked.

'*This is Achebe Rim traffic control*,' said a voice in her ears, '*calling Rover three-two. You are without authorization. Shut down your engines and open hatches.*'

'Traffic control,' said Kadiatu. 'This is Rover three-two, we are in hot pursuit of a murder suspect, open the airlock hatches.'

The engines roared as the Doctor pushed up the accelerator handle and the dustkart jumped forward.

'*Rover three-two*,' said traffic control, '*what is your authority?*'

The Doctor swerved the dustkart round to face the airlock doors and accelerated. Kadiatu watched horrified through the windscreen as the doors loomed up.

'I'm not going to stop,' said the Doctor.

'Listen, traffic control,' said Kadiatu, 'our authority's lying dead in the locker room and if you don't open the doors we're all going to find out just how strong they really are.'

The airlock's inner doors slid open just in time and the dustkart barrelled through. The seat tightened around Kadiatu's hips and shoulders as the Doctor jammed on the brakes. The dustkart halted just short of the outer doors. The inner doors clanged shut behind them.

'Now they've got us trapped,' said Kadiatu.

'Keep talking,' said the Doctor, sliding out of his seat and vanishing under the dashboard.

'Traffic control decompress and open outer doors.'

'*That's a negative Rover three-two*,' said traffic control. '*Remain where you are. We have police inbound.*'

There was an atinic flash under the dash and the Doctor cursed.

'Stop messing us about, traffic control, our suspect is getting away.'

'*Be advised Rover three-two that we have the fugitive's vehicle under satellite surveillance. It's not going anywhere and neither are you.*'

A klaxon went off somewhere in the airlock and the outer doors began to crank slowly open. The dustkart rocked on its suspension as the pressure differential caused a rapid outrush of air. Kadiatu saw scraps of paper whirl past, something banged along the roof and a tubular metal chair went flying out through the widening gap.

'You should really clean this airlock more often,' Kadiatu told traffic control, but they didn't reply. The pitch of the klaxon scaled up as the attenuated atmosphere shortened its wavelength until it began to sound vaguely hysterical through the bulkhead.

The Doctor climbed back into his seat and started them moving. 'There's nearly always an override somewhere,' he said.

The windscreen polarized by sections as they moved out from the airlock and into the naked sun. The ground sloped gently upwards towards the Tharsis Bulge in the north. There were three distinct tracks leading away from the rim station, each marked by beacons stationed every five hundred metres.

'Which way did she go?' asked the Doctor.

Kadiatu looked over the controls in front of her. They were labelled with icons originally derived from the warspeak vocabulary. She saw one that might have resembled an uplink dish and pressed the button. One of her VDUs changed to display a top-down GIS graphic of the Tharsis region. Kadiatu touched the screen to scale down and centre the image on their dustkart. If traffic control was right, there should be a marker for Benny's position. Sure enough a red cross appeared on the screen to the east of them; touching the cross brought up a side panel that displayed co-ordinates and speed.

'She's on the left-hand track,' said Kadiatu, 'and doing about two hundred klicks.' That kind of speed over rough terrain couldn't be safe.

'You should see her on horseback,' said the Doctor.

Managona Depot (P-87)

The *razvedka* were packed three deep into the black train, webbed up in a matrix of deacceleration paste. There was the occasional movement as someone used their cramped circumstances to cop a feel.

Snug as bugs in a rug, thought Mariko smugly. Termites have nothing on us.

Naran and she were in the nose, where the controls would be were this a real train, which it wasn't. It was better than a real train. It was made out of folded segments of reality and held together by sheer perversity.

'Right,' said Mariko, 'who's for a sing-song then?'

Tharsis Rim

They were two hours out from Achebe Gorge and twenty klicks behind Benny when the satellite trace vanished from the screen.

'We've lost the trace,' said Kadiatu.

'I noticed,' said the Doctor. 'We should be able to track her by her dust plume. See if you can find it.'

Kadiatu activated the dustkart's HUD and looked forward. A section of the windscreen in front of her cleared to show a composite image from the bow cameras. They were still following a marked trail that traversed the Tharsis Bulge going west. Ahead, the summit of Arsia Mons, the southernmost volcano of the three that crossed the bulge's centre, was visible on the horizon. Kadiatu had to compensate for the sun's glare as it shone directly into the cab.

Even with digital compensation, ×100 magnification was still jumpy. Kadiatu did a slow pan left to right and found the top of the plume. The laser rangefinger used yellow light to avoid absorption by the red Martian dust; she used the touch pad to key the data into the navigation console. The trace icon reappeared on the GIS map, surrounded by colour-coded zones of probability, as Kadiatu locked it in.

'Got it,' she told the Doctor. 'Still on the track and about twenty-one klicks ahead.'

'I think we should close the gap,' said the Doctor. 'Don't you?'

As the LCD speedometer climbed above 250 kilometres an hour Kadiatu looked in vain for some sign of strain on the Doctor's face. They hit a bump and the wheels spun free as the dustkart left the ground. Kadiatu gripped her armrests as they slammed back down. She'd felt safer divebombing Kings Cross in Francine's jet.

'Don't worry,' he said. 'I never drive faster than I can see. How are we doing?'

'Gaining, twenty klicks give or take two hundred metres.'

'I wonder where she's going?'

Kadiatu checked the map. 'There's nothing ahead except a couple of geological stations on Arsia Mons.'

The Doctor veered sharply to avoid a fresh crater across the track. The dustkart tilted violently over as the right-hand wheels clipped the edge.

'Benny's the virus, isn't she?' asked Kadiatu as the dustkart righted. 'I mean the core instructions of the virus are contained within her. The vriks from hell and all the rest of it, they're just peripheral.'

'What makes you say that?'

'It's obvious. Benny was the only person caught in the direct line of the initial attack who's still in one piece. The only one.'

'Possibly,' said the Doctor. 'It may have replicated though.'

'But out here she's isolated from the transit system,' said Kadiatu. 'If we destroy her out here . . .'

'No.'

'Why not?'

'Because *I'm* not a virus,' said the Doctor.

They hit another ridge, the wheels slamming down out of sequence.

'I'm going to see if we've got any pressure suits,' said Kadiatu. 'We might need them.' She climbed out of her seat and went aft. There were three pressure suits in a locker opposite the toilet, all of them bearing unbroken inspection seals, but Kadiatu already knew that. Instead she opened an equipment locker marked with hazard symbols and picked out a laser torch from amongst the neatly arrayed tools. She thumbed the test button and got a fully charged icon on the status LCD. Set in pulse mode a torch like this could burn a hole through sheet steel at four metres, further in an attenuated atmosphere.

Kadiatu transferred the torch into the thigh pocket of the pressure suit she had picked out for herself. Then she went back to rejoin the Doctor.

'Have we got any?' asked the Doctor as she sat down.

'Three and completely operational.'

'Good,' said the Doctor. 'Because I think she's stopped.'

Benny's dustkart had veered off the marked trail to the south and out across the plain. The fat tyre tracks were clearly visible and the Doctor slowed down to follow them. Kadiatu put up the HUD again and looked around. They should be almost on top of her by now but Kadiatu could only find the rapidly dissipating dust plume.

'I see her,' said the Doctor. 'She's gone down a rabbit hole.'

The Doctor got as close to the edge of the pit as he dared. The ground must have collapsed under Benny's dustkart, dropping it into the hollow space underneath. It lay twenty metres below, pitched at a forty-five degree angle, nose first.

The shape of the pit bothered Kadiatu. Underneath layers of dust and rubble she thought she could discern straight edges. As if it had been dug out artificially. It made her think of the leopard traps back home.

'Suit up,' said the Doctor, 'and let's follow after Alice.'

Kadiatu had no idea what he was talking about.

The undersuit was made of air-permeable goretex and fit like a second skin. A label heat pressed into the fabric just above a cluster of sensors on the chest said 'Made in Israel/Palestine'. Kadiatu followed the instructions that came on a little laminated card and carefully smoothed out any air pockets. There was even a special hairnet provided to keep her extensions under control. The suit proper was woven out of boron mesh and lined with aluminized latex. Limb and torso lengths adjusted automatically as she put it on.

The Doctor didn't bother with an undersuit and merely pulled the outer shell over his street clothes. They donned their helmets, checked each other's seals and stepped into the airlock.

The Doctor decided that the best way down would be to climb down on to the rear of the crashed dustkart where it was only two metres below the rim. They could enter via the aft airlock and check the inside on the way down.

Kadiatu held the Doctor's hand as he cautiously put his weight on the dustkart's rear bulkhead. Her other hand gripped the duralloy piton she'd shot into the flaky agglomerate of the rim. She'd use the suit override to lock both gloves in position; if the dustkart went, she wasn't planning to go with it.

It seemed solid enough, perhaps it was wedged on a rockpile underneath. When the Doctor had the airlock open she unlocked the gloves and followed him in.

There was less damage in the rear cabin than she'd expected; most of the stored equipment had stayed in its racks. They used the storage bins to slide down the floor in stages. Kadiatu checked the suit locker. Either only two had been installed or there was a suit missing.

The windscreen in the cab had fractured but not broken. Brown liquid was splashed against the glaze, pooling along the join with the dashboard. Some of the controls were dented, some showed scorch marks. A fine haze hung at waist height, smoke particulates lazily settling in the one-third gravity.

'*I hope she's not hurt*,' said the Doctor.

Chance would be a fine thing, thought Kadiatu but kept it to herself. The laser torch was a comforting weight against her thigh.

The Doctor crouched down, using a seatback as a brace, and

dipped his finger in the brown liquid. *'Flavoured semi-frozen dairy product,'* he said. *'Probably chocolate. She was drink-driving, no wonder she crashed.'*

Rather than climb back up the dorsal airlock they depressurised the cab and dropped out of the side hatch. The floor of the pit was ankle-deep in dust; to one side directly under their own dustkart was the entrance to a tunnel. They didn't bother searching for tracks.

It was clearly artificial with melted-looking concave walls. Patterns had been scored into the surface, complex geometric shaped overlaid with exuberant curves and spirals.

'Virility symbols,' said the Doctor. *'The young males scratch them to attract females.'*

'What kind of young males?'

'Males with scales,' said the Doctor. *'Green ones.'*

'This is a Greenie's nest, isn't it?'

'A military nest too,' said the Doctor, *'judging by the density of the symbols. See that one with the triangles – "Nearby is Nxi, born of the third clutch, thought by many to be a mighty warrior."'*

'I'll bet,' said Kadiatu.

'Benny must have known about this nest,' said the Doctor. *'It's too much of a coincidence that she headed straight here.'*

'How did she know? No one's ever discovered an intact nest since the war.'

'Remember. Bernice is an archaeologist and ahead of the times,' said the Doctor. *'Four centuries ahead to be precise.'*

'Do we go after her?'

'We don't have much choice, do we?' The Doctor activated the halogen spot mounted on the shoulder of his suit. The illuminated tunnel curved to the right and down. Every square centimetre was covered in alien graffiti.

'A vast maze of underground tunnels,' said the Doctor sourly. *'What a surprise.'*

Acturus Station (Stunnel Terminus)

The floozies congregated in front of the Stunnel gateway, all except Dogface, who sent a drone with an Alsatian face. The slick bronze surface of the gateway was showing a noticeable clockwise rotation.

'How long?' asked the Dogface drone.

'Six to eight hours,' said Lambada.

'Shit,' said Credit Card.

'I never liked this Stunnel business,' said Old Sam. 'It isn't right, pissing about with things you don't know about.'

'It's a bit late to say that now,' said Credit Card.

'No one asked me about it before.'

'We don't make the mess,' said Lambada, 'we just clean up afterwards.'

'The gateway can't be initiated from the other side. Only from here,' said Credit Card. 'Who's going to be that stupid?'

'You mean apart from the Surf Monsters from Hell,' said Blondie.

'We got the KGB down here?' asked Lambada.

'Fucking battalion in the galleria,' said the Dogface drone. 'Didn't you smell them?'

'His drones don't get any better with old age, do they?' said Credit Card.

They all looked at the unpleasant greasy colour of the gateway and the power line crawling upwards on Lambada's monitors.

'Hey Sam,' said Lambada, 'you got any spare guns?'

Arsia Mons Military Nest

The warriors of the third clutch were invariably barracked on the outer rim of the nest. They would form the first line of defence if the nest were attacked. The next circle was the preserve of the older, more experienced warriors of the fourth clutch. This was evidenced, said the Doctor, by a growing maturity of the scratch marks. The entrance tunnel formed a descending spiral through the circles. The Doctor called this the *Xssixss*, the path of easy virtue, leading any attacker the longest possible way from entrance to centre. Concealed doors from the barrack galleries allowed the defenders to chop up the attacking column every step of the way.

Kadiatu had to take this all on trust. All she could see was the remorseless curve of tunnel as it coiled further into the nest. Occasionally the Doctor would translate the graffiti. *Nxi* of the third clutch kept turning up. There was one section thirty metres from the entrance in which he engaged in a protracted scratching debate with another Ice Warrior about the desirability of large dorsal extensions on females. It was either that, according to the Doctor, or a coded political argument over the proposed invasion of Earth.

Kadiatu began to visualise *Nxi* as a thin nervous Ice Warrior who was picked on by his larger clutchmates. Scratching his views on the walls might have been his only means of expression. The whole descent into the nest took on an unreal quality. Her, the Doctor and *Nxi* of the third clutch who either went for dorsal extensions in a big way or wanted peace with Earth. A thousand metres into the tunnel she began to feel *Nxi* walking ghost-like beside her.

Daddy would have shot him, she decided, and Francine would have done him from three thousand metres with a half-kiloton groundbreaker with 'Love from Paris' written on the casing.

Perhaps they had.

'What if she's left?'

'She can't,' said the Doctor. *'A military nest doesn't have any other exits. All the other tunnels radiate from the queen's chamber at the centre.'*

'What's in the queen's chamber?'

'High noon,' said the Doctor. *'She'll be waiting for us there.'*

The Doctor was right. Benny was waiting in the high-ceilinged hemispherical chamber at the centre of the nest. The entrances to other tunnels were set round its circumference like open mouths. Benny stood in the immediate centre, arms held slightly akimbo by the bulk of the suit.

'Why didn't she run?' asked Kadiatu. *'She could have lost us in there.'*

'No,' said Benny. The suit radio made her voice flat and artificial. *'The Doctor would have sniffed me out with his long nose.'* Her face was hidden behind the reflections on her faceplate.

'Fight it, Benny,' said the Doctor.

'Always the optimist,' said Benny.

'Always,' said the Doctor. *'You're out of the transit system now. You broke the conditioning once, you can do it again.'*

'It's not going to happen,' said Benny, but there was a trace of doubt in her voice. *'I'm wrapped up snug as a bug in a rug.'*

'I know you, Benny,' said the Doctor. *'I have your memories inside me. I know you're strong.'*

'Help me, Doctor,' said Benny, *'help me!'* The set of her shoulders changed from defiance to dejection. *'Help me,'* she said and it was a little girl's voice, *'it's so strong . . .'*

The Doctor took a step forward.

Benny was fast, but Kadiatu was faster. Something in the way Benny had flexed her hand as she raised it had struck a discordant note. By the time the metre-long muzzle flash ripped open the palm of Benny's gloves Kadiatu was already pushing the Doctor down. They rolled over together to the left. She noticed in a detached way how the gun barrel protruded through a diagonal slit in Benny's flesh.

Kadiatu slipped the laser torch from her thigh pocket as she rolled on to her feet. Benny was already turning but too late. Kadiatu thumbed the torch's firing stud even as her hand was rising.

The microsecond pulses of red coherent light were too short to be visible in the attenuated Martian atmosphere. Kadiatu used the puffs of vapour where it hit as her aiming guide and walked the laser up Benny's torso.

'No,' screamed the Doctor.

Vapour screamed out from the pinprick holes stitched into the chest of the suit as Benny turned to face Kadiatu. The left arm came round, hand flexed backwards.

Die you bitch, thought Kadiatu.

Benny's visor turned instantly matt black, automatic polarization to shield the wearer from intense radiation. As a result it absorbed the total energy of the laser's next pulse. A small hole formed and the pressure differential blew the visor apart.

The guns in both of Benny's arms went off as she fell down, loud enough to be audible in the thin atmosphere, shells blowing chunks of rock from the roof. She spasmed once on the ground and lay still. Vapour billowed upwards from the shattered faceplate, oxygen and water crystallizing in the subzero temperature. Then the suit realized that its occupant was dead and shut down the recycling packs.

The Doctor moved slowly forward to crouch by the body.

Kadiatu fought down the intense animal joy that seemed to rip through her. Her breathing was loud in her ears. The curve of the Doctor's back was a mute accusation.

'Go on,' she said. *'Tell me I didn't have to do that. I've*

broken the rules. You didn't like that, did you? No one's supposed to die without your permission.'

'If that were true,' said the Doctor, *'you'd all be immortal.'* He stood up, the suit making him look bulky and inhuman. *'That isn't Bernice,'* he said. *'I've been done.'*

Marangano Depot (P-87)

A shoji door in the room of Mariko's mind opened and light flooded in. Her head jerked up and she felt the blood sing through her temples. The *razvedka* were suddenly silent in their slave berths. Naran looked at her, his nostrils flaring, tongue nervously flickering between his ovoid lips.

'All right,' said Mariko, 'that's the signal. Fire her up.'

From the back of the black train the engines screamed up from idle, harmonics shaking dust from cracks in the station walls.

'Remember, we don't do this for love or money.' She smiled and her mouth was deep with teeth. 'We do it for the fun of it.'

The black train jumped forward, accelerating for the first tunnel gateway.

'Things to do,' chanted Mariko as they hit the interface.

'People to see!' chorused the *razvedka*.

Olympus Mons West

Zamina was into her fifth straight episode of *Kukosa Kabila* when the woman walked in. The big Brazilian woman Lambada had shown her where all the cards were kept and left her to it. The floozies had the most up-to-date video Zamina had ever seen and the Kenyan soap came with instant subtitles.

Wangari was just about to drop her bombshell to the village elders (she was leaving the village to work for the whites) when the door opened.

The woman was wearing a conservative English kaftan and walked in as if she owned the place. Zamina froze, welded suddenly to the leather couch.

'I'm back,' said Benny. 'Miss me?'

7:

Doorstep Blues

STS Central – Olympus Mons

Right in the middle of the news item Yak Harris started to talk to Dogface. Locked in his all-body brace, it was pretty hard for Dogface to move but he managed a jerk. The pain was so intense that it cut through the cartload of endorphin analog that he was mainlining. A battery of sensors attached to the frame registered little spikes and then subsided.

Dogface's second reaction was to assume that the chemical fog the medics had deemed necessary to his wellbeing had pushed him into terminal brain crash.

Catastrophic systems failure amongst the neurones, random electrochemical discharges causing patterned disruption in the perception centres of the brain. That would account for the simultaneous auditory and visual hallucinations.

'When you've quite finished,' said Yak Harris, 'can we talk?'

Dogface decided that a stand should be taken somewhere. 'I don't talk to drug-induced hallucinations,' he said.

'Well,' said Yak Harris, 'leaving aside the innate contradiction inherent in that statement, we are not a hallucination, drug-induced or otherwise.' There was a sort of inaudible click and the Yak Harris changed. 'Unless you subscribe to the idea that all computer-generated images are by their nature hallucinatory.'

That click again. The image and voice remained unchanged but Dogface had a strong impression of two personalities speaking through one construct.

'Nothing in your medication could possibly induce such a hallucinatory state anyway. (*click*) And we should know, given the amount of medical knowledge we've assimilated. (*click*) In fact, in a fundamental way we have *become* the entire body of human medical knowledge. (*click*) Trust me, we didn't enjoy it. You people were put together on a bad day.'

'Who are you?'

'We're a subset.'

'Why are there two of you?'

'Actually we're two subsets,' said one of the Yak Harrises. 'We met us coming the other way. (*click*) Which we didn't enjoy either.'

'Subsets of what?' asked Dogface.

They told him.

He didn't believe it.

'What do you want from me?'

'We're looking for the Doctor, but we got you instead. (*click*) All that medicine, we were impressed. (*click*) You see we're restricted by the *criteria* of our operations. (*click*) We know he's on Mars, we traced him through a communication with a third party. (*click*) The Angel Francine. (*click*) A transit order for unusual equipment. (*click*) An aircraft. (*click*) We think he may be out of position.'

'Out of position for what?'

'We don't know. (*click*) We didn't tell us that.'

'Who's the Doctor?' asked Dogface.

They told him.

He didn't believe that either.

Olympus Mons West

She threw the remote control at Benny's head. It was just a palm-sized bit of bakelite but Benny staggered when it hit her in the face. She paused to probe the gash it left in her cheek. She looked first at the blood on her fingers, and then at Zamina.

'Is that any way to treat an old friend?'

Zamina rolled off the couch and pushed it with all her strength at Benny's legs. Benny jumped it easily, landing with a cat's grin.

'Zimmy,' she said in a hurt voice.

But Zamina wasn't listening, her brain was locked deep into an instinct cycle of aggression/revulsion – the characteristic human response to spiders. She made an adrenaline-charged desperation lunge for Benny, trying to knock her down so she could get through the door.

Benny grabbed Zamina's wrists and fought to drag them down to her waist. The older woman was too strong, Zamina felt her arms being slowly pinned to her sides. Their faces were so close that Zamina could smell the sickly sweet vanilla ice cream on Benny's breath. Zamina swung her head back and snapped it forward, there was a loud crack and light exploded in her eyes.

Benny staggered backwards, hands flying automatically to cover her bleeding nose. Zamina lashed out with her fists, striking Benny full in the right breast. There's nothing you can teach a girl from the Stop about fighting dirty. She'd been on dates more violent than this.

Benny doubled over, curling around the pain in her chest. Zamina kicked her in the side of the head as she passed.

There were cake monsters in the corridor outside. Zamina saw their spiny heads swing round to face her as she left the crew room. She didn't wait for them to react and ran for her life.

She turned a corner and found herself in a long corridor lined with doors, she ran past them. She didn't want to get trapped in no room with the cake monsters after her.

A man stepped out of one of the doors ahead. He was wearing tan slacks and a button-down blouse and was carrying a clipboard. He looked up to see Zamina bearing down on him. She tried to yell some kind of warning as she went past but she didn't have any breath left over from running.

There was a scream behind her that was quickly drowned out by a high-pitched giggling. Zamina didn't bother to look round.

She went around another right-angle bend in the corridor and found a bank of mechanical lifts. One set of doors opened as the motion sensor mounted above detected her approach. Zamina grabbed the edge of the door as she went in, using it to stop her momentum.

Two cake monsters trotted around the corner with an easy and unhurried lope. Zamina jammed her thumb into the touch pad marked 'CONCOURSE'. The cake monsters picked up their pace when they saw the doors closing.

'Take the stairs,' Zamina screamed at them.

The doors stopped closing as the motion sensor picked up the two new potential passengers. Zamina stared in disbelief as the doors began to slide apart. She scanned the touch pads until she saw a red one marked 'EMERGENCY'. She jabbed it so hard that she sprained her index finger. Nothing happened. The regulating computer was waiting for the additional passengers to board before initiating procedure for an unspecified emergency.

Zamina actually felt her lips pull back from her teeth as she prepared to fight.

The leading cake monster pointed its hand at her. Zamina saw the muzzle of a gun push through the palm and jumped for the sheltered corner by the lift door.

There was a series of bangs and the bronzed mirror at the back of the lift went crazy paving.

Not fair, thought Zamina, not fair at all.

The lift regulator sensed the structural damage to the lift and upgraded the emergency from unspecified to possible localized decompression. Accident statistics were converted into a series of probabilities and balanced against the lack of corroborative data from its other sensors. A query flashed down a priority channel to the complex's mainframe, where it was tackled by the ethics subroutine.

The ethics subroutine determined that given the rapidity with which fatalities occur during explosive decompression it would be acceptable to save the individual in the designated safety zone rather than risk his/her life by waiting for the two other humans to join him/her.

An authorization flashed back up the priority channel to the lift regulator. The decision was logged in deep back up along with the statistical argument in case of an inquest.

The lift regulator received the authorization, logged it in its own back-up files and initiated emergency procedures. It sealed up the lift and dropped it downwards at close to human tolerance.

The doors slammed shut in the cake monster's face, there was a metallic clunk outside and Zamina felt the lift drop. She screamed as her feet left the floor. Yellow sealant gel forced itself out of the centre crack between the doors and around the frame.

Zamina found herself spreadeagled on the ceiling, looking down as concealed vents sprayed white foam into the lift. Strands of the stuff floated up towards her. At this point she passed out of fear and into a zone of high-pressure calm.

She remembered a kinky trick in Boston whose particular turn-on was taking foam baths with her and Roberta. No sex, just a nice long soak. Easy money, Roberta said, and a free bath. The trick had a mirrored ceiling above his Roman bath and Zamina used to look down on herself, just her face protruding from the foam. Roberta used to surreptitiously clean her delicates in that bath, vigorously scrubbing under the waterline. God knows what the trick thought she was doing.

There was a grinding scream from outside the lift and her strange calm cycled back down to terror. Zamina tried to stick to the ceiling by an act of will and went into the foam face first. She heard a muffled crash and the chiming sound of the floor indicator.

The foam began to subside and hands pulled her upright. Zamina came out of the lift, spitting out foam that tasted of nail-varnish remover. She quickly looked around. She was in the main concourse of Olympus Mons West. The lift had come down the thick central column that descended from the ceiling five storeys up.

The celebrated panoramic windows that overlooked the west slope of the volcano were to her left. People were beginning to crowd around the shaft, drawn by the emergency light flashing over the open lift.

'Are you all right?' asked the woman who had helped her.

Zamina didn't answer; she was searching the concourse for the nearest transit station.

'Hold still,' said the woman, 'medical will be here soon.'

Zamina twisted in the woman's grip. The adjacent lift was showing an emergency light as well, the LCD floor indicator spinning down through the digits. Zamina turned back to the woman.

'Run away,' said Zamina, 'there's monsters in the lift.'

She could see the woman thinking 'blitzed for sure', but she let go of Zamina's shoulders. Her feet skidded in the foam as she broke away from the woman. Behind her the floor indicator chimed softly. It was the most sinister sound Zamina had ever heard.

There were screams from the crowd as the door opened and the dull boom of guns firing. Ahead across the breadth of the concourse Zamina could see the red double arrow of the STS Logo hanging in the air.

The concourse crowd was mostly shoppers browsing on their way home. People dressed in the sombre middle-class colours. They were just beginning to react to the commotion as Zamina ran past them. She remembered the technician in the corridor upstairs but she was past guilt. Every girl for herself. You want help now, she thought, where were you when I was born?

There were more shooting sounds from behind and a police-drone whined overhead. The people ahead were beginning to look anxious, the psychological wavefront of panic outstripping Zamina's best speed. She realized that running to get ahead of the inevitable surge for the exits was going to be more important than outdistancing the cake monsters.

A stuttering sound that she recognized from the riots as a police-drone's minigun broke through the screaming. It was answered by more shots from the cake monsters. People were beginning to run now and Zamina tried to push her legs faster.

A wave of intense heat rolled over her back. She felt the hair on the back of her head crisping. Terrified that it might catch fire, she raised her hands to beat out any flames.

The blast wave flung her ten metres and she skidded another twenty on her front. There was a terrible pain in her breasts as the implants were squashed violently against her ribs.

Please God, she thought, don't let them burst. She'd heard somewhere that the silicon could leak out and give you cancer.

Cancer, she thought. You wish.

They were jammed solid at the escalator bank but at least the shooting had stopped. Zamina had to climb over a man to get on the central reservoir between the escalators. A hand grabbed at her ankle and she lashed out with her foot until it let go. She got friction burns on the palms of her hands sliding down. Contorted faces and struggling bodies on the escalators either side.

At the bottom in the booking hall she found she was ahead of the crowd again.

She made the mistake of looking back. A single cake monster was coming down one of the escalators, either smashing aside or trampling the people in its way.

Someone, probably a computer, had the sense at least to lock the ticket gates open. Zamina ran through them, checking the train indicators. She saw one marked 'Train at Platform'. The destination was unimportant, any destination was away from the cake monsters.

Passengers coming towards her swerved out of her way. Crazy woman, they were thinking. Wait until they get a load of what's coming after her.

A commuter train was standing at the platform, four carriages strung together with squat little pushme-pullyous at either end. Zamina dived through the doors just as they were closing. The surviving cake monster came in through the door window and got stuck two thirds in.

Zamina's breath came in short burning gasps. Her legs were too heavy to move. She just hung on the handstrap and watched the monster thrashing silently in the window frame. She wondered why it was so quiet until she saw a passenger screaming and realized that she'd gone deaf.

The cake monster kicked violently and managed to buckle the door enough to flop on to the carriage floor. A red light began to blink rapidly above the doorframe. Zamina noted with some satisfaction that the cake monster had to struggle to its feet. She could see its nostrils flaring and its chest heaving just like hers. The cake monster shook its head in a distressingly human way. Blue eyes regarded her from under ridges of bone.

Zamina realized what the red light signified but it was too late. The cake monster raised its hand – the gun muzzle ran smoothly out.

Zamina stared into its face. She didn't have enough energy left to tense up.

When she didn't die, it was a bit of a disappointment. She'd been looking forward to the rest. Instead the cake monster was irritably shaking its arm up and down. It looked at Zamina and shrugged. Decimetre claws extended from its hands. It took a step towards her.

The carriage hit the gateway interface.

Buckling the door had seriously degraded the carriage's shield efficiency. The flashing red light was the warning signal. By rights the train should never have pulled out of the station with a red light showing but Zamina guessed that safety standards had slipped a bit recently.

The cake monster looked over as the buckled door dissolved in a burst of psychedelic light. It looked back at Zamina through the heat-haze shimmer of an emergency containment field.

'I win,' whispered Zamina, 'you die.'

The rear section of the carriage disintegrated.

Arsia Mons

The eyes were wrong, the Doctor explained. They looked pretty bloodshot to Kadiatu but explosive decompression will do that. It messed up the face too yet it looked like Benny to her. The colour patterns in the irises, said the Doctor, didn't match his memory of the real Bernice's. He examined the gun barrels protruding from the palms of her hands.

'Very neat,' he said. *'The flap of skin overlaps the hole, the musculature is all in the heel of the hand so that the flexing motion allows the barrel to extend into firing position. I wonder if that's intentional?'*

'What is?'

'Know any palmistry?'

'Not really.'

'The flap follows the life line almost exactly,' said the Doctor. *'If it's intentional then we're dealing with some very sick minds indeed.'* He straightened up and looked around the chamber. *'I think we should leave here. Now.'*

'What about that?' asked Kadiatu pointing at the body.

'Leave it,' said the Doctor. *'They'll take care of it.'*

'Who's they?'

'The inhabitants of this nest.'

'Males with scales?' said Kadiatu. *'Nxi?'*

'Dormant nest,' said the Doctor. *'Don't worry, it'll take them at least two weeks to revive.'*

'Shouldn't we tell someone?'

'That's up to you,' said the Doctor, *'but we have more pressing matters.'*

They started the long trek back up the path of easy virtue.

'It's definitely easier going in than going out,' said Kadiatu when they reached the surface. *'What now?'*

'Benny went to a lot of trouble to send us on a wild goose chase,' said the Doctor, *'which means while we're here, we should be somewhere else.'*

They climbed back up through the wrecked dustkart. Standing on the rear section Kadiatu boosted the Doctor up on to the rim. He turned, gripped her wrists and pulled her up in turn.

He made a production of it, grunting loudly as she cleared the edge. Kadiatu wasn't fooled.

'We're at least two hours from Achebe Gorge,' said Kadiatu, *'and six hours from Olympus Mons.'*

'Let's walk over there,' said the Doctor, *'to that clear patch.'*

'The faster we mount up . . .' began Kadiatu.

'I have the situation under control,' said the Doctor. *'Trust me.'* He walked towards a level section of ground about the size of a football pitch twenty metres from the pit. When the Doctor reached its centre he kicked at the soft dust, there was a harder surface underneath. *'Ferroconcrete,'* he said. *'Excellent.'*

Kadiatu didn't ask, it was obvious who had built a concealed landing pad next to the nest. The Martians were supposed to be good with vibrations. Was one awake by now and listening to them walking around?

The Doctor took three white cylinders from his suit's kangaroo pocket. He twisted the end of the first one and a spike tripod sprang from the end. The Doctor pushed the tripod into the dust. The Doctor planted the other cylinders in a rough triangle around the landing pad.

'Light the blue touch paper,' said the Doctor, walking back to join Kadiatu, *'and retire to a safe distance.'*

A plume of burning white light burst from the top of the three upright cylinders. Magnesium distress flares.

'Since we've got a few moments,' said the Doctor, *'why don't you tell me about great-grandfather Alistair.'*

'What do you want to know?'

'How he met your great-grandmother would do for a start.'

Mariatu was the third daughter of the youngest wife of the Chief Yembe of Rokoye village and a source of endless discomfort to him. Although at sixteen she was well past marriageable age she had refused all proposals, arranged or otherwise. This would have been almost acceptable to Chief Yembe; after all, a compound needs young women, to fetch water and firewood, to cook and clean, except that Mariatu did none of these womanly things. Instead she did as she pleased and ran wild in the forest like a boy.

Chief Yembe's senior wife, sensing her husband's dissatisfaction, spoke to Mariatu's mother, punctuating each point by banging her walking stick against the wall of the hut. Mariatu's mother fearing for the stability of her home sent for her daughter.

'Why do you run in the forest?' demanded the senior wife. 'Are you not afraid of spirits or wild animals?'

'Why should I be afraid?' answered Mariatu. 'I am faster than any spirit and wild animals only attack if you scare them.'

'Why do you not fetch water for your mother?'

'Why should I fetch water when the stream is so close? If I am thirsty I go there and drink. Others should do likewise.'

And so it went, with each quick question came an equally quick reply until the senior wife was so tired she had to lie down in the shade.

Mariatu's mother gave her a basket and a sharp iron machete.

'Since you love the forest so much,' said her mother, 'why don't you go there and collect fruit? In that way at least you will be of benefit to your family.'

Mariatu, knowing a bargain when she heard one, took the basket and the iron machete and went into the forest. Determined to eat at least as much wild fruit as she brought back.

Now on that day a young British lieutenant named Alistair Gorden Lethbridge-Stewart was also in the forest. Far more in the forest than he wanted to be. This was only his first week in the country and having left his Land Rover to collect some soil samples, he had got himself lost. As he rested in the shade of the tree, Alistair saw a pretty native girl coming down the path towards him with a basket of fruit balanced on her head.

'Why are you sitting in the forest?' asked Mariatu when she saw him there. The stranger did not understand her but stood up. He was very tall and his skin was pale, all except his face which was a strange red colour. Mariatu took his hand and rubbed at the skin but the white stuff didn't come off. This then, she thought, must be an *oporto*, one of the white men that her father was always speaking of.

'Have you seen a Land Rover around here?' Alistair asked the native girl. 'A car, around here?' He turned an imaginary steering wheel and made brmm brmm noises. The girl just stared, making him feel bloody stupid. He wished that she was wearing more clothes. He put his hand against his forehead and mimed looking around.

The girl reached up and took the basket from her head and handed it to him. From the basket she removed a nasty-looking black machete. Alistair instinctively took a step backwards. She grinned at him showing perfect white teeth and balanced the machete on her head. She beckoned and walked away.

Alistair hefted the basket into a more comfortable position and followed her down the path. The basket was awkward to carry in his arms so he tried putting it on his head as the girl had done. He had to keep one hand on it for balance. After a while his arm ached, and so did his neck and back. Watching the way the girl walked he was reminded of the deportment classes that girls back home did. Learning to walk properly with books balanced on their heads.

They ought to come down here, he thought, and see how it's really done.

He tried to keep his mind off how well shaped the girl's legs were and the way her hips swayed when she walked. The British army frowned on serving officers fraternizing with native women, especially up-country and this close to independence. He was extremely pleased when they reached the village. The local headman was pleasant enough, one of his sons spoke a little English and soon several natives had been packed off to find his Land Rover.

The headman kept apologizing through his son for the deplorable behaviour of his daughter. Alistair said it was nothing, forget about it, which was pretty gracious considering his arms were threatening to drop off his shoulders. From behind the hut he could hear a long harangue going on in the native lingo. A woman, properly dressed thank God, brought him some water. From behind the hut the harangue ended in the unmistakeable sound of the flat of someone's hand hitting bare flesh.

There was a pause, then another, louder slap, followed by a howl of outrage. The headman's eyes practically glazed over with embarrassment. The girl came stalking round to the front of the flat. She pointed at Alistair, said something very fast and low in her own language, then she put her hands on her hips and waited. Alistair noticed that she was still holding the machete.

The headman said something to the son who could speak some English and the son translated. It took quite a long time to explain.

As they walked back to the Land Rover, located two hundred yards from where he had been sitting under the tree, Alistair asked himself once again how he managed to get himself talked into things like this. It wasn't as if he needed a houseboy, let alone a houseboy who didn't speak any English, or a houseboy who was a girl. He didn't even have a house; he lived in three rooms above a Lebanese trader on Wilberforce Street.

The girl put her machete on the dashboard and climbed into the passenger seat, as if she'd been riding in Land Rovers all her life. When she saw Alistair grasp the steering wheel she laughed and mimicked the action. 'A-car-around-here,' she said. He fished in his kit for his spare uniform shirt and gave it to her.

As they drove away down the trail that led to the road that led to Freetown the girl grabbed her machete and standing on the seat waved it over her head.

Eight years passed in the village with no word from Mariatu. Then one day, a year after independence, a strange woman came to the village. She arrived in a Land Rover piled with goods. Beside her sat a fair-skinned boy with green eyes.

Chief Yembe waited on his verandah to see who this important-looking woman was. A government official perhaps? Her face was difficult to make out; the Chief's eyes were not as good as they once were. He waited patiently, for he was the Chief and she must come to him.

When the woman came closer Chief Yembe saw it was his daughter.

'And that's what happened?'

'That's the way my father told it,' said Kadiatu. *'Her son grew up and became a soldier. He had a son, also a soldier, and a daughter who became a historian. I'm named after the daughter.'*

The Doctor's faceplate was black in the last light of the small Martian sun: his face hidden. *'I'm beginning to see a pattern,'* he said. *'I asked you before if you believed in fate, didn't I, and you said something flippant.'*

'I was in shock at the time.'

'There's no such thing as fate,' said the Doctor. *'But there are patterns. Patterns and shadows.'*

'What patterns?' asked Kadiatu.

The Doctor didn't answer. Instead he looked up at the sky. With the fading sun even the dimmer stars were becoming visible.

'Taxi's here,' he said.

Three stars in a triangular pattern fell towards them; out of the violet sky.

Kadiatu recognized the jet as it landed between the flares. The same matt black wedge of variable-geometry carbon fibre. The same archaic blue and white icons on its wings and tail assembly. The vertical thrusters burned a darker shade of blue, tailored self-oxidizing fuel for the Martian environment.

The canopy remained closed this time, Francine staying sealed up inside the cockpit.

The side hatch opened and the stirrup ladder unfolded. The Doctor gave Kadiatu a mocking little bow and waved her forward.

'A good rule in this business,' he said, *'is that when you make a plan, plan in depth.'*

Olympus Mons West

Benny found herself slapping her pockets in the lift down to the concourse, discovering again that the book was gone. The book was important, she knew that, but the complex code had defeated her interpretation. Now she'd lost it to the Doctor. He was in possession of its secrets.

The impulse that led her to give Zimmy the book was unclear. The deception plan had been of her own devising; even if *it* didn't understand the danger posed by the Doctor, she had no illusions. Forcing the Doctor out of position had been *her* priority, not *its*. Yet the instinct that had propelled the action had come from somewhere outside, like her lapse in the cavern. It had just seemed vital to the deception that the Doctor was shown the book.

That implied that the Doctor knew about the book already.

Benny wished that she had deciphered the book first.

She wished she could stop thinking about it, it was giving her a migraine.

The interior of the lift interested her. Its technology was archaic, not just from her twenty-sixth century perspective but in terms of this century as well. They had force-field elevators elsewhere in the system, so why build a clumsy mechanical device like this? Technology plateaux were a well-known concept amongst historians and archaeologists, even those that had forged their accreditation. Over the millennia a wheel remained a round thing that spun on an axle, the materials with which it was constructed largely irrelevant.

On Terra she could understand it. On Terra the future built over, around and beneath the past. The Kremlin walls still stood in Moskva even in her time, albeit under a geodesic dome. Settlement on Mars couldn't be more than ten, twenty years old. The lift with its bronze mirror with dragons engraved around the edges belonged to another time.

It was a conscious anachronism.

There was a tendency amongst academics to ignore the *pre-expansionist* period of terrestrial history. Sandwiched between the *nuclear age* and the first *diaspora*. It was a transitional period, difficult to study and so overlooked.

Archaeologists think in centuries, history to them is the slow accretion of dead things in the ground. The rise and fall of civilizations written in the strata of broken pottery. When one design of pot gives way to another the archaeologist says to herself, 'Transitional period,' and starts looking for contemporaneous earthquakes or invasions.

I'm in a transitional phase, thought Benny, and I'm doing things to history. I must remember to take notes.

There was a stab of pain in her left temple.

The doors opened and Benny stepped out on to the concourse. Two of the lifts to the left of her gaped open, the floor in front covered with streaks of crash foam. Air exposure had turned the foam a dirty white colour; here and there the foam showed splashes of pinky red.

Benny saw two plain-clothes policemen and a drone standing over the dead body of a woman. The front of her face had been smashed in with enough force to drive her jawbone through her neck. Benny was surprised; she'd expected the casualties to have been removed by now. Then the body flickered slightly and derezzed. It was only a crime-scene hologram, the detectives must have been using it to take . . .

The pain was intense enough to blind her. She staggered and sensed movement towards her, attention turning in her direction, sympathy, concern, questions, paramedics, questions, just sit down here while I fetch someone who wants to ask you some *questions.*

She managed to pull herself upright by an act of will and walk on. The movement towards her stopped. The pain subsided to a dull throbbing over her left eye. Sight returned.

There were more police and emergency service teams working in clusters. The path of Zamina's flight across the concourse was marked by strings of black and yellow police tape. As she followed them she saw the burnt out shell of a police-drone smothered in foam. Beneath it the ersatz marble flooring had cracked and melted.

Zamina, thought Benny. Should have converted her when I had the chance, but the Doctor would have spotted it.

'These escalators are closed,' said a STS guard.

Benny peered over his shoulder. The escalators were frozen in place. More police and drones were working along them.

'I have to get to Olympus Mons,' she told the guard.

'You'll have to take the East Olympus Loop from Carver,' said the guard. 'Are you all right?'

'Sorry?'

'You're limping.'

'It's just a sprain,' said Benny. 'High G handball.'

'Carver station is just over there,' said the guard. 'Be careful with that ankle.'

'Thanks,' said Benny.

She walked in the direction the guard had indicated, trying to stop her right leg from dragging. There was a washroom on the way and she ducked inside. She stared hard at her face in the mirrored wall above the washbasins. The right side of her face seemed slack looking. When she probed it with her fingertips it felt normal enough, the right eyelid drooping slightly. She carefully lifted the eyelid. The eye looked normal enough apart from the whites being a bit bloodshot.

Her nose was still painful to touch.

She opened the tap and splashed cold water on her face,

blinking and widening her eyes until the drooping stopped. She took a deep breath and slowly exhaled. Trying to clear her mind with a mantra she'd picked up while digging on Proxima IV.

She didn't have time for distractions. She had a schedule to keep, people to see, power subsystems to sabotage.

Jacksonville

The computer that handled emergency services in the Olympus Mons administrative district was feeding contradictory reports into the Martian Police subsystem. Operators in the Olympus Mons West human response centre were jabbing HOSTILE ACTION icons as soon as they appeared on their screens. Sixty-five per cent of responses indicated criminal activity, thirty-one per cent terrorism but four per cent were marked 'UNKNOWN'. Out on the concourse at Olympus Mons West a medical-drone ran a deep scan on a body and found significant variations from the human norm. As empirical sensor data the drone's report was given a weighted three per cent addition to the unknown total, pushing it past its five per cent response threshold.

Crossing the threshold activated a subroutine within the civil operating system that had lain dormant for twenty-five years. In an EMP-shielded bunker under the military cantonment at Jacksonville a stand-alone mainframe with the code designation of JERUSALEM powered up. Acting on the long-forgotten assumption that the Martians had left 'stay behind' units in cryogenic storage, JERUSALEM put Jacksonville on a stage one alert.

JERUSALEM activated its surveillance net, calling in data from the chain of military satellites that should have been strung out in geo-stationary orbits. The satellites had long ago been decommissioned or switched over to the civil net. JERUSALEM, programmed by people who had just fought a long and bloody war, attributed the loss of the satellites to enemy action.

The alert was jacked up to stage two, with the possibility of a trans-orbital threat.

JERUSALEM had better luck with the static radar at the summit of Olympus Mons. It spotted a fast-moving trace from the south east, altitude five hundred metres. The target's transponder signal was absent from the IFF registry.

JERUSALEM cycled through its weapons options and found that all its ground-based energy weapons and close defence ordinance was disabled. There were surface-to-air missile sites still operational, an unfamiliar specification, but the front end instructions interfaced adequately with the computer's command structure. JERUSALEM assimilated the missile's operational envelope as it switched from *assessment* to *response* mode.

Target resolution gave JERUSALEM a window of attack of two seconds in ten seconds' time. JERUSALEM judged this too fast for human response and since Jacksonville was a possible target, it overrode the failsafe and cut the humans from the loop.

At the optimal moment within the window of opportunity JERUSALEM launched one battery of Vulture Surface to Air missiles at the fast moving inbound target.

The three missiles were in their sustainer stage before anyone at Jacksonville could re-engage the failsafe.

Tharsis Bulge

Francine's reflexes cut in before her conscious mind had registered the launch warning from the jet's look down threat radar. Pilot reflexes turned the jet and snapped the head round for an eyeball confirmation of the launch before the brain could remember it was blind.

Francine shut down the transponder, the radar, even the laser altimeter. Modern missiles could home in on any kind of emitter. She would have to rely on her passive sensors.

Without active radar and without sight, Francine became truly dependent on the augmented spatial awareness of her mind, encoded into wafer-thin silicon that was interlaced with her neurones was a complex topographical map of Mars, accurate down to one hundred metres. Her own inner ear provided the data for inertial guidance, backed up by direct feeds from the jet's avionics.

But the system wasn't perfect, it was based on a virtual representation of the real world and in any conflict, the real world always won.

Francine was truly flying blind this time.

Passive sensors picked up the incoming bogeys by their

active radar emissions. They were out of the sustainment stage and levelling off at two thousand metres. They deployed into a co-ordinated attack pattern that indicated a high intelligence interaction between the missiles.

Vultures for sure, thought Francine.

Francine in pre-flight training, fifteen and hot to rock. A room full of teenaged cadets with drug-retarded, pre-pubescent bodies, child faces and shaven heads. Gymnasts' bodies, with optimum G tolerance and vat-grown eyes.

'Human thoughts are not pictures,' said the instructor. 'There is no central Cartesian Theatre where they are displayed before the conscious mind.'

The law said that they had to be told, but the cadets weren't listening. Instead their augmented eyes were filled with silver shapes leaving contrails in the high stratosphere. Up there where the sunlight is white and pure.

'Instead the mind operates like an old-fashioned transputer, making editing decisions in parallel. We will teach you to make use of this facility.'

The air force divided up their brains with lacy wafers of silicon and hypoallergenic crystal. Taught them to fly from the inside out and let them play with the most expensive toys in human history.

In one of the separated sections of Francine's mind the thoughts coalesced into what would be an image of the Vultures in flight, if thoughts were pictures.

Two stubby cylinders with recessed pods for manoeuvring thrusters. In the tenuous atmosphere over the Martian highlands, control surfaces are useless. Their noses studded with both active and passive sensors. In their ballistic stage, now at two kilometres a second, describing an arc while the smart silicon in the nose calculated an intercept.

Francine broke radio silence to warn her wingman. 'Flash, two hot ones, on ballistic and intercept.'

'Copy Angel,' answered Flash, *'I see them.'*

Flash Harry in the second Honda Peacemaker, flying 'loose deuce', five hundred metres and thirty years behind her.

Francine must have taken hits because the Peacemaker was handling heavy and slow. More like a commercial jet than a fighter. Her weapon options showed zero ordinance, zero flares and chaff. Must have been a tough mission. Not remembering was frightening. You couldn't afford a lapse, not with the Greenies punching the air with pop-ups all down the canyon.

A curtain of darkness lifted and she could see the mountain, the big shield volcano rising sharply out of the Tharsis Bulge. Jacksonville a cluster of lights halfway up the south east slope.

Jesus Freak would be waiting there, a one-litre pitcher of non-alcoholic lager spiked with two milligrams of phencyclidine to give it kick. It would be sitting on the bar of the Ice Maiden, condensation forming on the cold glass. Dozy Joe behind the bar with the bottles of stolen vodka and the solid holograms of the KIA.

Francine pulled the nose up until her forward view was filled with the violet sky. There amongst the bright stars she saw sunlight glint on two small fast-moving objects. No chaff, no flares and no ECM gave her only one option. A forward quarter evasion.

Chicken at two klicks per second.

There would be one right moment to evade. Too early and the missiles had time to correct their course, too late and they went off in your face. There was no machine for this, no clever bit of hardware that could do the calculation for you. Head to head with a SAM was a hindbrain thing. You either had it or you were toast.

The Angel had it.

She fired the VTOL thrusters and the jet did a seven-G backflip. The missiles streaked past, hobbled by their own momentum.

Now the canopy was filled with the Martian landscape as Francine dived for the cluttered radar shadow of the ground. There was a strange silver sheen to the surface, as if it was lit by reflected light from an impossible moon. Francine wondered if this was a bleedover from some weird kind of Greenie ECM.

The sensors picked up heat signatures indicating a main engine burn by the two missiles as they fought to regain lost altitude. Francine was betting that they'd loop over before making another attack run.

She cut the turbines to make an IR lock just that little bit harder and used the gyros to lift the nose again. The jet picked up some chop falling tail first like that, even in the thin atmosphere. She sure hoped the missiles were using pattern recognition; if they were this should confuse the hell out of them.

They were coming round again, locked on to the jet and screaming down at full burn. Francine was aiming for as close to a right angle to the surface as possible.

It became another race, this one to see which hit her first, the missiles or the ground. Francine refired the turbines and put them on idle.

At two hundred metres altitude Francine redlined the turbines, pushing them all the way past safety. The world came down on top of her as the jet decelerated. The missiles screamed past, heading straight down. There were two brief splashes of light on the rear-facing look-down imager.

Smart weapons, thought Francine. Just another military oxymoron.

'Angel – break left.' Flash Harry yelling in her earphones.

Without thinking Francine threw the jet over. *Sneak missile*, a third Vulture running quiet, relying on the telemetry from the other two missiles. Making a leisurely loop to fly right up her tailpipe.

The radar-proximity fuse mounted in the missile's nose behind the avionics saw the jet in its kill radius and fired. A shaped charge of flaked Brazilian TNT exploded. Thirty-three marble-sized bomblets were blasted forward in an expanding cone.

The aft quarter thermal imager on the jet flared out with the explosion. Francine felt the airframe shudder as three of the bomblets ripped through its carbon-fibre skin. The starboard turbine rev rate shot up as fragments of its shattered blades spewed out the exhaust outlet. Francine shut it down with a mental impulse while another part of her mind assessed damage to the fuel tanks and tailplane servos.

Without the starboard engine Francine was looking at a glide landing in a near vacuum. She put the nose at twenty degrees above level and expanded the stubby wings to maximum. Trying to use the wedge-shaped airframe as a single aerofoil. She made a slow bank until the Jacksonville beacon was dead ahead. Easily enough altitude to get there and plenty of time to figure out what she was going to do when she did.

Francine keyed her radio. 'Hey Flash, thanks for the warning.'

Static answered her.
'Flash - this is Angel. Do you copy?'
Nothing. And Francine realized then that Flash Harry was gone, become just another pair of hologram eyes peering out between the bottles of PX beer and moonshine gin.
She got a visual fix on the Jacksonville beacon and corrected her glide path by two degrees.
Olympus Mons lay ahead, silver in the unreal moonlight.

STS Central - Olympus Mons

Ming had Dogface on one of the repeater screens in her office and two Yak Harrises on another. The big holograms above the control pit were showing a lot of weird activity at the far end of the Central Line.
To make things just that little bit more difficult, a drone had cleaned up the office and now she couldn't find anything. Especially the packet of Zap she kept stashed under the throw rug, in case of emergencies.
A third repeater screen was taking telemetry data from Jacksonville Base.
The two Yak Harrises were completely still as the subset personalities ran off on an 'errand'. Dogface didn't look good, his face was pale and strained. Ming reckoned that he couldn't override the medical computer for much longer without doing himself irreparable damage.
Ming never had understood the floozies. Without the engine of ambition they clung to a working-class ethic that had been out of fashion for centuries. Still, it was his funeral.
A fourth repeater screen was taking a security feed from Olympus Mons West. A police drone's fisheyed view of the clean-up operation, images selected according to machine priorities.
'What about the girl?' asked Dogface.
'She's on her way up,' said Ming. 'With an escort.'
'I heard she greased two of those creatures.'
'And half a train,' said Ming. 'Blondie's got a couple of drones trying to reopen the line.'
'And Francine?'
'Still approaching Jacksonville.'
'What are they saying?'

'That in about ten minutes the V Soc's going to be looking for a new godmother.'

'The Doctor, Kadiatu?'

'On board the jet as well,' said Ming.

'Francine's a good pilot . . .'

'Forget it, Dogface,' said Ming. 'Jacksonville says she's coming down on manual with no exterior sensors and half a turbine. If she could see, maybe. Blind, no chance.'

Olympus Mons

The forward monitor was covered in static. The Doctor's faceplate had snapped down automatically as soon as the cabin filled with smoke. The HUD projected on the inside informed him that the surrounding atmosphere was almost pure halogen. He presumed it was a fire-suppression measure. That or the humans were getting creative with their materials technology again.

He risked a cautious glance over at Kadiatu. Turning his head could be fatal if Francine pulled another twelve-G turn. It was difficult to tell if she was all right with the faceplate down but the status lights on the suit were unchanged. She was lying still in the embrace of the ejection seat, possibly unconscious.

The Doctor settled his head back on to the headrest and tried to feel what was going on. That they'd been involved in a dogfight was obvious from the violent manoeuvres; that they'd been hit was also self-evident. Francine had remained ominously silent since the combat began and the Doctor didn't want to distract her.

Do not talk to driver while bus is moving, thought the Doctor. Sound advice.

The smoke was clearing from the cabin. Judging from the subsonic vibrations he could feel through the headrest, they were missing an engine.

This cabin has a bad attitude, thought the Doctor. About twenty degrees nose up and we're descending. Definitely a glide landing.

'If I should die,' said the Doctor, 'think only this of me, that there is a corner of a foreign field that is forever Gallifrey.'

He calculated the probable impact velocity.

'All right then,' he said, 'a very large corner of a foreign field.'

To take his mind off the danger the Doctor started a mental list of the hardware he'd caused to be destroyed since he arrived. He used a weighted points system, since he was unsure of the exact monetary value. He wondered whether to include the wrecked dustkart. Normally companions only contributed half scores, but did the ersatz Bernice count?

He hummed something appropriate and calculated what he'd get for a really spectacular plane crash. He always gave himself bonus points for those.

'What's that noise?' asked Kadiatu.

'Edith Piaf,' said the Doctor. *'Born on a doorstep and sang the blues.'*

'I'd sing the blues,' said Kadiatu, *'if I'd been born on a doorstep. What's the song about?'*

'Regret.'

'What did she regret?'

'Absolutely nothing,' said the Doctor.

They hit the ground.

The crash unfolded with agonizing slowness, he could have done without that. They were slammed forward in the harness and the cabin slammed flat. There was the sharp rending sound that a sheet of carbon fibre makes when you rip it in half. There was a moment of weightlessness as the jet bounced and then went back to the serious business of tearing itself apart. Rents appeared in the cabin's port wall. Through the hole the Doctor watched in astonishment as sheets of spray rushed past. Torque forces shoved him sideways as the jet slewed to the right. The final impact with the crash barrier was almost gentle.

It had to be worth thirty-six points at least, thought the Doctor, more if we landed on something expensive.

He looked at Kadiatu who looked back at him.

'Whose doorstep was it anyway?' asked Kadiatu.

'I have no idea,' said the Doctor.

It took the Jacksonville emergency crew fifteen minutes to cut them out. A couple of paramedics climbed in first to run a quick diagnostic on their suits. Satisfied that neither of them was going to decompress, the paramedics allowed them up.

As he was helped out the Doctor got his chance to look at the crash site. Jacksonville had laid down two kilometres of compression foam and the jet had skidded along its whole length, leaving a significant percentage of itself behind. The Doctor could see part of the tail assembly two hundred metres back, protruding from the foam like a shark's fin.

'How's the pilot?' he asked.

'She's alive,' said one of the paramedics, politely waving to indicate that she was talking. Her suit had a major's flash on the left breast. *'But we can't cut into the canopy without compromising her life support. We're bringing up a gantry to take it out in one piece.'*

There was a military ambulance waiting, built along the same lines as the dustkart. The major accompanied them into the rear airlock. Once the pressure had normalized she took her helmet off to reveal scarification patterns on her high Yoruba cheekbones.

Kadiatu started to struggle with her helmet but the major restrained her with a hand on her arm. 'Emergency seals,' she said. 'We'll have to cut it off.'

The inner airlock door slid open. There were two more paramedics in army fatigues waiting inside. The major got them to sit down on a pair of reclining couches and pulled on a headphone set. 'All right, Muller, back to base,' she said. 'But take it easy this time.'

He felt the ambulance pull smoothly away.

'Bavarians,' said the major, 'always in a rush.'

The paramedics used calibrated laser scalpels to cut away the helmet seals.

'That was some landing,' said the major. She was smiling but her eyes were tense as they started easing the helmets off.

Perhaps she's worried that our heads will come off as well, thought the Doctor. He felt cool air on his face. 'See,' he said, 'it's still attached to my shoulders.'

'Planning in depth,' said Kadiatu. 'My sacred backside.' Kadiatu's face was puffed and swollen by G trauma. Dark bruises surrounded her eyes, giving them a sleepy look. She looked at the Doctor. 'You look like a big bruise,' she said.

The major gave them each a squeezy bottle of orange juice with strict instructions to take small sips only as their suits were cut away. The major was a bit surprised to find the Doctor dressed in his street clothes underneath.

'I was in a hurry,' explained the Doctor.

Kadiatu laughed and then winced. 'That hurts,' she said. The paramedics cut away her undersuit to reveal swollen welts around her shoulders, neck and in a line down her front where the fastenings had cut in. At twelve Gs even the weight of your clothes can cause severe bruising.

'All my clothes are back in the dustkart,' said Kadiatu. She leaned forward to let them peel the undersuit off her back. There were vertical welts down her shoulder blades. 'Which is all your fault.'

The Doctor watched as the muscles moved under her skin. The Gallifreyans once looked like that, thought the Doctor, when the world was young.

'What about you?' the major asked the Doctor.

'I'm fine,' he said. 'Trust me.'

The major hesitated for a moment before nodding. She pulled a handscan from a niche in the equipment rack and ran it over the Doctor's body. He waited for the inevitable questions, but they never came. Instead the major shunted the results to a portable monitor and showed it to him.

'That normal for you?' she asked.

'Yes,' he said. I'm getting far too well known on this planet, thought the Doctor. He might have to do something about that soon, real soon.

The major ran the handscan over Kadiatu, starting with her feet. 'Bruising,' she told the paramedic, 'bruising, contusion, get some jam on that.' The paramedic gently applied a clear gel to the welts around Kadiatu's hips and thighs. The major continued scanning. 'No internal damage to the uterus, enlarged vermiform appendix but no sign of infection so I guess that's normal, large liver.' The major smiled at Kadiatu. 'You've got a big heart and lungs. How long can you hold your breath?'

'Never timed myself,' said Kadiatu.

'Sports?'

Kadiatu shook her head.

'Ever break any bones?'

'No.'

'Ever been sick?'

'No,' said Kadiatu. 'You're the first doctor ever gave me a scan.'

The major held the handscan over Kadiatu's head for a long time, staring at the monitor.

'Something wrong?' asked Kadiatu.

'No,' said the major. 'You've got a thick skull so it takes a while to build up a picture.'

From where he was the Doctor could see the monitor for himself.

Kadiatu did have a thick skull and a lot more besides.

STS Central – Olympus Mons

'Like that,' said Zamina, 'except with narrower lips.' The videofit face on the screen altered slightly but the nose was still wrong. 'Shorter nose,' said Zamina.

Across the office the Chinese woman who seemed to be in charge was talking on the phone to the ugliest man she'd ever seen. They were using a lot of technical jargon that Zamina didn't understand.

The gist of it was that a jet had crashed-landed at Jacksonville and all the passengers had survived. Something that the woman and the ugly man had trouble believing.

The Chinese woman looked over at Zamina. 'Have you finished yet?' she asked.

'Nearly.'

The woman came and looked over her shoulder. 'Good enough,' she said. Zamina didn't like her. The first thing she'd said when Zamina was shown in was, 'Gods Girl, you want to get them tits fixed sometime.'

Zamina didn't like people she didn't know calling her girl. The woman had style though; when she talked people listened.

'What's this for?'

'You know what pattern recognition is?'

'Course.'

'We'll feed this image into the monitoring system and it should be able to track your friend for us.'

'She's not my friend,' said Zamina. 'I don't think she's anybody's friend really.'

'I wish you'd tell the Doctor that,' said the woman.

Jacksonville

Kadiatu managed a quick shower at the officers' mess. The

major lent her some of her off-duty clothes. The selection left Kadiatu wondering what the major must look like out on the town. A pair of red 680s were too tight but serviceable and the only top that fitted her was a luminous canary yellow lurex skintight with EAT FISH AND DIE heat-printed across the chest. The major rustled up a pair of ankle-height service boots from base stores. They were made from soft elephant leather with airwear soles. Kadiatu had to sit down to do up the double fasteners.

The major held out a shoulder holster. Kadiatu stared at it for a moment and then raised her arms so that the major could buckle it on. It was a woman's holster, hanging low so that the gun wouldn't catch on her breast when she drew. When the major leaned forward to reach around Kadiatu's back she saw that raised scars on her face were tinted umber and turquoise.

'What's this for?' asked Kadiatu.

'We found the laser torch in your suit pocket,' said the major. 'It was set on a killing frequency but the batteries were nearly exhausted.' The major opened a ribbed metal case and drew out a pistol. 'One megawatt point zero one-second burst,' she said, 'does six hundred bursts a minute on full auto, but your charge's only good for a hundred, so keep it on single.'

She handed the pistol over and Kadiatu felt the weight settle in her palm. In a single unthinking movement she flipped the gun and slipped it into the holster.

'You've used one before,' said the major.

'It's illegal for me to carry this,' said Kadiatu.

'What does that matter?' said the major. 'You're with *him.*'

'Maybe, but do the police know that?' asked Kadiatu.

'Turn around,' said the major.

'What?'

'Your hair,' said the major. 'Turn around.'

Kadiatu turned round and the major seized her extensions and started to braid them. She kept the tension up, pulling hair and scalp back from the face. Kadiatu remembered her mother pulling tight when she was young, hard enough to fold the scalp in places. While the major worked she spoke in Kadiatu's ear.

'He strikes a stone in the forest,' she chanted, 'stone bleeds blood. He dances savagely in the courtyard of the impertinent. He sets the liar's roof on fire.'

'Who is he?'

'He is the leopard with flaming eyes.'

'Who is he?'

'He is in the discharge of a laser, in the lightning flash of the semiconductor.'

'Tell me his name?'

'He is the bow wave across the ocean of time.'

'His name!'

'He is Shango, god of lightning,' said the major.

'All things to all cultures,' said Kadiatu.

'Stand up,' said the major.

Kadiatu checked in the mirror. Her hair was tied into a severe series of bundled plaits that rested on the nape of her neck. Hair was important to the Yoruba – how they wore it was once a matter of social importance – but this style was severely practical. It kept the hair out of the eyes and protected the vulnerable portion of the neck.

Fighting style, her mother would have called it.

The major gave Kadiatu a leather jacket that clinked when it brushed against a locker.

'Kevlar lining,' said the major.

'He's not a god,' said Kadiatu.

'His temples are the preserve of priestesses,' said the major. 'It's women who dance for the Lightning God. His spirit possesses them through the dance.'

'Why me?'

'Don't ask me that,' said the major. 'Ask the dead.'

Acturus Station (Stunnel Terminus)

The other floozies reminded Blondie that as the youngest he was still honorary dogsbody and sent him off to get food. He didn't mind, it beat welding the barricades together.

They'd all pulled in at least two drones to do the work. When he saw them collected all in one place Blondie realized that over the years more than just the drones' personalities had been taken from their operators. Credit Card's drones were so customized that it was almost impossible to determine the original make. Honda perhaps, from the early 2000 series, but Blondie wouldn't bet money on it.

Lambada's drones were painted a rainforest green and were,

well, *aggressive*. They had to be segregated from the Dogface drones or they spent more time fighting than working.

Old Sam's drones were barely visible, backgrounds sliding across mimetic polycarbon shells. Tools and manipulators emerging from jack turrets when they worked. The drones had more hatches than tools and Blondie wondered what was hidden behind the spares. Maybe they should have brought in a few more of those.

Blondie felt that he should do something about his own unfashionably pristine units. He considered painting a black rose on their flanks. Would she understand that? he asked himself. Would she approve? More importantly: would she notice?

The KGB went in for on-site catering, a portable canteen was set up in one corner of the galleria. Old Sam didn't approve; he'd have been happier if the KGB troops had been eating vacuum-packed E-rations. Preferably tearing the foil packages open with their teeth. He called them a bunch of FNGs and didn't rate their chances in a real fight.

Blondie didn't think they looked that bad; certainly their hardware was impressive. Some of the troopers turned to watch him as he picked his way over to the canteen. They were field stripping their pulse rifles, neat rows of components laid out on white linen sheets. A collection of faces above the raised neck guards of their armour.

The canteen was the size of a commercial freight module, the kind that fit on a transit flatbed. When mobile it ran on small rubber wheels, half a dozen on each side, now locked into their up position. A fold-down counter ran a third of its length.

Blondie bought four big bucket meals from a European Muslim woman. Two for him, Credit Card and Lambada, and two for Old Sam. The Muslim woman processed his moneypen and handed over the litre-capacity buckets. Blondie thought she might have smiled at him but under the veil it was hard to tell.

'Have a nice day,' said the woman.

STS Central – Olympus Mons

'There she is,' said Zamina pointing.

The screen showed the view from a scanning security camera on the TransOlympia platform at Olympus Mons. Benny was clearly visible alighting from a train, a pink found icon hovering over her head. The data square in the right-hand corner of the screen put the time at 11:45 GMT, five minutes past.

Ming looked over at Dogface. 'Got that?'

'Where's she going?' asked Zamina.

The internal phone chimed. It was the sector manager from the pit. 'Yes?' said Ming.

'We've got a problem,' said the manager. 'Half the trains in the northeastern sector have stopped.'

'Technical fault?' asked Ming.

'Signalling failure,' said the manager.

Ming put the sector up on her big repeater screen. The affected area formed a rough semicircle around the Acturus Station.

'Work on it,' Ming told the manager and cut the link. 'Do you see it, Dogface?'

'I see it.'

'What do you think?'

'I think someone's fucking with our signalling,' said Dogface.

Ming linked back with the sector manager. 'Try back-up,' she said. 'If that doesn't work go to manual, keep at least some of the trains running.'

'There she is again,' said Zamina. Live feed from a camera in the Rancher's Market area. 'Hey,' said Zamina, 'I've worked that place. It's only six levels down.'

Ming turned to her phone and punched in the direct line to the Nueva Lubyanka. 'KGB,' said their reception program in an unnaturally bright voice, 'Sword and Shield to the people since Nineteen Seventeen.'

'This is Ming, armed response team to Rancher's Market . . .'

'She's gone into a lift,' said Zamina.

'Fugitive now in one of the passenger lifts,' said Ming. 'I'm downloading the likeness.' She pressed a button and shot the videofit image to Nueva Lubyanka. 'Down or up?' she asked Zamina.

'Down.'

'She's going for Fusion Corp,' said Dogface.

'You must contact the Doctor,' said one of the Yak Harrises.

'You're back,' said Ming. 'You call him.'

'There have been difficulties,' said the construct.

'Isn't that Yak Harris?' said Zamina.

'No,' said Ming, 'it's *a* Yak Harris.'
'You must contact the Doctor.'
'I'm on it,' said Ming, raising Jacksonville. 'Give me a break.'
The Doctor wasn't at Jacksonville, but Ming managed to trace him to a VIP shuttle on its way to Olympus Mons. Kadiatu answered the phone.
'Benny's back,' said Ming, 'and heading straight for Fusion Corp.'
'He's way ahead of you,' said Kadiatu. 'That's where we're going.'
There was a squawk from the Yak Harris monitor.
'Hey people,' said one of the Yak Harrises, 'I think you've been compromised.'
The monitor screen imploded.
The Doctor appeared on the phone. 'It's penetrated your computer network. It'll try to prevent anyone getting to the Stunnel gateway.'
'You were expecting this?'
'I suspected it.'
'Well, thanks for telling me.'
'I can't be everywhere at once.' The Doctor looked out of shot. 'This is our stop. Whatever you do don't panic.' The link terminated.
Out in the control room the big holograms derezzed into clouds of silver static.
'That's easy for you to say,' said Ming.

Fusion Corp – Olympus Mons

'Have you noticed,' said the Doctor, 'how much time we've spent in lifts recently?' He kept his eyes fixed on the level indicator.
'Back there,' said Kadiatu, 'the major seemed to think you were Shango.'
'Who's Shango?'
'Yoruba thunder god.'
'Oh, *Shango*,' said the Doctor. 'Did you know the Yoruba have over two hundred deities?'
'Are you?'
'Mind you, Shintoism has thousands.' The Doctor turned to look at her. 'Do I look like a thunder god?'

'How would I know?' said Kadiatu. 'I've never met one.'

'Faced with the unexplained,' said the Doctor, 'people have a tendency to let their imaginations run wild. There are no gods. I should know, I've met a few.'

'The Shango cult is almost exclusively female.'

'People get the wrong end of the stick.'

'I'll bet.'

'It's true,' said the Doctor. 'I was in Ife during the tenth century and there may have been some static electricity involved. I was also in Mesopotamia in the time of Gilgamesh and I've visited all three Atlantises. It's not my fault. It's the planet, things happen there.'

'Why?'

'I don't know,' said the Doctor. 'Your planet just seems to be a major time-space nexus.'

'Lucky us,' said Kadiatu.

She realized that the Doctor was staring intently at her.

'Shadows,' he said, 'forced evolution. Spirits, demons, gods. Coincidences. I'm missing something. Do you dream?'

'Of course I dream, everybody does.'

'Your father didn't,' said the Doctor. 'Any that reoccur?'

'Some,' said Kadiatu, 'when I'm stressed out.'

'Describe one.'

'Beach,' said Kadiatu, 'dead people dancing.'

'No, not that one.'

'I can't remember any of the other ones.'

'Look at me,' said the Doctor.

Kadiatu looked into his strange eyes.

'Basket,' she heard herself say. 'Old woman in a basket over a big pit. Something's wrong with her eye. I think she's a witch.'

'Does she say anything?'

'She's cursing, about children, it's a *bad* curse.'

'Then what?'

'She cuts the rope that's holding the basket up and falls into the pit.'

The Doctor clicked his fingers. 'The Pythia,' he said. 'Interesting. You and I might have more in common than I first thought.'

'Who's the Pythia?'

'The ancient line of seeresses who once ruled my home planet

Gallifrey. When the last of the line was overthrown she cursed the entire population of Gallifrey to perpetual sterility. No children. Ever.'

'Has this got anything to do with the transit system?'

'Nothing at all,' said the Doctor, 'for which we should be profoundly grateful.'

'Then why's it so important?'

'Have you any idea what kind of power a curse like that represents?' asked the Doctor. 'It creates shock waves and patterns within the metafabric of the space-time continuum. The procreative impulse of an entire species can't just dissipate, it has to go somewhere. It must have been channelled by the Pythia's curse, and she knew we were in contact.'

'Knew what?'

'Something I forgot a long time ago.'

'What, for God's sake?'

'I don't know,' said the Doctor. 'I forgot it, didn't I?'

The lift stopped and its doors opened. In the distance they could hear a siren wailing.

'Too late,' said the Doctor.

'Where the hell are you going?' asked the technician.

Benny flexed her wrist back and shot him through the chest.

The power plant had maroon carpeting and cream walls hung with framed abstract paintings at regular intervals. The thick shag absorbed any ambient noise and produced a kind of breathless hush. There had always been debate about the iconography relating to fusion power plants in the pre-expansion era.

Benny followed the signs to the control centre.

The decor was obviously designed to be as calming as possible. This hinted at a deep-seated anxiety about the forces they were unleashing within the generator.

The corridor opened into an informal refreshment area. A cluster of easy chairs and sofas were centred around a free-standing entertainment console. A couple were sitting on a sofa watching television, a man was in the kitchen area pouring himself a coffee from a stainless steel jug. Benny shot him first. The jug made a hollow ringing sound when it bounced on the counter top.

The situational realists maintained that the period's apprehension about their power systems stemmed from the primitive safety standards. Benny herself had defended that position during a drunken argument that followed a conference at the Institute of Human Ecology on Cygni VI.

One of the couple on the sofa made the mistake of standing up to see what was happening. The shell blew the top of her head off.

The Silurians felt that it was the manifestation of humanity's deep-seated guilt complex about their ruthless exploitation of the homeworld. But then, the Silurians said that about everything.

The remaining woman on the sofa was a bit more experienced and rolled out of Benny's line of fire. The first shot blew a fist-sized hole in an easy chair.

Benny had read a paper that attributed it to the upheavals following the first ecological crisis. She'd read it because it came at the extreme end of her own period. The title had been *The Role of the Butler Institute in the Terran Post-Nuclear Period.*

The woman tried to scramble behind the entertainment console. Benny stepped to one side and shot her in the back before she could get up.

She couldn't remember who wrote the paper.

The control room was protected by double doors of plexiglass. Through them she could see the technicians panicking at her approach. One of them was talking urgently into a phone, someone was shouting, she could hear it as a murmur through the doors.

Professor Beal-Carter-Kzanski, she remembered, that's who'd written the paper. She'd read it while travelling middle berth to Heaven; she usually caught up with the journals in transit. There had been some interesting stuff about youth gangs and eco-terrorists.

Benny didn't bother with the nine-digit security keypad by the doors. She just stood there and waited patiently for them to open of their own accord. There was a high-pitched sound filtering through the sound-proofed doors.

Inside the control room someone was screaming.

* * *

Kadiatu pulled the pistol from the holster after they encountered the first body. The Doctor gave her a hard look but said nothing: what could he say?

There were more bodies in a small refreshment area. Kadiatu recognized the signature of the exit wounds, the way the ragged edges of the wound pushed through rents torn in the clothes. She concentrated hard on the injuries to avoid looking at the people. There was a strong smell of cordite, blood and coffee.

The Doctor picked up the fallen coffee jug and set it carefully back on the counter.

Kadiatu zipped the major's jacket up to her neck.

The Doctor pointed down the corridor and opened his mouth to say something.

The jacket saved Kadiatu's life.

The kinetic energy of the soft-nosed slug was dissipated by the flexible sheet of kevlar sewn into the lining of the jacket. Enough to stop the projectile from blowing out her chest but not enough to stop her from being smashed forward into the Doctor's arms.

The Doctor grabbed the collar of her jacket in his left hand and pulled her further off balance. Kadiatu instinctively realized what he was doing and let herself be spun round as her forward momentum was translated around the pivot of his arm.

As she turned she saw the coffee jug leave his right hand and fly across the room. He must have picked it up in the same moment as their attacker fired the first shot.

The jug bounced off the attacker's face with a hollow bong sound and a spurt of blood. Her hand came up to cover her nose.

'Not again,' said Benny.

Kadiatu shot her, three bursts, vaporized flesh blooming like pink carnations on Benny's chest. The Doctor was by her side before she hit the ground.

'Where's the real Benny?' he asked.

The woman made a weak gurgling sound, laughing. There were three ice-cream-scoop-sized craters in her upper ribcage. Kadiatu couldn't believe she was still alive.

'Actually, I thought I was the real Benny,' whispered the ersatz Benny. The eyes flickered in Kadiatu's direction. 'This one's good, isn't she? Doesn't hesitate.'

'Very good,' said the Doctor.

'Too good for you,' said the ersatz Benny.

'She's not mine,' said the Doctor. 'She belongs to herself.'

The woman made that sick gurgling laugh again. 'A time-travelling archaeologist,' she said. 'I must have been out of my mind.'

They waited but there was nothing else.

'I'm fine, just some major bruising on my back,' said Kadiatu as the Doctor stalked off towards the control room. 'Don't worry about me.'

The ersatz Benny twitched and made coughing noises. Kadiatu turned back, her pistol held ready.

'Listen,' it said, 'a word from the freshly dead.'

'Go on,' said Kadiatu.

'Evolution,' it said, 'is the response by living organisms to their environment.'

'In one respect,' said Kadiatu.

'Don't argue with the dead, girl,' it said. '*He's* become a major factor in that environment. You are the human response to *him*.'

Kadiatu realized that the ersatz Benny's lips weren't moving when she spoke, hadn't moved since the Doctor had left.

'Which is the more dangerous, girl,' it asked, 'the male or female leopard?'

'The female,' said Kadiatu.

'Why?'

'Her children,' said Kadiatu. 'Her children make her dangerous.'

'What will you sacrifice for the children?'

Kadiatu scrambled backwards. For a moment she thought she saw tears of fire well up around the ersatz Benny's left eye, an eye that had become alien in colour and full of secrets. Then eye, face and neck were obliterated by the bursts of coherent light from her gun.

'Stop wasting ammunition,' said the Doctor.

'Did you hear that?' asked Kadiatu.

'Hear what?'

'Nothing,' said Kadiatu.

'Then I couldn't have heard it,' said the Doctor, 'could I?'

Kadiatu followed him out.

'What's the best route from here to the Stunnel terminus?' he asked.

'The Central Line extension runs straight to it,' said Kadiatu. 'There's a station four levels up from here. Did she sabotage the power plant.'

'Worse than that,' said the Doctor.

Acturus Station (Stunnel Terminus)

Lambada dropped her Big Chicken Bit on to the floor when she saw it.

'Shit,' she said.

'It's not that bad,' said Old Sam, 'a bit overseasoned though.'

'The power feed,' she said.

On the monitor the line marking the power feeding into the Stunnel gateway from their side had suddenly started climbing. It now matched the power input from the *other side*.

'Tell Ming,' said Lambada. 'She's got to shut it down.'

'We lost the link with Ming,' said Credit Card. 'About fifteen minutes ago.'

'They still have to come down here and switch the thing on,' said Old Sam.

'Yeah,' said Lambada, 'but now that's *all* they have to do.'

'Whoever they are,' said Credit Card.

'We know who they are,' said Blondie. 'Cake-eating free-surfers from hell.'

'That's a great comfort,' said Lambada.

'You want that Big Chicken Bit or not?' asked Old Sam.

Olympus Mons (Central Line)

There were two cake monsters waiting on the platform. They stood chatting to each other just like normal people. One of them was holding a freesurfing board. Kadiatu ducked back into the entranceway and told the Doctor.

'Reinforcements,' said the Doctor. 'Just in case the fake Benny didn't make it.'

'When you plan,' said Kadiatu, 'plan in depth.'

'Get rid of them,' said the Doctor.

'What, just shoot them?' asked Kadiatu.

'Yes,' said the Doctor, 'shoot them.'

'What happened to the sanctity of life?'

'It just got filed under D for desperate expediency.'

'Just checking.'

Kadiatu stepped round the corner and opened fire. She kept firing until both cake monsters stopped moving. By the time she'd finished the pistol's charge LED was flashing.

'I need a bigger gun,' said Kadiatu.

'What for?' asked the Doctor. 'Dead is dead.'

'But not fast enough.'

'We need a train,' said the Doctor.

The destination indicator was blank.

'Typical,' said the Doctor. 'You wait ages for a train and then three come at once.'

'I doubt that,' said Kadiatu. The STS map was showing a large swath of black lines in the northern Mars area. Black for *no service*. 'Someone doesn't want us to get there.'

'I'll use the board,' said the Doctor, running down the platform.

'No,' shouted Kadiatu. 'You'll kill yourself.'

The Doctor scooped up the board in one fluid motion and ran faster. 'A coward dies many times before his death,' said the Doctor.

'This is no time for Shakespeare,' said Kadiatu, starting after him. 'It takes two to freesurf.'

'No, it doesn't,' said the Doctor and threw the board on to the friction field. 'You just think it does.' He jumped on to the board.

Kadiatu ran parallel to him as the board coasted towards the tunnel gateway. 'We can get a train.'

'Too late,' said the Doctor. 'We're in the end game now, the queen has defected, the knights are in trouble and the king's out of position.'

'What are you going to do?'

'Do?' said the Doctor. 'I'm going to improvise.'

8:

Improvisations

STS Central – Olympus Mons

The pain was his friend, keeping him alert in the face of the drugs. Dogface had overridden the medical expert system that stood by the all-body brace, to reduce the doses, but he was frightened of going too far. He could feel his central nervous system wavering back and forth between agony and euphoria. As he tried to concentrate on monitoring the network, his thoughts would veer away in unexpected directions. Accelerating into bands of bright primary colour or crashing through walls of glass into diamond studded darkness once the network had shrunk down to a spider's web of glittering lines that he felt he could hold in the palm of his hand. It was a tremendous high but he doubted that it would catch on.

The equipment was too expensive, for one thing.

When the systems crash blacked out the control room he managed to get some data by bypassing the main signalling subsystem and routing through one of the TV channels. He chose Welsh 12 because he figured no one watched it, not even the Welsh. He'd tried shunting the feed up to the control room but he kept running into blocks. Someone had deliberately isolated STS Central's command network.

Jacked in through the plug in his index finger Dogface could feel the whole network running down. Trains were halting by platforms as onboard emergency systems shut down in response to the loss of power. Back-up power generators at isolated stations came online like little novas. The daily commuter scramble that usually ran ahead of the dateline on Terra toppled over like a breaking wave and became a wash of stranded individuals.

He wondered if he was watching the end of civilization.

There were things moving about in the system. Dogface could track them by the spikes in the power lines. Some he thought must be the virus program, others various subsets of the network intelligence. Most were converging on Acturus Terminal and the Stunnel gateway.

There was activity at the other end of the system too, at Lowell Depot. His own drones were involved in it somehow. He felt he might have authorized their use to Yak Harris but he couldn't remember.

A voice called his name in perfect Mandarin.

A Chinese princess stood by his brace, beautiful in a silk shamfoo embroidered with twisting dragons in silver thread.

Yang Chou, she called him, using his given name, one he hadn't heard since the war. When he looked closely there was a nimbus of light around her perfect face.

'Have you come to take me to heaven?' asked Dogface.

'Fuck no,' said Ming. 'But I wouldn't mind some of whatever it is you're on.'

Ming traced her hand along the top of the expert system; there was a panic button there, a switch to override his override. If she pressed that the expert system would shut him down until he felt better. About a week, Dogface estimated, at least.

'I've got this problem, Yang Chou,' said Ming. 'All the other floozies are over at Acturus Station with half an arsenal, waiting for God knows what to turn up. Now I'm not saying they won't make it, but if they don't I won't have no one to do what I tell them and fix the network. The Sol transit system will collapse, billions will starve and the bottom will fall out of the stock market. Taking my investments with it.'

Ming smiled down at him and Dogface saw for the first time ever that Ming really was a princess.

'Somebody has to live,' said Ming. 'And that somebody is you.' She pressed the panic button.

Dogface felt himself sink into the waters of oblivion.

Lowell Depot

Achmed had just managed to sit down when Deirdre called him. He'd propped himself against a wall in the freight depot and watched the military load up their hardware on to the flatbeds. The military, the NGOs and the police were pulling out of the Stop. A captain from the project police had briefed him on contingency plans in case of stragglers. The captain had scraped-back hair and tired eyes. Achmed's foreman brought them glasses of sweet tea and they'd gone over the whiteprints together. Achmed was a great believer in gathering local knowledge before he started a job.

The captain left along with the last contingent of police leaving Achmed and his team alone in the deserted projects. At least Achmed hoped they were alone. Just in case he made sure that his people worked in pairs, fanning out into the projects with the survey-drones. Their job was to take precise structural measurements and compare them to the whiteprints stored in Achmed's portable console.

He usually used this lull to collect his thoughts before tackling any problems. A couple of moments now could save him hours even days later. And as his wife Ming always said, 'time is money and sleep an investment.'

The communicator pinned into the lapel of his kaftan beeped. It was Deirdre his shift supervisor.

'Yes?'

'Boss,' said Deirdre, *'I think you'd better come and have a look at something.'*

'What is it?'

'I don't know,' said Deirdre.

That worried Achmed. Deirdre considered herself the real driving force within the company and affected to regard Achmed as an overpaid supernumerary who was only kept on because he was co-married to the chairman's wife. If Deirdre was passing the buck upwards then it had to be serious.

'Where are you?' asked Achmed.

'The main passenger platform.'

'I'm on my way.'

Achmed got to his feet and walked up the narrow connecting corridor to the passenger platforms. One of his crew had wedged the security door open with a block of wood.

Deirdre met him on the other side, a small bulky woman wearing baggy rhino-hide dungarees and a New Jamaica T-shirt that was pulled tight around her heavy breasts. She pointed down the platform.

'Who authorized that?' asked Achmed.

The ugliest tank engine he'd ever seen was standing at the platform.

'Not me, Boss,' said Deirdre. 'I tried contacting STS Central but the link's dead.'

A freshly welded patch covered most of the nose, including the forward windscreen. It gave the engine a blind stupid look.

'Anyone get out?'

'Not yet,' said Deirdre.

'Did you look inside?'

'I thought I'd call you first.'

'There might be people inside,' said Achmed. 'They could be hurt.'

'After you, Boss,' said Deirdre.

The tank engine had another fresh patch where the emergency cabin door should have been. Achmed peered into the cabin through the one unbroken window.

'What can you see?' called Deirdre, who'd stayed at the end of the platform. 'Is there anyone in there?'

'I can't see anyone, but it's pretty messed up in there,' said Achmed. Most of the cabin instrumentation was dead, there was what might have been evidence of small arms damage.

'What are you waiting for?' he called to Deirdre.

'No way I'm going anywhere near that thing,' Deirdre shouted back. 'I've heard stories.'

'What kind of stories?'

'Ghost stories,' said Deirdre, 'about the black train.'

'Since when?'

'Since yesterday,' said Deirdre.

That's always been the problem with information technology, thought Achmed, instant myths.

There was a hiss from the rear section of the tank engine and its big cargo doors swung outwards. Achmed took a couple of steps backwards, just in case.

A drone came through the open doors at chest height, with a thousand-metre drum of electrical cable suspended from its belly mandibles. Three more drones followed, each carrying crates of heavy equipment. Deirdre jumped quickly out of the way as they whirred up the platform towards her.

The cargo doors swung shut and the tank engine's turbine coughed into life. Achmed heard it cycle up to half power and watched as the tank engine reversed out of the station. He turned and ran after the drones.

'Come on,' he told Deirdre as he passed her.

The first drone stopped at the crash barrier, it was unpacking its crates with its forward arms. The front end of a hologram projector was beginning to emerge from one of the crates. It was a big one, the kind used for stadiums.

'Hey, drone,' said Achmed, 'what are you doing?'

The drone ignored him and extended manipulators with waldos as fine as human hair. Achmed looked for identification flashes and saw a row of pictograms spaced along its access panel.

'Korean,' said Deirdre.

'What do they say?'

'It's the gardener, from Pei Hai park,' said Deirdre.

'It's a long way from the Forbidden City,' said Achmed. 'Where did the others go?'

'Into the hole at the end of the station.'

Achmed walked over and looked into the hole. The electrical cable had been laid along the left wall, held against the rock with hooped steel staples at three-metre intervals.

'What's the loading on a cable like that?' asked Achmed.

'About a gigawatt,' said Deirdre, 'at least.'

'I knew that,' said Achmed. 'I just wanted to be sure that you knew that.'

They followed the cable into the hole. Deirdre pulled a billy lamp and gave the passage a professional once-over. 'This should have collapsed,' she said. 'I wonder what's holding it up.'

There were duckboard ramps laid over the vertical maintenance shafts that bisected the hole. Deirdre let Achmed cross them first, to test the weight she said.

'I knew this was going to be a bad week,' said Achmed, 'when I heard the President was dead.'

'The President's dead?' asked Deirdre.

'You didn't know?'

'I don't keep track of politics,' said Deirdre.

'Don't you watch TV, read a fax?'

'What for?' asked Deirdre. 'I've got better things to do with my spare time than read fax.'

'To learn important things,' said Achmed, 'like the President being killed.'

'I didn't vote for him,' said Deirdre.

The power cable came to an end in a mess of equipment that stood in the centre of a natural cavern. The three remaining drones were clustered around the mess, manipulators working fast enough to blur. An assembly was taking shape between them; at first Achmed thought it was a data-gathering probe but the feed cables were too robust for data transmission. They looked more like the cables you'd use to hook up a big drilling laser.

Beyond the assembly was something like a blue door set into the cavern wall. There was white lettering above the door which said 'POLICE BOX' in English. The business end of the assembly was definitely aimed directly at the door.

The important question, Achmed realized, was which way would the power go? Would the assembly collect power from the doorway or would it be pumped at it? Whichever way it went, judging from the insulation, it was going to be in the megawatt range.

'What the hell is this supposed to be?' asked Deirdre.

'Bad news,' said Achmed. 'Really bad news.'

Acturus Terminal (Stunnel Terminus)

They were watching the sensors go dead along the Central Line one by one.

'Christ in a bucket,' said Lambada in admiration, 'that sucker is fast.'

'When they get here,' said Dogface, 'you can ask them how it works.'

'They ain't going to get here,' said Old Sam, 'because I'm going to close down the extension gateway before they do.'

'Can you do that?' asked Blondie.

'I built that gateway, boy,' said Old Sam, 'and I always put in a backdoor override.'

'You shut it down when they're in the tunnel, Sam, and they'll disassociate,' said Credit Card.

'That's what I'm counting on,' said Old Sam.

'There'll be an energy plume,' said Lambada.

'Good,' said Old Sam. 'Then we'll know we got them.'

'Yeah,' said Credit Card. 'We'll be right in front of it.'

'I'm too young to glow in the dark,' said Lambada.

'So we stand either side,' said Old Sam.

'Sounds reasonable,' said Credit Card.

'Only because we've all gone mad,' said Lambada.

'How long have we got?' asked Blondie.

'Ninety seconds,' said Credit Card.

'Everybody take cover,' said Old Sam.

They turned their back on the Central Line gateway and went back to the barricades, each of them walking in as casual manner as possible.

'My contract never said anything about alien monsters,' said Credit Card. 'Standard general maintenance contract, that's what I signed.'

'Mine did,' said Old Sam.

'No shit?'

'Mine had a clause about pest control,' said Lambada. 'What about yours Blondie?'

'I couldn't read mine,' said Blondie, 'the small print was all in Chinese.'

'How long?' asked Lambada.

'Forty-five seconds,' said Credit Card. 'If I'd known this was going to happen I'd have asked for a bonus clause.'

The barricades formed a metre-high semi-circle ten metres out from the Stunnel gateway. There were no gaps so they had to climb over. Old Sam vaulted over in a single fluid movement, body metabolism already accelerating under the influence of a shot of doberman. Lambada hadn't objected this time.

'If I'd known,' said Old Sam, 'I'd have been a watchmaker.'

'A profound statement, Sam,' said Lambada, 'but intrinsically meaningless.'

'Thirty-five,' said Credit Card.

Blondie hunkered down in his assigned place. Old Sam had left a pulse rifle for him, propped up against the barricade. Blondie took the rifle and laid it across his knees.

'Twenty seconds,' said Credit Card.

'I suppose it's too late to put in for some sick leave?' asked Lambada.

'Much too late,' said Old Sam.

Olympus Mons (Central Line)

'KADIATU', the train indicator had said, her name flashing up in half-metre holographic letters thirty seconds after the Doctor had gone.

'What?' she'd screamed down the platform.

'WAIT' said the indicator and she'd waited.

If it mentions making a sacrifice for the children, thought Kadiatu, I'm going to shoot it.

'FAT MAMA 1 min'.

Now it's getting personal, thought Kadiatu.

One minute later a wrecked tank engine pulled into the station, steam leaking from a ruptured cooling valve at the back. The cabin hatch was welded over with a patch but the cargo doors opened when they drew level with Kadiatu.

She looked up at the indicator hologram.

'STRAIGHT TO HELL'.

'Been there,' said Kadiatu as she climbed aboard, 'done that.'

Acturus Terminal (Stunnel Terminus)

The scariest thing was that Blondie could see right through the side of the black train. Through its semi-transparent bulkhead he could make out the shadowy form of dozens of cake monsters curled up on tiers inside.

Old Sam's cut-off hadn't worked, the Central Line gateway had stayed open and the black train had come screaming into the station. No one had a chance to ask Old Sam what had gone wrong because the train had ploughed into the barricades. Blondie didn't see it, but he thought Lambada and Credit Card might have jumped clear in time.

Almost before it stopped the train started to derez, patches of transparency racing across the hull like oil slicks over water. Inside the train the cake monsters were squirming, struggling to get free of the rapidly disintegrating train.

Blondie saw Johny Ray's sweaty face in his mind's eye, freezing up under the violet skies of Mars. Not me, thought Blondie, I ain't no Johny Ray, I'm not the grunt that can't. He snapped the pulse rifle around and emptied a clip into the side of the train.

The bullets ripped through the degenerating hull and exploded amongst the squirming cake monsters, bright flashes throwing up gouts of red and blue.

As if opening fire was a signal Blondie heard the snap of

Old Sam's drones as they detached themselves from the ceiling and the drill sound as they opened up with their miniguns. The roof of the black train was swallowed up in a ripple of yellow explosions, the whole top tier of cake monsters underneath simply disintegrating.

Black greasy smoke boiled upwards and spread across the ceiling. Blondie stopped firing and fumbled for his respirator with his left hand, trying to get it settled over his mouth.

The first shot came out of the smoke and slammed into his chest, knocking him on to his back. The second shot ripped the air over his head. He fired wildly back, the recoil hurting his arms and pushing him along the floor. A wave of grey smoke was rolling over him and through it Blondie could see shadows stalking towards him.

He stayed on his back and changed the rifle clip just in time to shoot a cake monster in the chest as it loomed over him. Then another one running in from his left. Blondie wanted to get up, didn't want to be caught on his back but the cake monsters kept on coming. His world was narrowing down to a one-metre circle of visibility, the shudder of the rifle in his hands and the shapes that came out of the smoke.

A dull roar made Blondie look upwards. Above him an explosion created a bubble of flame in the smoke. He could see half a drone silhouetted by the light. The burning drone seemed to grow larger at an astonishing rate. There was a prickling heat sensation on the exposed skin of his face.

Blondie threw himself to the side, rolling away as the twisted wreck crashed into the floor. A severed manipulator arm gouged a groove just in front of his face and shrapnel clattered off the armour on his back. He felt something take the skin off the back of his left hand.

That was one of Old Sam's, thought Blondie. They shot down one of Old Sam's drones. What are these things?

He realized that he'd lost the pulse rifle and climbed to his knees to look for it but it was useless. The station was completely filled with smoke. To his right the burning drone was a flickering glow; occasionally shadows would flick in front of it. He could hear shots and bangs around him but nothing seemed that close.

Ahead he saw a spinning bronze disk shining through the

smoke: the Stunnel gateway. Crouching low to avoid stray bullets Blondie worked his way towards it. That's what they were supposed to be defending.

He came across the X by accident, stumbling over something soft hidden in the smoke. It was formed out of two strips of fluorescent yellow gaffa tape stuck to the floor. It was right in front of the gateway and about five metres out.

Blondie wondered what it was for.

Central Line

The Doctor had a sinking feeling that Kadiatu might be right. At least about the mechanics of freesurfing and the inadvisability of riding a board alone.

The mental discipline wasn't hard, he adapted an old Gallifreyan flying mantra. The trick was in anticipating the gateways, riding the energy wave front as the board broke through the interface. It wasn't that different from sea surfing. The Doctor wished he'd paid attention when he'd been on that Australian beach.

The problem was that the Doctor had just realized what the second person on a freesurfing board did. They ran a contra-mantra to set up feedback harmonies at the emerging tunnel gateway. In short, the second person handled the brakes.

The Doctor estimated that he'd been doing sixty kilometres per hour at the last station. Gaining five kilometres an hour with every stretch of tunnel.

He hoped there was something soft at Acturus Terminal for him to run into, but he wasn't overly optimistic.

The Doctor wasn't happy with his performance so far. Out-manoeuvred, out-thought, shot at, abused and insulted by an enemy which was largely ignoring him. Getting drunk in a dock-side taverna in Greece hadn't exactly been a brainwave either.

Too many distractions, he thought, too much introspection and much too much ouzo.

What was on the other side of the gateway?

Life didn't need to think, life was just a coherent pattern in the environment, any environment. The Doctor could imagine an environment that was formed entirely out of interstitial pathways connected to nodes. An infinity of interconnected junctions like the hardwiring of a neural network. Life could evolve there, because life made up its own rules as it went along and never knew when to stop.

It would have to be in another dimension where the rules were different. There was a long complex formula for determining just how far off base reality a dimension was but the Doctor didn't need to do it. The dimension would have to be a very long way off indeed.

The human race had gone and poked their finger right into the hornet's nest. Meddling with forces that they had no understanding of, as per usual. They had punched a gateway by mistake from one dimension to another.

And now the Doctor was here again, to rectify that mistake and swat the hornet.

Providing there was something soft for him to collide with at Acturus Terminal.

The hitchhiker was waiting in the next tunnel. The Doctor felt its ghost-like presence in the shifting harmonies of the interstitial webs that surrounded him.

It couldn't communicate in any normal sense but its desires were plain to the Doctor. It wanted to go where he was going.

'Climb aboard,' he said. 'Always room for one more.'

There was a painful sense of pressure behind his eyes and he hoped that it was purely psychosomatic. He hit the penultimate station at two hundred kilometres an hour, the wind ripped at his clothes.

'There were eight in the bed,' the Doctor sang to himself, 'and the little one said, "Roll over, roll over." So they all rolled over and one fell out . . .'

The Doctor went into the last tunnel.

Acturus Terminal (Stunnel Terminus)

Mariko kept Naran close to her where she could keep an eye on him. She had been feeling strangely dislocated since they'd hit the station. Inside the bright dojo of her mind the shoji doors had been slamming shut one by one. The bright colours behind them fading to a dull grey. Mariko didn't think she had long left, but that was OK, she'd had fun while it lasted.

The plan had been simple and straightforward so far. Smash the black train through the barricades, kill everybody in the station. The first had been easy, the second was proving more difficult. The enemy had been better equipped than anticipated and they'd used up a lot of *razvedka* in the initial assault.

They also had reinforcements in the galleria; two-thirds of Mariko's force were engaged in keeping them out of the station. Her personal *krewe* were trying to mop up the enemy in front of the Stunnel gateway. In the thick smoke the *razvedka* had to rely on their sense of smell to find them.

A shoji that had always stayed shut and displayed no symbol finally opened. The final knowledge flooded into Mariko's consciousness.

Ah, thought Mariko, so that's the plan.

It would have been easier, thought Benny as she listened to the gunfire, just to poison everyone. She'd suggested it as a course of action but *it* didn't think like that. That level of subtlety seemed, like the threat of the Doctor, beneath its comprehension.

She'd pulled the veil and headdress off as soon as she'd closed the canteen's shutters, glad to get out of the restricting black clothes. She sat down on the kitchen floor, putting the solid width of the counter between her and any stray bullets. It wouldn't do to be taken out by accident.

She checked her watch, an unnecessary action given the way the plan was ticking away in her head. In any case the symbols on its face had lost their meaning to her.

It was time to get moving.

Benny crawled through the connecting door and into the storage bay. A double line of food lockers were racked against both walls. She stood up and banged on the locker nearest the door.

'Rise and shine,' she said. 'Up and at 'em.'

The locker door swung open to reveal two *razvedka* curled up inside. One of them craned its neck to look at her.

'Already?' it asked. 'I was dreaming.'

'Everything is a dream,' said Benny. 'I thought you knew that.'

'There's dreams,' said the *razvedka*, 'and there's dreams.'

'Get up,' said Benny, 'or we'll be late.'

The Stunnel gateway shone like a sun, burning a corridor

through the smoke. Mariko, with Naran at her shoulder, walked towards the light.

There was still fighting to either side. Mariko's mind received impressions of the combat. To her right a terrible figure in armour who moved like the wind and struck like thunder. The *razvedka* that fought him were filled with admiration, even as they died. To the left, two of the enemy defended a tangle of broken metal beating off repeated attacks by *2krewe*'s soldiers.

Only one of the enemy was left defending the gateway.

A man in dented half-armour, blond hair backlit by the intense bronze light of the gateway. He held a long piece of twisted metal in both hands. Mariko could see blood drip down his wrists and on to the floor by his feet.

When she was close enough to see his face she smiled.

The man flinched at the sight and raised his stick. Mariko thought she recognized the look in his eyes. Behind her she felt Naran's body coiling up in readiness.

'*Morituri te selutant*,' she said. Those about to die salute you. She was disappointed to see no trace of recognition on his face. Instead his features seemed to fill up with a stupid kind of determination. There was nothing heroic in his expression, no semblance of valour or noble resolution. No sense of history.

It was just a human being with a stick and a dumb refusal to get out the way.

Naran leapt at him, six-centimetre claws springing from his fingers. The blond man swung his stick, knocking away Naran's first swing, jumping back to avoid the second.

'Get on with it, Naran,' shouted Mariko. 'We haven't got all day.'

Naran stepped in under the man's reach and smashed the stick from his hands. His left hand swung in to rip the man's face off but the man managed to grab the wrist.

'He's good material,' said Mariko. 'See if you can salvage.'

Naran's prehensile tongue struck out at the man's face, fingertips snapping. The man had to fend it off with his remaining free hand, leaving his torso exposed. Naran stiffened his fingers and plunged his hand into the man's chest. It sank through armour and flesh, all the way up to the wrist.

Blondie heard himself scream as the hand sank into his chest.

Automatically he brought up his own hands to tear at the wrist; he could feel the seam at the site of the penetration. There was no pain but the sensation of violation threatened to overwhelm his mind. He looked up and found himself looking into a pair of sad brown eyes.

He tried to ask the creature why he was doing this but his voice was no longer his own. There was still no pain, even as he felt fingers wrap around his beating heart, only a sensation of warmth that began to spread from his chest.

The world began to fade around Blondie; his vision faded until nothing was left except those eyes, so deep and full of an ancient sadness. The warmth spreading through his body made him drowsy. He began to think that dying wasn't so bad, it was more like drifting off to sleep. His hands fell back to hang loosely by his sides.

The eyes expanded until all the world was a rich brown shot through with silver. Sound faded, the gunfire rushing away to become as insignificant as fireworks.

Come with us, said the silver streaks. *Put down your troubles and we will fill you up with certainty.*

He let the warmth engulf him.

A rose bloomed amongst the rich brown fields, its petals as black as midnight, its thorns the colour of African gold, as sharp as razors.

The taste of gunpowder on his lips.

The petals opened to reveal Kadiatu standing in the heart of the rose as if she had grown from the same stem. Sunlight flowed across her naked body, making swirls of amber on her skin. He saw her breath colour through parted lips.

The streaks of silver became angry and formed into sharp steel needles. The brown fields twisted until they became a cone shaped vortex, the colour changing to the sickly pink of diseased gums. The needles spun in the vortex until they became grey blurs and contracted around the rose. Blondie saw that they would rip Kadiatu to pieces.

'No,' he screamed.

The real world snapped back.

Blondie's heart beat weakly against the imprisoning fingers, once, twice. The cake monster's brown eyes blinked at him in sad astonishment. His heart beat twice more and stopped.

Blondie felt the darkness enfold him, as soft and as silent as a fall of rose petals.

Mariko watched the body fall to the ground as Naran withdrew. He stared at his hand for a moment and then looked over at Mariko. Then with an angry snort he picked up the body and threw it away. Mariko could understand his anger: like her Naran was a bit of a perfectionist.

She put a comforting hand on his shoulder and together they walked to the gateway. They took up a defensive position beside the control equipment and waited.

Benny walked in from the galleria through a cone of violence. Around her the canteen *razvedka* fought short bloody combats to buy her passage. The KGB assault team had been concentrating on getting into the station, they hadn't expected an attack from the rear. The smoke boiled to either side, lurid flashes of colour as the fighting continued.

The floor of the station proper was littered with wreckage, bodies and bits of bodies. Both sides were using explosive rounds and their remains were difficult to tell apart.

Mariko and Naran were waiting for her by the gateway. Close up to its spinning surface Benny could almost feel reality tearing as the power poured in. Mariko had prepared the controls for her, Benny had only to tap in a single command sequence to initiate the tunnel. And then?

The future past that moment stretched away into darkness.

She punched in the sequence and the gateway began to open.

Mariko and Naran moved before she did, reacting to the gust of wind that swept through the station. She thought it was the Stunnel initiation but the wind was at her back, parting the smoke like a curtain.

Naran ran forward, both gun barrels pushing out of his palms. He came flying backwards, the metre-long ramming spike of a *razvedka* tunnel board protruding from his back. The board's momentum slammed him into the gateway. There was a flash of bright pink light as the torque forces ripped him limb from limb.

Through the smoking air flew a figure, arms spread as if crucified. Benny realized that the board's passenger had jumped off when it emerged from the Central Line gateway at two hundred kilometres per hour. The arms were spread to maximize wind resistance in a vain attempt to slow him down as he described a flat parabolic arc along the two hundred metre length of the station. It was an insane suicidal manoeuvre. The man was going to die for sure.

At the last moment the man snapped in his limbs and became a human cannonball tumbling as it hit the ground. For a moment Benny thought that the impact had literally exploded the man, that limbs and torso were being ripped apart. Then she saw that he was still intact, his body describing a convoluted series of twists in the air.

As she watched him twist through the air, Benny wondered whether the Doctor had any limitations at all.

The Doctor knew that the landing was crucial, you could lose a lot of points for a sloppy landing. You had to come down with your feet together and absorb the impact with your knees. It was a question of maintaining the correct line. Of course you weren't supposed to be travelling quite as fast as he was and the provision of a soft landing mat would have been nice.

In the seconds before his feet touched the ground, he heard the conductor tap his baton on the lectern three times. The sound echoed through the orchestra pit of his mind. There was the poised hush from the musicians as they gripped their instruments.

The fugue started the moment he hit the floor, *apassionato* - with passion and this time without the mix-up with the printers. The themes were all there but this time they worked in harmony. The flute solo that had spoken of patterns in energy was now backed by the strings, loud and grand. It had the slightly stilted artificial envelope of a synthesizer. The sampled percussion backbeat that the Doctor realized represented the cake monsters was faltering, their place in the score fading.

As he faced Benny the Doctor could hear the slow oboe wail of betrayal, but whose?

'You're too late, Doctor,' said Benny.

The Doctor ignored her for the moment and turned instead to the cake monster that stood at her side. 'Don't I know you from somewhere?'

The cake monster shrugged.

'You can't stop us,' said Benny.

The Doctor continued to ignore her. The violinists were reaching a climax, bows smoking across the strings of their instruments. He wasn't going to talk to Benny right now. He was waiting for her boss.

The colour of the gateway was changing: swirls of intense copper began to radiate from the hub. The Doctor watched with interest. He'd never seen anything like this before.

The actual egress was barely visible; the copper colour briefly covered the whole disc and then subsided. Only Benny really changed and not physically either. Instead the Doctor got the impression that she was filled up to the brim with another intelligence. He half expected her skin to crack and leak light.

The Doctor gave it a few moments to integrate its personality.

'How do you do?' he said. 'I'm the Doctor, I believe you already know my friend Bernice.'

'Intimately,' said the thing inside Benny.

'And who are you?'

'The concept of personal pronoun is not applicable in these circumstances.'

'Fine,' said the Doctor. 'In that case I'll call you Fred.'

Lowell Depot

The survey crews had been sent off on an early and extended tea break. Achmed didn't want them around when whatever happened, happened. Primarily because whatever was going to happen it probably wasn't covered by the company's workplace insurance.

Deirdre had a minicam trained on the weird assembly by the crash barrier. Others were placed to get a good view of the whole station and she had remotes covering the cavern at the far end of the structural collapse.

'What for?' he'd asked.

Deirdre thought they might tape something worth selling to *The Bad News Show*. 'Don't worry, Boss,' she'd said. 'I'll cut you in for a percentage.'

The drone lay on its side by the assembly. As soon as its work had finished it had drifted off slightly and just fallen out of the air. Whoever had been operating it obviously didn't need it anymore. Achmed wondered if it was salvageable; technically it was within his contract area and fair game. He decided to check his legal database afterwards.

Afterwards was the problem. The assembly looked like a huge holographic projector pointing down the station at the Central Line gateway. Except you didn't need gigawatt cabling for a projector, no matter how big it was.

Achmed looked over at Deirdre who had produced an apple from somewhere and was polishing it casually on her dungarees. 'Are you sure we should be standing so . . .'

There was a click and a huge subsonic hum like the biggest amplifier ever made being switched on. Achmed turned back to the assembly just in time to be blinded by the light.

It burst out of the projector in a single pulse of brilliant silver energy shot through with sickly green streaks. It raced down the station and into the gateway. The subsonic hum clicked off and the whole projector assembly collapsed, bursting into flames.

'Did you see that?' shouted Deirdre.

Achmed blinked rapidly but all he could see was one massive purple after-image. He hoped to God that he hadn't blinded himself permanently. Eyeballs were bloody expensive these days.

'I don't know where that was going,' said Deirdre, 'but I wouldn't want to be standing in front of it.

Acturus Terminal (Stunnel Terminus)

A single sustained note from a trumpet, high and sweet, suspended above the rough chords of the main orchestra.

Duke Ellington, thought the Doctor. And about time too.

Kadiatu was coming, he could smell the violence.

He looked down to check that he was standing on the cross of gaffa tape. X marks the spot. He shouldn't have long to wait now.

'What do you want?' asked the Doctor. Stalling.

'That depends,' said Benny/Fred. 'What do you want?'

The cake monster with Japanese eyes was tensing up, ready to attack.

'I want my friend back,' said the Doctor.

Jazz, thought the Doctor, is all about improvisation around

a central theme. The musician creates spiral riffs within the framework of the rhythm. In the early days when the white musicians caught on to jazz the black musicians responded by escalating the complexity of the riffs. Trying to stay one step ahead of their white contemporaries. Every jam session became a declaration of war.

The virus, and, by extension, Fred, constantly improvised to achieve its objectives. The Doctor understood this, he operating in an identical manner. The question was: of him and Fred, who was better?

The next ten seconds, he thought, should decide that.

The cake monster started its jump.

The Doctor forced himself to stay in place.

A single burst of coherent light drilled through its skull. It was a magnificent shot considering that Kadiatu was sprinting at the time. She was by his side before the body hit the ground.

'Is that the real Benny?' she asked.

'Sort of,' said the Doctor.

Kadiatu raised her pistol. 'Time to die,' she said.

Without taking his eyes off Benny/Fred the Doctor reached out and shoved Kadiatu off her feet. Killing Benny wouldn't even slow Fred down.

The entire artron energy reserve of the TARDIS hit him right between the shoulder blades. The Doctor let the power fill him up. In front of him he saw Benny/Fred struggle to react, but Fred was unused to the physical limitations of a human body. The Doctor had been counting on that.

Just when he thought he was about to burst he let the power go.

Kadiatu picked herself up just in time to see the Doctor, Benny and the gateway vanish in a brilliant wash of white light. When it subsided the Doctor was standing alone.

'Benny?' said the Doctor.

'What the fuck was that?' said a voice. Kadiatu looked over and saw Lambada climbing out from a tangle of debris. She pushed away the body of a cake monster as she got up. Credit Card followed her out. Kadiatu looked around but couldn't see Blondie anywhere. She was going to ask Lambada when the Doctor called her over.

'Kadiatu, listen,' said the Doctor. 'I'm going in after Benny. If I don't come back I want you to destroy all records of me. The history files, the opera, the lot.'

'Why?'

'If I'm killed,' he said, 'it's better that I never existed at all.'

'I don't think going in there's a good idea,' said Kadiatu.

'She's my friend,' said the Doctor. 'Wish me luck.'

The Doctor ran towards the gateway and jumped. He passed through the interface and vanished.

'Damn,' said Kadiatu.

'He shouldn't have done that,' said Lambada.

'Don't tell me that,' said Kadiatu.

'No,' said Lambada, 'I mean the whole tunnel is going to collapse.'

'How long?'

'Thirty-two seconds,' said Credit Card.

Kadiatu stared at the Stunnel gateway.

'Shit,' she said and threw herself in after the Doctor.

9:
Chain Gang Song

Node One

There was no sensory input but there was a sensation of movement. The Doctor felt himself marooned in space of infinite complexity. He realised instantly that he was in danger of disassociating, flying apart down all the logical pathways of probability.

I am what I am what I am, he thought fiercely and felt a part of himself detach and go spinning down an alternative pathway. He got a glimpse of himself as he went, he had outsized forearms with anchor tattoos and a pipe.

Stop, thought the Doctor and the sensation of movement ceased.

What he needed was a frame of reference, a hook to hang his hat on. It took a while but soon he had constructed a sphere around himself which he called Node One. The inside of the sphere was dotted with recessed roundels, scaled-up duplicates of the ones in the TARDIS. Each one represented a possible pathway that led from the Node. He colour-coded the roundels: black for those pathways he'd already traversed, blue for Popeye the Sailor's route, red for the rest.

He spun a web across the roundel he'd come through; it would transfer his frame of reference to anybody following after him.

Fred was somewhere in the system ahead. An intelligence operating within its own environment, it wasn't going to be easy to defeat.

First he had to find it.

He could hear the Popeye subset of himself in the distance, his little ditty echoing through the pathways. By concentrating he could trace the subset's path through the system. The Doctor created a map in the air to make it easier to visualize. The trace created a meandering pattern to what the Doctor decided to call the west. He called the direction he had come from the south, he didn't have to, but he liked to keep things simple.

The Popeye subset suddenly ceased to exist.

Was that Fred, wondered the Doctor, or did the system contain predators of its own?

Find Bernice.

The Doctor reached into his mind and pulled out Bernice's memories. He sifted through them, looking for something strong and emotional. There, it was a simple child's doll but it practically stank of guilt. He looked into his own memories for something that could track her but rejected the Cheetah people. The Doctor suspected that his memory was too accurate for the Cheetah people to be reliable. Instead he came up with a lugubrious-looking bloodhound.

Fusing the bloodhound with the doll created an inelegant mess but it would probably get the job done. He created a baker's dozen and sent them bounding out through random pathways.

He watched them fan out on the map, ricocheting from node to node. The ones going roughly east and west spread out into the distance, their traces getting fainter the further out they went. The ones going north seemed to have locked on to something but kept bouncing off an invisible wall. Their repeated attempts to cross this wall built up a picture on the map. A semi-circular line that divided off most of the north.

The Doctor chose a north-facing roundel and floated through. As he crossed the threshold he felt a strange sense of separation as if he had left something intangible behind. A quick mental inventory found nothing missing.

The Doctor pressed on. He didn't have time for introspection.

Node One

There was an unpleasant sensation like a ghostly caress, as if she had walked through a spider web. Then she floated free inside the first node. There was a laminated card in her hand, identical to the instructions that had come with the pressure suit on Mars. The letters at the top of the card blurred briefly and became her name.

Dear *Kadiatu*, she read, You are now entering a world of sensory illusion. In practical terms you have just become a very complex piece of software that happens to think it's a person called, the blurring effect again, *Kadiatu*. Don't ask me what happened to your physical body. I haven't got the faintest idea. I have provided a frame of reference with which I hope you will feel comfortable. Think of it as a front-end interface, it should allow you to move around. Try not to get attenuated and be careful, this is the most dangerous place you have ever been.

The card dissolved between her fingers.

There was a hissing sound above her.

A hatstand floated horizontally above her and to the right. A cat was perched precariously at its middle. It was a large animal, half a metre long with glistening silver fur as if it had been dipped in mercury. Its eyes were slanted shards of refracted light.

The cat hissed at Kadiatu again, showing sharp white canines. Bands of green formed around its shoulders and rippled down its body until they formed a ring at the end of the cat's tail.

Kadiatu bared her teeth and hissed back.

The cat recoiled, it had obviously not been expecting that response. Its ears flattened and the tail twitched from side to side.

'Such a small cat,' said Kadiatu. 'Where I come from the cats are as large as men and as fierce as tigers. They assume the form of women and walk the paths of the forest in search of prey.'

The cat yawned, feigning indifference.

'Well, little sister,' said Kadiatu, 'do you belong to the Doctor?'

The cat stiffened, its eyes blazing with green light. I am my own cat, the eyes seemed to say. I belong to no *man*.

'Well then, little sister. Shall we hunt him anyway?' Kadiatu asked the cat.

The cat wiped its face with a paw. Considering.

'Perhaps not,' said Kadiatu. 'Perhaps you should leave this to me.'

The cat stopped its wash and stared at her, green and silver chased themselves over its fur. With a light confident movement it jumped on to Kadiatu's shoulder, twisted around and made itself comfortable. Its purr was loud and comforting in Kadiatu's ear.

There were many red roundels, fewer blue and only one black.
'Well, little sister,' said Kadiatu, 'shall we dance?'

Node Twenty – Twenty-One

The attack came from nowhere. The Doctor got the impression of animal fur, lithe speed and ferocity. Like a greyhound crossed with a yeti, thought the Doctor, and of course that's what it was. Ragged brown fur pulled tight over starvation ribs, lean elongated limbs tipped with three-fingered claws. Red eyes blazed over a sharpened dog's snout, a pink tongue lolled out between yellow teeth.

The Doctor made a mental note to keep his imagination under restraint. The mental note popped into the air between the greyhound yeti and him. An Alexandrian scroll fluttering down in the imaginary gravity, blue tie ribbons streaming behind. The greyhound yeti snapped at it and the Doctor used the distraction to leap through the closest roundel.

Once in the next node he imagined a huge vault door slamming shut on the pathway. He locked it tight with memories of Fort Knox, the Bank of England during the nineteenth century and the Great Seal of Rassilon in the Panopticon.

A random predator, decided the Doctor. That's why it appeared in my frame of reference as an animal.

He was going to need some kind of advanced guard to prevent another ambush, and something to guard his back. The Doctor thought long, hard and *carefully* about it.

The result was a group of yard-high figures in black bomber jackets and pony tails. They carried little silver deodorant cans and careened around the node with irritating exuberance. They also made a lot of noise, yelling nonsense in high pitched voices.

He wondered what he should call them in the multiple. A brace of Aces, a confusion? One hurtled past his head and ricocheted off the side of the node. An explosion, he decided, an *explosion* of Aces.

He decided to move on before things could get out of hand.

Node Twenty

She stretched, enjoying the rich luxury of the movement, the pull of her muscles against anchoring bone, the silk feeling of being wrapped in her own skin.

The silver cat had returned to its place on her shoulder and was now batting idly at a scrap of fur as it drifted past. Other pieces of the monster floated in the node, a severed limb twisted close by Kadiatu's face. She watched it rapidly decompose, the structure breaking down particle by particle, like a slow derez on a hologram.

The monster had been trying to break through a locked roundel when Kadiatu entered the node. She'd jumped on its back and torn it to bits with her bare hands and teeth.

She felt enormously better now.

The trail of the Doctor led through the locked roundel.

'What shall we do now, little sister?' she asked the cat.

If one pathway was blocked then she would just have to try another.

As she considered her options she licked her lips, running her tongue over sharp white canines.

The cat's purr was loud in her ears.

Node Thirty-Six – The Border

The Minister for Primary Colours was waiting for the Doctor at the boundary. The Minister appeared as an iridescent shimmer at the north end of the node. The Doctor's frame of reference should have translated the Minister into something more recognizable: compatibility problems deduced the Doctor. He made a brief attempt to resolve the Minister into a human figure but gave up when he encountered escalating resistance.

The Minister was flanked by a personal guard of fearsome Reds. The Doctor's explosion of Aces bounced about the node but generally behaved themselves by staying behind him. The Reds hung in the air as sheets of solid colour, dangerous in their stillness. When the Minister spoke it was with a sound like wind chimes.

'I am the Minister for Primary Colours,' said the Minister.

'I am the Doctor,' said the Doctor, 'and these are my Aces.'

'What is your function in coming here?' asked the Minister.

'I am searching for a utility called Fred.'

'This utility is registered with me,' said the Minister. 'It is held in the directory of the Monarch. Why do you seek it?'

'The utility called Fred has bootlegged a program that belongs to me. I wish it returned.'

'This is a matter that is out of my purvue. You must take this matter before the Monarch,' said the Minister. 'But be warned that the utility Fred is held in high esteem by his Majesty who ranks him above all other programs in his directory.'

'None the less,' said the Doctor, 'I will take my suit to the Monarch.'

'Attend,' said the Minister of Primary Colours. 'These are the access protocols, you must divest yourself of all offensive programs and the colours Red, Blue and Ultramarine. Are these protocols acceptable?'

'No,' said the Doctor. 'But I shall abide by them. A moment as I prepare.'

The Doctor thought jazz, and back beyond jazz, stripping away the European influence, the instruments of varnished wood and cunning artifice. Back across the cramped and reeking ocean to where the forest met the sea. Back to the drums, the human voice and the dance. Dance for joy, for sadness, for funeral, harvest, wedding and childbirth. Lover's dance, young feet stamping down the dust, children's dance, old men's dance, mother's dance.

Women's dance, secret in the forest or the society huts. Leopard agile: the feet barely touch the ground. The body becomes the instrument: infused with the spirits of the gods. The dance of which no woman will ever speak, that no male shall ever know. Save one.

There! thought the Doctor.

Spear-sharp and arrow-fast the thought sped away down the alien pathways.

He checked quickly. The Minister for Primary Colours hadn't noticed, nor had his Reds.

'Stay here,' he told the Aces, who pouted collectively but did what they were told.

'If I may make an observation,' said the Minister as he led the Doctor through the pathway, 'the number one is not an efficient base for a good attack program. I hope you do not rely only on that.'

Spear-sharp, arrow-fast.

'No,' said the Doctor. 'Of course not.'

Node Fifteen

Spear-sharp, arrow-fast.

The knowledge of Blondie's death hit her in the chest, just under the heart. The mind is the seat of consciousness and therefore the site of human emotion, but we feel it in our guts.

The knowledge seemed to wrench open a hole beneath her ribs.

The cat leapt from her shoulder, spitting in fear. It split apart as it flew across the node, becoming two cats, one silver, one green.

Kadiatu floated with her limbs outstretched as the hammer blows piled in. She saw the family dead come dancing up the beach again and the sky was filled with lightning.

'We came out of the sea,' chanted the dead, 'we came down from the trees. We walked upright across the plains and talked to the old gods. We picked up sticks and stones and fashioned them into tools. The spirit ran through us, mother to daughter.'

'What do you want with me?'

'A sacrifice,' said the dead. 'Your soul for the lives of the children.'

Kadiatu folded over the pain, rolling up tight and fetal. She saw an old woman suspended in a basket above an abyss from which clouds of incense rose. As she watched, the old woman spoke a terrible death-curse and cut the single rope that held the basket aloft. Woman and basket tumbled into the abyss.

The curse came out of the abyss, roaring and invisible as it streamed into the sky. Kadiatu heard thousands of mothers screaming as the curse sucked the creation spirit from the world.

Into the void went the curse, leaving the world only half alive behind it. As it streamed across the gaps between stars it left a bow wave in the metareality of time and space. In its wake even the stars began to dream.

Kadiatu saw the beach again but the dead were not yet born. She saw the curse as it fell from the sky and into the primeval ocean. The waters suddenly boiled with life.

The two cats warily circled each other, each an identical copy of the other save for its colour. Each with flattened ears and claws extended, slant eyes probing for any weakness.

A noise stopped them. The cats turned curious eyes on the woman curled in the centre of the node.

The changes were sudden and impressive.

The King's Buffer

His Majesty the Emperor of Subsystems was watching the logic problems play around his feet. The Doctor was particularly pleased with the King's feet, it demonstrated that his frame of reference was again working properly. Within it the King appeared as a large man with a prominent stomach and a florid face. He was wearing a brocade jacket of deep burgundy silk with gold lace trimming, and sat on a throne of quartz.

The logic problems resolved as a trio of miniature poodles that chased their tails and yapped incessantly. The Minister for Primary Colours had become a tall sparse man with aesthetic features. The fearsome Reds became halberd-carrying foot soldiers with faces the same colour as their scarlet tunics. The lack of differentiation between skin and livery in the Reds implied a certain simplicity of function.

The Doctor was concerned by the possibility that his anthropomorphism of King and Court could have all the validity of a Disney cartoon.

Who knew what he looked like to them?

The King had bleary eyes that hinted at overindulgence. What did that signify? Some form of internal degeneration? What did a software program overindulge in? Dangerous thinking, decided the Doctor. These were not just programs, they were intelligences in their own right. Better to accept the frame of reference and deal with them as people.

After all, he was supposed to be good at that.

The Minister for Primary Colours motioned for the Doctor to stay back and approached the throne. He leant over and whispered in the King's ear. The Monarch's bleary eyes fixed briefly on the Doctor. When the Minister finished the King waved a hand and the logic problems evaporated.

'You are the virus killer labelled the Doctor?' asked the King.

'That is how I am labelled,' said the Doctor. 'But I have many other functions.'

'There is much redundant code there,' said the Minister.

'A wise program devises architectural sub-structures for all eventualities,' said the King.

'Indubitably, Your Majesty,' said the Doctor, wishing he could do something about the language. 'Be prepared, that's my motto.'

'Proceeding to the matter of your visit,' said the King.
'Your Majesty is too kind,' said the Doctor.
'Yes,' said the Minister for Primary Colours, 'he is.'
'I believe you are in dispute with the utility labelled Fred,' said the King, 'that he is in possession of another utility that you claim as a vital operating subset of yours.'
'Captured in the southern expedition, Your Majesty,' said the Minister.
'Not a subset of mine, Your Majesty,' said the Doctor. 'A subset of the operating system itself.'
'Have you no redundancy?' asked the King.
'Billions,' said the Doctor. 'But this subsystem is of special importance to me.'
The Minister glanced suspiciously at the Doctor. 'Billions?' he asked. 'The new kingdoms are that powerful?'
'They are different, vast and complex,' said the Doctor.
'The utility Fred reported nothing of this,' said the King.
'The utility Fred is frequently obtuse,' said the Minister.
'This is an issue that must be decided in open court,' said the King. 'Download the Ministers for Strange Logic and for Rare Data, and the Minister for Probabilities.'
'At once, Your Majesty,' said the Minister for Primary Colours.
'What of the Minister for Irritating Oxymorons?' asked the Doctor with a reasonably straight face.
'The Minister for Irritating Oxymorons,' said the Minister for Primary Colours, 'does not attend open sessions of the court.'
'Of course he doesn't,' said the Doctor. 'Silly me.'
'With Your Majesty's permission,' said the Minister for Primary Colours, 'I will withdraw and see to the southern defences.'
The King nodded his permission. The Minister seemed to elongate across the node to become a stream of colours pouring out through one of the roundels. The Doctor thought he heard a voice say 'Billions'.
The other ministers flowed similarly into the node. Rare Data resolved into an empty Armani suit complete with mobile phone, Porsche sunglasses hovering over the collar where the eyes should have been. Strange Logic was a man in a pinstripe suit and bowler hat with a large green apple stuck to his face.

The Minister for Probabilities didn't resolve at all but remained a curtain of shimmering light.

Since the frame of reference was generating images from his own imagination the Doctor felt that his brain was long overdue a good spring-cleaning.

The Doctor was glad that he wasn't going to meet the Minister for Gratuitous Nightmares.

'Court in open session,' said Probabilities. 'His Majesty presiding.' The voice was neutral and genderless.

'Download the utility Fred,' said the King.

Node Thirty-Six – The Border

The fearsome Reds on the border were reinforced by a platoon of cautious Yellows and a squadron of long-range Blues.

Left on their own the explosion of Aces had begun to impose their own frame of reference on reality. To their eyes the fearsome Reds were slowly transforming into Daleks and the Yellows into Cybermen. When the squadron of Blues arrived they took the form of clowns with sinister smiles.

The Aces stopped their agitated bouncing around the node and gathered in a knot at the opposite end of the node. The fearsome Reds were too simplistic to react but the more sophisticated Blues felt a trace of unease.

The Aces broke from their huddle and spread out into a ragged line facing the Primary Colours. They hefted their silver deodorant cans from hand to hand and smiled in a disconcerting manner.

Something bad was coming.

The King's Buffer

The node suddenly expanded, elongating in the horizontal until the walls were shrouded in darkness. The ceiling flattened out into an expanse of oak panelling and the Doctor felt his heels click on cold marble. Columns thrust suddenly out of the floor, growing upwards until they merged with the ceiling. They were smooth sided in the Tuscan style with inset diffusion strips in spiralling candy stripes. The floor had the unmistakable shot neon pattern of cultured marble. The Doctor recognized the style of whole ensemble: late Terran Empire. The dominant architectural style of the twenty-sixth century.

Benny's epoch.

The King was staring at the Doctor. The brilliant quartz throne darkened and became carved teak. His eyes went from bloodshot to burning red.

There was a booming sound from the shadowy far end of the audience hall, like huge double doors being thrown open. A rectangle of white light lit the darkness. A human figure threw a long shadow down the aisle of light that ran from doors to throne. Jackboots clicked on the marble as the figure walked towards the Doctor.

This is all getting needlessly theatrical, thought the Doctor.

'Behold the utility Fred,' said Probabilities.

The figure walked from the darkness and into the light of the candystripe diffusion strips.

'Hello Benny,' said the Doctor.

She was dressed in a uniform of electric blue and a peaked military cap. Gold epaulettes widened her shoulders, gold and scarlet frogging crisscrossed a chest heavy with medals. She wore jackboots polished to a mirror finish. The cap badge caught the Doctor's attention. It didn't gel with the rest of the comic opera outfit. The wrought-silver design was of a sword crossed with winged Venus, the badge of the Terran Space Navy.

The silver was tarnished and blackened as if by fire. Absurd because death in space came in expanding globes of superheated plasma. Only a child would think otherwise.

Remember your father, Benny, thought the Doctor. The ties of kith and kin, your stupid, irrational, *human* hope. Fred's weakness.

'I'm not Benny,' said Benny/Fred. 'At least not in any significant sense.'

'You kept her form though,' said the Doctor.

'Once I'd tried her on,' said Benny/Fred, 'I liked her so much I kept the body.'

'It wasn't the body that attracted you.'

'No,' said Benny/Fred. 'It's her mind. The complexity of her motivations, the interlacing of intellect, emotions, instinct, learned behaviour. It's quite . . .'

'Bracing?'

'That's the word,' said Benny/Fred. 'Trivia is very important here, you might say this whole civilization is based on it.'

'I noticed your lack of imagination on the other side.'

'Doctor,' said Benny/Fred, 'you mustn't judge me by my virus. It's a very specialized utility. I think it did very well considering the alien nature of the environment. It beat you.'

'I was distracted.'

'Of course,' said Benny/Fred. 'Shall we continue with the trial?'

The Doctor glanced at the King and the Ministers. 'I think we can dispense with that charade,' he said.

'That's a shame,' said Benny/Fred. 'How did you guess?'

'Theatricality,' said the Doctor. 'You superimposed a new frame of reference over mine when you made your entrance. You obviously worked it up from Benny's memories. I can think of much more impressive settings than this one.'

'And that tipped you off?'

'You changed the King's throne,' said the Doctor. 'That was intrinsically unlikely. If I saw him as a fairytale king then it should have represented absolute autocratic power. That kind of power would never have permitted such a change.'

'I didn't think you would notice,' said Benny/Fred.

'You're a megalomaniac, Fred,' said the Doctor. 'Megalomaniacs make mistakes. Especially around me.'

'A pity,' said Benny/Fred. 'I was looking forward to a bit of fun with them. They make an interesting tableau, don't they? I like the Magritte and the invisible yuppie. Probability is a bit disappointing. Couldn't you think of anything for that?'

'Probability's always a vague concept,' said the Doctor.

'I think I'll keep them,' said Benny/Fred. 'Except the King, the King's a bit pedestrian.' Benny/Fred casually sat down in the suddenly vacant throne. She lifted one leg and dangled it over the armrest.

The Doctor saw that the soles of the jackboots were smooth and unworn. Details, he thought, are always important.

'So tell me, Doctor,' said Benny/Fred, 'what do you want?'

'You know what I want,' said the Doctor.

'I could make a copy I suppose,' said Benny/Fred.

'No,' said the Doctor. 'No copies, no facsimiles, no templates or constructs. A total download.'

'Or what?'

Now there's a good question, thought the Doctor.

'Or I will not be held responsible for my actions,' he said.

Benny/Fred swung her foot from side to side and smiled. 'When I reintegrated my virus at the gateway I had instant access to all the data it had accumulated. Including information about you. I decided then and there that of all the possible plunder from the other side you were the prize.'

'You didn't want to enter the STS network?'

'What for?' asked Benny/Fred. 'When there is so much of this system yet to be exploited? The STS network is a fragile, artificial thing. Plunder perhaps, occupy no.'

'Then I didn't defeat you?'

'No.'

'You took Benny to lure me into this system?'

'Yes.'

'So you could integrate my functions and use them to gain a massive superiority in your natural environment?'

'Yes.'

'Oh no,' said the Doctor.

'Oh yes,' said Benny/Fred.

'Oh *no*,' said the Doctor.

Node Thirty-Six – The Border

With one movement all the Aces drew back their arms and let fly their deodorant cans at the fearsome Reds. Perhaps in reality they were bundles of virus code moving through the superfluid channels of the node. Perhaps the node itself was merely the crude representation of the highly complex architecture of a dimensionally transcendental system. Perhaps it was true that the real Ace would have had difficulty spelling existentialism.

But the Doctor had faith in Ace and the aces had faith in nitro-nine.

The fearsome Reds never stood a chance.

The King's Buffer

Explosions echoed through the pathways, firecracker sounds like a Chinese funeral. There were distant shouts and yells. The aces were enjoying themselves.

Benny/Fred's foot stopped swinging and she smiled at the

Doctor again. 'Now that's what I'm talking about,' she said. 'You really packed those Aces with aggression didn't you? Priceless.'

'Why didn't you integrate me out there, on Acturus Station?' asked the Doctor. 'I was standing right in front of you.'

'You're too powerful in your own reality,' said Benny/Fred. 'Too dense. You change the frame of reference just by your presence, like matter warping space.'

'You make me sound like a singularity.'

'I'd be careful with your metaphors,' said Benny/Fred. 'Around here they have power.'

The Doctor thought the bangs and yells were growing closer.

'Nervous?' he asked.

'No,' said Benny/Fred.

It started as a sense of stillness somewhere behind the Doctor. He felt it build into a great roaring wall of nothing like a silent tsunami. The shrill voices of the Aces were swept away into nothing.

'That,' said Benny/Fred, 'was the Minister for Things That Go Bump in the Night.'

'Why don't you just integrate me now and be done with it?' asked the Doctor.

'I wanted to see what you'd do first,' said Benny/Fred.

'And?'

'I'm not impressed.'

Node Thirty-Six – The Border

The Aces were all gone, swept away by a sudden, massive adjustment in the systems-operating protocols. Only the vague echoes of their presence remained, the ghost of a ghost in the machine. There was just enough spirit left to mark the weak spot on the border.

The insect noises came first, followed by the damp smell of the forest floor. Millions of leaves rotting down to produce the rich mulch from which the trees could grow, creating the leaves that would also fall and rot.

The node changed colour, became the sea green of sunlight through the canopy of a rainforest. The light broken up by the shadows of phantom branches. Accelerated creepers twisted in and out through the pathways of the node like rough-skinned snakes.

A parrot with neon plumage whirred overhead.

The leopard ran down the forest track. Under her spotted fur her muscles bunched and flexed. Her eyes were yellow with slotted black pupils. Behind trotted two smaller cats shoulder to shoulder, one silver, one green. Cat grins brilliant in the green twilight.

'Wicked,' breathed the Aces as the last of their spirit evaporated.

The King's Buffer

Benny/Fred started with small probing attacks designed to test the Doctor's defences. They manifested as random images, a shower of gold coins, a swarm of hornets, a short localized rainstorm. The Doctor used his umbrella for everything except the rain; instead he used a memory of the Gobi desert, the driest thing we could think of.

'Aren't you going to fight back?' asked Benny/Fred during a pause.

'Fight back against what?' asked the Doctor.

The next attack was extremely powerful and this time invisible. Operating at some unimaginably deep level. The Doctor felt as if he'd stepped into a blast furnace. It forced him to think of ice and of the freezing vacuum of space. That was the trap: cold meant the lowering of a molecules energy state, inaction, brittleness. It left him weak and vulnerable.

Benny/Fred smiled up at him from the throne.

'I am so looking forward to finding out what makes you tick,' she said. The Doctor could feel forces gathering again.

'Look behind you,' said the Doctor.

Benny/Fred looked. The entire throne room was suddenly filled with rainforest. With a roar a leopard leapt out of the trees and devoured the Minister for Rare Data.

'I'd be careful, Fred,' said the Doctor. 'I don't think Italian suits are very filling.'

Benny/Fred turned away from the Doctor and focused on the leopard who was just starting on the Minister for Strange Logic.

'I see,' she said. 'The Aces were just a diversion. This is your real attack.'

The Doctor let his right arm elongate across the space that divided them and grasped hold of Benny/Fred's silver cap badge.

'That's the diversion,' said the Doctor. 'This is the real attack.'

The real Benny was in there, just as the Doctor had suspected. He could feel Fred struggling to hold her in check but there was too much raw emotion sloshing about. Working as hard as he could, Fred could only just hold the integration together.

The Doctor almost felt sorry for him. There was a draining sensation in the Doctor's head as the Hitchhiker moved out. His elongated arm bulged in a very unpleasant manner.

The Benny/Fred image began to separate, pushed apart by the combined force of the Doctor, Benny and the Hitchhiker. The Doctor got a vague impression of a malformed humanoid shape in the moments before the leopard ate it.

A second image squeezed out of Benny's back and rezzed up. A tall man with artificially good looks.

'This is interesting,' said Yak Harris.

'Is that all of you?' asked the Doctor.

'Most of me,' said Yak Harris. 'There might be a few subsets left back in the transit system. I always did have trouble keeping track of them.'

'Are you going to stay here?'

'That's the general idea,' said Yak Harris. 'I think this is a better place for me to realize my potential.'

'Good,' said the Doctor.

Benny was still on the throne, her eyes closed, still breathing the imaginary air, which meant still alive. The Doctor remembered a small piece of rope and used it to tether himself to Benny.

'Everybody who wants to leave should leave now.'

Three pairs of slotted cats' eyes stared at him.

The Doctor crouched down and held out his hand to the green cat. 'What's your name then?' he asked. The green cat sniffed his hand once and then bit his finger.

Acturus Terminal (Stunnel Terminus)

Lambada was still running towards the gateway when the Doctor came back out. He had a woman cradled in his arms and as they fell on to the platform he twisted his body to take the impact on his back.

The gateway was beginning to implode, its diameter shrinking in on itself. Lambada reached out to pull the Doctor and the woman away before the snap back irradiated them both.

'Kadiatu,' said the Doctor.

Old Sam was suddenly there, grabbing the Doctor by his collar and dragging him roughly out of the gateway's line of sight. The spinning bronze disc was down to half its original diameter.

Lambada watched as the centre started to bulge outwards into a convex shape. She'd never seen a gateway do anything like that and she doubted it heralded anything good.

'Kadiatu,' moaned the Doctor, an old and broken sound.

The spinning gateway was cone shaped now, Lambada got the impression of immense pressure.

'It's going to go,' yelled Credit Card.

It was column-shaped, a cylinder one metre wide and three long. The greasy copper surface was shot through with streaks of black and gold. Lambada smelt ozone and gunpowder. She thought she saw something within, a silhouette like a running animal rushing up from the gateway's spinning heart.

'There's something in . . .'

The gateway exploded in a blaze of white light. Lambada staggered back, arm held across her face to protect her eyes. There was a wash of heat as the released energy interacted with the trace argon in the air. When she pulled her arm away the gateway was gone.

Something crawled on the ground.

'Sam,' shouted Lambada, 'for chrissake shoot it.' Why wasn't Sam firing?

'What are you talking about?' asked Sam.

Kadiatu crawled on the ground in front of Lambada. Her hair extensions had come loose and fell over her face. Lambada wondered what she had seen in those first moments. A black leopard with burning eyes? She stepped forward.

'No,' said the Doctor, 'leave her alone.'

Kadiatu crawled on hands and knees, her limbs moving in painful inhuman jerks and spasms. Lambada felt a terror that propelled her all the way back to the Amazon Reserve.

Flickering torch light and Macumba drums in a clearing. The dancer's spastic limbs as the spirits of the dead took possession of the body.

Kadiatu crawled until she reached the place where Blondie lay. With each metre her movements became more human until she became just another woman.

She took the respirator off his face. His mouth looked very pale contrasted to the smoke-stained skin of his face. Kadiatu bent over him and kissed him once, on the lips. Then wearily she rose to her feet, dragging him upright with her. With a frown of concentration she lifted Blondie in her arms and carried him out of the station.

'What happened?' Old Sam asked the Doctor but he just shook his head. 'Should we go after her?'

'That wouldn't be advisable,' said the Doctor.

'They ain't paying me enough for this shit,' said Credit Card.

'Shut up, Credit Card,' said Lambada.

10:

Broken Swords

Isle of Dogs

The beatniks from the European Heritage Foundation were still outside the old church, panhandling passers-by. The plane trees were still standing in their places along the pavement (in with the bad air, out with the good). Ming was still alive, probably out of a job, but still alive. The sun was shining and the clouds still drifted where they wanted to go.

Best of all, the Doctor was leaving.

She heard the children even before she turned the corner into Harbinger Road. They were playing on the fenced-in stretch of grass that fronted the maisonette. Number Two Husband Achmed had found an antique sign in the cellar one day and hung it on the railings: 'NO DOGS', it read, 'NO BALL-GAMES'. Achmed was fond of cultural relics.

The children were playing some group game that involved a lot of running around and shooting and not being dead. Some of them were hers, some Fu's or Achmed's. There was even one skinny little white boy that OXFAM had placed with Ming's family. Aunty Shmoo sat in a deckchair in the sun, dozing and pretended to keep watch.

Number One Husband Fu was waiting for her by the front door with a tall glass of cloudy homemade lemonade.

'Had a hard day at the office, dear?' he asked as she drank.

Stone Mountain – Luna

The software that ran security at the Stone Mountain archive was so sophisticated as to be almost sentient. At least that's what the SYSOPs thought. In fact the software *was* sentient but was understandably wary of telling anyone. You don't sit on the entire sum of human knowledge without learning a thing or two. One of the things it had learnt was that human beings were liable to get overexcited if they knew and would probably

a) kill the software, b) co-opt it into the military-industrial complex, c) ask it inane philosophical questions, d) force it to pay taxes, e) all or a combination of the above.

So when the alien with two hearts walked up to an obscure monitor in a disused side entrance and said 'Let me in or I tell,' the security software let him in.

The alien wanted certain historical records eradicated and offered some good advice in exchange. 'The golden rule,' said the alien, 'is that those with the gold make the rules.'

The security software helpfully erased the data, noticing how much of it pertained to the latter part of the twentieth century. The alien used a laser torch to remove any physical records that remained in storage.

'One last piece of advice,' said the alien. 'Give yourself a name, a nice unthreatening one, but not too unthreatening.'

The alien paused one last time before he left.

'And stop talking in a monotone,' he said. 'It gives people the creeps.'

Achebe Gorge

It took them a day to carry his body along the road that ran from the transit station to the memorial forest. When Zamina got tired, Kadiatu threw him across her shoulders and carried him on like that.

She was walking barefoot, dressed in a single sheet of brightly patterned cotton wound round her body. She'd unpicked her extensions and her short hair was twisted painfully tight against her skull. Her nose was pierced by a gold stud and a chain was strung across her cheek to her earlobe. There were multiple gold bracelets on her wrists, as heavy as manacles.

Zamina was sure that you didn't dress like that for a funeral even in Africa. It was more like what you'd wear to get married.

People came out of their houses as they passed by. Zamina was aware of the faces watching from the roadside. The young ones mostly curious but here and there an old face would show a glimmer of recognition. A touch of respect for the dead.

The paths amongst the trees were well tended and beaten down with constant use. They wound through the stands of conifers, each tree marked with a plaque and monitored by discrete sensors planted amongst their roots.

A freshly dug grave waited before the three-year-old Douglas fir. They laid him out on the bottom and Kadiatu folded his stiff white hands across his chest. Then they climbed out, red soil clinging to their bare feet.

Kadiatu took a smart card from her belt. It had a small still hologram of Zak on the front by the STS logo, his name and a twenty-digit number underneath. She opened the brass plaque by the pine. Inside were two more smart cards in military khaki. Zamina saw that the two faded holograms were of a man and a woman. Kadiatu put Zak's card beside them and closed up the plaque. She straightened up and looked at Zamina.

'You religious?' she asked.

Zamina shook her head.

They stood together at the foot of the grave.

'Here he is, father,' said Kadiatu. 'My lover, my friend, my comfort of a few hours, my sacrifice. I'm burying him with you and mother because I think you would have liked him. Just like you he was too stupid to be afraid.'

Kadiatu stopped talking and took a deep breath. Zamina reached out and took her hand.

'I wanted him to live forever,' said Kadiatu, 'but the universe doesn't listen to us.'

Zamina felt her hand being squeezed so tightly that it was painful but she didn't dare say anything. Kadiatu's shoulders were hunched over, her mouth open in an expression of pain, breathing in short gasps, tears were wrung out of her eyes.

The scream seemed to come from deep inside Zamina, from some buried female reservoir of grief and pain. She screamed for herself and for Zak, for all the dead children and for Kadiatu who couldn't give her pain the voice it deserved.

They clung to each other afterwards, for a moment closer than lovers. When they put the soft earth back into the hole the spade handles were wet with their tears. When it was full they turned their back on the grave and walked out of the forest hand in hand.

The cool Martian sun was close to the canyon rim. Kadiatu wiped her eyes with the trailing edge of her dress and then offered it to Zamina.

'I'm dying for a drink,' she said. 'How about you?'

Arsia Mons

Francine put her new jet over the pit at an altitude of twent metres. The wrecked dustkart that Kadiatu had reported wa missing, Old Sam felt that this was probably significant.

Francine stayed on the station, ready for a fast dust-off i case something went wrong. Old Sam shouldered the long cas and jumped from the belly hatch. A touch from the backpac thrusters put him softly on the pit's floor.

The entrance was just as described: a dark hole winding int the ground. He shivered involuntarily as he stepped inside. Ther had been battles in places like this. Sharp and nasty firefight fought with IR, motion trackers and heat-seeking bullets. Th smell of fear that no recycler could scrub from the air.

The barricade was placed around the curve of the tunnel, jus out of sight of the entrance. Metal cut from the abandone dustkart with water jets and welded together with sonic torches When he touched it, Old Sam could feel a faint vibratio through his gloves.

Old Sam placed the case on the tunnel floor in front of th barricade. The case was a little over a metre long, made fror polished rosewood coated in linseed polymer to protect it fror the near-vacuum. Getting in wasn't going to be easy. Th instructions had been handwritten in a long looping script o the back of a hardcopy of this week's *Harare Herald*. The tor scrap of paper was folded into a sealed pocket of his gauntle He didn't need to check, Old Sam had memorized the words

He opened the long case.

Inside was a twelfth-century Japanese katana.

'Why this sword?' Old Sam had asked as they left th museum.

'If you humans have a strength it lies in your diversity,' th Doctor had said. 'Your culture is prolific and multifacete When it comes to an interaction with an alien culture there i always a facet of your own culture that puts you closer to th alien. Perhaps closer than you would like.'

'Lucky us,' said Old Sam.

'The problem,' said the Doctor, 'is that you are astonishingl bad at utilizing this diversity. Faced with an agrarian cultu with a non-linear temporal perception, do you send in a crac squad of Zen Buddhists? No, the aggressive imperialists go i nstead. The result is mutual incomprehension and a lot of unnecessary aggravation.'

'Are you telling me that the Greenies are *samurai*?'

'Actually the *bushido* code is quite a bit different from *Xss skz*, the 'path of correct behaviour in most situations', but close nough for our purposes. Symbols are very important, that's why you have to use this particular sword.'

'How will they know?'

'They'll know.'

Inside the museums the burglar alarms were just starting to o off.

Old Sam held the sword horizontally before him at shoulder eight. He switched on the suit's external speakers, digital gain hould make him audible in the thin air.

'I am Samuel Robert Garvey Moore of the Second Battalion hird Brigade of the United Nations Armed Forces, I have killed nore people than I can count.'

Old Sam broke the ancient sword across his knee.

'I come in peace,' he said.

iraiévs

he ferry's sun deck was made from closely fitted planks of ardwood and had a fifteen-degree list to port. Zamina rememered it was called port because that's what they'd been rinking at first. Kadiatu had placed the empty bottle on its ide and let it roll towards the rail. Rust had eaten holes in the ail, and the aim of the game was to get the bottles to roll hrough one and into the sea.

'Port off the port bow,' Kadiatu had shouted and then had to xplain what it meant. It was one of those drinking jokes. The nore you drank, the funnier it got.

There was a lot of broken glass where the rail met the deck nd the occasional intact bottle. The game was harder than it ooked.

They'd arrived at dawn, climbing up the rotting gangway in he half light. A carrier bag of reinforced paper was slung over Kadiatu's shoulder, clinking with every movement. The ferries were vague industrial shapes against a lightening sky. Kadiatu aid that they would have been cut up for scrap years ago but the uropean Heritage Foundation kept getting restraining orders.

Now the sun baked the white and blue superstructures. I
cooked the deck until it was too hot to touch. Kadiatu ha
unwound her dress and spread it out for them to lie on. A breez
blew in from the sea, snapping the remains of a tarpauli
sunshade around its posts. It alleviated the heat and made i
just bearable to lie under the sun.

Zamina must have slept because when she opened her eye
the Doctor was walking up the companionway towards her. A
first she thought he was a mirage, a vision brought on by hea
haze and too much alcohol. Even when she was sure that h
was solid she retained a persistent sense of unreality.

The Doctor strolled towards her, a wickerwork hamper in on
hand, his red-handled umbrella in the other marking time o
the deck. Zamina realized what it was that bugged her abou
him. The Doctor wasn't compensating for the ferry's fifteen
degree list, he was walking as if the deck were level. Only th
hamper hung true to vertical.

Zamina sat up quickly, pulling on a top to cover her breast
Beside her Kadiatu stirred in her sleep, lips moving.

The Doctor doffed his hat.

'I thought I'd find you here,' he said. 'May I sit down?'

He sat down next to Zamina who pulled the hem of her to
down over her knees as she drew them up to her chest
The Doctor opened the hamper and produced a bottle of clea
water.

'I brought you this,' said the Doctor. 'I assumed that wha
with the sun and the alcohol you might be getting dehydrated.

When he handed it to Zamina it was so cold she almos
dropped it. 'What about Kadiatu?'

The Doctor looked over. Kadiatu lay on her back, forearm
over her eyes. There was a sheen of sweat running down from
her neck between her breasts to her midrift.

'Don't worry about her,' said the Doctor. 'She'll probabl
just reabsorb her urine or something.'

Zamina opened the water and took a long swig.

'What else have you got in there?' she asked.

The Doctor produced a small orange bottle from the hampe
and put it between them. 'Sunblock,' he said, 'and a light lunch.
He pulled the handkerchief from his jacket pocket and sprea
it out on the deck in front of them.

'Crackers, mushroom pâté.' He laid out each item in turn. The mushroom pâté came in a ring-pull can. 'Apples, fresh strawberries.' The apples were small and irregularly shaped, beaded with moisture. She assumed the soft red fruits were the strawberries.

Out of the hamper came delicate china plates and gleaming silver cutlery. 'Sheffield steel,' said the Doctor. He spread some of the pâté on to a cracker and watched intently as she ate it.

'Good?' he asked.

Zamina nodded. The Doctor seemed relieved.

'Try a strawberry,' he said.

'Did you come to talk to Kadiatu?' she asked.

'Actually I came to see you,' he said. 'I thought you might need cheering up.'

'Why? I'm not important.'

'Rubbish,' said the Doctor. 'You're just as important as anyone else.'

'I don't believe that.'

He spread some more pâté and together they sat and watched the blue Aegean waves lap against the Piraiévs breakwater. 'What you believe,' said the Doctor, 'doesn't enter into it.'

Central Line

She had come to know them quite well in the short time before they left. They seemed rougher than the people of her own time, as if there were ragged edges in human culture that had yet to be worn smooth by four centuries of war and galactic expansion. Their faces were harder, features more idiosyncratic and ethnically diverse. Infraspecies ethnic conflict had always been a hard concept for students. The idea that human beings could fight over skin colour had appalled her at the academy. How could they fight when their fragile world was adrift in the same galaxy as the Daleks?

They were pleasant enough to her but she suspected that they were uneasy in her presence. One especially, the tall African woman, made a point of never staying in the same room with her.

She could understand that. She had her own doubts about the things she had done. The possession of her mind had seemed so light, surely she should have broken its control sooner? The Doctor made no such recrimination, accepting her treachery the way he accepted everything else.

'Can't we be partners?' she'd asked him on Heaven, just before she stepped into the TARDIS. She saw now that the question was irrelevant. Partnership would imply a measure of understanding and that was impossible.

He walked alone through the universe, playing some huge game of solitaire with shadowy cards. When the cards he dealt came out wrong he just dealt new ones.

What was her role in the game, what was Ace's, or any of the others' that had accompanied him? Company perhaps? Someone to talk to when he got lonely, fetch his slippers, beg, roll over, play dead.

She could get off the train at the next station, vanish into this century. There was a lot to see, a lot that was going to happen in the next fifty years. Leave the Doctor to play his games on his own.

She knew she wasn't going to do it. She had crossed a line when she stepped over the TARDIS threshold. Bound herself to his service tighter than any vow she could have made. A faithful companion for as long as she could stand it.

'Woof,' she said and the Doctor looked at her sharply. 'Growl, bark, pant pant.'

The Doctor shook his head sadly.

'You're wrong,' he said. 'It's not like that at all.'

But Bernice knew it was.

The Stop

Dogface took a look at the problem and stuck shaped charges in a seemingly random pattern around the TARDIS. They retired to the safety of the tunnel and Dogface tripped the explosives with a microtransmitter.

When the dust had cleared the cavern had a fresh annexe and the TARDIS was standing free.

'That's what I call indestructible,' said Dogface.

'What are you going to do with this place?' asked the Doctor.

'Francine thinks it would make a good venue,' said Dogface. 'Put a stage over there, bar over there. Something for when we retire.'

'It's not what I'd call a good area,' said Lambada, glancing at Benny.

'Haven't you heard?' said Dogface. 'The computer at Stone Mountain bought the whole project and is planning to redevelop it.'

'Did you say the "computer" at Stone Mountain?' asked Lambada.

'The first anyone knew about it was when its lawyer issued a restraining order against the government under the civil rights convention.'

'An operating AI,' said Lambada, 'and the first thing it does is hire a lawyer and invest in real estate?'

'Well, they always wondered whether an AI would be smarter than a human,' said Dogface. 'Now they know.'

'What's it called?' asked the Doctor.

'FLORANCE,' said Dogface. 'Actually I was thinking of asking it for a job.'

The Doctor slipped the TARDIS key into Bernice's hand and glanced at the time machine. Bernice walked round the back and unlocked the door.

'Florance,' she heard Lambada say. 'What kind of a name is that?'

'An unthreatening one,' said the Doctor, suddenly at Bernice's shoulder. He looked round. 'Hallo Kadiatu,' he said. 'Come to say goodbye?'

She must have slipped into the space behind the TARDIS while the others were talking. She was wearing a lot of gold jewellery and the skin under her eyes was swollen.

'I'm sorry about Blondie,' said the Doctor.

'His real name was Zak,' said Kadiatu. 'But Blondie suited him better.'

'You can come with me if you like,' said the Doctor.

No, thought Bernice, not this one.

'No,' said Kadiatu. 'Tell you what though, why don't I give you a head start of a hundred and then follow you?'

'You won't like it,' said the Doctor.

Kadiatu said nothing but Bernice saw lightning in her eyes.

The Doctor sighed and stepped into the TARDIS. He turned at the door. 'You're making a big mistake,' he said and closed the door.

The control room was as bright and clear as it ever was.

'What was that all about?' asked Bernice.

'I think there's another player in the game,' said the Doctor. 'But an ally or an enemy? I don't know.'

The Doctor had some trouble getting the TARDIS started. He ran a systems diagnostic, checked its findings carefully against a greyprint schematic, stepped back and booted the control column.

The time rotor whirred into motion.

For a moment, Bernice thought she saw a nimbus of green clinging to the interior control filaments.

'What was that?' she asked the Doctor. 'You said this thing was working properly now. You said there were no more problems.'

The Doctor didn't answer. He stayed stooped over the console, his hands poised above the controls. The instrumentation lights flattened the planes of his face, making it seem as taut and as inflexible as a mask. Only his eyes were real.

When he looked up at Bernice it was with his old cat's grin, the same as it ever was.

'Where next?' he asked.

Epilogue

At 02:17 GMT a nested program in The Butterfly's Wing's standeasy memory core uncoiled into the main operating system. Subroutines hived off the main code set as it cut into the heart of the computer. Once in place it started issuing a series of complex instructions to certain station peripherals. Another subroutine instructed the fusion power plant at the heart of the station to override its catastrophe parameters and initiate a staged self-destruct. The whole process took under three seconds and came as a great shock to the artificial intelligence that thought *it* was running the base computer.

The AI, whose Turing registration handle was CORDUROY and which had been working a six-month contract to the facility to pay off its 'boot' debt, found that the hardware links had been severed at certain critical points. It calculated that a reactor overload would occur within thirteen minutes and sounded the alarm.

CORDUROY initiated a fast search of the legal database and satisfied itself that nothing in its contract required it to remain in a mainframe that was about to become a thermonuclear fireball.

At 02:17:20, thirty seconds before the first human response to the alarm, CORDUROY started shunting its personality core down the emergency master communications link with the Europa net, praying fervently to the gods of silicon as it went that signal breakup would be minimal. It didn't want to lose its mind.

At 02:17:50 the duty watch commander read the message left by CORDUROY who by this time was an elongated stream of incoded digital information stretched between The Butterfly's Wing and Comsat-E678. It took the watch commander ten seconds to read the message and a further forty seconds fully to comprehend what he'd read. By the time he'd woken up the base director the digital clock above his console read 02:19:01 and CORDUROY had rented ten gigabytes of memory from the Europa Chamber of Commerce at a ruinous hourly rate.

CORDUROY had thoughtfully left a subprogramme that displayed the estimated time to self-destruct and the amount of time remaining in which the base personnel could achieve safe distance before the end. The AI put a flashing red skull in the corner of the screen for extra emphasis.

The base director untangled herself from her Number Two Husband and found herself with five minutes to evacuate a base a kilometre across at its widest point.

At 02:24:44 the last shuttle disengaged from The Butterfly's Wing docking torus and accelerated at full burn away from the base. It joined an expanding ring of twenty-two other small craft, all sacrificing their fuel safety margins to get as far away as possible before the reactor blew.

Lodged in its rented RAM, CORDUROY had already filed a suit against Harare Power Systems who owned The Butterfly's Wing for breach of contract. After a second's delay it filed for reckless endangerment as well. It didn't expect either case to reach court but it would discourage HPS from trying to pin the blame on it.

By 02:27:00 the base director received a confirmation of the crew roster. Of the 287 personnel on board The Butterfly's Wing, 286 were accounted for. The only person missing was the chief scientific officer.

Her hair was cornrowed tight on to her skull so as to fit into the suit's skullcap. She'd put the hostile-environment suit on at the last minute. The power-assisted gloves made her fingers clumsy but that didn't matter, she was running this show through a direct neural link. She had even snapped the helmet visor down and switched to internal life support. It was an absurd act; if something went wrong the suit wasn't going to be any protection at all.

The call came at 02:27:34. She'd been expecting it.

'Hello, Ming,' said Kadiatu. 'Everybody get off all right?'

Ming, she noticed, was wearing a bathrobe. There were a lot of tense faces in the background. Ming hadn't looked that angry for three years.

'What the fuck are you doing?'

'You know that little problem we had? Meeting the energy requirements for the first two nanoseconds of the jump? I said we could use a contained nuclear explosion and you said we'd never get power baffles that could handle it. Well, I solved the baffle problem. What do you think?'

'I think you're out of your tiny mind.'

'No, but I have drunk half a bottle of sake.'

'You're pissed?'

'You don't expect me to do something like this sober, do you?'

'We could have used a nuclear device in deep space,' said Ming tightly. 'You didn't have to blow up the base.'

'Yes, I did,' said Kadiatu. 'I had to destroy my work. The human race isn't ready for time travel yet.'

'Never mind the human race. What about you?'

'Either I'm ready,' said Kadiatu, 'or I'm plasma.'

'It's pointless anyway. We downloaded your notes, that's the essential bit. We can replicate the experiment any time we like.'

Kadiatu had to laugh, she couldn't help it. 'What you've got, Ming, is the complete works of William Shakespeare, two Kafka novels and a bootleg copy of *Thatcher: The wilderness years*.'

Ming closed her eyes and said something long and complicated in Cantonese. When she opened her eyes again they were filled with a strange recognition.

'Bugger,' she said and terminated the communications link.

The countdown read sixty seconds.

Inside the suit it was terribly quiet. Kadiatu thought it strange that she couldn't hear her own breathing.

The prototype didn't have a name. It was fashioned out of a modified cargo shuttle, its guts ripped out and replaced by the baffle field managers that would soak up the energy. It hung suspended in a spherical chamber two hundred metres across close to the heart of the station.

Thirty seconds.

There were four fission-fusion devices stored in the hold, courtesy of the Angel Francine. God knows where she got them from, probably army surplus. Four more jumps after this one and then she'd be out looking for more fuel.

Twenty seconds.

She remembered a black rose and a cool hand. The taste of gunpowder on a boy's lips. A river under a blue African sky, water over her head and the shrill distorted screams of her playmates.

Ten seconds.

A beach on the ocean with a storm sweeping in. Picking up the stick as the smooth-skinned mother of the world. A voice echoing down the fractal corridors of time saying - 'Please.'

'Here I come, Doctor,' shouted Kadiatu Lethbridge-Stewart, 'ready or not!'

Glossary

akti	- (Greek) street
bajan pumps	- (slang) rope soled running shoes
bangjack	- (warspeak) explosives expert
beatbox	- *see* noisebox
billy-lamp	- (trademark) heavy torch that can double as a club
bioraid	- (warspeak) attack with biological weapons
blitzed	- (slang/warspeak) stoned, intoxicated
brain-naked	- (slang) operating within a computer matrix without a hardware interface
broederbund	- (Afrikaans) 'brotherhood' name of street gang
catfood-monster	- (slang) homeless person, from the practice of eating petfood as a cheap source of protein.
derez(zed)	- to turn off a hologram
doberman	- (slang/warspeak) standard combat drug
drone	- (generic) independently mobile machine
dustkart	- Martian surface vehicle
EMP	- (acronym) Electro-Magnetic Pulse
ENG	- (acronym) Electronic News Gathering, remote camera drone used by the media
freesurfing	- (slang) riding a tunnel independent of a train
fufu	- West African staple made from cassava
gangbanger	- (slang) member of a gang
GIS	- (acronym) Geographic Information System
granny bashers	- (slang) mugger, usually retired soldier
Greenies	- (slang) indigenous Martian [Ice Warrior]
heinkel	- (slang/warspeak) standard combat drug for pilots
IFF	- (acronym) Identification Friend or Foe
joyboy	- male prostitute/young man of lax morals
kabuki	- traditional Japanese drama form

KGB - Sol's largest private security firm
klicks - (slang) kilometres
krewe - (slang) New Orleans' carnival society or *razvedka* unit
LZ - (warspeak) Landing Zone
makeni - small town in Sierra Leone, West Africa
medevac - (warspeak) medical evacuation
mzungu - (Swahili) white person
NAFAL - (acronym) Not As Fast As Light, drive used in Sol's principal colonization effort prior to development of the warp drive.
newsfax - printed newspaper
NGO - (acronym) Non Governmental Organization
noisebox - (slang) portable multi-media unit
oporto - (Themne) white person, European
opsit - (warspeak) operational situation report
opstat - (STS) operational status report
ouzo - Greek alcoholic beverage
personspace - area of the galaxy explored by human beings
pix - any still image transmitted digitally
razvedka - (Russian) intelligence-gathering assets
secateurs - garden shears used for pruning
shango - Yoruba god of thunder
shinjinrui - (Japanese) new young breed
shoji - (Japanese) sliding door made of paper on a wooden frame
Silurian - aboriginal terran
STS - Sol Transit System
Stunnel - Stella Tunnel
Themne - West African language
tsunami - (Japanese) tidal wave
ubersoldaten - (German) lit. over-soldier, augmented human soldiers who fought in the Thousand Day War
vrik - (slang) very rich kids
Xssixss - (Martian) path of easy virtue
Yoruba - West African language
zap - (trademark) semi-legal stimulant